MW00559755

BAD
RIVER

BAD RIVER

MARC CAMERON

KENSINGTON
PUBLISHING CORP.

www.kensingtonbooks.com

KENSINGTON BOOKS are published by

Kensington Publishing Corp.
900 Third Avenue
New York, NY 10022

All Kensington titles, imprints, and distributed lines are available at special quantity discounts for bulk purchases for sales promotion, premiums, fund-raising, educational, or institutional use. Special book excerpts or customized printings can also be created to fit specific needs. For details, write or phone the office of the Kensington Special Sales Manager: Attn. Special Sales Department, Kensington Publishing Corp., 900 Third Avenue, New York, NY 10022. Phone: 1-800-221-2647.

Library of Congress Card Catalogue Number: 2024934894

The K with book logo Reg. U.S. Pat. & TM Off.

ISBN: 978-1-4967-3763-2
First Kensington Hardcover Edition: August 2024

ISBN: 978-1-4967-3764-9 (e-book)

10 9 8 7 6 5 4 3 2 1

Printed in the United States of America

For Aunt Billie—
who surrounded me with books well before I could read.

*"Waste no more time arguing what a good man should be.
Be one."*

—Marcus Aurelius

BAD
RIVER

PROLOGUE

THE FIRST BULLET ZIPPED THROUGH THE FIREWEED JUST INCHES from Arliss Cutter's ear. His partner, Lola Teariki, crouched low beside him, in the middle of an animated one-sided conversation about her kid brother, who was telling her that if law enforcement didn't work out, he could always get her a gig dancing at Te Vara Nui on their home island . . .

It was as good a time as any for a gunfight.

The passing shot sounded like an angry wasp—with a can opener—a quick whirring buzz followed by a metallic *thunk* as it punched a hole in a rusted oil drum less than five feet to the left. Cutter and Lola rolled away from the sound toward a pile of dead-fall to the right of their makeshift hide. Deputy United States marshals, they'd been shot at before.

Two more rounds whirred overhead, absent the *crack-boom* of supersonic bullets.

"He's using a suppressor," Cutter hissed, his face pressed against the frosty ground. He'd let his binoculars fall against the strap around his neck, swapping them for the M4 carbine that lay beside him.

Bullets continued to punch holes in the rusted drum, forcing Cutter and Lola to keep their heads down.

Lola hooked a thumb over her shoulder. "They're coming from behind us."

Cutter stayed flat on his belly, spinning a hundred and eighty degrees—away from the vacant travel trailer they'd come here to check. Rifle to his cheek, he scanned the wood line through the red circle of his holographic sight. Brush and debris had been piled up on both sides of the road during its construction, giving their ambusher plenty of places to hide. Cutter directed his breath toward the ground. No reason to let this guy dial in on an exact position.

The shooter wasn't quite so smart.

Another shot clipped a willow branch to Cutter's left. Moments later, a cloud of vapor blossomed from a line of spruce trees across the gravel road.

Two quick shots, one on either side of the tree, would have found a target, but Cutter wasn't in the habit of killing something he could not see. For all he knew this was some grandma who thought they were trespassing. If said grandma didn't stop shooting at him, though . . .

Head down, Cutter worked through the details of a rudimentary plan while he scanned his surroundings.

Crystalline frost flocked the tiny leaves of the blueberry bushes and Labrador tea shrubs that covered the mountainside. Some, already yellow from the crisp fall weather, were now a burnt orange under the glow of the sun that was just peeking over the ridgeline. A mile below, the Turnagain Arm of the Cook Inlet stretched along a ribbon of pavement. Even from this distance the vast brown plain and muddy ditch-like guts made it clear the tide was out.

The collateral lead request had come in over CAPTURE, the Marshals Service's internal warrant and prisoner tracking network. Lola had called it a nothing burger—the lead, not the bad guy.

From all accounts, Caldwell Vickers was six feet five inches of bearded gristle and guile, the kind of man who'd grown up seeing something he wanted and taking it. Cutter's grandfather had called such thinking "right of way by tonnage" and taught his grandsons to despise it.

Vickers was wanted on state robbery and assault charges in both Idaho and Washington, but his federal warrant stemmed from a DEA case where he'd apparently been the muscle for a methamphetamine lab outside Yakima. The DEA had looked for him hard for a solid week after the initial raid. Then, having other cases to deal with, turned the fugitive hunt over to the Marshals Service. Eastern District of Washington deputies sent a list of possible associates to task forces and warrant squads in the respective areas, no matter how thin the connection. Shotgunning wasn't a bad tactic as far as fugitive work went. Cutter just preferred more information than "travel trailer belonging to Vickers's past associate registered to property near Indian, south of Anchorage."

Cutter liked to know the whole story.

Lola got what she thought was most of it. The E/WA deputies holding the original warrant didn't expect to find Vickers at the property in Alaska. They believed he was holed up somewhere in the mountains of northern Idaho. The woman who owned the Alaska trailer was wanted on a state DUI charge. What the deputies hoped was that the Alaska Fugitive Task Force would find and leverage this woman into giving up information on Vickers's location.

So far, that wasn't working out too well.

Another bullet slithered through the brush.

Cutter caught a flash of movement across the road. He snapped his fingers to get Lola's attention, then nodded toward the tree line.

"I want you to put a couple of rounds into that biggest spruce while I move to the other side of this slash pile."

"Unless I get a clear shot," Lola said. "Then I'm capping his ass."

"No doubt," Cutter said, already walking his elbows over the brush, dragging his legs. Cover was virtually nil, little more than blueberry bushes and willows—nothing that would stop a bullet. But concealment was good. He was able to settle into a low swale behind an overturned stump, giving himself and Lola roughly a forty-five-degree spread from the shooter.

He gave a curt whistle to let her know he was ready, then, aiming in with his M4, announced, "United States Marshals! Put down your weapon and come out of the trees with your hands up!" Then, just in case the shooter was living under a rock and didn't know what a marshal was, "Police! U.S. Marshals! Drop your gun and come out now!"

Another shot, this one from the shadows ten feet to the left of where he'd seen the previous flash. Were there two, or was this the same guy?

Cutter stayed aimed in, ready to press the trigger the moment he got a shooter in his reticle. He didn't have a chance.

A car horn blared from farther up the mountain, barely audible at first but growing louder by the second. Cutter kept his focus on the tree line. Moments later, a rattle-can black Dodge minivan came bouncing down the gravel road, horn beeping, driver yelling.

The shooter picked up his pace, alternating fire from Lola to Cutter, probing the brush.

The minivan driver's head and left arm hung out the window, waving frantically as the vehicle careened back and forth from ditch to ditch like something from Mr. Toad's Wild Ride.

The van crunched to a stop, throwing a cloud of dust into the morning haze. The driver, a twenty-something man wearing a ballistic vest under a tattered Carhartt jacket, bailed immediately. Shoulders bobbing, arms flailing, he was near apoplectic. He put himself between the deputies and the van.

"Hold your fire! Please! Please! Hold your fire!"

Behind him, a man in a hat and a similarly tattered Carhartt jacket darted from the wood line with a rifle, shooting as he ran. Same hair, same facial structure. Cutter assumed they were brothers.

Lola took a shot but pulled it, surely fearing she'd hit the unarmed brother. Cutter sent a round through the back window as the man with the rifle dove into the van. The bullet smacked the A-pillar on the far side, in line with where the man's head had been a half breath before. The driver continued to wave his arms and plead as he backed his way to the van. Rifles raised, Lola and Cutter barked orders for him to stop. When he reached the door, he jumped in and threw the van in gear, tearing down the road toward the Seward Highway below.

Cutter stayed put, watching the wood line. He'd been in too many ambushes in Afghanistan to take it as a given that there was only one shooter. Bad guys often sent out a rabbit and then shot the dogs that chased it.

Eventually though, his predator drive won out and he whistled for Lola. He needn't have bothered. She was already running toward him, rifle at port arms, binoculars swinging around her neck. Her crawl through the weeds had knocked loose her usual high bun of jet-black hair, and it now hung loose around broad shoulders.

Their Marshals Service Tahoe was parked up the road in the direction the minivan had come from. Lola had the key fob in her pocket, but Cutter reached the driver's door first. He jumped in and pushed the ignition as she swung herself into the passenger seat.

"Get us some backup," he said, calm, laser-focused on the road. He might as well have been saying "*I'll have the pie.*" He punched the gas, throwing gravel and fishtailing around the first of many switchbacks before the road intersected with the Seward Highway a mile below.

The radio mic was already in Lola's hand. "I got a plate on the minivan," she said.

With shots fired, Anchorage PD cleared the channel immediately and dispatched every available unit south to assist. The Seward Highway was theirs all the way to Girdwood, but the nearest unit was at Dimond—fifteen miles to the north. An Alaska State Trooper captain on his way up from Homer had just crossed Turnagain Pass. An hour away, but good to know if these idiots decided to run south.

Cutter drifted around a tight corner, hanging a wheel over the ditch. He kept up his speed and steered into the skid, buying some distance between him and the fleeing minivan.

In the meantime, Lola was on the phone with Task Force Officer Nancy Alvarez, who performed a lightning-fast workup on

Ryan Thornton, the registered owner of the minivan. Alvarez emailed Thornton's driver's license photo, confirming he was the one in the ballistic vest.

Lola put her on speaker. "He's got a younger brother," Nancy said. "Reese. Both have records, but Reese is the star of that shit-show."

"Address?" Cutter said, drifting around another turn at speed. The minivan's brake lights flashed only one switchback ahead now.

"An apartment in Wasilla," Alvarez said. "And . . . looks like some property up the Twenty-Mile."

Cutter gripped the wheel tighter, exchanging glances with Lola.

The Twenty Mile River met the ocean at the Seward Highway and the southern end of the Turnagain Arm. There were no roads up the valley.

Lola shrugged. "Maybe they're making a run for a boat they've stashed—"

The minivan was going at least fifty miles an hour when it reached the bottom of the mountain. Instead of slowing, it appeared to speed up.

Thornton hit the highway on two wheels, darting into the path of an oncoming side-dumper gravel truck on its way out of Anchorage. Smoke poured from the trucker's tires as he locked his brakes. Momentum kept the load of heavy gravel going south while the tractor pointed east toward the mountain, jackknifing the rig and ultimately spilling over thirty cubic yards of gravel across the roadway. Between the overturned rig and its load, the entire highway was blocked.

Cutter made it to the south end of the spill as it was happening, in time to watch the hapless minivan fly over the guardrail, out of sight.

"Holy hell!" Lola whispered. She called for an ambulance and someone to clear the roadway.

Cars, morning commuters heading into Anchorage, were already stacking up on the northbound lane.

Cutter skidded to a stop on the far shoulder and flung open his door to peer over the edge. Tracks for the Alaska Railroad paralleled the highway some fifteen feet below. The minivan had jumped them completely, rolling down another twenty feet to land well out in the sticky mud of Turnagain Arm.

Lola turned to go check on the driver of the gravel truck, but he waved her off. He'd climbed out his side door, which now pointed skyward, and stood on the cab, giving him a bird's-eye view of the scene.

"I reckon this guy's going into shock," Lola said.

Cutter took his eyes off the minivan long enough to see the truck driver waving frantically, pointing to the north.

"Oh shit," Lola said, figuring it out the same time as Cutter. "Bore tide!"

The combination of Alaska's huge tidal swings and the narrow neck of Turnagain Arm periodically set up the perfect circumstance for a single wave on an incoming tide. Walls of frigid water as high as ten feet, these bore tides rushed up Turnagain Arm from Cook Inlet like mini tsunamis at speeds over ten miles an hour.

Cutter cupped his hands toward the gravel truck, shouting at the driver.

"How far out?"

"A mile," the man yelled back. "If that."

Cutter looked at Lola, then the minivan. It lay on its side, spewing steam from the radiator, sunk almost to the license plate in the worst kind of mud, a shining slurry of glacial silt. It was only fifteen feet or so out from the rocky bank, but the drop was a steep one, making it plenty far to be underwater when the tide came in.

Like roaches, the Thornton brothers had survived the flying leap over the tracks, the rolling tumble down the rocks, and the sudden impact with the mud. Reese, clearly not the brains of the outfit, kicked out the cargo window and jumped, trying to make a run for it. Cutter heard the man's knee snap as the mud grabbed his ankle like an iron fist while the rest of his body fell forward. Fortunately for him, his brother snatched him by one arm and hauled him back into the van, screaming in pain. The unforgiving mud took his boot as payment.

Cutter had his Colt Python out in the event Reese decided to make the van his Alamo.

"Keep your hands where we can see them!" he barked. "Listen to me. Bore tide is coming in. This mud will eat you alive. We've got about five, six minutes tops to get you out of there before the water gets here and you drown or die of hypothermia."

Given the odds of survival without help, the Thornton brothers kept their hands up and waited to be rescued.

Lola retrieved the ballistic shield and two of the Tahoe's rear floormats made of hard plastic. The driver of a pickup truck donated a plywood bedliner. Several other stranded drivers had hard floor mats and other items, including a whiteboard meant for a business presentation—all of which could be used to create a workable "floating bridge" to dissipate the brothers' weight over the quicksand-like mud. It wasn't so deep as to sink past your knees, but once it had you, it was like standing in a cement block.

The truck driver gave tide reports as they worked and the wall of water got closer. Cutter could hear the roar of the oncoming wave as he and Lola laid out their own ballistic vests to complete the last few feet of bridge.

Ninety seconds after they'd coddled and dragged a whimpering Reese Thornton and his brother to safety, a ten-foot wall of ice-cold seawater slammed into the rocks, then continued onward to the south, taking the makeshift bridge and the minivan with it.

"Why were you hassling us?" Ryan Thornton asked, his teeth chattering from shock while a paramedic who'd climbed over the spilled gravel worked on his brother's broken leg.

"You shot at us, nimrod," Lola said. "We didn't even know you were there."

"You weren't looking for Reese? I thought he might have a warrant . . ."

"Nope," Cutter said.

"Marshals," Ryan nodded. "You were hunting somebody."

"Caldwell Vickers," Lola said.

"I haven't seen Vickers for months." Ryan Thornton swallowed hard. "But I tell you what. If you go easy on me and my brother, I can give you someone better."

"I remind you again," Lola said. "He shot at us."

"You'll want this guy," Ryan said. "I guarantee it."

"And just who would that be?" Lola asked.

"Eddie Dupree," Thornton said.

Cutter raised a brow at the name. Apart from having to write memos to the chief about their lost ballistic vests—and getting shot at—this was turning out to be a pretty good day.

CHAPTER 1

Wainwright, Alaska
Two Years Ago

THE ZIPPER-PULL THERMOMETER ON SEVENTEEN-YEAR-OLD WILLADEAN Benson's baby blue Costco parka read nine below zero. It was almost two in the morning, but it had been dark for a long time. Weeks. The sun had disappeared in mid-November and would not peek above the horizon again for another month—not until late January. Just a glimpse of a cold orange sliver—and that's if the sky happened to be clear.

And then more dark.

Willadean gritted her teeth and tugged the collar of her store-bought parka tighter against her neck, chilled more at the thought of the boys from the party than the angry wind that screamed through overhead power lines. Frigid air pinched her nose, seared her lungs, seeped into her joints. Crystals of frost rimmed her long lashes.

Willadean's father had a strict rule about late-night parties, especially parties with boys from neighboring villages, so she'd crawled out her bedroom window and left the much warmer caribou fur *amauti* on a peg by the front door.

Her house was on the other side of town—not far if she hadn't had to worry about the bone-numbing cold or polar bears or Gordon Ivanov and his creepy friends.

She picked up her pace, trying to ignore the white-hot pain in her lungs. Over her head, a river of green fire bathed the night sky. *Aksarnirq*—the aurora borealis. Beautiful, sure, but it was just one more thing to worry about.

According to Willadean's grandmother, whose name was Tiqriganiannig, but everybody called Foxy, the old ones believed the aurora were walrus spirits playing kickball across the frozen sky with a human head. This, Grandma Foxy assured Willadean, was pure foolishness.

Mostly.

The aurora were not walrus spirits at all, but spirits of the long dead guiding the recently dead toward the afterlife with their colorful torches. If the lights happened to be especially active, these long dead spirits might indeed be playing a game of kickball, but it was very, very rare for them to use a human head.

Inside by the warmth of the oil stove, Grandma Foxy's stories seemed nonsensical, but out here, alone in the frigid darkness, the sky awash with swaying curtains of green and red and purple— walrus spirits and human heads were not that difficult to imagine.

Another gust of wind barreled in off the frozen Chukchi Sea, shoving Willadean sideways. A storm was coming. She could hear it shrieking out on the ice. Dark clouds and blinding snow would soon chase the lights south across the tundra. She broke into a shuffling trot, breathing through her nose and teeth to curb the burning in her lungs. She needed to be home before the storm hit—before Gordon Ivanov realized she'd left the party.

A heavy scraping noise loud enough that she heard it even above the moaning wind yanked her attention to the left.

Her neighbor, Charlie Leavitt, had seen a humongous polar bear over by Wainwright Inlet just a couple of days ago. Polar bears were quiet, though. You rarely heard them coming.

Ghosts of swirling snow kicked up around Willadean's boots, herding her this way and that as she moved. It would have looked like she was staggering had anyone bothered to peer out their window to check on her.

No one did.

She nudged her flimsy hood back with a sealskin mitten and strained her ears, enduring the icy sting as she scanned the shadowed spaces between junked snow machines and weathered wooden homes. In some ways, she hoped the noise was a bear. At least she would know what she was dealing with. Bears considered you food. It was nothing personal. They never pretended to be nice and then tried to corral you all alone in a back bedroom like Gordon Ivanov did.

The party had been a stupid idea. Willadean had things to do after she graduated high school, places to go. She'd dominated the North Slope in girls' cross-country earlier that year and had come in second overall in the state. She was star forward on the Wainwright Huskies girls' basketball team and somehow managed to impress the admissions people in New London, Connecticut, enough they gave her an early admission offer to the United States Coast Guard Academy. She wasn't about to let some dipshit from Nuiqsit get her pregnant and screw up what was basically a four-hundred-thousand-dollar scholarship.

Another sudden movement to her left caused her to stop in her tracks. The crunch of boots against the snow fell silent, leaving nothing but the flapping clatter of something metal on the moaning wind. She sniffed the air and looked half away from the place she'd seen the movement. Grandma Foxy had taught her to rely more on her peripheral vision when it got dark. That did the trick. A dark form slowly came into focus over George and Martha Solomon's front porch—a frozen seal skin draped over a line flagging in the wind like a weather vane.

Another rattle, this one to her right, nearly sent Willadean out of her skin. She ducked instinctively, like a snowshoe hare at the cry of a hawk. Her rational brain assured her it was just the wind. It was definitely not a spirit coming to play kickball with her head. A prolonged gust shook the broken plastic cowling of a junk snow machine mere feet from where she stood. If it had been a bear, she'd be food by now. Her hand dropped to her pocket and the knife she kept there. It might help some against the boys, but it was small comfort when she thought about polar bears or marauding walrus spirits.

Behind her, somewhere in the darkness, rough voices tumbled and fought on the back of the wind. Gordon Ivanov and at least one of his asshole friends—maybe more. Boys like that always seemed to run in packs.

Dammit.

Drunk on home brew—alcohol made from baker's yeast, sugar, and, in this case, a couple of cans of fruit cocktail. Their slurred taunts grew louder.

She was out in the open, a sitting duck against a field of white snow under the glowing northern lights.

Ivanov called out—a nasty growl.

He'd seen her.

Willadean did what any smart prey animal would do when threatened by a predator. She ran for the shadows and didn't look back.

Gordon Ivanov slid to a halt, his freakishly large—but warm—white, military surplus, rubber bunny boots chattering on the driven snow. He raised a fist, signaling for the other boy to stop. An oversize field parka—also military surplus—made him appear much more imposing than he actually was. The ratty fake-fur ruff looked like he'd slept in it. He was winded from his short sprint, and clouds of vapor enveloped his long face. A wisp of a black mustache added to his natural sneer. He pointed his chin at the weathered hulk of a junked snow machine, then crept slowly around it, motioning for his companion to follow.

Nothing.

Ivanov threw his head back and howled. "Where the hell did you gooooo?" Then, to his buddy, "She was right here . . ."

Allen Brown, two years younger than Ivanov but six inches taller, took a half step back and shot a nervous glance over his shoulder. "We should just leave her alone. Come on. I know where my uncle hides his whiskey—"

"If your uncle ever had any whiskey, he drank it already," Ivanov sneered. He grabbed the other boy by the collar of his parka and jerked him closer, as much to steady himself as to get his point across. Wobbly from the home brew, both boys swayed on the uneven ground.

"Tight-ass bitch thinks she's better than us," Ivanov said. "All because she's goin' away to some East Coast college. You can't tell me that don't piss you off."

Brown's halfhearted shrug was nearly lost in his huge parka.

"I guess so."

"Well, it pisses me off," Ivanov said. "I mean, she left the party without even saying good-bye." He jammed his mittened hand at the other boy's chest. "We're gonna hang out. She just doesn't know it yet."

Brown jerked away. "Five minutes ago, you were worried about polar bears—"

"Correction, numb nuts," Ivanov said, his voice dripping with disgust. "I was *talking* about polar bears. I'm *worried* this bitch is gonna get away. Now, see if you can muster up some balls and help me hunt her down. She's probably hiding behind one of these piece of shit machines, listening to every word we say."

Marvin Benson woke up to the thump of an Arctic storm buffeting his house—and another sound he couldn't quite wrap his head around. A low and mournful moan. Creepy as hell. If he'd heard a noise like that when he was a kid, he would have run to his mom and dad. Now he was the dad, so he sat up in bed and listened, trying to figure out what was making the eerie racket.

It was dark, which meant nothing in the Far North. It could have been midnight or ten in the morning at this time of year. Benson blinked away the fog of sleep and glanced at his clock. Five minutes after four. No wonder he had to pee. His wife snored softly beside him, on her back, an open Bible splayed across her chest. She often fell asleep reading the Good Book while he surfed his phone for YouTube tutorials on how to fix snow machines or soup up his four-wheeler. She worked hard, and when her head hit the pillow, she was out. It would take more than a blizzard to wake her up.

Heavy winds shook the house and rattled the doors. Benson liked a good storm. It cleaned things up, scouring away trash and covering up the little piles of the neighbor's dogshit with little white snowdrifts. The trash just blew somewhere else, and the dog-shit was still there, but he didn't have to see it. He counted that as a blessing.

He swung his legs out of bed, then gave a little start when his wife suddenly spoke in the darkness.

"You hear that, Marvin?"

"Mmm," Benson grunted. "I'm going to check after I pee."

The moan grew louder with each step as he shuffled up the hall, so loud he forgot he had to go to the bathroom. Willadean's room was on his right. Four decades of hunting seals on the ice had rendered his feet numb to the cold. It took a moment before he noticed the river of frigid air flowing from under the door.

He knocked. The last thing he wanted to do was barge in on his sleeping teenage daughter.

No answer.

He knocked again.

"Willadean! Are you okay?"

Still nothing but the ghostly moan.

Panic that only the father of daughters can know gripped his chest as he eased open the door. A sickening dread chilled him to the bone. Snow howled in from the bottom of Willadean's window where it had been left open little more than an inch. Her quilts were neat and undisturbed.

Marvin's wife crowded in beside him, still clutching her Bible, took one look at their daughter's empty bed, and began to scream.

CHAPTER 2

Anchorage, Alaska
Present Day

SUPERVISORY DEPUTY US MARSHAL ARLISS CUTTER AND HIS PART-
ner, Deputy Lola Teariki, sat in the early morning darkness, listening to the bark of a distant dog and tick of the slate gray
government-issue Chevy Tahoe as it cooled under the patter of a
steady rain. A running engine would have given away their position.

There was a hierarchy to the hunting of men. Some of the rules
were spoken; some were understood instinctively by those who
did the hunting. Crimes against persons trumped property of-
fenses. Fraudsters and embezzlers were hunted in the margins
when time allowed, often by newer deputy marshals still learning
the ropes. Violent felons rose to the top of the stack—and went to
the real man hunters, deputies with former law enforcement experience or just a particular acumen for the job.

Fugitives like Kevin Edward Dupree, wanted for crimes against
children, earned a scrutiny akin to the light of a thousand suns.

Ordinarily, Cutter would not have bothered kitting up for a surveillance, but this morning the Alaska Fugitive Task Force was
dressed in full battle rattle—ballistic vests with trauma plates over
their hearts and lungs, oblong pouches with individual first-aid

kits, and M4 carbines. A green Kevlar helmet sat on the floorboard between his leather boots.

An arrest was imminent, and Eddie Dupree had a lot to lose.

Information from the Thornton brothers had given them Dupree's latest burner phone. The number had gone active around five in the morning three times over the last seven days, pinging in or around the Holiday gas station and convenience store at Boniface Parkway and DeBarr Road in midtown Anchorage. Two visits could have been a fluke. Three was a pattern, and patterns were a man hunter's friend. Patterns got people caught.

It was ten minutes until four in the morning. Wanting to be early, the task force had already been on station for half an hour. Technically, it was still summer. The first day of autumn was still a couple of weeks away—but Alaska hadn't gotten the memo. Each day was five minutes shorter than the day before, and the first snow of the season—termination dust, they called it—had fallen on the craggy Chugach Mountains to the east of the city. Here at the lower elevations, a steady rain sent chilly rivulets cascading down the windshield. The syrup-sweet smell of wet birch crept into the vehicle with the chill, mingling with the pleasant odors of fresh coffee and Lola Teariki's coconut shampoo.

Periodic wind gusts tossed the birch trees and ripped away leaves, plastering the lonesome Tahoe with mottled yellow spots. In the passenger seat, Cutter found himself grateful for the heavy ballistic vest, even though it threw him forward at an angle that caused his sidearms to dig into the flesh above his belt.

Cutter moved the Colt Python revolver over a skosh, adjusting it and the smaller .40 caliber "baby" Glock 27 that was doing a number over his right kidney below the base of his ballistic vest. He'd carried guns of one kind or another professionally for almost twenty years—nearly four "lustrums," his grandfather would have said. Grumpy always had loved his dusty words.

His weapons now situated over fresh pieces of meat, Cutter took a sip of coffee and reconciled himself to the fact that he'd have permanent divots in his hip by the time he retired—in another couple of lustrums.

A battered Dodge Ram pickup ripped past on DeBarr Road, its tires hissing rooster tails off the wet street.

Deputy Sean Blodgett's voice broke squelch over the radio. He and his partner, Nancy Alvarez, a TFO (task force officer) on loan from the Anchorage Police Department, were parked under a small stand of fir trees at the base of a cell-phone tower in a gravel lot across DeBarr.

"That had to be Troy Swenson in the Dodge," Blodgett said. "We have paper on him for jumping bail on that robbery a month ago downtown by the Performing Arts Center."

The fact that a robbery suspect would be released on bond boggled Cutter's mind.

"Eyes on the prize," Cutter said. "We stick with the plan and focus on Dupree. We'll grab up Mr. Swenson later."

Cutter's grandfather, Grumpy, a Florida Marine Patrol officer who raised Cutter and his older brother, had always said there were only three kinds of people out between midnight and four a.m.— cops, paperboys, and assholes. Paperboys were a dying breed, but in Cutter's experience, Alaska had just the right amount of ass-holes to provide plenty of job security for a professional man hunter.

Kevin Edward Dupree was a prime example. The thirty-nine-year-old convicted sex offender had federal and state warrants for impersonating a federal officer, misconduct involving a child under sixteen, and manufacturing child pornography. The kind of warrant that floated to the top like the turd he was.

Lola Teariki, a fit twenty-something deputy US marshal, held a pair of government-issue Vortex binoculars to her face with one hand while she tucked an errant lock of black hair back into her bun. Her mother was a slight Japanese woman, but the Polyne-sian genes of her Cook Island Māori father seemed to have won out. Muscular arms bulged under the dark-blue USMS mock turtleneck that protruded from her own ballistic vest. The high bun tended to make her face look harsh, belying her bubbly per-sonality. Cutter shared the resting mean-mug, but not the bub-bles.

Sighing like a rambunctious child cooped up inside on a rainy day, she lowered the binoculars and used the steering wheel to push herself back slightly, then drew a deadly looking little knife from a sheath hidden behind her buckle. The black handle fit her hand perfectly. A wicked three-inch blade that resembled a steel claw extended straight out of her clenched fist.

"Nifty get-off-me blade, eh, Cutter?" she said, holding the weapon up between them.

Her husky voice carried the pleasant Kiwi accent of her Cook Islander father, throwing away her Rs and clipping her vowels. Cutter's name became "Cuttah."

He recognized the little blade as a Clinch Pick. Small but lethal.

"My Japanese auntie and one of my brothers each gave me one of these puppies for my birthday." She reached into the pocket of her vest and produced an identical knife in a black Kydex sheath, passing it across the console to Cutter. "I'm not sure about giving a sharp instrument to an emotional time bomb such as you, but what am I gonna do with two supercool little stabby things? Besides, it seems like you're always dropping your grandfather's revolver. I figure a last-ditch weapon like this might come in handy one day."

Cutter took the Clinch Pick in his fist and used his thumb to pop the blade out of the Kydex sheath.

He had to admit, it was a cool little stabby thing.

He pushed it back toward her. Though they operated as partners, Cutter was actually her supervisor.

"Lola . . ."

"Bullshit," Lola chuckled. "Screw policy. I reckon we can call it a birthday gift."

"It's not my birthday."

"It will be."

"How about I borrow it for a while?" he said. "Try it out."

"Sweet as," she said. "Borrow it as long as you want." She tucked her Clinch Pick back into its sheath on her belt and raised the binoculars again. "I haven't heard anything about Ethan's case lately. How's that coming?"

Cutter's older brother had been killed in an oil rig explosion on the North Slope of Alaska two years before. At first, it was thought to have been an accident. New clues pointed to a murder. Cutter didn't talk about it to most people, but he and Lola had been through enough that she'd become more like a kid sister than a partner. She'd earned herself a pass. That didn't necessarily earn her an answer—frankly, because Cutter didn't have one. It had been a busy summer with mandatory supervisor school in Georgia and an excruciating stint as acting chief while Jill Phillips rotated to USMS headquarters on TDY. When he did find time to follow up, he found that virtually every lead had dried up.

"Working on it," he said.

Deputy Blodgett broke squelch again, rescuing him from going into more detail.

"We've got movement outside the stop-n-rob . . . At the east end, in that little alcove by the ice boxes."

Lola threw her binoculars to her eyes.

"*Popongi!*" she said.

It was the Cook Island Māori expression for "good morning," but Teariki often used it when a target showed up on an early morning surveillance.

There was momentary silence while everyone studied the situation through their binoculars and attempted to identify the players through rain-streaked glass.

"It's just some dude talking to Squish," Alvarez said at length. "Definitely not Dupree. Repeat. Negative on Dupree."

"Copy," Lola said over the radio. Then, just to Cutter. "Squish Merculief . . . I feel for that kid."

"Squish," Cutter mused. "That's an interesting name . . ."

He peered through his binoculars again to find a wisp of a woman loitering outside the convenience store. Even from that distance, he could see the sunken eyes and gaunt hollows of her cheeks. She moved in short, jerky motions, as if startled by every sight and sound.

"Poor kid was in bad shape when I saw her a couple of months ago," Lola said. "Couch surfing at a place we hit at Penland trailer park. We had to give her two doses of Narcan just to save her ass. She bolted awake in a full-bore panic, looking for her next fix."

"Narcan'll do that," Cutter said, his voice muffled against his hands as he continued to study the scene.

His heart sank. Squish's baggy yellow plastic raincoat swallowed her up and made her look like a child. She was probably only in her early twenties, but life on the street had taken the bark off her and added years. Small and weak, she reminded him of someone from a long time ago in a very faraway place.

Lola brightened. "Hey, Dupree's been popped for fentanyl possession before. Maybe he's dealing now and she's here for a meet with him."

"Could be," Cutter said, not counting on it.

A blessed silence fell over the car, but as usual, Lola didn't wait long before filling it.

"Mim told me the boys want a dog."

Taken aback, Cutter turned sideways in his seat. The thought of Lola chatting with his widowed sister-in-law was like sailing in uneven seas.

"When did you talk to Mim?"

Lola gave a little shrug. "I ran into her when we were both doing laps at the Dome a couple of days ago."

"Ah," Cutter said.

She raised her eyebrows up and down. "That girl's got a set of legs on her."

Cutter kept his eyes on the windshield. He couldn't help but picture Mim's legs. He'd met her when they were only sixteen, fallen in love with her right then and there, moments before his smooth-talking older brother had swooped in and . . .

"I had a dog for a while," Lola said. "He was like a bad boyfriend. Warm enough in bed . . . but needy as hell."

Cutter eyed her again.

"I don't want another dog," she said. "But I reckon the boys should get one."

"Of course, you do," Cutter said.

Conversations with Lola could change directions at the blink of an eye. Thankfully, she'd veered back to the case at hand. She snatched up the powder-blue warrant file from between the seats and looked at the photo taped to the cover page.

"Why do these dicks always have to say they're deputy marshals when they decide to pretend to be cops?" It was a rhetorical question, so Cutter simply left it alone.

"Eddie . . . Edward . . . Edwardo . . . ," Lola mused. She curled her lip, scrunching her nose as if the name were bitter. For her, every warrant was personal. A mission. Cutter knew exactly how she felt. "He looks like a normal dude," she said. "But North Las Vegas coppers found a fake Marshals badge on him and a USMS raid jacket along with heaps of sex toys in a tackle box in the back of his car." She shook her head in disgust. "I mean, give me a break. An FBI badge and a trunk full of sex toys . . . that would make sense—"

Nancy Alvarez's voice crackled over the radio.

"You guys seeing this?"

Cutter threw the binoculars to his eyes.

Squish Merculief had gone inside the store. She stood at the counter engaged in an animated conversation with the clerk.

"I know this guy," Alvarez said. "Micah something or other . . . He's a level-ten *pendejo*. Tells me every time I see him how he woulda been a cop but for . . . insert excuse of the week. Likes to let folks see the butt of his Hi-Point he keeps in his waistband. Last time I went in, he was sporting an ankle monitor."

Cutter watched as Micah reached over the counter as if to touch the young woman. She took a step back. It was impossible to tell from all the way across the street, but it looked to Cutter as if she'd suddenly grown smaller.

Sean Blodgett spoke next. "Anyone got eyes on Dupree?"

"Negative," Lola said.

Inside the convenience store, Micah came around the counter, putting himself between the girl and the door. He was at least a foot taller than her. The short sleeves of his convenience store uniform shirt were rolled up to show off mirror-muscle biceps. He put a hand on her shoulder.

She jerked away.

A low growl rumbled in Cutter's chest.

Squish took another step backward, clearly scanning the store as if for an escape.

Micah scanned too, glancing out the window to see that there was no one in the parking lot.

He leaned in toward Squish, as if to kiss her.

She crawfished backward, bumping into a display of potato chips and falling to the ground.

Micah followed, looming over her.

Lola had her binoculars up now.

"This guy's got some nerve—"

Cutter slammed his hand against the dash. "Go!"

Lola looked at him, incredulous. "He hasn't—"

Cutter undid his seat belt and started to open the door to get out.

"Okay, I'm going!" Lola snapped.

"Then go now!" He pounded the dash again, still ready to bail if the G-car didn't start to roll.

She threw the Tahoe in gear and, after a quick check for oncoming traffic, stomped the gas to shoot across DeBarr Road, hitting the concrete median at an angle to bounce and bump over the top.

Blodgett's headlights came on in the trees to the west of the store. "Did you guys spot Dupree?"

Cutter snatched up the mic. "Negative." Then to Lola as he threw open the door and jumped out of the still-rolling Tahoe, "Tell them what's going on."

"All righty," she said. "As soon as I figure that out . . ."

Cutter only heard part of it, already sprinting straight for the door.

Inside the store, Squish tried to shrug off Micah's advances, wanting no part of whatever he was suggesting.

The muscular clerk grabbed her by the hood of her raincoat and dragged her across the floor toward the candy aisle, apparently so hyper-focused he failed to hear the ping of the door chime. The hapless kid didn't even look up until Cutter snatched a handful of greasy hair and lifted him onto his tiptoes.

"US Marshals!" Cutter barked. "Knock it off!"

Screaming in surprise and pain, the clerk dropped the young woman like a hot potato.

"Hands!" Cutter growled. "Let me see your hands!"

Micah stretched his arms to the side like wings, hands open wide, eyes clenched tight.

The door chime pinged again as Alvarez entered the store, her pistol drawn, angled toward the floor.

"Micah," she said. "You got your handgun on your belt?"

The kid kept his arms so straight it looked like his elbows might pop. He nodded, then opened his eyes to look up and find a frowning Arliss Cutter—and lost control of his bladder.

"Well, this warrant shit the bed," Sean Blodgett groused while Cutter turned their prisoner over to a responding APD patrol officer. "What happened to 'eyes on the prize,' boss?"

Cutter didn't answer. There was no point. Blodgett and everyone else on the Alaska Fugitive Task Force had worked with him long enough to know what he would and would not stand for.

Nancy Alvarez took a statement from Squish Merculief.

"I'd be glad to press charges against that pervert." The young woman rocked from one foot to the other, hugging herself tight. Her face twitched and squirmed, like she had a bad itch. "Guys like him think they can give you a cup of coffee and . . . you know . . ." She swayed in place, blinking at Alvarez. "Can I go?"

The task force officer folded her notebook. "Have you got any outstanding warrants?"

Squish gave a noncommittal shrug. "How am I supposed to know that?"

"I'll take that as a no. You need a place to get warm?"

"I'm good," Squish mumbled.

Alvarez gestured with her chin toward the sidewalk. "Go on then. I'll check to see if you're wanted some other time. You've been through enough shit for one night."

Squish brightened some now that she wasn't going to jail, but her face continued to twitch and jerk. "Who are you guys here looking for?"

"What?"

Squish laughed. "I may be a junkie, but I'm smart enough to know you guys didn't just swoop in to save my skinny ass."

Alvarez chuckled and hooked a thumb over her shoulder at Cutter.

"Pretty sure he did."

"Come on," Squish said. "Maybe I can help you, get a little crime-stoppers money or something."

Alvarez glanced at Cutter, her brow up at the possibility. He gave a slight shake of his head. If word got out on the street that they were looking for Dupree, this location would be blown for good.

"Nobody in particular," Alvarez said to Squish.

Squish shrugged again, not buying it but not caring, either. She put her yellow hood up against the drizzling rain and walked out from under the awning without another word and disappeared into the darkness.

"We'll get him, boss," Lola said once the girl was out of earshot.

Cutter's phone began to buzz before he could answer. He glanced at his watch and stifled a groan. Ten minutes past five. Calls at this time of the morning rarely carried good news. It was Jill Phillips, chief deputy US marshal for the District of Alaska. He'd dispensed with the heavy ballistic vest, trading it for a raincoat. A cascade of chilly water ran down his back when he pushed back the hood.

"Mornin', Big Iron," Phillips said as soon as he answered. She never missing the chance to poke a little fun at his choice to carry a revolver when the rest of the Marshals Service carried Glocks. (The baby Glock 27 kept him in compliance with USMS policy, but just barely.) The chief's soft Kentucky drawl poured out of the phone, cotton-mouthed and fatigued like you'd expect the mother of a toddler to be when she is woken from a sound sleep an hour before her usual time. "Are you still sittin' surveillance on Dupree?"

"We had a couple of complications," Cutter said.

"Is that a fact?" Phillips groused. "Did somebody get throat punched?"

"All throats on the scene remain unharmed," Cutter said. "Good guys and bad."

"I'll get the details in your report," she said, obviously in no mood for early-morning jokes. "Listen, the AST need your help tracking a couple of hikers on Pioneer Peak."

AST was the Alaska State Troopers.

Lola stepped around to his side of the Chevy, eavesdropping as good partners did. She whispered, "Joe Bill and I hiked Pioneer Peak on Saturday."

"Lola can stay on the hunt for Dupree," Phillips continued. "But I need you heading north. Captain Krieger will meet you at the trailhead."

"You bet," Cutter said. "So you're aware, Lola and her boyfriend hiked that same mountain just a couple of days ago. Her experience might come in handy."

Phillips gave an exhausted sigh, then she said, "Never go anywhere for the first time," quoting one of Cutter's grandfather's well-known rules.

Lola, still listening in, gave Cutter a thumbs-up.

"Exactly," Cutter said. "And since Lola's already set foot on the mountain, I wouldn't be going in blind."

"You have the gear you need for rural work?"

Lola nodded, a puppy eager to get on the trail.

"We're both good to go," Cutter said. "Never leave home without it."

"All righty . . ." Phillips gave a tired cough. "Call me when you're en route. I'll brief you on the way. And don't spare the horses. It's kind of a big deal that the Troopers actually thought to call us for help."

CHAPTER 3

Wainwright, Alaska

"*I* AM NOT JOKIN' BOYS!" NAOMI IPALOOK SMACKED HER HAND against the kitchen table. Hard. She wasn't going to hurt it. The wood surface was cut and marred from two decades of butchering seals and caribou and blackfish and tomcod.

Her sons, ten and twelve, were glued to morning cartoons and hardly moved at the sudden racket.

Today, the table was covered with Tupperware bowls, each filled with two gallons of waxy, red lowbush cranberries. Naomi was in the process of dividing them into meal-sized portions and then dumping those portions into sandwich baggies, ready for the freezer. In the old days, they would have been mixed with tallow and frozen. The family had already stocked away gallons of golden salmonberries, blueberries, and tiny nagoonberries, which looked like perfect little half raspberries but grew low to the ground on the Arctic tundra. Lowbush cranberries, often called lingonberries, were the last to come in, much sweeter after a good frost. The boys preferred to eat them in pancakes. Naomi's husband, Abner, one of the local whaling captains, liked them in a sauce over just about any kind of meat—especially bowhead whale.

The Iñupiaq woman looked over the top of purple cat-eye

reading glasses and gave a frustrated shake of her head. The boys had an hour before they needed to leave for school. That was plenty of time if they'd just get their butts in gear.

Garth and Clinton, named for their grandfathers, sat cross-legged in front of the TV. Both were dressed in sweatpants, two-sizes-too-big Wainwright Huskies T-shirts, and basketball shoes. Each boy had a wool blanket pulled around his neck against the morning chill. Winter came early to the shores of the Arctic Ocean. It was cold enough in the Ipalook house to run the stove, but heating oil was pushing seven bucks a gallon, so Naomi put on a sweater and resolved to leave it off for another week at least.

She gave the table another smack, rattling the berries far more than she rattled her sons.

Neither boy was afraid she would actually spank them. She could, however, hit them where it hurt in other ways.

"Your dad met with the other whaling captains last night to decide when they're going out. He was gonna have you help clear out a path for the boat sleds, but I guess you'll still be home getting the cellar straightened up instead."

Clinton, the younger of the two, crinkled his nose and knitted his brow—an unspoken sign of dissent in Iñupiaq.

Garth rocked under his blanket, eyes glued to the cartoon on TV. His voice was deadpan, mimicking his father. "Clinton's scared to go down inside the ice cellar."

The younger boy recoiled as if he'd been slapped. He toppled forward, crashing into his brother and knocking him over.

"*You're* the one who's scared."

"It's dark down there . . . and cold," Garth said. "Maybe we should wait for grandpa to help us."

"We're not gonna make your grandfather climb down that ladder!" Naomi snapped. "How's it gonna look if the whale boat captain doesn't have a clean cellar to store our meat? It disrespects your dad, and it disrespects the whale."

Clinton's nose remained crinkled, like he'd just eaten something bad. "I watched this TikTok where these girls said we shouldn't even be catching whales . . ."

"Well," Naomi said, not feeling up to the debate. "We have been for a thousand years. And we keep clean ice cellars too, so get a move on."

Feelings about whale hunting ran deep and strong on both sides, but to the Iñupiaq people of Alaska, landing a whale was as much a part of life as going to the grocery store was for people who lived on the road system. Both Naomi and Abner Ipalook held the deep and abiding belief that a subsistence lifestyle—gathering, hunting from land and sea—kept their boys healthy, both mentally and physically.

Naomi would do whatever it took to keep her boys grounded in tradition—to their heritage.

"That's fine." She shrugged and returned to bagging berries. "I'll tell your dad you are gonna stay home with me instead of going out on the ice with him."

The boys were up in a flash. Throwing on their coats and scrambling for the door.

A blast of Arctic air rolled in before they got the door shut, shivering the hairs on Naomi Ipalook's neck. She'd never admit it to her boys, but she didn't much care for that ice cellar, either.

Ten-year-old Clinton Ipalook hunched in front of the plywood door like a deviled porcupine and clicked his flashlight nervously on and off. His older brother turned up the collar of a hand-me-down coat and snugged a wool hat down low over his ears. A dark wind blew off the broken sea ice—from out where his father would soon go for bowhead whale. Garth threw back the metal hasp and, with his little brother's help, pulled open the piece of plywood that served as a door. Their dad was proud of the fact that he didn't lock his ice cellar. He was a whale boat captain. The Ipalooks *fed* the village, he told his sons. They didn't lock food away.

"This wind sucks," the older boy said. "Funny that we gotta climb into the ice cellar to get warm."

Clinton leaned a heavy piece of driftwood on the edge of the plywood to keep it from blowing shut while they were inside. That had happened once, and it scared him so bad he'd nearly clawed Garth's eyes out trying to get to the ladder. It was embarrassing, and the boy vowed to never let anything like that happen to them again.

Garth leaned over the open pit and braced himself with both hands on the wooden tripod of rough timbers, pushing the rusted pulley out of the way. A sturdy two-by-four ladder and a yellow extension cord disappeared into the blackness of the dark hole.

Roughly a yard wide at the mouth, the pit dropped straight down almost ten feet before it widened into a ten-by-ten-foot round room. The hollow space was shaped like an upside-down mushroom in the dirt and permafrost. The boys' grandfather had dug it, or maybe their great grandfather. Clinton couldn't exactly remember, but it had been here a long time—forever.

"Helloooo!" Garth shouted, poking his head into the hole. "We're coming down. Please don't eat us, Mr. Hairy Man!"

"Shut up!" Clinton elbowed him in the ribs. "You go first," he said.

"Happy to," Garth said, unable to resist doing what older brothers did best. "If that's what you want. It's still dark, and Long Nails lives up here on top. I'll be way safer down there."

Long Nails was the name of the mythical old woman who ate children that played in the beach grass near the water. Her toenails were said to click on the frozen ground as she galloped after you on all fours.

"That's . . . not true . . ." Clinton tried to put on a brave face but wasn't so sure. "Can we please just go down and finish this?"

Garth flicked on the shop light hanging at the end of the extension cord as soon as his feet touched the ground. The bare bulb threw creepy shadows across the rough walls of dirt and permafrost.

The musky odor of something very close to blue cheese hit the boys in the face. Centuries of living in these harsh Arctic conditions had taught their forebearers how to preserve food for maximum nutritional value over the long winters. It was not

uncommon for meat to be left to ripen or "ferment" out of the
sun, rendering it a delicacy that would turn the nose and stomach
of people from other cultures.

Normally, the smells would have made Clinton's mouth water,
but he wasn't thinking about food this morning. He squinted like
his stomach hurt, but went right to work, straightening up waxed
cardboard boxes and the few pieces of remaining meat that had
fallen over since the spring hunt. The back leg of a *tuttu*—caribou—frozen solid and wrapped in an old pillowcase, leaned
against one of the boxes. Several frantic up-and-down trips by the
boys on errands from their mother over the past months had
caused many of the food piles to slump or fall into disarray.

The bulb twisted and swung as the wind nudged at the extension cord above. Clinton's eyes flitted around the room, following
the shadows.

"Hurry up," he said.

"What do you think that is?" Garth aimed his flashlight on what
looked like a tangle of gray-green fuzz. "I think Hairy Man's been
down here . . ."

"I said stop it!" Clinton said. "It's just roots and stuff. You know
that." A sob caught in his throat. "Seriously, Garth. Please . . ."

The fact that Clinton was about to cry only seemed to increase
the older boy's resolve. He wasn't about to pass up the opportunity
to scare the crap out of his little brother. Clinton could see it in his
face. If something ran, a predator had to chase it. It was the law.

Garth's voice grew somber.

"Something's been down here." He took hold of the exposed
roots and put the flashlight under his chin with his free hand, giving a ghostly moan. "Whoooooo—"

The roots pulled free much easier than either boy had anticipated, causing a sudden avalanche of dirt and ice as a section of
the wall fell away.

Clinton turned and covered his face with both hands, screaming inside, half expecting to be buried alive. He breathed a sigh
of relief when he looked down and saw the mound of dirt and
milky ice had merely piled around his boots.

Garth had fallen backward when the grass gave way, but he was still facing the wall. He raised a hand and pointed, claw-like, stricken, over Clinton's shoulder, like something was behind him.

The oldest trick in the book.

"Nice try," Clinton said. "You're not getting—"

He turned, expecting to see more root balls. Instead, he found himself nose to nose with a mummified girl who stared back at him from behind a layer of crystal-clear ice. Her dark brown eyes wide and life-like, her mouth open, with pale blue lips drawn back to expose her teeth as if frozen in the middle of a terrified scream.

Garth Ipalook broke out of his stupor and tripped over his own feet scrambling for the ladder. He slipped on the bottom rung, splitting open his chin and nearly knocking himself unconscious.

Ten-year-old Clinton stood rooted in place, his eyes locked on the frozen girl.

"She . . . she used to babysit us when we were little," he whispered. "It's . . . Willadean . . ."

CHAPTER 4

Anchorage

LOLA FUDGED THE SPEED LIMIT AS SHE HEADED NORTHEAST OUT OF town on the Glenn Highway. They were going to assist the troopers, after all, so who was going to stop them?

Tracks and any associated sign left on the ground were perishable. They were ruined by weather and time, of course, but more often than not were obliterated by the careless footprints of other rescue personnel. It wouldn't take long before the entire area was trampled so completely it would be rendered useless.

Cutter held his Battle Board on his lap and took notes while Lola drove and Chief Phillips briefed them over Cutter's phone.

Twenty-one-year-old James Burleson and nineteen-year-old Miranda Hill had gone missing on Pioneer Peak, a six-thousand-foot-plus mountain in the Chugach Range that towered above the farmland and glacial valleys of Palmer. Six thousand feet didn't seem especially tall when compared with other mountains in the lower forty-eight, but the trailhead was near sea level, so virtually every foot was vertical gain. Much of the climb was above the tree line and completely exposed to the weather. Neither Burleson nor Hill had much backcountry experience, but according to Burleson's mother, who was waiting at the trailhead, they had the necessary gear to protect them from the harsh elements. They'd not taken a gun, but both carried cans of pepper spray and wore jingling bear bells to warn the big brownies of their approach. They'd camped for one night somewhere off the ridgeline trail, then hiked to the south summit the following morning. Their plan had been to be back at the trailhead that afternoon, but Burleson had called his mother around six p.m. to say he'd gotten turned around on their descent. He'd called again two hours later, saying they'd sorted everything out but didn't expect to reach their truck until midnight.

That was the last Mrs. Burleson had heard from her son.

Lola grimaced at that news.

"Pioneer Peak trail can be hella gnarly coming down if you take a wrong turn." She stared straight ahead at the thumping windshield wipers as she drove. "There are heaps of bears on that mountain."

"That's what I hear," Phillips said.

Cutter looked up from his Battle Board, turning his head to speak into the phone he'd set on the console between him and Lola. "I'm surprised the Troopers are holding the scene for us."

"That's why you need to scoot," Phillips said. "They're not. Not really, anyway. Alaska Search and Rescue volunteers are gearing up as we speak, and a couple of troopers are heading that way from Palmer. Captain Krieger called to ask for you personally. He's seen you track. The other troopers are going to want to move on up the trail. The captain is on his way from Chugiak, probably just ahead of you. Hopefully, he gets there before his troops do."

Cutter leaned sideways, pressing his head against the passenger window so he could get a better view of the weather. The sun wouldn't be up for an hour and a half. The valley faced north and was socked in with clouds, meaning the shadows would linger until much later in the day—if they ever left.

"Weather's too bum for any air assets," he said.

"Trooper pilots are guessing it's supposed to clear later this morning," Phillips said. "But you're right. This business is going to start off as a ground search." The sound of an unhappy toddler overwhelmed the connection. Phillips paused, groaning as if she was picking up something heavy. The child fell silent. The chief had a way with kids and deputy US marshals, often pointing out that there wasn't that much of a difference. "Let me know if you need anything . . . and Arliss, Sergeant Yates is one of the troopers coming in from Palmer. Do me a favor and don't kick him in the nuts."

It was Cutter's turn to groan, but he kept his thoughts to himself.

Lola picked up the slack. "That guy's a dick," she said. Her accent turned it into "*deek.*" For some reason, that sounded like an even better description to Cutter. Yates was a deek.

"Agreed," Phillips said. "And your job is to keep your partner from killing him."

Cutter ended the call with the chief and used his phone to pull up a topographic map of Pioneer Ridge on the AllTrails app. The tiny screen wasn't optimal but it looked straightforward enough, and he had a lifetime of land nav skills—and Lola.

Pioneer Peak was a broad wing-like mountain named for the "pioneers" who had been sent to homestead the region by the US government during the Great Depression, many of whose families still lived and farmed in the fertile Matanuska-Susitna Valley. The indigenous Dena'ina peoples who had lived in the shadow of the great mountain long before any White settlers from the lower forty-eight called it Dnla'iy—the one that watches us.

Fitting, Cutter thought.

Planning ahead, Cutter went over the contents of his gear bag in his head. Beyond the tools of his trade—i.e., his sidearms and handcuffs—he started with the three basics, a knife, a light, and something to make fire, then built from that. He carried two knives—his late brother's 3DK sheath knife and a small folding pocketknife he used to whittle when he needed to ponder on something important. His key ring held a Surefire Titan flashlight and a two-inch ferrocerium fire-steel. Cutter's grandfather, Grumpy, had always said you could tell an expert woodsman by the stuff he *didn't* need to pack. Cutter planned on being back before dark but was prepared to bivouac overnight if it came to that.

He'd been in enough tight spots with Lola Teariki to trust her abilities when it came to fieldwork—urban or rural. She knew what gear worked in Alaska. Hell, she'd taught him a thing or two when he'd made supervisor and transferred up from Florida to help his recently widowed sister-in-law. If Lola said she was prepared to hit the woods, she was ready.

She turned and glanced at him, seemingly aware that he was thinking about her. "This," she said, jamming her index finger into the console between them. "This here is exactly what I love about a typical day with the United States Marshals Service!"

"Tracking turned-around hikers and dodging brown bears in the dark?" Cutter said, though he knew exactly what she meant.

"Hell yeah." She grinned. "That—and I love that I can come to work thinking the day is going to be one thing and it turns out to be a half dozen adventures before lunch that I hadn't even considered."

"Or we sit in court all day," Cutter offered.

"Sure," she said. "But come on, Cutter. Think about it. This morning we used sophisticated telephone and computer tech to track Dupree, you kicked some shithead's ass—"

"I didn't kick his ass."

"You kinda did," she said, breathless. "Anyway, now we're heading for a slog up a muddy mountain trail to find a couple of lost hikers, who, for all we know, got themselves eaten by a bear." She tapped on the steering wheel and nodded to herself. "You just never know what we're going to get into. That's why they call us the action service."

"You sound like a recruiting video."

"Hey," she shrugged. "It's who we are . . ."

"True enough," Cutter said. "But Burleson's mother's waiting at the trailhead. Let's keep the man-eating bear talk to ourselves."

"For sure." Lola nodded at the empty highway ahead of them. "We got smooth sailing. No pokey RVs to slow our roll this time of the morning."

"Tell me about the mountain," Cutter said. He kept the All-Trails map open on his phone for reference.

Lola sighed. "It's beautiful," she said, "and sinister, too. We'll have good switchbacks for the first couple of miles, through thick trees. It's relatively steep right off the bat. It was muddy as hell when Joe Bill and I went up, but that's good as far as tracking is concerned. Right?"

"It can be," Cutter said.

"Anyway, some wooden bridges, and heaps of bear scat while you're still in the trees, then you break out and you're basically ridge running for a bit before a scramble to the top. Hard to get too lost above the tree line. I mean, you can see the road."

"You'd be surprised."

"The way down can be tricky, though. Heaps of false routes that can ding you. You basically keep to the left going up, so you'd think you'd stay to the right coming down, but there are a couple of little side trails you might miss on the way up that can put you at some gnarly canyons that are between you and the parking lot."

Lola got off the highway onto the Old Glenn, heading almost due west on the narrow two-lane. Braided channels of the Knik River lay to the left. Tree-choked vertical walls of the Chugach Mountains rose to their right. Neither was visible in the heavy fog.

"I want to hit the ground running as soon as we get there," Cutter said.

"It's still dark."

"Yep," Cutter said. "And raining. I'd like to get ahead of the other searchers and see what the ground tells us. What are we, ten minutes out?"

"If that," Lola said.

Cutter punched in Captain Krieger's number and put the phone on speaker. He and Lola had worked with the captain just months before, tragically identifying tracks at the crime scene of a murdered Alaska State Trooper. Krieger was of Iñupiaq and Tsimshian heritage and had grown up in the rural village of Un-alakleet. Search and rescue operations and the tracking that went along with them were nothing new to him.

"Thank you for coming out here so quickly," Krieger said when he picked up. "I'd just pulled into the parking lot and was speaking to the boy's mother when you called. Weather's still too low to get a helo up there, but it's supposed to clear soon. I've got an ambulance en route along with my troopers. ASAR folks should be here any minute. I'll keep 'em off the trailhead."

"Obliged for that," Cutter said. He pointed to a Honda Accord parked on the south side of the road. He'd never been to the trailhead before and thought they'd arrived.

Lola slowed but shook her head and whispered. "Parking lot's still a quarter mile up."

Cutter nodded. "We're two minutes out," he said to Krieger. "See if Ms. Burleson knows what brand of boots her son is wearing."

"Roger that," the captain said. "I've got her moving her car away from the boy's truck. Keeping that area clear for you—though I'm not sure what good it will do. It's been pouring all night here. The ground's not much more than muddy soup."

"Are we fairly certain they're still on the mountain?" Cutter asked.

"You mean did a bear drag them off when they reached their car?" Krieger said. "There is that possibility. Are you still carrying your grandad's old Colt Python?"

"I am indeed."

"That's good," Krieger said. "I chased off a brown bear sow when I pulled up. She hauled ass across the road toward the river, but there's always a chance she circled back in the pucker brush."

Lola shot a side-eye at Cutter, then looked at the phone. "Did she have cubs?"

"If she did, I didn't see them," Krieger said. "My Glock .40 is better than teeth and fingernails, but your .357 Magnum would be mighty handy to have."

"And a twelve-gauge," Lola said.

"True enough," Krieger chuckled. "To answer your earlier question, I haven't ruled anything out at this point, including a bear dragging them into the woods—though I saw no sign of that . . . other than the sow nosing around. I'm thinking she was looking for something to drag into the woods. To be honest, I was hoping you'd be able to look at the trail and give me some insight . . ." He paused, said something Cutter couldn't make out, then, "Listen, Mrs. Burleson is coming up to my vehicle, so I'd better curtail the bear talk . . . I've got eyes on a pair of headlights coming up the road through the foliage. Guessing that's you."

Lola looked at Cutter as he ended the call, as if waiting for him to weigh in. He didn't, so she plowed ahead.

"If they're just lost, they're probably in the trees. I'm guessing the visibility is pretty much nil up on the ridgeline. Storms come howling off the Gulf of Alaska and funnel up Cook Inlet into these mountains. Joe Bill and I hit a window of good weather on Saturday morning when we started up, but it was raining sideways by the time we reached the tree line coming back down."

She slowed, waited a beat while she made the turn into the trailhead parking lot, then said, "What's your opinion?"

Cutter looked at her, tapping his pen on the plexiglass front of his Battle Board. "Right now, my opinion is that I should listen to your experience and expertise."

"I reckon that's mighty cool of you, boss," she said. "But I want to know what you think about what happened here. What's *your* opinion?"

"I don't have one."

She grimaced, unconvinced. "Not even a guess?"

He shook his head. If he'd been a smiling man, he would have sent one her way. Instead, he gave the slightest of shrugs. "It's okay not to have an opinion this early in the game. I'm sure I'll get one after I study the ground for a while. We'll see where the tracks lead us."

Lola put the Tahoe in park and killed the engine. "Well, in my opinion, if we find any tracks at all, there is a significant chance those tracks lead us to a steaming pile of bear shit full of pepper spray and jingle bells."

CHAPTER 5

*T*O HIS CREDIT, CAPTAIN KRIEGER HAD PARKED AT THE EAST END OF the gravel parking lot, well away from the lone Nissan Pathfinder and any remaining tracks that might give Cutter at least a portion of the story. The Nissan would be the "point last seen" or "last known point" as far as the trail went. It was presumed that the lost couple had hiked up to Pioneer Ridge, but Cutter preferred to let the tracks tell him what happened.

Krieger's shadowed figure stood beside the door of his unmarked AST Durango. He adjusted the plastic rain cover over his dark blue Stetson campaign hat with his left hand. His right hand rested on his pistol as he stood guard while Mrs. Burleson locked the door to her car and hobbled toward him on a set of wooden crutches. Her dark-green raincoat caused her to all but disappear in the downpour.

Cutter and Lola made a run for the captain's Dodge. As badly as he wanted to hit the trail, they needed information, so they climbed in the back seat behind Krieger. Mrs. Burleson sat in the front passenger seat, crutches between her knees.

"I would have gone looking for them myself," she said after the captain made introductions, "if not for this stupid hip."

"You did the right thing," Krieger said. "Calling us."

The poor woman gave a whimpering sigh. "Because of the bear?"

"There is that," Krieger said.

Burleson twisted in her seat, looking at the captain first, then to Lola and Cutter in turn. Her voice was frail and breathy, unsure. "Do you think that's why my son hasn't called me back? Do you really think a bear has—"

"That's not likely, ma'am," Cutter said. It wasn't unlikely, either, but there was no reason to traumatize the poor woman any more than she already was. Better to get her mind on something else. "Can you tell me what kind of footwear your son is wearing?"

"I know exactly what he's got on," she said. "Size ten Asolo hiking boots. I bought them for him at REI last year when they were on sale."

"Any health conditions?"

"None," Mrs. Burleson said.

"And Ms. Hill's boots?" Cutter asked.

"I'm sorry, I—" Burleson's cell phone rang. "It's Miranda's mother," she whispered, before putting the phone on speaker. "Hello, Georgia. I have troopers and US Marshals trackers here with me. They're about to start up the mountain."

She said nothing about the possibility of bears.

"Still no word from James?" Georgia Hill asked.

Mrs. Burleson's voice cracked. "I'm afraid not. Not since yesterday." The poor woman's eyes sagged to half-mast. Worry and waiting had taken a toll. "He . . . he was going to propose."

"Seriously?" This from Miranda's father. The man's derisive tone made Cutter sit up and take note. Georgia Hill chided her husband, whispering through clenched teeth for him to calm down. He didn't. "Brainless little shits . . ."

An airport intercom blared in the background.

"They're calling for us to board," Mrs. Hill said. "We'll be there in" . . .

"Two hours," her husband groused. His voice grew distant. Cutter could picture him walking away.

"Give us a call when you land," Captain Krieger said. "We'll text you if we have any updates. You should be able to get them in the air."

Lola started to say something, but Cutter shook his head. "We should get started."

Captain Krieger left Mrs. Burleson warming herself in the SUV and followed Lola and Cutter to the back of the Tahoe while they geared up.

Cutter took off his jacket and braved the pelting rain long enough to shrug on a chest rig that contained most of his gear. He'd originally thought to leave the long-gun duties to Lola, but considering the presence of the brown bear sow, he decided to sling the shorty Remington 870 over his shoulder. Boasting an eleven-inch barrel and ball-like bird's-head grip, the extremely concealable weapon was known in the Marshals Service as a "Wit-Sec shotgun." Lola grabbed her issued 870 from the truck, this one with a full stock and a maneuverable fourteen-inch barrel. Both weapons were loaded with a combination of Brenneke Black Magic lead slugs and double-aught buckshot, carried patrol ready—chamber empty, four in the tube, safety off, trigger pulled. If a threat presented, all one had to do was rack a round in the chamber and fire.

Headlights arced across the parking lot as two more trooper SUVs wheeled in from the road, followed by an ambulance and a couple of civilian vehicles. The lead SUV, obviously driven by Sergeant Yates, pulled up directly behind Lola's Tahoe, high beams glaring until the captain waved at him to turn them off. Cutter kept his right eye shut to retain at least a modicum of night vision.

Lola shielded her face with the flat of her hand, letting her middle finger inch out to salute the idiot sergeant.

"You know he did that on purpose," she whispered.

"Yep."

"I always liked those Trooper Stetsons," she said. "But Yates looks like a roofing nail . . ."

Krieger gave a dry chuckle.

The sergeant jumped out of the SUV with his pack, took one look at Cutter, and started for the trailhead, no doubt wanting to get a jump on them.

The captain gave a shrill whistle and called Yates by name. "He'll chip his teeth about it," Krieger whispered under his breath. "But I need him here helping me with the command post." The captain glanced skyward, getting nothing but a face full of rain. "Nobody's going to blame you, Cutter, if you want to wait for first light. Especially with the bear out there. Looks like it might be clearing some. With any luck we can get the AST helo and some ASAR folks up in the air before too long."

"All good," Cutter said. "Teariki has my back. We'll look for wherever our couple got off the trail, then get you a direction of travel so the chopper will have a place to look."

Cutter glanced at Lola.

She gave a thumbs-up, grinning to show a mouth full of teeth in the darkness. "Ready as, boss," she said, turning up the Kiwi.

Cutter raised his Motorola handheld radio, speaking over his shoulder. "We'll be on cell as long as we have service, channel three on the radio after that."

Cutter stopped when they reached the trailhead, taking a moment to check the Alaska State Parks signpost for any notes left behind by hikers. Nothing, except two warnings about recent bear sightings in the area.

"Those were there last week," Lola said. She gestured forward with the shotgun. "I got you covered, boss."

The trail began to climb as soon as it left the parking lot. Snotty with mud at first, it became more passable as they ventured a dozen or so yards into the trees. Slightly protected from direct impact of the rain, the trail under the canopy also produced more discernable tracks.

Cutter moved methodically, noting several distinct footprints from among the jumble of tracks, one of which he took to be the high arch and swooping fish-like forefoot of an Asolo hiking boot. He studied the tracks for a time, noting foot size, stride, straddle, and pitch of the individual print. As usual, his gut told him something was off well before he could put his finger on exactly what it was.

Lola crowded in closer, looking down long enough to try and see what he was seeing. She'd caught his change in mood.

"You have an opinion yet?"

Cutter caught her eye in the periphery of his headlamp.

"Nope," he said.

* * *

A strapping Alaska Search and Rescue volunteer who looked like an L.L. Bean flannel shirt model sloshed up behind them as Cutter stood up and started moving again. The reflective SOLAS patches on the shoulders of the ASAR man's red rain jacket dazzled brightly in their headlamps.

"Holy hell!" Lola held up an open palm as if to ward him off. "Best not to sneak up on armed people in the middle of bear country."

"Sorry about that." The volunteer extended his hand. Like most of the ASAR folks Cutter had met, this guy looked to be half mountain goat. In addition to the radio in his chest harness, he carried a sizable medical kit and a large coil of climbing rope. "Marty Palmetto," he said.

"Like the bug," Lola said.

"The captain said I could tag along in case you guys need an EMT. I promise to stay behind you at all times and not screw up any tracks."

"Are you armed?" Lola asked.

"Bear spray." Palmetto gave her an impish wink. "And my naturally disarming personality."

"Just don't get either of them on me," Lola said.

Cutter was already moving. He and Teariki were Captain Krieger's guests. If he wanted them to have a medic in tow, then they would have a medic in tow, even a flirty one.

A hundred yards in, Cutter held up his fist, motioning for the others to stop. The roots of a large poplar tree crossed the path, forming terraced steps in the soil, one of them almost a foot higher than the one below.

Cutter felt a flush of pride when Lola began to explain what he was doing to the ASAR guy. She'd been paying attention.

"Root steps like this make perfect track traps," she said. "They form a barrier to natural stride, all but forcing someone to put their foot in a given spot on the trail as they step up."

Cutter stooped, using his headlamp to cast shadows over the mud. The angled light giving him a better view of any tracks. He counted at least seven different tread patterns of various shapes and sizes.

"Miranda's described as being around five feet nothing," Lola noted. "It's a good guess her tracks would be small."

"Unless she has hobbit feet," Palmetto said.

Lola turned and gave a you're-not-helping frown, catching the kid in the eyes with her headlamp.

Cutter ignored him. He was harmless. Wearisome, but harmless.

"I have one set of size fives or sixes that look promising," he said. "The only other set small enough look to be going up and coming down." He snapped a couple of photos and then dropped the cell back in his pocket. "All this rain degradation, it's impossible to tell without getting more samples."

Palmetto hustled up beside Lola as the trail widened.

"Can I ask a question?"

"No," she said.

"Be nice," Cutter chided her over his shoulder.

"Geez," Palmetto said, giving a nod toward Cutter. "And here I thought he was going to be the mean one."

"That's not a question," Lola said.

"Okay . . . How about this? You seem to know a lot about this stuff too. How come you're both not tracking? Wouldn't two sets of eyes be better than one? I mean, I know bears are a problem, but hundreds of hikers take this trail every year. This seems like overkill for a search and rescue."

Lola looked like she wanted to chew the kid up and spit him out. Cutter almost felt sorry for him.

"A long time ago," Cutter said, "my grandfather took me and my older brother hunting. When I was around ten—"

"About your age," Lola said, stink-eyeing Palmetto.

"Anyway," Cutter said. "I shot a deer, but it ran off. I thought I knew some stuff, so, head down, I led the way. It was *my* deer. I would be the one to put meat on the table. I had to be the one to find it. I followed the tracks and telltale drops of blood. A couple hundred yards later the trail just vanished. Completely stumped, I searched and searched, even getting down on my hands and knees, working methodically out from the last bit of sign I'd found in an effort to cut the trail again. I was about to give up when I heard my older brother laughing under his breath.

"Laughing about?"

"Not fifteen feet in front of me, in the wide-open clearing, lay my deer. I'd been so focused on the tracks I'd forgotten to look up." Cutter tipped his forehead toward Lola. "She's my eyes. I need to focus solely on the sign and what it tells me. We track a lot of folks who want to kill us. It's easier to do it that same way every time. Now, let's go."

"And that little speech," Lola said, "is more than he talks in a year."

Cutter ignored her, moving slowly but surely, pausing here and there to examine every viable piece of evidence. He wasn't just looking for tracks, but scraps of left-behind candy wrapper, toilet stops, smears in the mud where someone slipped and fell—or blood. They crossed bear tracks four times in the first mile and a half, some of them on top of the boot prints, meaning the animal that made them had come along after the hiker. One set was disturbingly small. The second to the last thing Cutter wanted to run into was a grizzly cub.

"Let's keep an eye open for mama bear," he said. "And make plenty of noise."

The little group carried on, stopping, studying, and singing out "Hey, bear!" every fifteen or twenty steps.

Here and there, rivulets of water from the all-night rain cut across the trail. Some tiny, some wide enough to force the trackers to jump across. Thick brush formed black walls on either side of the path. Eerie shadows darted and danced, chased away with each glance of a headlamp. Every stone and stump looked like it might have teeth.

Cutter's uneasiness grew stronger with each passing step. But it wasn't the shadows or the creepy surroundings. Something else was nagging him. Something in the tracks.

The morning had turned a cold metallic blue by the time they reached a lone picnic table at the edge of the tree line. The sky was still overcast, but the clouds were higher now and seemed to be getting tired of spitting rain. Even with the cover, the sun was beginning to heat the Knik River valley below. It wasn't enough to start a breeze blowing up the mountain, but it was enough to slow the downward flow, bringing a relative calm.

They were two miles in, stopped on the lee side of a gurgling mountain stream, when Cutter realized what was bothering him.

Another set of boot prints periodically overlayed Burleson and Hill's tracks. This wasn't concerning in and of itself. Half a dozen other hikers looked to have been on the trail at the same time as the missing couple. It was only after Cutter noticed how this particular set of impressions periodically stopped, feet parallel, heels lifting while the toes dug into the soil that he saw the big picture. It was the same impression his own boots made when he hunkered down to get a better view of an instep or heel strike.

"Someone else is following them," he said, explaining his theory to Lola as they continued. "Studying their tracks."

Rather than looking down to confirm, she took his word for it and scanned the mist around them. A lock of black hair blew across her face. She pushed it aside with one hand, never lowering the shotgun. "Another lost hiker?"

"Could be," Cutter said. "But three times now he's stopped to study Miranda's tracks."

"That false trail shunts off up here on the right," Lola said.

Miranda and James's tracks continued straight toward the ridge and then returned, veering right on their way down. The third set of tracks continued down the mountain past the junction, stopped and turned around to start up the mountain again. Cutter pictured him. Intent on following them down the correct route, he'd missed their wrong turn and passed the side trail completely. Judging from the difference in weather degradation, he had come along several hours later.

Cutter stooped to confirm his suspicions and then grabbed his radio.

"You were right about their wrong turn," he said to Lola, before keying the mic. "Hello, Krieger."

The captain broke squelch immediately. "Go for Krieger."

"Cutter here. Looks like our couple took a dead-end trail on their descent. I'll send you the GPS coordinates and an azimuth for direction of travel. They may have realized their mistake and just hunkered down to get out of the weather."

"Copy," Krieger said. "I was just about to call you. The situation has changed. I need you to be on the lookout for a white male, possibly armed, six-one, a hundred and ninety pounds, twenty-seven years of age. Name's Jason Gove, Miranda Hill's ex-boyfriend. His blue Nissan sedan is parked up the river road a quarter mile or so. My guys found half a dozen spent nine-millimeter cases scattered on the floorboards."

"Copy that," Cutter gave a quick readback to show he got the pertinent information. "We'll keep an eye open for Miranda's ex-boyfriend, possibly armed. I believe we've found his tracks. He was moving the same direction as Hill and Burleson for a time, but he appears to have missed where they took their wrong turn and went back up the mountain looking for them." He exchanged frowns with Lola, catching her eye to make sure she'd heard everything. She gave him a curt nod and faced outbound, hood back, scanning the trail to the west.

Krieger continued. "The Hills were able to get in touch with one of Miranda's former roommates when their plane touched down in Anchorage a few minutes ago. Sounds like this Gove character has a temper, used to smack the shit out of Miranda every time he'd get a couple of beers in him. She has a restraining order against him now. Unsure if he knew about the pending marriage proposal, but there's apparently no love lost between him and James Burleson."

"We'll be watchful," Cutter said.

"Pilots say this cover should lift in the next forty-five minutes or so," Krieger said. "If you want to hold where you are, three troopers are about halfway to your position on the trail. With luck, we'll get some backup heading your way in the helo."

"We'll proceed with caution," Cutter said. "Turning my radio volume down. Call my cell if you have more intel."

"Copy that," Krieger said.

Cutter slipped the radio back in his chest rig. If he'd been certain Miranda's ex was ahead and not circling through the woods behind him, Cutter would have sent Marty Palmetto scampering back down the trail. As it was, he could do little but make sure the ASAR volunteer stayed well behind him and Lola. Palmetto gave him no argument.

Lola scoffed. "A damned restraining order."

"Isn't that a good thing?" Palmetto said.

"Not so much," she said. "Bullets shoot through paper . . ."

Rather than clearing, the clouds slumped. The rain picked up again as if the weather had gotten wind of the new situation. Cutter picked up his pace. There would be no Trooper helo anytime soon. Any reinforcements would be forced to come in by land—and halfway was a hell of a long way.

The false route dropped into the trees again where thick stands of alder and prickly devil's club loomed close on either side of the trail. Every so often game paths veered off, disappearing into trees and adding to the confusion. Cutter pulled up short at one of these junctions.

He raised a fist and whispered, "Listen!"

The group froze for a full minute. Nothing but the raindrops pelting the trees and pattering against their jackets.

Cutter took a deep breath and let his gaze fall back to the ground.

Head up, Lola took three steps to Cutter's right. She kept the shotgun to her shoulder. The gun's muzzle followed her eyes as she scanned their surroundings.

"How far ahead is that dead end?" Cutter whispered.

"Maybe half a mile." She matched his volume.

Marty Palmetto swayed in place. "What is it?"

"This isn't good," Cutter said. He moved to get a look at the ground from a better angle. Rain had degraded the footprints, but this section of the muddy trail was relatively protected by a thick stand of alder, leaving a decent track trap.

Cutter pointed out the raised portion at the toe of Miranda's track where she'd stopped abruptly, the kick-ridge of earth in front of subsequent tracks where she'd backpedaled. The larger tracks beside hers, left by Burleson's Asolos, showed similar signs of sudden surprise and retreat. Bits of thrown mud and floundering toe-digs showed these two sets of tracks transitioning into a dead run. The third set of boot prints, presumably belonging to Gove, came in from the side trail, overlaying those of the lost couple.

"You have an opinion now, boss?" Lola asked.

"Yep," Cutter said, starting briskly down the trail. "Gove was hunting—and he found them here."

CHAPTER 6

Wainwright

"WE GOT A DEAD BODY. I NEED YOU TO FLY ME OUT A SAW."

They weren't the words Officer Janice Hough expected to hear on the other end of her phone early in the morning.

Or anywhere. Ever.

Newly promoted to detective, she'd spent more than a decade policing the largest geographic municipality in the United States. If the North Slope Borough Police Department's jurisdiction wasn't the biggest in the world, it was awfully damned close. Often referred to simply as "the Slope," the municipality, or borough, encompassed roughly the top quarter of Alaska—most of that tundra, caribou, and mosquitos in summer. Snow and ice picked up the slack in the fall, winter, and spring.

The wake-up call had been from Woody Boatman, the North Slope PD officer on rotation to Wainwright that week. Even with grisly news of a young female frozen, somehow locked in the ice, Hough was happy to open her eyes. She'd been smack in the middle of a dream about the big boar polar bear spotted poking around out on Cake Eater Road. Hough swung her legs over the edge of the bed and rubbed a hand across her face, trying to make sense of the bear dream and this new information about saws and dead bodies. She slapped herself on the cheeks.

"They're unrelated," she said to herself, her voice thick with

morning breath. Luckily for her husband, he was away on a business trip in the lower forty-eight. Probably having the time of his
life. Those accountants sure knew how to party.

Hough stumbled to the kitchen to pour herself a cup of coffee.
Praise the Lord for automatic coffee makers. Two sips in, she was
reasonably awake. A quick half cup later, she'd cobbled together
the basics of her plan.

The requested saw was the fourteen-inch circular variety used
by fire rescue to cut people out of mangled metal in wrecked vehicles. Not much need for something like that in Wainwright, a
village of six hundred, most of whom drove ATVs or snow machines. The hub village of Utqiagvik, formerly Barrow, had plenty
of cars and a robust fire department that, after some begging,
loaned Hough one of their twenty-two-hundred-dollar Husqvarna
rescue saws.

Ninety minutes after Boats had roused her from a warm bed,
Hough pressed her forehead against the window of her chartered
Cessna 208 Caravan as the pilot crossed over Wainwright Inlet on
a downwind approach. She was the only passenger if you didn't
count the stacked cases of Pepsi and instant ramen noodles
strapped to the floor. A green David Clark headset mashed her
bedhead of blond curls into a tangled mess. She didn't care. You
got what you got when you woke her up half an hour before her
alarm went off. Just as she'd had to settle with drawing Tony, the
"Baby Bush Pilot," on her last-minute charter. He was a good kid,
Tony, but incredibly green. Hough went out of her way to keep
from flying with him.

From the air, Wainwright Inlet looked disturbingly like a ginormous alien with long, spindly legs and outstretched arms. A bul-
bous ET head looked back over a bony shoulder. Hough shivered.
The shapes were even more unsettling in the gathering dawn, the
water inky black against a parched tundra. "Bush Pilot Tony,"
twenty-seven-years-old and building hours in hopes of one day
getting an airline job, banked over the ocean, then into the wind
back across the alien's head to line up with the gravel airstrip at
the south edge of the village.

Hough braced her black, insulated Danner boots against the

removable, and therefore relatively flimsy, seat in front of her as Tony added flaps, flaring to settle over the end of the runway. The stall warning squealed, and the young pilot wrestled with the yoke and pedals in a wallowing dance to get the airplane to stop flying and stay on the ground. He bounced it twice and then came off the throttle.

"Not bad this time, Tony," Hough said into the tiny boom mic on her headset. "We have cheated death once again."

The pilot chuckled and gave her a tentative thumbs-up. He glanced over her shoulder with a tense look that said he needed to pee . . . or maybe already had.

Boats hadn't exactly been forthcoming with information about the body. All Hough really knew was that some local kids had found an unidentified female frozen in the ice. Odd for this time of year. She'd retrieved bodies off the coast that had been ground nearly to hamburger between flows of pack ice and pulled out bodies half frozen in lakes during midwinter. She'd dragged rivers with giant treble hooks and dug a couple of college kids out of the snow after an avalanche near Anaktuvuk Pass. But sawing a corpse out of a block of ice? This was a first, even for the bush.

Boats had only been with North Slope PD for sixteen months, the first year spent training in the big village of Utqiagvik, learning the ropes with his field training officers—Hough among them—working out of the big blue box that served as their headquarters. Wainwright was his first village assignment, eighty-five miles west of Utqiagvik and accessible only by plane, boat, or, in the winter, a bumpy—and iffy—snow machine expedition. Working two weeks on and two weeks off, he was still getting to know the ins and outs of the community. They didn't quite trust him yet. Not the way they trusted Hough.

Linda Skidmore, the principal of Wainwright's consolidated school, stood outside a dusty white minivan parked on the gravel apron adjacent to the runway. Tony taxied up and rolled to a stop a dozen yards away, adding power to turn the Cessna so it nosed slightly downhill. When it was time to leave, he'd be able to start rolling again without having to give too much throttle and damaging his prop with gravel. Hough nodded to herself. He was learning. He'd turn into a capable bush pilot someday. Probably. If he lived that long.

Skidmore, a normally cheery Arkansan from Fort Smith, gave Hough a somber halfhearted wave. She wore a gray alpaca wool sweater and a hat that also matched her long silver braids.

"Jan," she said. She grabbed Hough's soft-sided duffle and left the bulky rescue saw to her. "Boatman said he needed to stay with her body. I'm your ride."

The way Skidmore said "her" made it clear she knew the victim well. Hough wasn't surprised. The K–12 school served as the center for most community events in every village. Principals knew everyone. Skidmore had been in Wainwright for eight years—a lifetime for a bush educator. She knew everyone's secrets. Her eyes were red, and not from the wind.

Skidmore sniffed back a tear. "It's Willadean," she said.

Hough closed her eyes, gut punched at the news. "She's been missing, what—"

"Over two years," Skidmore said. "I have hope for all my kids, but I'm also realistic. That kiddo . . ." She swallowed hard. "She had real promise. Village life can be hell. You know that. Teen pregnancy, suicide, drugs, domestic abuse . . . I mean, it goes on everywhere, but in the village, it's all right in your face. Hard for a girl to get away from. Willadean somehow seemed to rise above it. She'd just come to my office that week to let me know she'd been accepted to the Coast Guard Academy . . . then poof! She disappears, gone off the face of the earth. All death is tragic, but Willadean Benson was a bright light. The entire village felt it when that light vanished."

"I'm just sick about this," Hough said.

"A warm wind blew through the day before she went missing," Skidmore said. "A peculiar wind, out of place for midwinter. That night the temperature plummeted, and a terrible blizzard barreled in off the ocean."

Hough nodded, feeling a sudden chill. "I remember."

"The older kids remember too. Hell, it's like it was yesterday to most everybody here in Wainwright. Folks from the village consistently report hearing Willadean's voice singing on the wind before a storm. Warm winds are the worst. The kids tell stories about seeing her ghost in the school windows, always wearing the baby-blue parka and sealskin mittens she had on the night she vanished." Skidmore shot Hough a side-eye. "The Ipalook boys are the ones who found her. They say she's wearing the same parka and mittens."

They turned out of the airport and onto Ahloaksageak Road, taking them toward the scattered plyboard houses and weathered buildings perched between the tundra and the Arctic Ocean.

"I don't get it. She's *in* the ice?"

"How am I supposed to know?" Skidmore snapped. "That son of a bitch Boatman won't allow anyone down in the cellar."

"Come on, Linda," Hough said. She had to concentrate to keep her voice soothing and nonconfrontational. "Boats is just doing his job. If this is a crime scene—"

"I know that," Skidmore said. "Rationally, anyway. I shouldn't take it out on him. It's just that . . . this is all so . . ."

"Futile?"

Skidmore sniffed back a sob. She rubbed her nose with the back of her sleeve and nodded emphatically, driving the rest of the way to the Ipalooks' house without another word.

Officer Boatman took Hough aside as soon as Skidmore dropped her off. Four snow machines and an old three-wheeled ATV sat in various stages of disrepair around the muddy yard. Far from abandoned, they continued to give up cannibalized parts for the still serviceable machines that were stored under blue tarps nearer to the front porch. A slab of black meat and rib bones hung under the eaves of the house, in the wind but out of the rain. Hough had been in the Arctic long enough to recognize it as a piece of *ugruk*, bearded seal. Women worked together in large communal groups that resembled Southern quilting circles to expertly sew *ugruk* skins into covers for *umiaks*, the open boats used for centuries to hunt whales. The seal's blubber was rendered into precious oil into which all kinds of dried and frozen meat and fish were dipped for warm winter meals. Hough had never acquired a taste for it. It was potent stuff. To the uninitiated, so much as a teaspoon often acted as an extremely powerful—and near in-

stantaneous—laxative. Hough's stomach churned, partially from
memories of her last bout with the seal-oil two-step, but mainly
from the task she knew lay ahead.

Virtually everyone in the village who wasn't in school milled in
small groups in the Ipalooks' yard, eyes on the yellow crime scene
tape that fluttered in the breeze across the plywood cellar door.

Boatman spent most of his off time in the gym and liked to
wear tight, muscle-mapping shirts. He pinned his shoulders back
when he walked so his chest led the way wherever he went, carrying himself with the certitude of a young peacock. He had a
we're-cops-and-you're-not attitude that didn't exactly ingratiate
him to the village elders. But they could tell he was young, with
plenty of room to mature. Woody Boatman was to law enforcement what Bush Pilot Tony was to charter pilots. They'd both be
all right . . . if they survived long enough.

Hough shot a sympathetic nod toward the Ipalooks. The two
boys scrunched their foreheads and noses, the customary Iñupiaq
equivalent of shaking their heads "no." They'd seen what was in
the frozen pit, and the fact that Hough was going down there apparently brought the unpleasant memory back to them.

She turned to Boatman. "You already got the story from the
homeowners?"

"For all that's worth," Boatman said. "The boys were stacking
what was left of last season's whale to make room for the new
haul. Part of the wall caved in on 'em."

Hough started for the cellar door.

"Show me."

Boatman led the way. "Heard y'all had a big bear nosing
around out toward the point."

"Off Cake Eater," Hough said, distant. She wanted to focus on
the problem at hand, not a phantom bear a hundred miles away.
"No whale carcasses to scavenge yet, so it's moved on, I'm sure."

She strapped on an elastic headlamp and watched Boatman
disappear into the hole, waiting until his boots crunched on the
frozen ground below before committing her weight to the ladder.
She'd lived and worked in the Arctic long enough to have been in
plenty of ice cellars—large underground freezers dug out of the

permafrost. They were dark and cold and predictably stuffy, being full of ham-sized chunks of frost-covered whale and other meat that people needed to keep through the winter. Many had resorted to aboveground freezers they bought from the Stuaqpak store in Utqiagvik. A few, particularly the whaling captains like Abner Ipalook, vowed to stick to the old ways as long as the land allowed them.

The odor inside these cellars never ceased to surprise her. If it smelled like anything, the red meat and *muktuk*—the tire-like skin and thick blubber of the bowhead whale—carried the faint odor that some might describe as the sea. The most prominent odor came from a concoction called *mikigaq*—bits of whale tongue, *muktuk*, and other cuts of meat left to age in a dark place above ground for a period of several weeks. It was stirred three or four times a day, then frozen in the cellar for later use. When Hough first heard of this "fermented" whale, she'd expected the rotten-egg odor of fermented shark she'd once tried on a dare during a trip to Iceland. *Mikigaq* looked like a bloody mess, but the taste was not at all unpleasant. To Hough, it smelled like something between red wine and oil paint.

The mixture of smells hit her in the face before she reached the bottom rung of the ladder. She dropped into the frosted womb of the ice cellar, ten feet below the surface, and took a deep breath. There was really nothing like this on earth.

Boatman had already strung three light bulbs, but Hough kept her headlamp on for close work.

The interior was a remarkable feat of human ingenuity and engineering, not much different in design than it would have been centuries before—a roughly ten-by-ten room at the bottom of the narrow tunnel dug at least ten feet down into the frozen ground. The chief difference being that now they could use shovels to dig, where their forebearers used whalebones and caribou shoulder blades. Four rough-hewn six-by-six timbers pressed squares of plywood against the domed roof, shoring up the permafrost that formed the ceiling. A half dozen waxed cardboard boxes full of slabs of frozen whale and gallon baggies of blood-red *mikigaq* from last season were stacked against the wall at the base of the ladder. Twice as many collapsed boxes, presumably what the boys had been down to clear out, lay on the floor directly in front of Hough under a pile of dirt and crystalline frost that had sloughed away from the wall.

Willadean Benson stared out from the sheet of exposed ice. She stood upright, right hand at her waist. A sealskin mitten was suspended on a woolen string in the ice beside her thigh, as if floating. Bare fingers, skinned and raw, reached for the knife that stuck half out of her coat pocket. Her left arm was raised above her head, torquing her shoulder backward in an unnatural and what would have been a painful angle. A lock of black hair lay across her face as if blown there by the wind. Her mouth was open, frozen in midscream.

"No obvious signs of trauma," Hough whispered to herself as she walked slowly along the wall, examining the body from mere inches away. "This is absolutely bizarre."

"No shit," Boatman said. "One for the books. Someone killed her, then stuffed her down here."

"She's locked in the ice," Hough said, running through all kinds of implausible scenarios. There were dozens of ways to get rid of a body in the Arctic. "It makes no sense," she said. "Willadean disappeared in December. The middle of winter in the middle of the night. Dark twenty-four seven for weeks. If someone killed her, all they had to do was make a quick trip by snow machine out on the sea ice and dump her. She would have been gone. Why go to all the trouble of burying her in town?"

"That's why you make the big bucks," Boatman grunted. "To solve mysteries like this while we mortals patrol the barren tundra."

"You're making yourself easy to ignore," Hough said. "Let's think this through."

Boatman patted the plastic case that held the saw. "It'll be easier to tell what happened when we cut her out."

Hough stepped closer, nose to nose with Willadean. "Boats, look at her face and tell me what you see."

"It creeps the shit out of me," Boatman said. "Like she's freezer burned but still alive, staring out through the ice, trying to talk to us."

"Exactly," Hough said. "I'm thinking she was screaming for help." Hough played the beam of her headlamp down by the knife that protruded from Willadean's coat pocket. Her breath caught hard in her throat when the light settled there.

"That's impossible!"

"What is it?"

Hough took a half step back, playing her light back and forth across the sheet of ice.

"We're going to be here a while."

"So, you're ready to cut her out?"

"In time," Hough said. "She's been here two years. No need to rush. Besides, I'm not too keen on firing up that gasoline-powered rescue saw in this enclosed space without more ventilation."

"Okaaaay," Boatman said, unconvinced. "What *is* your plan then?"

"We're going to wait," Hough said. "There's a couple hundred pounds of frozen whale in this cellar that the Ipalooks and their dependents need for food. We're about to raise the temperature enough to threaten some of it with spoilage."

Boatman turned up his nose. "I'm not so sure we could spoil any of this nasty shit if we tried."

Hough gave a vehement shake of her head. "You can't think like that, Woody." She used his given name to make sure she had his attention. "Not if you want to make it in these bush communities. They've been living here for thousands of years. We are newbies here. Strangers in a strange land. If we're going to go nosing around in their food supply, the least we can do is bring an electric freezer in from Utqiagvik to keep from wrecking their shit while we process our crime scene."

Boatman took a deep breath. "You're right," he said.

"Of course, I'm right, Weed Hopper," Hough said. "Let's get topside. I have a phone call to make."

"Hang on." Boatman shined his flashlight toward Willadean. "I saw you react there when you saw something in the ice. What was it?"

Hough pointed down by the girl's hand. "Fossils," she said. "More specifically oreodont teeth."

"What the hell is an oreodont?"

"Pretty sure it's a clue to another murder that happened about the time Willadean Benson disappeared. An engineer who worked on the Slope named Ethan Cutter." She took out her phone and scrolled through the contacts. "I need to go topside to get a signal."

"Are you calling ABI?" ABI was the Alaska Bureau of Investigation, an arm of the State Troopers.

"Nope," Hough said.

CHAPTER 7

Anchorage

CUTTER HEARD GOVE LONG BEFORE THE MAN CAME INTO VIEW, HIS voice a whining chainsaw that cut through the trees and fog.

With her right hand holding the shotgun, Lola waved Marty Palmetto to stay behind her with her left.

"I think they're at the drop-off I told you about," she said to Cutter. "We should send Palmetto back to the main trail."

"Agreed," Cutter said. He slipped the radio from his chest rig and radioed their new coordinates to Krieger. The oncoming troopers still had to come half a mile before they reached the orange tape Cutter had left on the junction of the false trail.

"You don't need to send me back," Palmetto said. "I can be of—"

A whimpering scream carried through the devil's club and cut him off.

"Stay here!" Cutter hissed. His tone left zero room for an argument. "We may need a medic. Don't come forward until Lola calls you on the radio or the troopers arrive. Got it?"

Palmetto nodded.

Lola turned to face him, hissing, "Say you understand!"

"Okay, okay. I understand." Both hands up as if fending her off.

Cutter motioned forward through the brush with an open hand, knowing that Lola would follow him.

Getting themselves killed would do Miranda and James no

good at all, but neither would sitting around on their thumbs. Cutter was not one to dally when he heard screams. Steady rain and wind from the valley floor rustled the leaves and helped to cover their approach. Cutter left the WitSec shotgun parked on the sling over his shoulder. The Colt Python would come in handier if Gove turned this into a hostage rescue situation.

Cutter and Lola moved shoulder to shoulder, skirting the devil's club as best they could in favor of alder thickets and stands of buckbrush. Almost two years and countless hours of working together saw them moving in concert, each reading what the other was about to do. First on their knees, they'd dropped to their bellies by the time they reached the edge of a clearing, west of the false trail, some thirty feet from the deep canyon that ran parallel to the mountain's broad face. Lola was right. The trail was blocked—unless you climbed straight down more than a hundred vertical feet.

Yards away, Miranda slumped against the root ball of an upturned poplar tree, cowering against the tangle of mud and stone. Gove loomed over her, waving a stick the size of a walking cane as if to drive home his point. A Glock pistol sat at the center of his chest in a black nylon holster—easily accessible. James Burleson was nowhere to be seen. Worse yet, Gove's chest heaved with convulsive sobs every few seconds. Cutter had no problem with men who cried. He'd been known to shed a tear. But under these circumstances, tears most often signified danger rather than compliance. This guy had followed his ex into the mountains with a gun and now stood over her with a club, weeping and slinging snot. He was at the end of his rope.

Low in the brush, Cutter felt Lola tense alongside him.

"Gun," she whispered. "I'm loaded with all slugs. Ten yards is no problem."

"Agreed," Cutter trusted Lola's judgment enough not to give her parameters of when to shoot—or not to. "You see the boy anywhere?"

"Negative," Lola whispered.

Miranda sniffed back her tears. "Jason, please . . . You don't have to do this."

"Do what? I'm just trying to get a minute to talk to you." Still clutching the stick, he pounded his own forehead with his free hand. His bloodshot eyes burned, visible even from thirty feet away. At first Cutter thought it was from the way he kept hitting himself, but a whiff of capsicum on the breeze said Miranda or James had given him a snout full of pepper spray.

Good for them, but it hadn't been enough.

Gove threw his head back and sent a screaming yowl toward the sky. This guy was losing it.

He gave himself another couple of smacks to the face, then glowered down at Miranda, his chest heaving.

"How am I supposed to make you understand if you won't even let me talk to you? Huh? You ever think about that? This whole thing is your fault, Miranda. Not mine."

She folded her arms tight across her chest, visibly shaking. "Okay," she said, obviously giving it everything she had to control her voice. "What is it, Jason? What do you want to tell me?"

"I . . . I just . . ." He dropped to one knee putting them at eye level. Quieter now, slowly shaking his head, his tone almost tender. "Tell me what that guy has that I don't?"

A third voice carried up from beyond the lip of the canyon. James Burleson. "Jason! So help me, if you hurt her—"

Gove waved away the threat. "You cannot honestly think this smarmy little prick could make you happy . . . I mean, how long have you known him?"

"Jason . . . I can't—"

Gove started to laugh, as if it were all so simple. He dropped the stick to the ground. "You know what? You're right. You can't. You two can't get married if one of you is dead—"

Miranda sprang at him, screeching, clawing. He caught her midjump, grabbing her by the throat.

A talented NFL player could run a sub-two-second ten-yard split. Cutter and Lola had to contend with wet ground and knee-high scrub, but still managed to close the distance to Gove in less than three. Miranda saw them first. Her eyes flew wide. She turned sideways, screaming something unintelligible under her attacker's grasp. Whether he noticed a change in Miranda's behavior or heard their approach, it took Gove a full second before he turned to face two hundred and forty pounds of frowning Arliss Cutter and a grimacing Polynesian woman wielding an 870 shotgun as they emerged at full speed from the mountain mist. Both looked as though they considered him food.

Gove shoved Miranda away as if she were on fire and threw both hands out in front of him, crawfishing backward to fend off these oncoming demons. A garbled cry escaped his throat, his frayed brain unable to decide whether to scream or cry.

"US Marshals!" Cutter barked. His deep voice bounced oddly in the swirling fog, disembodied, otherworldly. "Hands in the air!"

Fortunately for Gove, he didn't go for the pistol. Unfortunately, he kept moving backward until he dropped over the edge and disappeared.

Cutter shot a quick glance at Lola, motioning for her to slow down and spread out. Gove still had his handgun.

A nervous laugh came up from somewhere over the edge. It was James Burleson.

Then, a whimpering plea from Gove, "Help me . . ."

Colt Python in his hand, Cutter sidestepped, taking care to watch his footing as he cut the pie to do a quick peek over the edge. He found Miranda's ex clinging to a gnarled spruce trunk that was growing out the side of the rock wall fifteen feet below. The tree-choked canyon yawned beneath him as if part of the mountain face had leaned away, leaving a nearly eighty-degree slope with nothing but loose talus to arrest his descent for at least a hundred feet.

Gove wrapped his arms tightly around the twisted spruce. His legs pedaled against loose rock, failing to find purchase. The pistol was still in his chest rig.

He glared at Cutter, his lips pulled back in a quivering sneer. "You're a cop. Pull me up!"

Cutter stayed aimed in with the Python. "No rope," he said. "My partner's calling down by radio, but you'll need to hang on. It's going to be a minute."

James Burleson stood on a coffin-sized ledge to Gove's right, out of his reach. Blood from a deep gash in his forehead covered the right side of his face. He waved up at Cutter.

"There's rope lashed to my pack."

Gove let go with another tormented howl. Cutter had worked with people who had limbs blown off that carried on less. "I don't want your help!" Gove snapped. He looked back at Cutter, eyes blazing with rage. "Just shoot me! If I draw my gun you'll have to, right? Suicide by cop."

"Yep." Cutter stared down the barrel of his revolver. "But it ain't like the movies. No clean hole to put you out of your misery. From this distance, I would turn your neck into a stump and splatter your brains all over the rocks for the ravens." He took a long contemplative breath through his nose, as if he'd reached an important conclusion. "But we're not going that route. You've got plenty to live for, Jason. You don't really want to die."

Gove gulped. "And you're sure about that?"

"I am," Cutter said. "You don't need me to shoot you, that's for sure. All you gotta do is let go."

Lola contacted Captain Krieger on the Motorola and advised him all parties were safe. Cutter and Miranda worked to pull Burleson up, rescuing him first to rob Gove of a target if he decided to do something stupid with the pistol when given the opportunity. Even if he had been inclined to shoot someone, his arms were noodles by the time they finally got the rope to him.

Three Alaska State Troopers arrived and helped bring up Gove. Marty Palmetto, the ASAR volunteer, tended to Miranda and James's wounds, while the troopers took custody of Gove. The lumbering thump of an approaching helicopter echoed off the rocks.

Lola stepped in close to Cutter as she coiled Burleson's climbing rope. "Wow, boss," she whispered. "You should put in for crisis negotiator school. 'You wanna die, *all you gotta do is let go* . . .'" She chuckled. "I'm gonna get that on a T-shirt."

Cutter rolled his eyes. "He wasn't gonna kill himself."

"He was pretty whacked," Lola said. "Haven't you ever been spun up over a girl . . ."

Cutter looked at her but didn't say anything.

Lola grimaced. "Of course, you have. Sorry, boss. I didn't mean—"

She gave a little start, clutching the collar of her vest. "Well, thank the Lord." She dug out her phone. "If I can pry my foot out of my mouth, I'll get this call."

She listened for a moment, then pushed the phone to Cutter. "The chief wants to know why you're not answering your cell."

"Hello, Chief."

"Arliss," Phillips said.

Cutter and the chief deputy shared a great deal of mutual respect. Good friends. Even then, they rarely used first names to communicate when they spoke over the phone. Something in the tone of that single word made him brace, like when his grandfather said, "You know I love you boys," before he broke the news that their favorite dog had died.

His instincts proved correct.

"I've spent the past five minutes on the phone with Officer Janice Hough with North Slope PD," Phillips said. "She's been burning up the lines trying to get in touch with you . . ."

CHAPTER 8

*L*OLA THREW HER TAHOE INTO PARK ALONGSIDE THE CURB AT TED
Stevens Anchorage International Airport departures. She twisted
sideways in her seat to give Cutter one of her famous squinty-eyed
nods.

"This is exactly what I was talking about," she said. "Another
day in the life. I love this job." She canted her head, her hair still
damp from a quick shower in the office gym after they'd come off
the mountain. "Mind you, boss, I'm not whinging, but I sure as
hell wish I was going with you."

Whinge meant "to whine," one of the many words and phrases
she'd imported from her Cook Island/New Zealand heritage.

Cutter gave her a wink of his own and opened the door, eager
to make the 2:30 p.m. flight to Utqiagvik. "I need you to keep at it
with Dupree. Every moment he is on the street means he has access to other victims."

"I know." She pooched out her bottom lip. "Still, you make
stuff happen. Can't help but have a little FOMO."

"This is you not whinging?"

"Nah," she said. "You'd know it right off if you saw me whinge.
I'm a seasoned expert. You're my partner. I want to help with this
thing you're doing."

Cutter got out, pulled up the collar of his jacket against the
rain, and opened the back-seat door to grab his bag. He didn't in-

tend to RON—remain overnight—but he'd learned not to go anywhere in Alaska without taking a change of clothes . . . and a bit of extra ammunition.

"You do help," he said. "Right now, you can help by focusing on slapping the cuffs on Eddie Dupree."

"I'll get Joe Bill working on it with me." She nodded. "I'm glad the chief is letting you go north."

"As am I, Lola." Cutter smacked the top of the door frame with a flat hand to let her know he was ready. "Be safe."

She gave him a finger-gun salute and pulled away from the curb.

It was just after noon, and they'd both already put in a full day of work. Knowing Lola, she was on her way to the gym—"to relax."

Jan Hough's revelation that she'd found a dead girl with ore-odont teeth had come out of nowhere, putting Cutter on his back foot. These fossils weren't native to Alaska. Cutter had never heard of them before his nephews pointed out their deceased dad's knife handle was made out of the things. Willadean Benson went missing around the same time Ethan was murdered. Surely, there was a connection. Cutter had to go see this crime scene for himself. The problem was, homicide investigations weren't his job, even homicides that might provide clues to his brother's death. Hell, especially those homicides.

But Jan Hough had asked for him, and good chief that she was, Jill Phillips understood interagency cooperation. She'd found Cutter a "carrying paper." It was perfectly within USMS policy to assist state or local law enforcement when requested, even with a possible homicide investigation. The problem came with paying for the travel. The bean counters at headquarters took a dim view of chiefs expending district funds to send their deputies jet-setting around a state as large as Alaska unless the travel was mission essential. Fortunately, Phillips was well respected by those who counted the beans. As long as she provided a viable reason, no one offered a peep. A carrying paper—a summons, subpoena, or arrest warrant that, while not a top priority, still needed to be served—provided that reason.

CDUSM Phillips signed the USM Form 356 authorizing Cutter to fly the seven hundred plus miles to Utqiagvik, the city formerly known as Barrow, to serve a civil summons on a fuel company that was being sued by another fuel company in federal court. While he was in the area, he was free to assist Jan Hough with her crime scene.

Cutter was sure Lola really wanted to help get to the bottom of Ethan's murder, but it didn't take two people to serve a civil summons.

Cutter stopped at Alaska Airlines customer service long enough to show his credentials and get an armed boarding pass. He was shunted around the main security checkpoint to a small office, where a TSA agent cross-referenced the Marshals Service's agency-unique code provided by Cutter and then called a uniformed Airport Police officer. The officer double-checked Cutter's credentials and boarding pass before sending him on his way with a grunt, mumbling something about being glad he wasn't the one who had to go to Utqiagvik, where temperatures were already dropping into the low thirties.

Armed boarding meant Cutter got on the aircraft first, giving him time to meet the crew and any other agents and officers who were traveling strapped. On flights to and around the lower forty-eight, there were usually at least a couple of agents scattered among the passengers, but today he was the sole gun on the airplane.

He preferred an aisle seat on the left side of the aircraft, so his right hand was free and his sidearm didn't dig into the passenger sitting next to him. Spur of the moment plans left him nothing but a window seat. Fortunately, it was on the right side of the plane, putting his bulky Colt Python against the wall and not gouging into anyone but him. He didn't care for headphones when he flew—or any other time for that matter—preferring to stay aware of what was going on around him, even if it meant he had to ignore a blabby seatmate.

Like his grandfather, whom friend and foe alike called Grumpy, Arliss Cutter had been born with a resting-mean mug. Flying only added to his sour countenance. Flying to investigate a connection to his brother's death . . . that made him downright unapproachable.

His seatmate turned out to be a matronly Iñupiaq woman wearing a pink floral *atikluk* tunic and a wan smile. She occupied her time knitting and kept to herself.

Cutter settled in as best he could, turning slightly so his knees wouldn't be obliterated if the person in the row ahead of him decided to lie down in his lap. He stuck a small Moleskine notebook in the seat pocket in case he wanted to jot something down during the two-hour flight. He'd stopped at Mosquito Books in the airport and picked up a copy of a Don Reardon book the chief had been recommending—and the latest issue of *Cruising World*. He saved the book for later and opted for the sailing magazine, hoping to take his mind off the flight for a few minutes with stories of white sandy beaches and blue water. It didn't work. He ended up with his forehead against the window gazing down at the Knik arm of the Cook Inlet and the mountains he'd been in just hours before. Alaska was a wild place, most of it devoid of roads or people. It was easy to see why Ethan had loved it, why he'd dragged Mim and the kids all the way up from Florida.

Cutter had never pictured himself being promoted to management in the Marshals Service or living in Alaska, not for a second, but when Ethan had been killed in a rig explosion on the North Slope, leaving Mim a widow and their children with no father, Arliss had put in for the open supervisor vacancy on the Alaska Fugitive Task Force. At first, it was to help Mim and the kids. That mission had now morphed into finding Ethan's killer.

"Oh, I wish you were here," he whispered, fogging the window with his breath. "Even if that meant I wouldn't be."

Cutter's older brother had swooped in and taken the first girl he'd ever loved, eventually marrying her. But he'd also looked out for Cutter when he was a little runt.

1982
Port Charlotte, Florida

Grumpy said Daddy's funeral would probably make them miss a whole week of school. That was okay with Arliss. At kindergarten, they made you take naps on a little bathmat and make crafts out of toilet paper tubes. At Grumpy's house, he got to go out in Gasparilla Sound on the boat and track hogs in the glades and whittle with a real pocketknife.

It was a warm night, even in November. Arliss kicked off the bedsheet with bony legs and banged his head against the pillow, damp with sweat but not tears. The preacher said heaven was a happy place. Daddy was a good man. He'd gone to heaven, probably, even if he was sad all the time. Maybe he was happy now. It was hard to know things like that.

A box fan hummed on low on the other side of the smallish room that had up until a couple of days ago been Grumpy's study but now served as Arliss and Ethan's bedroom. At seven, Ethan was two years older and a full hand taller. He could have put most of the fan on himself, but he made sure it was divided fair and square. If anything, he gave himself less of the breeze.

Arliss's ears perked up when he heard a car engine turn down the quiet street in front of Grumpy's house. He hoped it wasn't another visitor. There'd been a lot of drop-ins after the funeral. Arliss's throat got all tight just thinking about it.

Grumpy never smiled much. He didn't talk much, either, so it could be kind of a trick for the boys to tell how he was feeling. Arliss figured he had to be sad right now, though. Daddy was Grumpy's son. When Arliss had sons, he figured he'd be real sad if one of them died.

Outside, headlights reflected off the twisted gumbo limbo trees along Grumpy's driveway as the approaching car neared.

Most of the drop-ins after the service had spent their time tousling Arliss's blond hair and telling him stupid things like "chin up, sonny boy" and "it'll get better," if they even talked to him at all. Mostly, they just patted him on the head and looked like they wanted to get out of there. It was a relief when everyone finally cleared off so he could eat some of his aunt's purple hull peas and cornbread without being deviled by a bunch of weepy grown-ups.

A giant silkworm moth as big as Arliss's hand fluttered feather-soft against the window screen. If it was still there tomorrow, he vowed to catch it and put it in a Mason jar. Outside, crickets chirped in the grass and the little frogs along the muddy gut called Alligator Creek sang behind Grumpy's house.

The headlights suddenly flooded the room, throwing long shadows across the big plastic billfish that hung on the far wall. Tires popped over the crushed oyster-shell drive.

More visitors . . .

Arliss pulled the pillow over his head and gave a whispered curse.

"Dammit!"

It wasn't the only curse word he knew, but it was the only one Grumpy didn't seem to get too mad about.

The car's engine went quiet about the same time the screen door squeaked open and Grumpy eased it shut. The old man had a rule against slamming doors any time of the day. He crunched his way over the driveway to meet the visitor. Muted voices carried up the driveway on humid air.

It was a woman.

The sound of her voice took Arliss's breath away. Soft and rich and buttery smooth.

Ethan recognized it too and knelt on the foot of Arliss's bed to peer out the window.

Arliss pushed the pillow out of the way and crawled up beside his brother, shoulder to shoulder, two little foreheads pressed against the screen.

A flutter hit Arliss's chest, softer than the silkworm moth had hit the window.

"Mama," he gasped, then shot an excited glance at his brother. "You think she's come to get us?"

Arliss had always thought of her as tall, but she looked smaller now than he remembered. She wore a green dress, just like the last time he'd seen her, the kind that wrapped around and left her shoulders out for the sun and little boys to snuggle.

Ethan took a deep breath. "Hush," he said, sounding a lot like Grumpy. "I'm trying to catch what they're sayin' if you'd be still."

Mama must have heard them talking because she looked directly at the window, blond hair down around tan shoulders, her long face bathed in the glow of the streetlamp.

Grumpy didn't say much, but when he did talk, it was neither quiet nor particularly loud. "Be matter-of-fact, boys," he'd always say. "Get to the point of your business and then listen." He took his own council, because Mama was talking way more than he was.

She called him Wayne, which never did sound right. His name was D. Wayne Cutter, but that was just weird. As far as Arliss knew, everybody had called the old man Grumpy from the beginning of time.

Arliss heard a lot of the words through the buzz of insects and frogs, but Ethan could understand more of them, especially the ones from Mama. He'd had two years more with her than Arliss had before she left.

"I get her meanings," Ethan said.

"What does she mean then?" Arliss asked.

"She's askin' about Daddy's house."

Arliss bounced on his knees. "You think she might come back and live in it with us?"

Ethan listened a while longer, then gave a slow shake of his head. A tear ran down his cheek. "Nope," he whispered.

"What then?"

"How am I supposed to know?" Ethan sounded an awful lot like he did know but wasn't going to say.

Arliss smiled softly to himself. "Remember when we were little and she would take us on adventures?"

Ethan coughed a little, like he might start crying any time. "I wish you'd hush."

The bugs outside fell into a lull, and Mama's voice drifted up the driveway over the holly bushes and through the window screen.

"Were you thinking of selling the house for the boys' upkeep?" she asked.

Arliss half turned to his brother, whispering. "What's upkeep?"

"Like food and Levis and stuff," Ethan said.

Mama carried on. She kicked the driveway with the toe of her sandal. "I'm just . . . I could really use . . ." Crickets covered the last bit.

Grumpy took some keys out of his pocket and put them in her hand. Arliss caught a glimpse of a white rabbit's foot. Daddy's keychain. It never brought him any luck at all.

"Take the house," Grumpy said. "Do what you need to."

"What about his truck?"

Grumpy looked at his watch and then let his hands fall to his side. "It's all yours. I'll look after the boys."

She glanced up at the window.

Arliss raised a little hand and waved, forehead still against the screen. He held his breath, waiting for her to wave back, to give him one of her warm smiles. Instead, she turned back to Grumpy and held up her fist with the keys in it. "I appreciate this, Wayne. I really do. I'm just in over my head, that's all."

Ethan fell back against his own bed, but Arliss kept his forehead glued to the window screen as she drove away.

"Go to sleep, little brother." Ethan sniffed back a tear. "Best to forget about her. Grumpy'll look out for me . . . and I'll look out for you."

Turbulence over the Alaska Range shook the plane and jostled Cutter out of his stupor.

The Iñupiaq woman in the seat beside him glanced up from her knitting, brow raised in concern.

"Ursula," she said. "That's not a very common name."

Cutter looked at her, genuinely startled. "No," he said. "It is not."

The woman resumed knitting. "I only bring it up 'cause that was my granny's name. You said it a couple of times." She gathered a series of wool loops onto her wooden needles as she spoke. "Seems like this Ursula is pretty important to you."

Cutter forced a smile. "No, ma'am. Just thinking out loud. She's not important at all."

CHAPTER 9

THE ALASKA AIRLINES 737 TOUCHED DOWN AT THE WILEY POST– Will Rogers Memorial Airport at a quarter to five, one minute ahead of schedule. Cutter helped his seatmate retrieve her bag from the overhead, grabbed his own, then made his way down the roll-up airstairs in spitting rain—just like home. A sign above the arched entry to the blue terminal building welcomed him in Iñupiaq.

PAGLAGIVSI.

The scene inside the Barrow terminal resembled a rugby scrum . . . Ten rugby scrums. Arriving passengers had to shove their way through those departing on the turnaround flight who were waiting to get through the single security checkpoint. The lion's share of the crowd was Native Iñupiaq. Blue eyes and blond hair like Cutter's were few and far between. Whaling season was approaching, and many of the crews, from teenagers to grandfathers, wore jackets or hoodies with the name of their captain on the back. It was battling backpacks and carry-ons as people turned to welcome arriving friends or find where they were in line. Taller than most, Cutter looked over a sea of black heads and caught the eye of a uniformed North Slope Borough PD officer on the far side of the crowd. Jan Hough had said his contact would have a red beard. Cutter gave him a chin nod.

All bags came out at a single point. The airport was absent a luggage carousel, so they were stacked immediately by whomever got to the claim area first while they waited for their own luggage to come out, often leaving a bag trapped under a chest-high pile of plastic totes, which made up at least half the checked luggage of the Far North.

"Dillon Levi," the North Slope officer said, returning Cutter's chin nod. He glanced woefully at the crowd pressed against the growing mountain of luggage.

"Please tell me you didn't check a bag."

Cutter held up his duffle. "I'm good to go."

"Outstanding." Levi turned to work his way through the packed bodies and out the door. "Geez, Louise," he gasped when they were outside. "I can deal with a little rain. There's not enough air in that place for everybody."

"Can't argue with that," Cutter said.

"We're over here." Levi pointed across what Cutter knew was the only stretch of paved street in town. "Been to Utqiagvik before?"

"I have," Cutter said. "A couple of Decembers ago."

"Roads are so much better in the winter," Levi said. "We're all potholes and quagmires this time of the year . . . and that's talking about the good sections."

"Where exactly are we going?"

"Down a couple of hangars," Levi said. "It's a short charter ride to Wainwright. I've already got the freezer loaded on board."

"Freezer?" Cutter asked. "Not a silver bullet?"

The brushed-aluminum coffins used to transport human remains by air were often called silver bullets.

"Oh, there's one of those too," Levi said. "Jan wants you to fly out a chest freezer for the whale meat."

"Whale meat?" Cutter gave a confused nod. "I suppose it'll make more sense when I get there."

"I wouldn't bet on it," Officer Levi said. "This is bush Alaska. Every day levels up a notch to increasingly weirder shit . . . Folks out on Cake Eater got some video of a humongous polar bear two days ago. Some of the gas plant guys ran him out of a vacant shack. That bruiser's ass is so big it got stuck in the door frame for a couple of seconds before he busted out the front. Hilarious to watch. I'll show you when you get back."

"That would be a large bear," Cutter mused.

"Massive," Levi said. "Butt like a barmaid, my granddad would have said."

Cutter nodded. "Mine too."

Levi nodded at the high wing Cessna Caravan parked on the other side of a ten-foot chain link fence. "You are in luck. Bush Pilot Tony's off this evening. He's a good kid, but . . . Anyway. You're safe. You get Neil."

Other than mentioning the recent polar bear sighting, Neil, the Cessna's pilot, was mercifully quiet through the entire flight, leaving Cutter alone with his thoughts and a million acres of fog-shrouded tundra.

The scattered houses of Wainwright hove into view as the Caravan descended out of low clouds on a downwind approach just over half an hour from wheels-up. A gathered crowd milling near the east end of the village left no doubt about Cutter's destination. The altitude and weather made it impossible to make out faces or, in most cases, gender, but Cutter suspected Willadean Benson's parents were in the group. Raindrops pelted the plane, streaming along the windows and spraying off the wing struts. Heavy waves rolled in from the Chukchi Sea to crash against the beach.

Cutter heard the telltale click as Neil switched from radio to intercom, which was surprising since the man hadn't spoken two words since he'd given the initial safety briefing in Utqiagvik.

"See that silver line off the left wing, maybe a mile out?"

"Ice?" Cutter said.

"Yep. It'll move in tonight if they're lucky. This weather's beating the hell out of the shoreline. The pack ice will do 'em good."

The Wainwright airport was a simple 4,494-foot gravel strip with no tower and no lights. The centerline was marked by a series of bright orange barrels off the ends of the runway. Neil used the CTAF, or command frequency, to call out their position over the radio to any other aircraft that happened to be in the area.

He switched back to intercom again.

"I start my take-off roll at seven-fifteen p.m. sharp."

Neil was one of the few men Cutter knew who could pull off wearing an Elmer Fudd hat under his headset, and his grizzled beard and narrow eyes left no room for debate. His expression was even gloomier than Cutter's.

Cutter looked at his watch.

"I've got an hour and a half to do what I need to do."

"Depends on how long it takes you to climb in the plane," Neil said, lining up on the gravel strip. "It's a hell of a lot easier if I'm not already moving."

"Roger that," Cutter said. "I'll get here early if I'm leaving tonight."

Neil's weathered face came with years of experience flying bush planes into remote airstrips. He set the high-wing workhorse down on the gravel without so much as a chirp and rolled to a stop just yards from a muddy pickup truck and a ten-passenger van idling on the apron. Both vehicles were marked with North Slope Borough School District decals on the doors. Three young men, probably still in high school and all wearing black rain jackets with "IPALOOK WHALING CREW" stenciled on the back, helped Neil unload the chest freezer from the cargo door at the rear of the Cessna. Cutter was impressed, not only with their physical strength but also the way they worked as a quiet team—a crew. Rough hands and strong backs said these were not boys who sat for hours playing video games—at least not this time of year. The woman driving the van introduced herself as the principal of Wainwright school. She gave Cutter a ride to the Ipalook residence, a stone's throw from the Glad Tidings Assembly of God church.

Jan Hough was waiting in front of a weathered gray house beside a couple of cannibalized snow machines. A raw caribou hide, still bloody, hung on a two-by-four banister behind her, flapping in the stiff wind of the Chukchi Sea some two hundred yards away.

The muddy street and trampled yards of the storm-bleached wooden houses were filled with pockets of onlookers. They stood in the rain, eerily silent, watching a whole lot of nothing. From the air, they'd been ants, little different than rocks or pieces of driftwood on the beach. Now Cutter was close enough to see their faces, to feel the gravity of their mood. Neil, the school principal, the boys from the whaling crew, the entire village—they all looked as if they might break into tears at any moment. It made perfect sense. Willadean Benson was one of their own. As long as she was missing, there had been hope. Now that hope was gone.

Cutter couldn't help but think that a people patient enough to hunt caribou while dressed in rain gear made from dried whale intestines or to sit for hours on the frigid Arctic ice to catch a bearded seal would have no trouble waiting in modern North Face and Frogg Toggs raincoats to see what had happened to Willadean Benson.

CHAPTER 10

A Native couple and two boys not much older than Cutter's nephews stood glumly by the wooden steps leading to the house. The woman clutched the boys' shoulders as if they might try to escape. The man stood stoically beside her, eyes half closed, black hair buffeted by the wind. All four of them appeared impervious to the spitting rain.

The Ipalooks.

Willadean's body had been found on their property, so, of course, they were persons of interest.

Hough gave a wan smile when she saw Cutter and pulled him into a tight, back-patting embrace. "Thanks for coming, Arliss."

She tended to call him by his given name, reserving "Cutter" for Ethan, who'd apparently been her dear friend and confidant prior to his death. Just how much of a confidant was still up for debate. A muscular man in his late twenties wearing a blue North Slope PD ballcap and ballistic vest carrier stepped up and shook Cutter's hand, squeezing as if they were in some kind of contest.

Cutter matched the grip, raising a brow.

"Easy there, Bamm-Bamm," he said, stone-faced. "That's my shooting hand."

Hough heaved a tired sigh. "Officer Boatman doesn't know his own strength sometimes," she said. "Or frankly, his ass from a hole in the ground. He can learn though . . ." She put a hand on Boatman's shoulder to show she was only kidding. Mostly. "He was first on the scene. I'll let him take you through what happened on his arrival, then we'll go down into the cellar."

She nodded to the timber scaffolding behind the snow machines. A large X of yellow crime scene tape fluttered over a plywood door.

The pickup truck with the chest freezer sloshed through the potholes and came to a stop in front of the house. Abner Ipalook and several other men helped the high school boys unload it and carry it to a plywood pad he'd already prepped beside his front porch.

"For the whale," Hough said, as if that made perfect sense.

Cutter shrugged it off. That was the least of the mysteries that faced him at the moment. Hough had told him about the oreodont teeth. Ethan had given his kids specimens of this same kind of fossil, even commissioned a 3DK hunting knife with them embedded in the handle. But they were found in the Dakotas, not Alaska. Cutter hadn't figured out the connection yet, but these little prehistoric teeth had to be a clue to Ethan's murder.

Cutter took a slow breath, holding it in, concentrating on not getting ahead of himself. He wanted to rush down and get a look at the fossilized teeth, but that was a sure way to miss something. He surveyed the area while Officer Boatman gave him a grudging blow-by-blow of his interviews with the Ipalook boys and their parents—who apparently had no earthly idea why a dead girl had shown up in their ice cellar. They knew Willadean. Everyone in the village did. She'd babysat the boys. Apart from the Arctic Ocean and the strong possibility of polar bears, Cutter could have been standing in many front yards in rural Florida. Animal hides blowing in the wind, stinging rain (albeit fifty degrees colder), and the rusting hulks of old vehicles, the parts of which just might come in handy someday. A jumbled pile of weathered driftwood, some the diameter of telephone poles, most no larger than Boatman's arm, lay on the far side of the cellar entrance. Several freshly cut pieces were propped against the trackless remains of a Ski-Doo Skandic snow machine that was seeing new life as a sawhorse. Wood chips littered the ground, matting the mud.

Cutter glanced from the woodpile to the house. "Chilly day," he said. "Surprised they don't have a fire going inside."

"They heat with oil," Hough said. "Firewood's at a premium around here. This is for the steam house." She pointed to an eight-by-eight plywood shed between the Ipalook's house and their neighbors. Chunks of blackened meat and rib bones that Cutter took to be from a seal swung like a wind chime on a line that hung under the eaves of the neighboring home.

Cutter shot a glance at Hough. "Let's get to it then."

The odor surprised him, musty, a hint of acetone, like the old paint-by-numbers sets Grumpy had gotten him and Ethan when they were kids. It wasn't what he'd expected, considering the stories he'd heard about indigenous diets in the Arctic.

Willadean Benson was just as Boatman had described her. She stood upright, frozen in time like a flower pressed between the icy pages of a book.

Cutter crouched down so he was at eye level with the three fossils suspended in the ice. Had he not already known what oreodont teeth looked like, he might have thought they were rocks. Three almost perfect slate gray molars, peaked like small mountains, each attached to a bit of slightly paler fossilized jawbone from the sheep-sized mammal.

Boatman crowded in beside Hough. "You guys really think it'll take all night for us to solve this?"

"Nope," Cutter said. He glanced up at Hough from his crouch. "I'm guessing you already have a theory as to what happened."

"I'm reasonably sure I know how she died," Hough said. "I called you in case there's more to these fossils when we get her out of there."

"Wait." Boatman bounced on the balls of his feet. The exuberance of a rookie youth. "I get it. You said there was another murder connected with fossils like these ones. You guys think we've got a serial killer leaving oreodontal bones at the crime scene?"

"Oreodont," Hough corrected. "And no, Willadean Benson wasn't murdered by a serial killer."

"Wait," Boatman said. "You've already figured out who put her in the ice?"

Cutter gave the young officer a slow nod. "How about you run your theory by us."

"Well," Boatman said. "Abner Ipalook seems like a good guy. I'm not liking him or his wife for this. No motive. But it's a point of pride that he doesn't lock the cellar door. The Bensons discovered the morning after Willadean went missing that she'd snuck out to go to her boyfriend's party across town. His parents were down in Anchorage, so there was some weed being passed around and plenty of bootlegged alcohol. Half dozen witnesses said the boyfriend didn't leave with her, so he was ruled out as a suspect." Boatman raised his index finger like he was about to make an important point. "But, there were two boys who apparently left the party shortly after she did. According to witnesses, both of them had been drinking. One, last name Ivanov, I can't remember his first name, but it's in the report, he supposedly tried to hook up with the victim at the party, but she rebuffed him. I just learned an hour ago while we were waiting for the freezer that Ivanov was killed in a hunting accident last spring. Just because he died already doesn't mean he didn't murder Willadean. We can still bring his friend in for questioning. Brown, I think his name is."

"So," Hough said. "The boys killed her . . . and then what?"

"Willadean was killed in December, when this place would have been chockablock full of whale meat from that October hunt. Anybody could have come down and chipped a cave in the ice and then packed the Benson girl in it. Some fresh snow over the top and she'd be sealed in."

"I suppose that's physically possible," Cutter said. "But if she was dead, it would have been difficult to keep the body standing upright like this while she froze. And if she was alive, she would have just pushed her way out of what was essentially a giant snow cone of loose ice. She wasn't restrained . . ."

"Maybe she was unconscious," Boatman offered. "And maybe they stacked boxes of whale against the body until the ice froze solid."

"That's one theory," Hough said. She stooped next to Cutter, studied the body for a moment, then glanced up at Boatman. "What do you see here, in the clear ice all around the body?"

He shrugged. "Dirt, I guess. And roots."

"What else?" Cutter asked.

The young officer leaned in. It took him a long minute, but he finally got it.

"Wood chips!" he said. "There's a woodyard by those snow machines right above us. They must have killed her up there! That's the murder scene—"

Hough pushed off her knees to stand with a low groan. "Or . . ."

"Or . . ." Boatman shook his head. "Or . . ."

She toed the waxed fruit boxes of frozen whale. "Let's go ahead and get Abner to start a line to carry this stuff up to the chest freezer."

"Aren't you worried we'll give up some bit of evidence to the homicide if we let them carry out the boxes?"

"No," Hough said. "Because there wasn't any homicide. Remember what the weather was the night Willadean disappeared."

"I wasn't here," Boatman said. "But the report notes a big-ass blizzard blew in off the ice pack."

"Does the file say anything about the weather before the storm?"

Boatman nodded. "A warm front," he said. "Like a chinook wind."

"Now look at how her arms are situated. One trailing upward, over her head. The way her face is pushed against the clear ice. The wood chips."

"Holy shit!" Boatman said. "I see it now. She fell in a sinkhole in the permafrost. The storm blew in and covered up all the evidence with drifts before morning. The snow must have just packed in around her . . . She was wedged in alive until she suffocated . . ." He gave a full-body shiver. "Maybe even until she starved to death."

"That tracks with what I see," Cutter said. "My guess is that she was trying to wriggle her hand down to her knife, hoping she might be able to cut her way free or even climb back up. See how the rest of the ice is fairly cloudy, milky almost, but how right around her is clearer, like glass."

Hough exhaled a long, slow breath and gave a sad shake of her head. "She was alive long enough for her body heat to melt the permafrost. Then the ice refroze around her. The poor kid probably screamed herself to sleep . . . or drowned in the meltwater."

"Well, that's gonna give me nightmares," Boatman whispered, vapor blossoming in front of his face. "Dozens of women go missing every year in Alaska, mostly taken by bad men . . . but sometimes, it's the land itself that gets them . . ."

"The autopsy will tell us if our suspicions are correct," Hough said. "In the meantime, there's still the issue of the fossils. That's too big a coincidence to ignore."

"It really is," Cutter said, distracted. He leaned closer for a better look, using his phone as a flashlight. He snapped photos from all angles so he could study them later. "It appears she accidently dragged the fossils out of her pocket when she was trying to get to her knife."

"The big question is who gave those fossils to her." Hough said. "It could have been Ethan."

"That's possible," Cutter said. "We'll have to see if they were connected in some way."

"Listen," Hough said. "Did Mim mention—"

"The Tunik kid from Wainwright who thinks he's Ethan's son? Yep. Mim's come to grips with the fact that Ethan helped a lot of people she wasn't aware of. Travis Tunik's name comes up quite a bit when we're talking about Ethan's past . . . As does yours."

"Okaaay," Hough said. "Not sure how I feel about that, but it is what it is. Anyway, Tunik is from here in Wainwright, but he's working in Utqiagvik at the moment. We need to talk to Willadean's parents before we leave town. They may know where she got the fossils."

"Speaking of leaving town," Cutter said. "We couldn't hear it fifteen feet down in this ice pit, but I'm pretty sure Neil has already flown away in our ride."

Hough checked her watch. "Seven-twenty. Oh yeah. He's scooting for home before it gets dark. He's not a bold pilot . . . which has allowed him to become an old pilot."

"I assume we're spending the night in the school?" Cutter asked.

"The PD has an itinerant apartment," Boatman said. "It's next door to my place. One bedroom and a passable couch if you don't mind a spring in the small of your back."

"I started work at . . ." Cutter shut his eyes, too exhausted to do the math. "I'll be able to sleep in a closet if I have to."

Hough rolled up her sleeves and heaved a somber groan. "First, we have to fire up the saw and cut this poor kid out of the ice."

CHAPTER 11

Anchorage

LOLA TEARIKI POUNDED A FIST AGAINST THE STEERING WHEEL AND cursed in frustration. Her hair, thick and unruly to begin with, refused to stay confined in the bun on top of her head—and it was beginning to piss her off. She was young, beyond fit, and not normally one to need much sleep, but the last few days had left her with a pit in her stomach and the feeling that her body had been scrubbed with coarse sandpaper.

She was parked in the strip mall west of the Yakishabu Japanese restaurant on Dimond Boulevard, peering through a rainy windshield and willing Eddie Dupree to show up. The restaurant was one of the few spots where the mope's phone had pinged more than once. It was a long shot, but it was better than sitting in the office. If Teariki had learned anything during her tenure as a deputy United States marshal—and especially working with Arliss Cutter—it was that good warrant analysis was vital, but sometimes, you just had to take the intel you had and beat the streets.

Twenty-six-year-old Anchorage police officer Joe Bill Brackett pressed a green can of Red Bull to his lips and peered over the top from the passenger seat of the Tahoe. His dark hair was wet from making the run from his pickup to Lola's G-car.

"Don't take this the wrong way," he said, "but I think you might be fighting a losing battle."

She stared at him, eyes wide, nostrils flaring. She'd teased him about being a lumber-sexual in his gray flannel shirt and Kühl jeans, so whatever he meant, she probably had it coming.

"Are you talking the warrant for Dupree?"

"Of course not," he said. "You're a fugitive-hunting genius. I mean trying to corral your hair."

Her lips drew back in a terrifying grimace to display perfect teeth—her best Polynesian warrior face.

He chuckled. "You don't scare me, Teariki."

She stuck her tongue way out and turned just enough in her seat to slam her elbow across her body into her opposite palm, growling—the beginnings of a haka.

"Okay," he said. "You scare the shit out of me, but that's why you're so fun to be around."

If man hunts for serial killers counted in the mix, Teariki and Brackett had been dating for the better part of a year. He was assigned to graveyard shift—ten p.m. to eight a.m. On a good day, they had maybe a couple of hours of overlap to grab dinner and compare notes. She'd been tracking with Cutter on Pioneer Peak that morning when Joe Bill got off work and hit the rack—and she was still hard at it, hunting Dupree when he woke up.

"Thanks for hanging out." She softened just a touch but kept one eyebrow up to let him know she was still a little grouchy. "Sitting on surveillance on a scumbag like Eddie Dupree ain't much of a date night. I reckon most guys would be whinging for me to call it a day and come home. It's just that this one is—"

"Personal?"

Lola shrugged. "I don't know if I'd say that."

"I think they're all a little bit personal with you," Joe Bill said. "That's what makes you so good at what you do."

"Maybe so," Lola said, chewing on that idea.

Joe Bill glanced at his watch. "You've been runnin' and gunnin' for days on nothing but predatory drive and caffeine. You want me to run to Lucky Wishbone and get us some dinner?" He raised his eyebrows up and down. "I know how you love your protein . . ."

"Maybe in a minute," she said. "Just sit with me for a bit if you don't mind." She slid the warrant folder from between the seat and the center console and passed it to him. "Skim over this and see if anything jumps out at you."

Joe Bill opened the file and studied it in silence. Lola continued to watch the Yakishabu parking lot, glancing sideways every few moments to gauge his reactions to the file.

"Sometimes fresh eyes see something we missed," she prodded.

"Maybe," he said. "I guess I'm just baffled by his mugshot . . ."

"How's that?"

"I don't know," Joe Bill said. "This guy looks like he could be running a PTA meeting. He's so—"

Lola started to say something, but Joe Bill raised his hand. "I know. There's no way to tell if someone's a perv by their appearance . . . but looking at Eddie Dupree's criminal history, you'd expect to see horns growing out of his head."

Lola caught movement in the parking lot and threw the binoculars to her eyes. It turned out to be a false alarm.

"I know what you mean." She relaxed a notch. "I worked an assignment on a high-threat trial when I was still a baby deputy—only a couple of months out of the Academy. Our prisoner had kidnapped a couple of kids, took them across state lines, and murdered them. He took video of the whole sick mess. The things this shitbag did were so evil and deranged . . ." She tried and failed to blink away the memory. "Anyway, usually we rotate duties when we're on assignment, but the powers that be on this deal split us up for the duration of the trial, so deputies who sat with the bad guy in court weren't the ones to transport him to and from jail."

"So he wouldn't get in your heads?"

"Nope," Lola said. "So we wouldn't drive him somewhere secluded and shoot him in the face. I mean, every one of us who sat through that trial and saw the crime scene photos, heard the witness testimony, we knew the world would be a better place if that dude took a dirt nap. To look at him, though . . . he could have been your mailman or high school physics teacher . . . When we hunt a guy like Eddie Dupree, I think about what I saw at that trial. It spurs me on, you know. So, yeah. I guess I do make these cases personal."

Joe Bill waited a beat to see if she had more to say—he was a hell of a boyfriend that way. When she didn't, he said, "My mom's constantly ragging on me not to let a law enforcement career get me all jaded."

"Jaded," Lola scoffed. "Or realistic? Nothing against your mum, but I think a hell of a lot of people are just more comfortable when they're blissfully unaware . . . you know, thinking that most people are good."

"You don't think they are?"

Lola groaned. "I'm honest enough with myself to admit that I just plain do not know. I'd like to think that there are a lot of good folks in the world, but there are more evil bastards than most people realize. I am absolutely sure of that." She looked through the binoculars as she spoke.

Joe Bill held up Dupree's warrant folder. "Let's talk about something cheerful—"

"Dude," Lola said. "You are a bright light in a pit of—" Her phone began to buzz like crazy, cutting her off. Nancy Alvarez came over the radio at the same time.

"Lola, Lola, Nancy," she said, using the "hey you, you, it's me," radio format.

"Go ahead, Nance," Lola said while she dug the vibrating phone out of her pocket. "Whatcha got?"

"Are you getting the info dump on Dupree's cell?"

"Notifications are coming in as we speak." Lola looked at the phone and hit the ignition. "He's gone active at Dimond Mall. We're about a mile away en route from that sushi place in the old Village Inn."

"We?"

"Brackett's with me."

"Ahh," Alvarez said. "I see . . . Anyway, Sean and I are coming in from south of O'Malley on Old Seward. Traffic sucks and we're hitting every red. You'll beat us there. ISU's working another case in midtown. I'll get them rolling this way to help us box him in."

"Copy that." Lola banged the wheel, willing a break in the traffic. She found one and made a snap right turn, throwing Joe Bill against the door as she sped east toward the mountains and Dimond Mall.

APD's Investigative Support Unit—ISU—was much more tactical than the name implied. Composed mostly of officers from the department's SWAT team, the plainclothes group's primary focus was hunting dangerous felons who were wanted in connection with cases investigated by the city. Considering the similarity of their missions it was only natural that ISU would frequently cross paths with the Alaska Fugitive Task Force. Many on ISU were sworn in as special deputy US marshals/part-time task force officers.

Lola caught a break and goosed it, fishtailing as she took the Tahoe out of a hole in the traffic to jet into the faster lane. She settled into her seat and shot a quick sideways glance at Joe Bill. "Are you going to get in trouble working with me when you're technically off duty?"

"Probably," he said. "But it'll be worth it if we get Dupree."

Alvarez came across the radio again, the tension in her voice speaking volumes.

"Location, Teariki?"

"Two minutes out." Lola gave her the cross street. A little white Ford Fiesta changed lanes in front of her without signaling, forcing her to slam on her brakes or eat the lady's bumper. "This traffic's for shit though . . ."

"Step it up if you can," Alvarez said. "Sounds like Dupree's making a run for the back parking lot off Old Seward."

Lola glanced at Joe Bill, then clarified on the radio. "Behind Best Buy?"

"Affirmative," Alvarez said.

Lola shot around a car, slammed on her brakes to avoid rear-ending a city utility truck, then juked left when she found another hole. "What's he doing running already?"

"Remember that deputy donut we met at the mall?"

"Yep," Lola said. "The chubby security guy. You gave him your business card."

"I told him to call us if he saw Dupree," Alvarez said. "The dumb-ass just called to tell me he thinks Dupree 'made him.' Then the call dropped. I'm trying to get him back on the line now."

"What the hell do you mean, made him?" Lola smacked the console with her fist, wanting to scream. "That idiot's not sup-posed to follow—"

"Preach, sister," Alvarez said. "I guess our deputy donut came down with a case of the ass-magnet and got a little too close. Dupree's phone has gone dark again."

"Do we have a make on what vehicle he's in?"

"Not yet," Alvarez said. "Hang on, ass-magnet is calling back . . ."

Lola ignored the red light at Old Seward, squirting through a break in the traffic to drift around the corner by the Burger King drive-through. Joe Bill braced both hands on the dash as she poured on the gas.

"I see him!" Lola tossed the radio mic to Joe Bill. "Make yourself useful and tell the cavalry Eddie Dupree is in the southeast park-ing lot of Dimond Mall, hauling ass toward a yellow dirt bike—oh, and he just stopped to kick the shit out of that security guy."

CHAPTER 12

LOLA JUMPED THE CURB, SENDING RED BULL CANS AND POWDER-blue warrant folders into the air. Joe Bill gave a muffled grunt as he hung on to the Tahoe's grab handle with one hand and worked the radio with the other.

Eddie Dupree hadn't stayed in the wind as long as he had by being stupid. He'd parked his motorcycle near the mall entrance, but in the open and far enough from other cars to make it difficult to pin like Lola and the other responding units would have done with a four-wheeled vehicle. Shitbag pervert that he was, their objective wasn't to run the guy down, but to slap him in cuffs without anyone getting hurt. That was easier said than done. The bike, a smallish Suzuki DualSport, was meant for street or dirt, highly maneuverable—but also highly unstable on the rain-slick pavement.

Lola zigged in and out of parked cars, working her way across the crowded parking lot in the straightest line possible.

Nancy and Sean were coming in from the south. A white Ford Expedition Lola recognized as one of the ISU guys roared in behind the Tahoe and then veered off to take a position farther to the east while Lola and Nancy pinched the bike from north and south.

The mall security guy had scrambled back to his feet almost as soon as he went down and was now pounding the pavement just steps behind Dupree, arms pumping, head back like he was sprinting for the finish.

"That guy runs fast for a fat kid," Lola said under her breath—and stomped on the gas.

"Hey, hey, hey!" Joe Bill's hand shot out to brace against the dash. "You planning to run him down?"

"No, mate," Lola said. "We're gonna box him in."

She gritted her teeth as she hit the gas and yanked the wheel hard to untrack the rear wheels and skid sideways, putting her door next to the little Suzuki.

Dupree grabbed the bike by the handlebars and threw his leg over the seat, nearly going down in the process.

Lola flung open her door and threw the Tahoe into PARK while they were still rolling. The transmission chattered in protest. Lola ignored it—and ran. Sean Blodgett bailed out of the passenger side of Nancy's rig and sprinted toward them.

She and Sean reached the bike at the same time, just as Dupree coaxed the engine to life.

"US Marshals!" Lola barked. "Get on the ground now!" She left her pistol in the holster but drew her Taser. Nancy had her handgun out, providing lethal cover if Dupree went for a weapon. At the moment, both his hands were visible on the handlebars. He was only a threat if Lola didn't get out of the way—which she did not intend to do.

Dupree rolled on the throttle, spinning the rear tire on wet asphalt.

Blodgett was almost on top of him, ready to bulldog Dupree to the ground, when the mall security guy came screaming up and planted a boot into the rear of the bike's frame. "Deputy Donut" was a big man, pushing three hundred pounds. Momentum and wet pavement carried him past the motorcycle and directly into Sean Blodgett. Both men went down in a tangled mess, sliding and splashing through an oily parking lot puddle.

Dupree horsed the bike back into control, yanking hard on the handlebars to keep from dumping it.

For a split second, Lola thought he was going down. Instead, Dupree grabbed a handful of brake and rolled on more throttle, spinning the rear tire again. Centrifugal force kept the little bike upright.

"Tase! Tase! Tase!"

She'd thumbed the switch on the side of her Taser, letting the red dots from the laser settle on Dupree's torso.

His left foot planted on the ground, the other on the opposite peg, Dupree kept the front brake locked and spun the bike in a half circle, forcing Lola to step offline at the same moment she pulled the trigger. A tiny canister of compressed gas blew the plastic gates off the cartridge and sent two barbed electrodes toward the target, unspooling on gossamer thin wires. Her shot went wide. One of the darts struck Dupree in the neck, but the second continued impotently under his arm.

Lola regained her footing and sprang forward, intent on grabbing a handful of rain jacket and burying the nose of the Taser into Dupree's rib cage, "drive-stunning" him off the bike.

Sean Blodgett had untangled himself from the mall cop and now lunged for the motorcycle. The ISU officer, a brute of a guy who looked like he'd have no trouble clotheslining the fugitive with a stiff arm, was only two steps behind Lola.

But two steps were a half-step too far away.

Lola's fingers closed around the clammy raincoat, but Dupree shrugged it off at the same time his tires found traction. Engine yowling, the motorcycle reared like a terrified horse into an unstable wheelie and then shot out of the scrum heading east, leaving Lola holding an empty coat.

Hopping mad and buzzing with adrenaline, Lola made a futile attempt to run after him but stopped a half dozen steps in and sprinted back to her Tahoe. Joe Bill Brackett followed, jumping in beside her. Nancy, Sean, and the responding ISU officer gave chase in their vehicles as well, but it was too late. Dupree was already under the Seward Highway and had ripped down a side street by the time anyone with a badge reached Dimond Boulevard.

Alvarez jumped on the radio immediately, directing inbound APD units in an attempt to cordon off the area.

She and Lola split up after they passed under the Seward Highway, with Lola hanging a left toward an industrial area and the Midnight Sun Brewing Company. She slowed the Tahoe and rolled down her window. Brackett did the same. They strained their ears for the whine of a motorcycle engine.

Nothing.

Lola glanced at Joe Bill, nodding at the rain jacket she'd tossed in between them. "Look in the pockets and see if there's anything to tell us where he's going."

She brightened for a moment when he pulled out a cell phone. He shook his head. "It's locked."

"Of course, it is!" She pointed to the glove box. "There's a Faraday bag in there. Drop the phone in it to block this son of a bitch from wiping it remotely."

"Cool," Joe Bill said, doing as she asked. "My girlfriend carries around a Faraday bag . . ."

"Anything else?"

"He's got a small ziplock baggie with three M-30s."

"Fentanyl?"

"Blue pills with "30" on the side, so yeah, fentanyl."

Lola scanned as she drove. Joe Bill kept rummaging, careful to watch out for the fishhooks and razor blades these idiots liked to hide in their clothes as a surprise to unsuspecting law enforcement officers.

"A scrap of spiral notebook paper that says 'claytonia green.'"

Joe Bill's shoulders slumped.

"What?" she asked.

"A pacifier . . ."

"A baby pacifier?"

He nodded.

"Well, hell. I don't even want to think about . . ."

"Could be he does some Ecstasy," Joe Bill offered. "And you know, uses the pacifier to keep his teeth from chipping."

Lola pounded the steering wheel. "We need to get this bastard in cuffs. Now!"

Twenty fruitless minutes later, one of the ISU guys found Dupree's Suzuki motorcycle abandoned two miles east, near the Abbott Loop ball fields. APD started a canine track but that yielded nothing.

The thick woods around Campbell Creek and Bicentennial

Park formed a black wall behind the ball fields, where Lola and APD had set up a temporary command post.

Nancy, Sean, and four APD officers, not including Joe Bill, had come back in from the woods. Midas, the Belgian Malinois, stood dutifully by his handler, Officer Theron Jenson—Nancy's boyfriend.

Lola rubbed a hand over her weary face. She couldn't remember what a pillow felt like, but she'd do it all again right now if it meant finding Eddie Dupree.

"Ideas?"

"Bicentennial Park just melds into the Chugach mountains," Alvarez said. "I don't see Dupree as one to try and hide out with the wolves and brown bears." She looked into the night sky and got a face full of rain. "Not in this weather anyway."

"Midas couldn't get a lock," Jenson said. "Even with Dupree's rain jacket." He rubbed the Malinois's ears. "He'll go after the scent of fear in the air, but he wasn't getting any hits in the wood line. I agree with Nance. Our guy didn't go that way. I'd say an accomplice picked him up."

"We need to get a warrant for the phone," Lola said when the APD units had gone and only task force officers and Joe Bill Brackett remained.

"Easy-peasy," Blodgett said. "But a warrant is one thing. Busting the code will not be. The manufacturers don't like that slippery slope, even for a pervert like Dupree. I've heard the Bureau might have a back way through the encryption, but they save that shit for terrorists. No way they're giving it up for a fugitive."

"What do you make of this?" Lola laid a clear plastic bag containing the scrap of paper from Dupree's raincoat on the hood of her Tahoe.

"Claytonia," Blodgett said. "Sounds made-up."

Joe Bill looked up from his phone. "It's a little flower. Also known as miner's lettuce or spring beauty."

"I gotta tell you," Blodgett said. "Thinking about this guy walking around with a baby pacifier is creeping the shit outta me."

"Kids at raves use them," Joe Bill offered again. "Keeps them from damaging their teeth when the dope makes them—"

"We know, Young Blood," Alvarez said. "Those pacifiers are always chewed to hell. This one doesn't have a tooth mark on it." She put a hand on Lola's shoulder. "We'll get him. But you need sleep." She stifled a groan. "We all need sleep."

Lola scooped up the baggie and looked across the hood at Joe Bill. "Let's go. I'll take you back to your truck."

"You have a plan," Joe Bill said when he shut his door. "I can see it in your eyes."

"I know a guy with the FBI who might be able to help with the phone," she said. "He hates my guts, but he hates shitbirds like Eddie Dupree more."

CHAPTER 13

Wainright

JAN HOUGH AGREED THAT IT WAS BEST TO GIVE THE BENSONS AN evening before an interview. They needed time to reopen their grief and at least try to come to terms with the terrifying way their daughter had died. Homicide investigations weren't usually in a deputy marshal's swim lane, but Cutter had been around death enough to learn that one of the first questions survivors asked was if their loved one had suffered. This wasn't a homicide, but Willadean Benson had died trapped in the ice, slowly and alone. An interview would keep until the following day.

Cutter opted for Boatman's couch and left the itinerant apartment to Hough. Gossip—tundra drums, they called it—traveled fast in the North, and there was already enough talk about Jan and the other Cutter brother.

The Bensons were understandably stunned that their beautiful teenaged daughter, smart, driven, with the world in front of her, had simply fallen into a hole and died. Countless people went missing every year in the Far North, the vast majority of them young Native women. People expected foul play, mysterious circumstance, bad men doing bad things, not something so . . . ordinary.

When asked the next morning, neither of Willadean's parents remembered ever seeing the oreodont fossils. Her father, still

processing, let his grief spill out as anger and railed at the "pointless questions." They wouldn't bring his little girl back. Mrs. Benson, her face a mask of calm, stared out the rain-streaked window,
mute except when questions were directed specifically at her. Cutter understood. Talking to her felt cruel, and as her husband had
angrily observed, pointless. In the end, she left her shattered husband brooding on the couch and showed Cutter and Hough to
the door, forcing a plastic smile.

"Thank you for coming by," she said. "I apologize for my husband, he's . . ."

Cutter put a hand over his heart. "There's nothing to apologize for."

A single tear ran down the grieving mother's cheek. "She was . . .
Willadean was so smart." A sudden memory brought the hint of a
smile. It faded quickly. "Did you know she got a college internship
when she was still in high school. The youngest ever to do it."

Cutter gave a soft smile but said nothing.

Mrs. Benson closed her eyes. "She was amazing with numbers."

"I wish I could have met her," Cutter said, meaning it. "Could I
ask, where was the internship?"

"Accounting business in Utqiagvik," she said. "Beck and Associates . . ."

Outside, Hough tucked her clipboard between the seats of the
pickup they'd borrowed from Officer Boatman and used the
steering wheel to settle herself into the driver's seat. She turned
to look Cutter in the eye.

"You'd have made a hell of a homicide investigator. You have a
way of connecting with people. A tender side . . ."

Cutter raised his brow, straight-faced. "Tender? Pretty sure
that's the first time I've ever been called that."

"For a badass, outlaw-trackin', son of a bitch, I mean."

Cutter scoffed. "I don't know about all that, but I think I'll
leave the crime solving to you pros and stick with chasing down
the ones that run."

"Shoot where you're pointed . . ."

"Yep," he said. "Life's simpler that way."

* * *

Eager to return to Utqiagvik, Cutter stowed his duffel behind the web netting in the rear of the Cessna Caravan and then settled into his seat across from Jan Hough. She'd just ended a phone call and was wrestling the phone back into her jacket pocket.

"So?" he said, situating the green David Clark headset over his head, leaving one ear uncovered so they'd be able to talk until the pilot started the engine and the intercom went live.

She clicked her cheap ballpoint pen against her notebook. "Your hunch was correct. Beck and Associates do handle accounts for Johnson, Benham, and Murphy."

"Okay," Cutter said. "So, Willadean interns for an accounting company that does work with my brother's old engineering firm . . ."

Hough clicked the pen against her front teeth, thinking. It was only then that Cutter realized she'd put on a fresh coat of lipstick. She pointed the pen at him, focusing on a sudden thought. "She runs into Ethan at some function, and he, being a nice guy, gives her a couple of fossils."

"It could be just that simple," Cutter said.

"I'm not buying it." Hough shook her head. "Ethan seemed like a generous guy but . . . Doesn't it seem weird for him to be handing out rocks from South Dakota all willy-nilly? He must have had a reason to give them to her."

"Maybe he gave them to someone else," Cutter said. "And that person gave them to her."

"I told you you'd make a good homicide investigator . . ."

Outside, at the back of the aircraft, the pilot, a young man with a nest of bed-head hair and wide eyes as if he'd just seen something unbelievable removed the stanchion that kept the tail of the loaded plane from squatting as everyone boarded, then he climbed in the front door behind the yoke. He turned in his seat and gave Hough and Cutter the quick, mandatory safety briefing—seat belts, fire extinguisher, survival gear in the belly locker—slightly unsure, as if he were trying to convince himself.

Hough gave him a wide, reassuring smile and a thumbs-up. Cutter nodded to show he understood as well.

"May I present Tony Caprese," Hough said.

"Like the salad," the kid said.

"Like the salad," Hough nodded. "But I call him Bush Pilot Tony."

Tony made a joke about using the fire extinguisher to put him out first if they burst into a ball of flames. The pleading look in his eyes made Cutter think he was actually serious.

"Heading down to Anchorage for a float check ride in Lake Hood," Tony said, as if to bolster confidence in his abilities. Headset in hand, he glanced over his shoulder at Cutter. "You're from Anchorage, right?"

"I live there, yes," Cutter said.

"I'm kind of stoked about it," Tony said. "The guys at the school are throwing a big party at the Peanut Farm on Thursday night if I pass."

"*When* you pass, Caprese!" Hough said. "Backup plans are for wusses."

"My life is one big backup plan."

Bush Pilot Tony buckled his harness and adjusted his headset. He leaned out the open window and shouted "Clear!" to no one in particular before starting the Caravan's engine, then craned his head to look up and down the runway before calling out his intentions over the radio. He hit the brakes twice while taxiing out to the gravel strip, causing Cutter and Hough to lurch forward against their belts.

Hough folded her notebook and clutched it across her lap, glancing across the narrow aisle at Cutter.

"I hope you have your insurance all paid up."

"I do," Cutter said.

Another sudden tap of the brakes.

A twenty-knot wind, gusting to thirty, blew in from the southwest, buffeting the plane as Tony taxied to the east end of the gravel strip. Using brakes and throttle, he made a stoppy-starty turn into the wind.

Cutter had never relished the idea of flying. Small planes were the worst—which could be a real issue, considering Caravans and 185s were considered SUVs in Alaska. Often the only way to get from point A to point B. The lead-up to the flight bothered him the most, but once he was on board, Cutter had learned to leave his future to fate. Bush Pilot Tony, last name Caprese, "like the salad," was in control, not him. There was little he could do about it at this point anyway. He let his head fall sideways as Tony pulled back on the yoke and the plane began to fly.

Hough gave a mock grimace.

"As for me," she said. "I'm too old to die tragically young."

"That's funny." He scoffed. "You're not old. You're what? Thirty-five?"

"That is exceedingly kind of you," she said. "I happen to be forty-two."

"That's young."

Hough leaned forward in her seat, arching her back. "My bones beg to differ," she said. "And my old bones have things they want to get done today—like check out what Willadean was doing on her internship." The Caravan hit a pocket of air and bumped as if the pilot had run over something in the road. Hough grimaced. "Fingers crossed we survive this."

Tony's voice came across the intercom. "You guys know I can hear you, right?"

CHAPTER 14

*J*AN HOUGH'S NORTH SLOPE BOROUGH TAHOE WAS WAITING AT THE airport when they arrived in Utqiagvik after a mercifully uneventful flight. Heavy flakes of wet snow mixed with intermittent rain as Cutter followed Hough down the foldout steps. Brooding clouds added to the gloom of the muddy village and made it feel colder than it actually was. Cutter dug a fleece jacket out of his duffel and layered it under the Helly Hansen rain shell.

"Sometimes I'm afraid I might give Bush Pilot Tony a complex," Hough said as she buckled in. "To hear him tell it, he's dreamed of flying ever since he was a kid. I don't want to wreck somebody's lifelong dream."

"There's a time for learning a new skill," Cutter said. "When I'm on his airplane is not that time. If I put my life in someone else's hands, I don't really care if they have dreams of becoming a surgeon or fly bush planes. I want them to be the best doctor or pilot I ever even heard of. Same goes for partners backing me up in the field."

"Is that so?" Hough gave him a long stare.

"My grandfather always said there were basically two kinds of partners in this business—those who will . . . and those who won't. Basically, someone who has the skill to get the job done and the fortitude to do it—by any means necessary. The kind who would back up their partner in a pinch . . . or the sort who talk a big game but pee down their leg and run screaming into the trees the moment things go rodeo."

"Awfully broad spectrum there, hoss." Hough turned and shot a grin at Cutter. "There *are* points in between."

Cutter leaned back against the headrest and closed his eyes, still exhausted from a short night on a shorter couch. "Maybe," he said. "It's metaphorical."

Hough turned on Stevenson Street toward the Police department, nodding to her left at Osaka Restaurant, a tiny Korean-Japanese place with wooden pallets out front to act as a walkway over the quagmire of mud that made up the small parking lot. "They make a great hotpot if you're hungry."

"I had a Clif bar," Cutter said. "I'd rather go visit these accountants before they leave for lunch. I'm interested to hear what they have to say about Willadean Benson."

"Agreed," Hough said. "Just wanted to be a good host . . ." She was quiet for a beat, then, both hands on the wheel, looked sideways at Cutter. "So, dare I ask how I stack up?"

"Stack up?"

"You know," she said. "On the back-you-up-or-pee-down-my-leg continuum."

Cutter smiled at that. He could see why Ethan had gotten along with this woman.

"Well," he said. "Let's see . . . Not long after I first met you in Deadhorse, I watched you bail out of your SUV without hesitating and pop a monster polar bear in the rump with a rubber bullet to run him out of town. Judging by that behavior, seems like you're plenty capable of shooting straight under pressure—and you aren't afraid of facing a bear the size of a Volkswagen Beetle."

"I'll take that." Hough slowed the Tahoe to a crawl, sloshing through a series of potholes that formed a kind of muddy moat in front of the five connected ATCO trailers that made up the Beck and Associates offices.

The front door chimed when they went inside, Hough leading the way. The presence of local law enforcement helped take some of the emotional sting out of a deputy US marshal suddenly darkening your door.

The building itself was man-camp chic, with panel walls and robust metal fixtures meant to be transported to drilling and con-

struction sites. Plain as it was, someone had taken the time to dec-
orate the boxy interior with a good deal of Native and Western
art. A hefty whaling harpoon with a thick wooden shaft took up
most of the wall to Cutter's right. The toggling barbed head was
nearly the size of his hand. A sharpened brass tube at least an
inch in diameter ran parallel to the shaft, a foot behind the
barbed point. A brass shoulder gun hung over the back wall. If
the gun was as authentic as it looked, it was probably worth upward of ten thousand dollars. The weapons were interesting, but
Cutter stopped in his tracks to admire the other art. One, a small
watercolor, showed a log lodge set along a meandering river,
smoke curling out a stone chimney.

"There are spruce trees," Cutter muttered. "It's obviously
somewhere far from here."

"I do miss me some trees," Hough said.

A slight Iñupiaq woman poked her head out of a nearby office.
Dressed in faded jeans and a pink hoodie, she looked to be in her
teens or early twenties. Cutter thought she might possibly be another intern.

"Mr. Beck's wife painted that," the young woman said, beaming.

Cutter read the Iñupiaq word penciled in neat block letters
below the painting.

"*Imigiksaaq.*"

"Your pronunciation is pretty good," the young woman said. "It
means 'fresh water.' Mrs. Beck's ancestors are Black River people.
A lot of the rivers south of the Kobuk are kind of dark and
swampy, but the one in front of the Beck's cabin comes straight
out of the mountains, so it's nice and fresh. *Imigiksaaq.*"

Still stooped over and looking at the watercolor, Cutter glanced
at the young woman. "You've been there?"

"No," she said. "But Mrs. Beck talks about it a lot."

Hough nodded. "She's from Shungnak if I recall."

"That's right."

Cutter took a half step sideways to check out a large canvas
painting to the left of the watercolor. He'd seen this one before,
and it took his breath away. *The Missing Horse* by Mark Maggiori—
a lone rider tracking from the saddle through the sagebrush.

Massive thunderheads roiled in the background, surely bringing rain that would soon obliterate any sign of the missing animal.

"This is remarkable," Cutter said under his breath. "I wonder if it's an original."

"That one's a print," she said, nodding at the painting. "But Mr. Beck has a couple of Maggiori originals. He's great."

"Mr. Beck?" Hough asked.

"No, I meant Mark Maggiori," the young woman said. "The way he paints clouds . . ." Then, glancing quickly over her shoulder, "I mean, Mr. Beck is great too . . . Anyway, how can I help you?"

The Iñupiaq woman, whose name was Maureen Akpik, recognized Jan Hough as North Slope PD, even in civilian clothes. Cutter introduced himself and showed his badge and credentials. Maureen gave a polite nod when she saw his badge. Like many people Cutter came into contact with, Miss Akpik probably wasn't aware US marshals were still a thing outside Hollywood or steamy romance novels.

Hough took the lead.

"We understand that Willadean Benson was an intern here a couple of years ago."

Maureen's eyebrows shot up. A silent yes. Her nose crinkled a half a second later. Distressed. "I'd just started working here when she started. She was a good kid. Hard worker. Wicked smart. I heard about her going missing. We're still hoping she turns up safe in Fairbanks or Anchorage or somewhere . . ."

"She did turn up . . ." Hough spilled a few details about the tragic accident to gauge her reaction.

Maureen leaned against the door frame. "That's just awful . . . I . . . I guess it was a blessing to her family to finally find her . . ."

"It sounds like she had a bright future," Cutter said.

"Willadean was amazing. Did they tell you she had a big scholarship to one of the military academies?"

"I did hear that," Hough said. "Do you guys get quite a few interns coming through?"

Maureen shook her head. "Not many. The main office is in Fairbanks so there are a few more down there through UAF. Mr. Beck and Ilisagvik College have an arrangement for students on the Slope. Willadean was still in high school but taking some classes through Ilisagvik. She really stood out, you know, so she got one of the college spots that way."

Cutter half turned, continuing to study the Maggiori painting.

"Did she intern for the whole office?" he asked over his shoulder.

"This office is small," Maureen said. "As you can see. Willadean mostly worked with Denny Foye, the main accountant in here . . . other than Mr. Beck, I mean."

"May we speak with Mr. Foye?"

"I'm sure he'd be happy to talk to you," Maureen said. "But he's in the lower forty-eight, visiting his brother in South Dakota."

Cutter forced himself not to turn toward her too quickly. When he did, he kept his expression passive. Hough looked down at a notebook, masking her sudden interest.

Maureen stepped into the cramped lobby and sat behind her desk to peck away at her computer. "Looks like he comes back to Utqiagvik on the a.m. flight tomorrow. I'm taking a subsistence day in the morning to help my dad hunt caribou, but I can leave a note for him."

"That would be most awesome, Maureen," Hough said. "Much appreciated."

Cutter nodded to the harpoon on the wall. "This is extremely realistic."

"It should be," Maureen said. "Mr. Beck commissioned my uncle to make two of them. They're exactly the same kind the whaling crews use. Mr. Beck insists his art is authentic. You may know this already, but sometime in the 1800s, I can't remember when exactly, thirty-three whaling ships out of Boston got trapped in the ice off our coast. All the crews made it off safely, but the ships went down." She hooked a thumb over her shoulder at the harpoon. "All these years later, bits of brass from those ships keep washing up on the beach. My uncle uses them to make the *qialgun*—the harpoon head."

"Impressive," Cutter said, meaning it. "Thank you."

Hough started for the door, then turned. "One more thing. Did you ever work with an engineer named Ethan Cutter?"

"From JBM? Oh yeah. He and Denny, Mr. Foye, were friends . . ." Her voice trailed off as she looked at Cutter, making the connection. "It was horrible, what happened to him."

Cutter gave a tight-lipped nod.

"It was."

"Thanks, Maureen," Hough said. "If you'd be so kind as to leave that message for Denny Foye. We'll check in with him tomorrow."

CHAPTER 15

A FAMILIAR SQUEAK CAME FROM DOWN THE HALL BEHIND MAUREEN Akpik the moment the chime rang and the front door shut behind the two visitors. Mr. Beck's office chair. She thought she'd heard him come in the back while she was talking with the cops. She didn't mention it, though. Mr. Beck had a standing order not to tell anyone he was in the office unless he'd cleared it beforehand. That's why he always parked a half a block away and sneaked in through the back door when he was in town.

It was weird, but he was rich, and from what Maureen had seen of rich people, weird went right along with it. He did a lot of good, donating to schools and all kinds of Native causes and organizations. His wife and her friends sewed him an authentic caribou-skin parka with a massive wolverine ruff on the hood. He wore it every day when he was in town during the winter. He bought a ton of Native art. Maureen had never been to any of his houses, but she'd figured they were dripping in ivory, baleen, and whalebone carvings. Most everybody in town—except Maureen's mother—thought he was great. He had no reason to sneak, but he did. Maureen supposed it was just his nature. Anyway, it was his business.

Another creaking noise. An office door opening wider. Boots slapped the hallway tile. Instinctively, Maureen put both hands flat on the desk, bracing herself for what she knew would happen next. As she suspected, Mr. Beck moved in behind her chair. His fingers began to knead the muscles of her neck and shoulders.

That was his thing. Any female who worked here knew they were going to get a shoulder rub at some point during the day. Still, he was a nice guy, really, and nothing ever went beyond a neck massage. Maureen learned to live with it. All the girls did.

Six-two and a fit one ninety, Leo Beck sported a silver goatee and a short buzzcut that made Maureen think of Jason Statham. He was strong, and not bad looking for someone older than her father. His eyes though. Maureen's mother said he had the black eyes of a *puktuktuk*, a dead animal that had sunk to the bottom of the water and then rotted enough to bloat and pop to the surface again. A stinker. Maureen didn't see that, but she had to admit, Mr. Beck did have scary eyes.

"Who was that?" he asked.

She steeled herself. He didn't sound mad. Not yet, anyway. Maybe this was nothing.

"Do you remember Ethan Cutter, that JBM engineer who was killed in the rig explosion near Kuparuk?"

"Mmm," Beck grunted. "Didn't he and Denny used to hang out?"

"That's right," Maureen said. "That big guy that was here . . . the marshal. He has got to be Ethan Cutter's brother. The other one was Jan Hough. She's North Slope PD."

"I recognized her," Beck said. "What did they want with us?"

His voice was nonchalant, but his grip on her shoulders grew firm enough to send a sharp pain up the side of her neck. She squirmed in her seat.

He patted her shoulder, smoothing the fabric of her sweater. "Sorry about that."

"It's okay." Maureen faced her computer, face flushed. He didn't like it if you acted like it hurt. "Anyway, they were asking questions about Willadean Benson. I guess they found her body."

"Foul play?"

"She fell into a hole."

She thought he might ask for more details about the accident. A normal person would ask details. Wouldn't they? Instead, he asked, "Why did they want to talk to Denny?"

"Because he was Willadean's main point of contact while she interned with us, I guess," Maureen said.

"How did they know that?"

"I . . . I told them." A sinking dread pressed against her stomach. "Was I not supposed—"

"That's fine, my dear," Beck said. His hands found their way to her shoulders again, kneading and pressing, much harder than before. "It's fine. Just fine. I'll talk to them when they come back tomorrow."

She flinched reflexively, jerking sideways without intending to. It didn't matter. Once Mr. Beck started in on a back rub, there was no stopping him. It came with the territory.

"You should relax, my dear," he said. "Your shoulders are way too tight." He grabbed even harder, pinching nerves and bruising muscle.

There weren't many jobs on the Slope that paid this well, so she settled into her squeaky office chair and took her punishment.

He suddenly pulled away and stepped back. "You should probably take the day," he said. "Start getting ready for the hunt with your dad." His voice trembled a hair, embarrassed.

Mr. Beck was probably a good guy . . . but if you wanted to work for him, you learned fast that it was better not to look at him when he was embarrassed. He swelled up like . . . Maureen's mother was right.

Mr. Beck's eyes did look like a *puktuktuk*—a bloated carcass floating in the sea.

CHAPTER 16

*C*UTTER AND HOUGH DROVE DIRECTLY FROM BECK AND ASSOCIATES to the PD, a boxy dark-blue building located kitty-corner across the mass of potholes called Agvik Street from the Wells Fargo bank. Hough briefed her lieutenant on Willadean Benson and filled out the paperwork to make sure the Stuaqpak store got paid for the chest freezer that now held the last of Abner Ipalook's whale. Cutter put in a good word with the brass for Officer Boatman, who, from the sound of things, could use all the positive press he could get.

Two uniformed officers in the squad room glanced up and acknowledged Cutter and then went back to working on their reports. Cutter found an empty desk that looked like it was out of the way. He tried to call Mim but couldn't get the line to connect. It was maddening but not at all surprising. Sometimes it felt like bush Alaska communication was little better than two tin cans and a string. He pitched the phone on the desk in frustration and got out his pocketknife to whittle on a little knot of cottonwood he'd found that held some promise.

Hough sauntered over—seemingly her preferred mode of moving—and set a file folder on the desk beside him. She looked at him for a moment as if coming to some decision before hopping up to take a seat on the desk, hands under her knees. She began to swing her legs off the edge like a schoolgirl, far enough to stay out of range of the pocketknife but close enough to Cutter some might think she was flirting with him. Maybe she was.

She looked at her watch and then put her hand back under her knee. Yeah, she was flirting.

"Not much to do until Denny Foye flies in tomorrow," she said. "Here's the deal, my friend. It's almost two o'clock. I can take you to a late lunch at Osaka, or Sam and Lee's, or there's a Mexican joint that's good." She tilted her head and let her blond curls fall sideways, batting her lashes. "Or . . . you can eat another Clif bar or something to tide you over and I'll make dinner at my house. You might as well spend the night. We have an extra bedroom."

"I'd better get a hotel."

"My husband comes home on the evening flight," she said. "He'll be there, if that's what you're worried about."

"Dinner would be terrific," Cutter said. "But I don't want to be a bother. I'll stick with a hotel."

Hough gave a slow nod, feigning hurt feelings. "The Top of the World has good rooms. It ain't the Hough House, but at least it's out of the wind and rain."

"I've got a lot to think about," Cutter said. "And I'm a loud thinker."

"Sure you are," Hough said.

"And some calls to make." He nodded at the blue folder on the desk, eager to talk about anything else but where he planned to spend the night. "Willadean's file?"

Hough nodded.

"Would it be possible for me to get a copy?" he asked.

She pushed it across the desk. "This is your copy. I called *you* for help. Remember?"

"Thank you," Cutter said. "Hey, if you're making dinner, you want me to pick up your husband at the airport when he gets in?"

"Oh, hell no," she said. "We keep a car staged across the street whenever we fly out."

Hough studied him for a long moment, chewing on her bottom lip, eyes narrowed. "Promise me you'll come for dinner."

"I said I would."

"Promise though," she said. "I don't want you to get to the

hotel and then all of a sudden feel like you're imposing on my husband's first night back or anything."

Cutter raised a brow. "Should I not—"

"No," Hough said. "I mean, yes, I want you to promise that you'll be there, but sometimes the flight is late, so we probably won't be eating until around six-thirty. The Top of the World Hotel has a restaurant that makes the whole place smell like cheeseburgers and fry oil. It can be awfully tempting."

"That does sound good right now."

"Arliss . . ."

"I said I'd be there, Jan," Cutter said. "I promise."

"Thank you," she said. "I'm holding you to that."

"Are you seriously worried that I won't show up?"

"No," she said. "I'm worried that you'll get there and then leave once you meet my husband. Bryan's an extremely intelligent man, but he can . . . Well, he can be a lot." She shrugged and left it there.

"Is he going to try and kick my ass?"

"Oh, hell no," she said. "Don't tell him I said this, but you'd wipe the floor with him. I married a lover not a fighter. This has got absolutely nothing to do with you." Hands in her lap, she leaned forward so her face was just inches from Cutter's. He had to hold the pocketknife against his chest to keep from cutting her. She gave a little shrug, confiding her secret bit of intel.

"He thinks I'm a teensy bit too flirty . . ."

Hough dropped Cutter off at the steps leading up to the Top of the World Hotel, a boxy, three-story affair. The muddy parking lot was pockmarked with countless potholes, as though it had endured a series of mortar attacks. An angry Arctic Ocean chewed away the land beyond a row of weathered buildings across a similarly cratered street, ignoring the car-size sandbags and metal bollards borough officials had put in place until the sea ice came in. Brown was the color of the day—brown water, brown earth, brown buildings. As much as he loved the sunbelt, scuba diving, and surfing on the Florida coast, there was something undeniably wild and almost sinister about this frontier. It was the literal edge of civilization, a place that suited Cutter more than he would have imagined. The Iñupiaq had been here for thousands of years, probably more, negotiating the ice, the dark, the bitter, bone-numbing cold. He resolved to learn what they might teach him.

Cutter tromped up the metal stairs, stomping the excess mud off his boots in an effort to endear himself with hotel house-keeping. The eight-and-a-half-by-eleven piece of paper taped to the glass doors of the Top of the World Hotel reminded visitors to WATCH OUT FOR POLAR BEARS, a sobering thought, considering the close call Mim had had during her last visit to Utqiagvik. Cutter was certain she'd downplayed the danger of the encounter. It was impossible to envision any scenario with a mama bear and cubs that was anything but life threatening—especially since polar bears grouped human beings right alongside seals on their food pyramid.

The homey odor of cheeseburgers and beer-battered onion rings hit him full in the face when he opened the second set of doors. Jan Hough had been right on the money.

A smiling Iñupiaq woman sat behind the desk, watching a doc-umentary about her people on a big screen television across the lobby. The walls were decorated with scrimshawed whale baleen, walrus tusks, and a piece of skull from a small whale.

Down the hall to the left of the reception area was the restau-rant, the source of the greasy comfort-food odors. Niggivikput—Iñupiaq for "our place to eat."

The clerk slid the key for room 210 across the counter. "Ocean view," she said. "Watch out for polar bears if you don't have a car. If you do, they saw a big boar out on Cake Eater. You might be able to see it."

"I heard."

"My boyfriend sent me a video, but it's not downloading." She shrugged. "Our Internet is shit sometimes. I'll bring the video in tomorrow if you want to have a look."

Mim called before he could answer.

"I'd like that," Cutter said. Apologizing for the interruption.

"Go ahead," the clerk said. "If your phone works, you gotta take advantage of it when you can . . ."

Cutter let her get back to her documentary and answered the call.

"Good to hear your voice," he said as he lugged his duffel past a display of ivory handicrafts and more photos of polar bears and beluga whales. Like so many places off the road system in Alaska, it was easy to imagine he'd been dropped into the pages of a *National Geographic* magazine. She'd called him, so he waited to see if she had anything pressing. If she did, she held on to it for later.

"At least it's something," she said, once he'd brought her up to speed on the possible connection between someone at Beck and Associates and Ethan's former employer.

"You have to stay in Utqiagvik another night?"

"Yep," he said. "It's easy to feel—"

"Trapped?" she said.

"Exactly."

"I know what you mean. It feels like the answers should be there on the Slope where he died, but all I got was more questions."

Cutter took a deep breath, held it, then let it out slowly, willing himself to be calm.

"We're getting closer," he said. "This guy Dennis Foye is flying home from South Dakota tomorrow morning. There's got to be some sort of connection between him and Ethan. I'm fairly well-read, and I'd never heard of oreodont fossils until all this. Dennis Foye and Ethan both have specimens of them. Too big a coincidence."

"The name Foye rings a bell," Mim said. "But I'm thinking Ethan talked about a David, not Dennis."

"His brother maybe," Cutter said. "Anyway, I have to stay put if I want to talk to Dennis Foye when he comes in tomorrow."

"What about dinner?"

"I'm eating at Jan's."

"Hmmm," Mim said. "Am I on speaker?"

"No," Cutter said. "I'm at the hotel. Same place you stayed when you were here. Same room, I think."

"I'm surprised Jan didn't invite you to stay with her."

Cutter chuckled. "She did."

"I'll just bet she did," Mim said. Cutter could picture her not-so-mock pout over the phone.

He suddenly felt the pressing need to see it in person. "Want to FaceTime?"

"I'm driving," she said. "Later tonight, though, after you get home from your date."

"It's not a date," he groused.

"I've met Jan Hough. I'm sure she thinks it's a date."

"Her husband will be there."

"Lucky for you."

"She's just—"

"I know," Mim said. "What's that Grumpy used to say? 'I'm just hankin' on you.'"

They were quiet for a time. There was a gravity in Mim's voice when she spoke again that hadn't been there before.

"Coop Daniels is still avoiding my calls," she said.

Daniels was an attorney who'd acted as if he was helping Mim get the benefits she was owed after Ethan's death, all the while representing the interests of JBM Engineering, the people who owed her the money. Cutter felt certain the man had only helped out to get her into bed, but Mim, the eternal optimist when it came to human nature, couldn't bring herself to believe that someone could be so duplicitous.

Sadly, she was learning.

"His office said he's still out of the country," she continued. "One of my coworkers has a cell with an Arizona number, so I tried him from that."

"And?"

"Get this, Arliss," she said. "He picked up that time. I felt all marshally, like you. Anyway, he got super flustered when he found out it was me. He apologized, said he had to go but would call me later . . . and then hung up."

Cutter stared at the raindrops on the window, pondering what he'd like to do to Coop Daniels. "I'm getting sick of this guy. We will have a meeting with Mr. Daniels if I have to track his ass down like a fugitive."

"Hmmm," Mim said. "I wonder if the biggest reason we can't find him is because he's afraid you might beat him to death."

"I feel sorely misjudged," he lied.

CHAPTER 17

Anchorage

LOLA TEARIKI LEFT HER G-CAR AT THE OFFICE AND MADE THE TEN-minute walk northwest, cutting through Town Square Park behind the Performing Arts Center to shoot down Fifth Avenue, one of downtown Anchorage's main through streets. A homeless woman eyed her from a bench in the park, looking distant and forlorn. Lola dug a Subway gift card out of her back pocket and gave it to the lady, taking a second to ask her name. Ida, from the Bering Sea village of Savoonga, thanked her for the card.

She walked on, scanning knots of people loitering in the park as she passed. Her cynical deputy marshal brain told her half of them were wanted for some crime or another. Her rational brain told her that number was likely closer to a quarter. Still a target-rich environment when she thought about it.

Joe Bill Brackett was waiting for her in the lobby of the Hotel Captain Cook.

Cook Islanders routinely greeted each other with a cheek-to-cheek air-kiss. (One side only—Lola's aunties deemed a kiss on both cheeks in turn to be "too French.") Brackett dispensed with the air all together, greeting Lola every time as if they hadn't seen each other in months. She didn't mind at all.

He noticed the rain on her jacket. "You walked from the Federal Building?"

"I needed to stretch my legs," she said.

Brackett turned to lead the way down the hall, past the shops to the elevator on the other side of the building. They passed several large murals of the British explorer James Cook, depicting his voyages to the South Pacific. Although he'd been a colonizer, Lola had always identified a bit with the old captain's ties to Alaska and the Pacific, particularly her father's homeland, the Cook Islands.

Brackett held open the elevator door and let her go in first, pressing the button for the Crow's Nest restaurant located on the top floor of the hotel.

"Your FBI frenemy have any luck with Dupree's phone?" he asked.

"No way we're getting into that phone short of a miracle," she said. "That's why I needed the walk. He did have some interesting information, though. Remember the scribbles on the paper from our guy's jacket?"

Brackett nodded.

"Claytonia," he said.

"Right. Claytonia Garden is apparently a porn site on the Dark Web. My contact thinks this sick puke is one of the site administrators."

"I read somewhere that the Dark Web is like ninety percent of the total Internet."

"You're thinking of the Deep Web," Lola said. "Stuff that's unsearchable like bank records, your email, DMs, etcetera. According to my FBI guy, the actual Dark Web—stuff you need a special browser to search—is only around three to five percent."

"Ah," Brackett said.

"Honestly, Joe Bill," Lola said. "I'd worry if you knew very much about this depraved shit. I just got a crash course from the Feebs, and it made me want to heave up my lunch. Another name for Claytonia is spring beauty. You know, a pretty young flower . . ."

"Yeah," Brackett said. "I'll leave the Internet crimes to folks with stronger stomachs."

The elevator doors opened to the Crow's Nest. The tinkling of glasses and the murmur of restaurant patrons carried into the wood-paneled lobby along with the heady odor of grilled steak and steamed crab.

"Protein," Lola whispered. She grabbed Brackett's hand and gave it a playful squeeze. "You know the way to a girl's heart."

The server seated them at a window table with a view of downtown Anchorage and the snowcapped Chugach Mountains to the east.

Brackett pushed her the wine list. "I have to work after this," he said.

She pushed the list away. "And I have to drive home in a G-ride." She spread her napkin and slathered butter on a warm olive roll—a benefit of all her hard work in the gym. "This is nice, babe," she said, gazing out the window and then back at Joe Bill. The light hit him just right in the eyes. "Enough icky talk about the Dark Web and pervs like Eddie Dupree. Did you dream about me . . . ?"

Lola ordered the espresso-crusted rib eye, medium rare. Joe Bill was heading to work the midnight shift in few hours, so this was really breakfast for him. He stayed on the lighter side with halibut and a wedge salad.

He was the easiest person to talk to she'd ever met, but it was just as easy to sit quietly and enjoy each other's company. If anything, the relationship was scary—too perfect.

She'd just tucked into the cap of her perfectly cooked rib eye when she got a call. Brackett heard it and, fork in hand, gave her a nod. "Aren't you going to get that?"

"I said it would just be us tonight—"

Brackett grimaced. "Knock it off. This is what we do."

"I don't want to scare you off," she said as she dug the phone out of her pocket. "But you're one in a million, Joe Bill Brackett."

"It's a 202 number," she said. "Dr. Mike, the chief psychologist in our Behavioral Analysis Unit." She slid one of her earbuds across the table for Brackett and put the other in her ear as she answered the call.

"Hey, Doc," she whispered. "I have Officer Joe Bill Brackett from Anchorage PD on the line with me."

"It's Deputy Te-ah-ree-key," Dr. Mike said. "Am I saying that right?"

"Right as," Lola said. "Thank you for returning my call."

"Happy to help," he said, getting straight to business. "Listen, I looked over the file you sent. The Bureau is tying up this Dupree guy's bitcoin off the Dark Web so he needs another source of income. He's likely to go back to what he knows. In addition to the child porn, his priors are . . ."

"Distribution of fentanyl," Lola said.

"Humans are creatures of habit," Dr. Mike said. "He'll return to what he knows, especially if you guys are on his ass. It takes cash to stay on the run."

"True," Lola said. "I reckon we've looked at everyone he's had contact with . . . that we're aware of."

"How bad do we want this guy?"

"Bad," Lola said.

"You're in Anchorage, right?"

"Yes."

"It might be small enough for this to work. If your chief's giving you the resources, I'd suggest that instead of looking for Dupree specifically, target everyone you can think of who's selling fentanyl. A sweep of sorts. Human traffickers or drug traffickers, fentanyl or underage girls, chances are there will be some crossover between the two camps. Nobody trusts an addict. You need to find someone in sales—a middleman. Normally, you'd flip him to work your way up the supply chain—"

"But this time we flip them to get to Dupree," Lola said. "I like it."

"You got it," he said. "Anyway, you know what you're doing."

"We need to get you out to Alaska," Lola said. "You can teach us your BAU magic and we'll show you around the North Country."

"Your lips to God's ears," the doc said. "Call me with anything else. I'm all about getting guys like Eddie Dupree off the street."

Lola ended the call.

Joe Bill passed her earbud across the table.

"I know someone we can talk to," he said. "Brett Pelkey on night shift popped a guy a couple of nights ago with fifteen thousand M-30s in a Stanley thermos."

"I know Pelkey," Lola said. "Good guy."

"And a good copper," Joe Bill said. "Anyhow, there was another mope in the car—a guy named Russel Whittaker. I've arrested him a couple of times before, once for DUI, another time for MICS 2." MICS was misconduct involving a controlled substance. A felony.

"Did Whittaker go to jail too?"

Brackett shook his head. "Still on the street. The DA said we only had evidence to charge the driver—and he's already bonded out. If I can figure out where he is, we can talk to him too. I think Whittaker will be easier to find."

"You got an address?"

"He lives at Karluk Manor—"

"The old Red Roof Inn," Lola mused.

"That's right," Brackett said. "But he hangs out at the bar across the street or one of the weed shops on Fifth."

Lola took another bite of her steak, thought about it a moment, then said, "How would you feel about getting the rest of this to go—and taking this date on the road?"

"I've got four and a half hours before I need to be at fallout," Brackett said. "Can't think of anything I'd rather do than hunt outlaws with you."

Lola looked up from another bite of meat. "I reckon that's not quite right."

"Okay," Brackett grinned. "Almost anything."

Lola waved for the check. "Let's get going then. If we catch Dupree tonight, I'll take tomorrow off. We can celebrate . . . with that other thing . . ."

CHAPTER 18

Utqiagvik

JAN'S HUSBAND, BRYAN, ANSWERED THE DOOR WHEN CUTTER WAS ON the backswing of his first knock.

"Saw you on the Ring camera," he said.

He was tall, just an inch or so shorter than Cutter, with thinning hair and a stout build that showed just the hint of a belly. Khaki slacks and a cotton canvas shirt with a shooting pad on the shoulder made him look as though he was about to go on safari. He stood in the threshold, one hand on the door, the other behind the frame. In other circumstances, Cutter might have been concerned about a hidden weapon.

"Janice is my wife," he said.

Interesting way to introduce yourself, Cutter thought. *Not, I'm Janice's husband.* It was a verbal way to mark his territory.

"Arliss Cutter." He held out a bag of oranges he'd picked up at the Stuaqpak store.

Hough eyed the bag, still blocking the door. "What's this?"

"My grandfather taught me not to arrive with my hands swingin' empty," Cutter said. "I'd have brought wine, but that doesn't seem to be an option in Utqiagvik unless you join some private co-op."

"We have a weed shop." Hough shrugged. A sly grin spread across his face. "I'm just kidding."

"No," Jan called from somewhere behind him, probably listening to everything on the doorbell camera. "He's not kidding even a little bit."

Hough rolled his eyes, finally stepping out of the way. "Pot is legal now, ya know."

Cutter gave a tight-lipped grin. "Not for me."

"Me neither," Jan called out.

Hough cocked his head to one side and took custody of the oranges—a treat in the Far North, where they cost three to four times as much as they did in Anchorage. He lowered his voice. "Why are you here again, Marshal Cutter?"

"First of all," Cutter said. "It's Deputy—"

Hough raised his hand, grinning again. "I'm just pulling your chain." He took Cutter's jacket and then turned suddenly, causing Cutter to stop short. The grin vanished again, replaced with a hint of something crueler. "But seriously, why *are* you here?"

Jan appeared in the nick of time, drying her hands on a dish towel. Her blond curls damp from a recent shower, she'd changed from her work clothes to a form-fitting gray sweatshirt, capri jeans, and fuzzy pink slippers. A large pair of black-framed glasses replaced her contact lenses. Her tight jaw and flushed cheeks made Cutter feel like he'd interrupted an argument. She bumped her husband out of the way with a hip and took the bag of oranges.

"I told Bryan you wouldn't show up empty-handed," she said. "You have that look about you."

"What look?"

"The same look that says you guys are about to offer to help me in the kitchen. . . ."

Jan put Cutter to work slicing the deep-red caribou backstrap into quarter-inch slices—across the grain. Bryan chopped at a pile of onions and mushrooms like they owed him money. Jan started a small amount of oil heating in a cast-iron frying pan and threw a handful of rock salt into a pot of boiling water on the back of the stove before dropping in a box of linguini pasta.

Bryan had apparently gotten the caribou the week before, not far out of town.

Jan seasoned the caribou slices with salt and pepper before dropping a single piece into the fat to check the temperature.

"*Tuttu* is normally best medium rare," she said. "Mim probably told you I have a tendency to overcook things, but this recipe cooks the hell out of the caribou. I call it Caribou Marsala. Bryan calls it—"

"*Aluuttagaaq*," Bryan said. "An Iñupiaq woman in Kaktovik taught me to make it when I first moved up to the Slope. I just used caribou and onions over rice or potatoes—the Iñupiaq way. For some reason, my wife feels compelled to jazz it up by adding mushrooms and having it over pasta."

"So, you met up here on the Slope?" Cutter washed the caribou blood off his hands.

"We met the first time when she was working in Vegas." He gave a sideways nod. "She tripped me up with this pseudo-wholesome Marilyn-Monroe-at-home look like she's got going on tonight for some reason . . ."

"This is the way I always dress, Bryan," she said. "You act like I'm wearing pasties and a G-string."

"You were when I met you."

"You're such a dick," she said. "Cool it a little while we've got company."

"I'm only joking," Bryan snitched a piece of sliced mushroom and popped it in his mouth. "Anyway, it's my own fault for marrying Jessica Rabbit in a cop uniform."

Cutter refused to return Jan's disgusted look. Whatever this was, he didn't want to step in the middle of it . . . any more than he already had.

Jan busied herself dusting the rest of the caribou in flour and then browned the pieces in the hot grease—just enough to cover the bottom of the pan. When it was done, she added a knob of butter along with the mushrooms and onion, stirring constantly. She added a couple of splashes of marsala along the way, cooking it off until the onions turned translucent, at which point she added two cups of beef broth. She let that simmer while they set the table and then added her secret ingredient, a quarter cup of heavy cream. The light dusting of flour on the meat along with the cream formed a rich brown gravy.

Bryan dipped a spoon and passed it to Cutter, almost friendly. "What's your verdict?"

"Damn good," Cutter said, meaning it. "My grandfather would have approved."

"It ain't really *aluuttagaaq*," Bryan said. "A little more flour and my grandfather would have called this shit on a shingle."

Cutter grabbed the bowl of pasta and followed Bryan to the table.

"Leave out the marsala and it's good on biscuits," Jan offered, like she wasn't in the middle of an argument with her husband. As far as Cutter knew, cruel banter was the norm in the Hough household. His second wife had been that way.

Bryan dished up his own plate while Jen was still in the kitchen. Arm encircling his plate like he thought Cutter might steal his food, he motioned to a chair across the table with a fork full of caribou and gravy.

"You'll starve if you wait on her," he said. "She'll flit and hover forever before she finally takes roost and starts to eat."

Cutter took a seat and spread the napkin over his lap.

Hough scoffed, speaking around a mouthful of food. "Of course, she digs out the cloth napkins for you. She's perfectly content to use paper towels when it's just me."

Jan laughed, finally coming to take her seat. "Who are you kidding, hon? You use the back of your hand."

"Fair enough," Hough said.

The rainy chill had made everyone hungry, and they ate for a time in stony silence.

"You guys have big plans for the morning?" Bryan said once he'd wolfed down most of his caribou.

"Interviews," Cutter said, relieved to talk about something that didn't feel like an argument. "We're meeting another accountant from Leo Beck's firm."

"Beck." Bryan pursed his lips. "There's an interesting guy."

Cutter paused midbite. *Interesting* was a copout word, allowing the user a hell of a lot of wiggle room when it came to an opinion. "What do you mean?"

"I don't know," Bryan said. "His main office is in Fairbanks, but he's married to an Iñupiaq woman from somewhere down on the Kobuk River. Ambler or Shungnak, I can't remember which. Anyway, he has an office in Utqiagvik. Close enough city to keep him in good with all the oil companies, and she gets to be nearer her Iñupiaq culture. He makes some significant donations to all kinds of causes. That and having a Native wife gives him a hell of a lot of political clout here on the Slope." Bryan raised a wary brow. "Is Beck involved in this thing you're working on?"

"It's too early to tell," Cutter said.

Jan took a drink of lemonade. "The guy we're meeting is supposed to come in on tomorrow's flight. Dennis Foye. Know him?"

Bryan gave a slow nod. "You think he has something to do with Willadean's death? I thought that girl fell into a hole."

"She did," Jan said. "So, you do know him?"

"Of course, I know Denny Foye." Bryan glanced up from his plate, a hair on the defensive side. "He's another accountant competing with me for clients in the booming metropolis of Utqiagvik. What manner of malfeasance is it you guys suspect him of doing?"

"You know everyone we talk to isn't a suspect, right?" Jan dropped her napkin beside her plate and pushed away from the table, making it clear she intended to change the subject. "I'll dish up the pie."

Bryan frowned. "We're feeding him pie too?" He paused for effect, then said, "I'm joking . . . but seriously, Jan, there's only half a pie left, and I want to take some for work tomorrow so go easy on the slices . . ."

CHAPTER 19

*C*UTTER PASSED ON THE PIE AND THANKED HIS HOSTS FOR AN INteresting evening before making his excuses for an early night. The hotel was just under a mile walk, on the other side of the Isatkoak Lagoon. The strong possibility of coming nose to nose with a polar bear in the dark made him think better of it. Grumpy's Colt Python was a capable weapon, but it felt infinitesimally puny when compared with an animal whose head would brush a basketball rim if it stood on its hind legs. Jan insisted on driving him—to talk about the case. Her husband didn't seem too keen about the idea, but Cutter decided it was better to just shut up and get gone rather than argue while he stood around waiting for a cab.

"Well, as dinners go, that was pretty damned horrible," Jan Hough said as soon as Cutter shut his door and they were alone in the SUV.

"No worries."

"I'm serious," Hough said. "Bryan can be a jerk, but he usually doesn't go all in like this."

"I suppose I bring it out in him." Cutter patted the dashboard and forced a chuckle. "How about you drive before he decides to take a shot at me from your kitchen window."

"Good plan." She did a quick shoulder check and backed into the street, bouncing across several potholes in the process.

"Did you ever have Ethan over for dinner?"

Hough gave a contemplative nod. "Sure. Several times."

"How'd Bryan feel about that?"

"A little bit like tonight, I guess," Hough said. "The rumors were kind of hard on him, I'm sure. Anyway, it's a little game we play. You know, fight and then have some torrid makeup sex—" She jumped in her seat and began to dig for the phone in the pocket of her sweatshirt as she drove. "I need to take this." She glanced at the phone. "It's Jason Tuia from the office."

She listened for a moment, thanked Officer Tuia, then ended the call.

A frown crossed her face as she pocketed the phone. "Get this. Dennis Foye flew in to Utqiagvik on this afternoon's flight."

"Alaska Airlines?"

She ripped off her glasses, holding them in the same hand she used to steer while she rubbed her face with the other. "The same plane my shithead husband came in on."

"Bryan must have missed him . . ."

"Not a chance," she said. "Bryan always flies first class so he can see everyone who walks by him as they board. I'm not sure why he held on to that little tidbit of intel . . ."

Cutter kept his thoughts to himself while Hough worked through this new information. Then, when she pulled up in front of his hotel, he said, "I hate to ask, but—"

"You want to know if I think my husband is involved?"

Cutter let her talk.

"I just do not know," she said. "I mean, I don't think so, but . . ." She looked up suddenly, her face stricken, like she had a stomachache. "What do you think?"

Cutter took a deep breath and exhaled it slowly.

"I think there's a lot going on here that we don't yet understand. At times like this, the list of people I trust gets shorter, not longer."

"Do you trust *me?*" Hough asked.

Cutter gave a slow nod. "Ethan apparently did."

"That's not an answer."

"Yes," Cutter said. "Mostly."

Cutter climbed up the hotel steps and performed the foot stomping ritual to rid his boots of mud outside the door. Someone had taken a ballpoint pen and scrawled a new message at the bottom of the polar bear warning that was taped to the door.

IF IT'S BROWN, LIE DOWN. IF IT'S BLACK, FIGHT BACK. IF IT'S WHITE, GOOD NIGHT!

He pushed aside thoughts of a predatory Nanook and ticked through his more immediate problems.

Maybe Bryan Hough was just pissed at his wife and decided not to help her with the investigation. Maybe he was simply not as observant as she believed him to be. Or maybe there was something more sinister afoot. Cutter had a feeling he'd find out soon enough.

He called Mim as soon as he got back to the room, standing by the window for better cell reception. She answered on the first ring.

"I was just about to check in," she said. "How was dinner?"

"Not as good as the caribou gravy and pasta you make, but—"

Mim scoffed. "I've never made you caribou gravy and pasta."

"Well," Cutter said, "if you had, it would have been delicious. This wasn't bad. The conversation was uncomfortable, though."

"Any conversation is uncomfortable for you," she said.

"Yep."

"Speaking of uncomfortable," she said. "Coop Daniels is back in town."

Caught off guard, Cutter took a beat before answering. "That *is* a surprise," he said at length.

"We need to talk to him, Arliss. When are you coming home?"

"Tomorrow." Cutter cranked open the window. A breath of cold air and the sound of rain would help him think. "Find out when he'll meet you this week and set it up."

"That's a tall order," Mim said. "He's scared to death of you."

"He wouldn't be coming over to talk to me. Tell him I'm out of town and you want to meet with him. You'll be telling the truth when you say it."

"What if he doesn't agree to meet?"

"Then I'll go see him myself," Cutter said. "Believe me, he'd like the first option better."

CHAPTER 20

*L*EO BECK PUT HIS PHONE ON SPEAKER AND SETTLED DEEPLY INTO the overstuffed leather chair in his home study. He ran his fingers along the business end of the whaling harpoon and its "bomb" laid out across his desk blotter while he waited for Foye to pick up. The harpoon—*nauligaun* in Iñupiaq—wasn't just a wall hanger. The brass had to be polished and kept in good working order. Beck didn't believe in the concept of free time. That and a healthy disdain for following the rules of other men had made him rich. He could get a lot done during a phone call. Beck had no doubt the other man would answer. He didn't pay to leave voicemails or send texts. He paid for you to pick up your damned phone when . . .

"Hello." Tentative. This guy always seemed one jump-scare from pissing his pants.

"Denny," Beck said, quieter, chastising. "Denny, Denny, Denny. What are you up to at this moment?"

"I'm at the office finishing up some accounts."

"Outstanding," Beck said. "How's David holding up?"

"For the millionth time," Foye said. "David just wants to cowboy. Not a problem. He's minding his own business, just like I told you he would."

"Good to hear." Beck picked up the harpoon, enjoying the weight of the thick wooden shaft. He'd polished the barbed brass point to a high sheen. Shoulder guns were interesting enough, bulky, blunderbuss things like a four-bore shotgun, but harpoons carried the history of millennia. He studied the weapon while he waited. Silence could draw out disloyalty like a poultice on poison—and carried the added benefit of keeping the other party on edge.

"What is it?"

"There's been a development," Beck said. A verbal shrug.

"What . . . ?" Foye's voice quavered. "What kind of development."

"Best not to discuss over the phone," Beck said. "We've had some visitors drop by the office today. I need to run a couple of things by you. That way you'll know what to expect when they talk to you. It won't take long."

"Law enforcement visitors?"

"Not over the phone," Beck chided. "Are you still with Lilian?"

"Yeah . . ."

"Out on Cake Eater—"

"Listen." Foye cut him off. "I'd rather not get Lilian involved in any of this."

"You told me we could trust her." Beck examined the pointed brass barrel of the harpoon as he spoke. Forward of the wooden shaft but to the rear of the toggling brass spear point, this bomb would detonate and send a heavy dart into the whale when the harpoon was thrust in far enough.

"And we *can* trust her," Foye said. "It's just that . . . lately, she's been in a mood."

"A mood?" Beck waved that off. "Never mind. I need you to meet me out by the college."

"I'm at the office," Foye said. "We can talk here."

"The college."

"How about we knock off this spy shit," Foye said. "Just tell me what this is all about—"

"For the third time," Beck said, forcing himself to sound calm. "I am telling you not to talk about this over the phone. I need to fill you in so we're on the same sheet of music when . . . I'll explain when we meet. Shall we say eleven?"

"Fine," Foye said.

Leo Beck stood, harpoon in hand, and wondered idly what a whale bomb would do to a pigeon-chested guy like Dennis Foye . . .

CHAPTER 21

Anchorage

JOE BILL BRACKETT DROVE LOLA FROM THE CAPTAIN COOK TO THE Federal Building, where they switched to her G-car. On the way, Lola contacted APD Vice and a buddy with DEA to deconflict any cases they happened to be working on Russel Whittaker. Both agencies gave the all clear.

The APD dispatcher sent Whittaker's driver's license photo to Lola's cell at the same time she was pulling out of the underground garage onto Eighth Avenue.

"Charming," she said, glancing at the photo as she stopped and waited for the rolling door to rumble shut behind her. "He's going to be hard to miss."

Three marble-sized knots from subdermal implants started just above Whittaker's nose and formed a dotted line up the center of Whittaker's forehead. Ear gauges the size of half dollars and an assortment of brow and lip rings rounded out his face jewelry. Wild black hair that looked as if he'd stuck a fork in a wall socket nested into a frizzed man bun.

"I'm all for self-expression," Lola said. "But if lizard man decides to fight us, I reckon he's got plenty of murder handles to grab on to."

"I forgot to mention," Joe Bill said. "Whittaker's had a bad runny nose every time I've seen him."

"Noted," Lola said.

"I'm talking really, really runny," Brackett said. He blew air into his cheeks pretending he might throw up. "Like don't-get-any-on-ya runny."

"Fantastic," she said under her breath.

Lola let APD Dispatch know she would be out at the Karluk Manor conducting an interview. Blodgett, Alvarez, and the rest of the task force had already called it a day. If things turned rodeo, any backup would come from APD Patrol.

Approaching from the west on Sixth Avenue, Lola hung a left on Karluk Street, intending to make the block and get the lay of the land before they tried to make contact. Karluk Manor was a public housing facility aimed at the chronically homeless with alcohol problems. It was wet, meaning no one had to quit drinking to get a room. The notion was to get them housed and then address the substance abuse. It had been converted from the old Red Roof Inn. Considering the clientele, disgruntled locals derisively called it the Red Nose Inn.

Law enforcement wasn't necessarily welcome.

Karluk Manor on her right, Lola stopped at the intersection with Fifth Avenue.

"I'll swing around one more—"

Brackett leaned forward in his seat, like a dog suddenly on point. "Check out the weed shop across the street," he said. "Whittaker just exited the front, walking toward Lucky Wishbone. He's in an orange-and-black raincoat."

Lola's head whipped back and forth, looking in vain for a break in traffic to cross Fifth Avenue. It was one-way, but she'd been surprised more than once by some drunk or discombobulated driver.

"I'm gonna run the light," Lola said.

"He's coming toward the crosswalk," Brackett said. "Probably on his way home."

Whittaker made it past the Lucky Wishbone restaurant to the Karluk intersection at the same time the signal changed and traffic stopped, allowing Lola to cross.

Her unmarked Tahoe had no visible lights or radio antenna, but to a person who made his living selling fentanyl, it virtually screamed law enforcement. The big Chevy may as well have had a spotlight pointed directly at it. Russel Whittaker made it two steps into the crosswalk before he turned into a statue midstride and stared down the oncoming SUV.

"Shit!" Brackett snapped. "I think he made me."

"You think?" Lola chuckled as Whittaker shook off his stupor and spun on his heels. His feet slipped on the damp pavement, causing him to run in place like a Wile E. Coyote cartoon. Lola stomped on the gas, glancing sideways at Brackett. "I love it when they run!" Then, realizing they'd just come from a date, "Tell me you're armed."

"Lola," he scoffed, patting his belt.

He leaned forward, one hand on the dash, the other on the clasp of his seat belt. "He's going behind Lucky Wishbone."

"Toward the jail," Lola chuckled. "That's rich."

Brackett popped the clasp of his seat belt and jumped as soon as they crossed Fifth, pouring on the coal about the time Whittaker ducked into the alley behind the restaurant, going west. Lola cut left as well, gunning the Tahoe to parallel Fifth Avenue. She turned right on the far side of the Lucky Wishbone, standing on her siren to open up the line in the restaurant drive-through, then barreling through the parking lot. She reached the alley just in time to cut off Whittaker's escape, pinching him between her Tahoe and an oncoming Joe Bill Brackett. A chain-link fence ran along the north side of the road, beyond which the land fell away some fifty feet to the roof of the Anchorage jail complex below.

Whittaker juked right and then left like a trapped rat as Brackett closed the distance. A sly grin scrunched the lizard knots on Whittaker's forehead as he spied what he must have thought was a way out past the Tahoe's front fender—and bolted. His lead foot hit a rain-filled pothole that was much deeper than he'd anticipated. He went down hard, eating the pavement and dousing himself in oily brown water as he slid to the other side of the alley.

Realizing he was caught, he pushed himself to his knees. He'd raised both hands above his head by the time Lola got out of the Tahoe.

"R . . . running from the cops ain't a crime," he said. He wiped his face with his arm, keeping his hands in the air, sniffed, then wiped his nose again.

"Right-o," Lola said. She nodded to the two plastic sandwich bags on the grimy pavement beside Whittaker's knee. "But I reckon a couple of baggies of dope warrant a chat at the very least."

Whittaker glanced down. "Those aren't mine. I never saw them before."

"Nice try," Brackett said from behind him. He'd drawn the Glock from his belt when he stopped running and now held it in Sul position—tight against his chest with the barrel down.

Lola patted Whittaker down for weapons, cuffed him behind his back, then stood him with his back against the Tahoe. She considered putting him in her car, but like Brackett had warned her, the guy's nose ran like a firehose. It was a wonder he wasn't dehydrated. They had the alley to themselves so far, so she left him where he was, preening his runny nose against his shoulder every few seconds like a bird.

"That's a fair amount of heroin," she said, retrieving the baggies after she'd gloved up. "Not looking good for you."

"Cut the bullshit," Whittaker said. "You want something or else you'd be hauling me down the hill to jail already."

"Perceptive," Lola said.

"I'm not rolling on anybody," Whittaker said. "Those guys would cut my junk off and feed it to me. I'll be out in three or four days, anyway."

"Probably will," Lola said. "But that's a long three or four days without a fix."

"I can handle it." Whittaker wiped his nose on his shoulder again.

"You say that now," Lola said. "But I know what you're thinking. You're thinking you can get your hands on some stuff on the inside. That may be true, if you are not kept in lockdown." She pointed to the circle-star badge on her belt. "US Marshals. This would be a federal arrest. We'd want you kept separated."

Whittaker grimaced like she'd kicked him in the groin. His forehead flushed red, leaving the knots over the subdermal implants a pale yellow-white.

"That's cold . . ."

"Yep," Lola said. "Cold as hell. But here's the deal. I'm not a dope cop, Russel. I'm completely uninterested in you flipping on whatever cartel you get your shit from. I'm looking for one particular guy who's into the same things you are."

"Forget about the *slow*, and I'll give you whoever you want." Whittaker used the street name for heroin. "That is, as long as this particular guy you want ain't Dominican."

Lola shot a glance at Brackett. "Nope," she said. "Not Dominican. I'm looking for Eddie Dupree."

Whittaker gave an exhausted sigh. "I don't know Dupree personally," he said. "But I know he's into some . . ." He rolled his lips and shook his head. "That dude is bad news. And I gotta admit, that's sayin' something coming from a junkie like me."

"Where can I find him?"

"I wish I could tell you," Whittaker said. "I really do."

"Let's try this," Lola said. "Hypothetically, if a person needed to buy some, say, M-30s from Dupree, how would they make contact. A phone number is fine."

"Phone number?" Whittaker scoffed. "You guys ever heard of the Internet? I don't know about Dupree, but a lot of guys are using buy-and-sell sites. Books, boats, meet-ups, you can set up a code for pretty much any kind of shit you want to buy, from M-30s to mushrooms."

"You're wasting my time," Lola said. She twirled her finger over her head, motioning that it was time to wrap things up.

"Wait, wait, wait!" Whittaker said. "I said I don't know Dupree, but I know people who know him."

Lola looked at Joe Bill and groaned. "Let's drop this asshole off at the jail," she said. "More productive if we follow up with that other—"

"Hang on now," Whittaker said. "These people I'm talking about . . . I'm pretty sure they're in production with Dupree."

"Production?" Brackett said. "Meth? Fentanyl?"

Whittaker shook his head. "No," he said. "Production. Like movies. Really dark shit . . . from what I hear. They shoot in a couple of hotel rooms around Anchorage. Word on the street is that he's looking for new talent. Young, if you know what I mean. I could make some calls and find out for you . . . if I wasn't in jail . . ."

CHAPTER 22

Utqiagvik

CUTTER WOKE UP ANGRY AND FLUSHED WITH ADRENALINE, READY to kick the shit out of Coop Daniels as a matter of principle. It took him a few fevered seconds to realize he was in a hotel and his cell phone was ringing on the table next to his bed. He blinked, squinting to see the caller ID in the dark.

It was Jan Hough, calling at four twenty-two a.m.

Cutter unplugged the phone from the charging cord and fell back on his pillow to answer. Hough was far too energetic for this early in the morning.

"Figured you'd want to be called for a double death."

"Double death?" Cutter sat up and swung his feet off the bed. "You mean a double homicide?"

"I'd bet that is exactly what it is," Hough said. "But my bosses are calling one death a bear mauling and the other a suicide."

"Did you say a bear mauling?"

"More like a 'bear consuming,'" Hough said. "As in Nanook, the polar bear. And from the photos they texted me, mauling doesn't even come close to describing what happened. This victim has been partially . . . eaten. Did you know bears will often eat a person's kidneys first? Because I did not know that . . ."

Cutter rubbed his eyes with a thumb and forefinger, attempting to will away the headache that had ambushed him the moment he woke up. "What's this about a suicide?"

"That's the primary reason I called you," Hough said. "The victim is Denny Foye. And get this, his girlfriend, Lilian Egak, is the one who got eaten by the polar bear. A borough maintenance worker found Foye's body in a parked car out by the gas chiller plant off Cake Eater Road, about a half mile from Egak's house. My guys on the scene tell me it looks like maybe he discovered her and then offed himself out of grief."

"With carbon monoxide?"

"That's what it looks like.

Cutter ran a hand over his face. He should have shaved before he went to bed.

"And get this," Hough continued. "He left a note . . ."

"Sounds like you're not buying the suicide theory."

"Do you? I mean, Willadean's body shows up frozen in the ice, and the person she used to intern for kills himself the very next day. The day before we're going to talk to him no less."

"Sounds fishy."

"That's putting it mildly," Hough said. "Wanna go for a ride with me? I'm two minutes from your hotel."

"I'll be down in four." Cutter ended the call.

Hard experience and a meticulous grandfather had taught him the value of getting ready for the day the night before. Cutter had done everything but shave. His pocket litter—knives, flashlight, wallet, and orange Zippo lighter—was placed neatly on the bedside table. His guns were right where he'd left them, resting on a folded washcloth in the top drawer of the same table—out of sight but within easy reach. He checked them, anyway, depressing the slide on the Glock 27 just enough to assure himself there was still a round in the chamber and swinging open the Colt's cylinder. All was still right with the world . . . at least when it came to ammo.

It took him longer to lace and tie his Zamberlan boots than it did to brush his teeth and slip out the door, careful not to let it slam at this ungodly hour.

It was four-twenty-eight.

Jan Hough sat waiting in her idling Tahoe when he tromped down the metal steps to the parking lot. Her windshield wipers thumped vigorously against a steady rain. Cutter turned up the collar of his jacket, happy to have a pair of Smartwool glove liners in his pocket if he ended up standing at the scene for very long. The temperature hovered around thirty-four degrees, but the wind and rain made it feel much colder, chilling Cutter to the bone.

September in Alaska. It would be fall soon . . .

"You said four minutes," Hough said. "And I'll be damned if that wasn't four minutes on the nose. What's the matter with you?"

"Plenty," Cutter said. "You'll have to drill down on a specific area if you want the truth."

Hough stared across the console, sizing him up. "It took me four minutes to pee this morning . . ."

Cutter raised a wary brow, changing the subject. "Does Bryan know Dennis Foye is dead?"

"I told him as soon as I heard," Hough said.

"And his reaction?"

"Complete surprise," Hough said, "He still seems to be operating on our assumption that Foye wasn't supposed to fly in until later today."

"So Bryan didn't see him on the plane?"

"Either that," Hough said, "or my husband is an extremely skilled liar who is up to his nuts in this mess."

What was left of Lilian Egak was on the way to the suicide scene. Hough stopped there first.

Sunrise was still almost three hours away, and the emergency vehicle headlights and strobes created a pulsating bubble of light in the middle of a black tundra. Reds and blues bounced off nearby houses and turned the rain into colorful streaks. A palpable curtain of darkness separated the houses and the tundra beyond. Hough must have seen Cutter looking at it.

"Don't wander off," she said. "They had to put down this bear, but there are plenty more where he came from."

"Don't intend to," Cutter said.

Construction lights illuminated a mountain of off-white fur less than thirty feet away from what Cutter suspected was Lilian Egak's body.

"Will they do a postmortem on the bear?" he asked.

"If I ask them to," Hough said. "Who knows what we'll find . . ."

Hough escorted Cutter through a skirmish line of North Slope PD officers, borough officials, and Cake Eater Road residents who'd crowded their way as close to the body as they could.

"He's with me," she said to the heavyset uniformed officer guarding the gap in the crime scene tape.

The officer grunted. "You're the boss."

Dozens of feet had trampled the scene. Tracking was pointless, but Cutter tried anyway. Looking at the ground was instinctive.

"Just as described," Hough said under her breath. "Looks like he went straight for her kidneys . . . among other things."

Cutter played his flashlight around the body, face down in a muddy puddle of blood and gore. The whiteness of bone was always startling, more so under the glaring beam of the flashlight. A dark-colored T-shirt and all but one leg of a pair of pajama pants lay in tatters in the grass around the body. Lilian Egak had not been a large woman, and Cutter estimated less than fifty or sixty pounds of her remained.

"Why do you think she came outside?" Cutter asked. "In the rain . . ."

Hough gave a slow nod. "And in her pajamas no less."

Cutter aimed his flashlight at a small shed fifty feet behind the house. "Maybe she was heading to get something from that." He stepped well away from the most probable path and moved toward the outbuilding. There were plenty of tracks, but most of them were going laterally between the two buildings. The three sets coming and going were large boots, not the canvas sneakers that lay shredded on the ground beside Lilian Egak. The lateral tracks probably belonged to the officers who were first on the scene.

"We're definitely getting a postmortem on her," Hough whispered. "Though I have to be honest. I wonder if there's enough left to tell us anything."

"I hate to sound macabre," Cutter said, "but whatever isn't here will be inside the bear."

A bear predation case wasn't likely to land in Hough's lap, but she took photos, anyway.

Cutter stooped to look at another set of boot tracks in the mud behind the house, two of which appeared to be under Lilian Egak's sneaker prints. He set his pen on the ground beside the most legible track to give it scale and then snapped several photos. He held his flashlight at an angle for better depth and definition.

"Who found her?" he asked, slipping the phone back in his jacket pocket.

A tall man with thinning salt-and-pepper hair and stars on the lapels of his North Slope Borough PD uniform strode up from the nearest crowd.

"Morgan Strawbridge," he said, extending his hand to Cutter. "I'm guessing you're Jan's US marshal friend."

"Arliss Cutter." He shook the offered hand.

"Chief Strawbridge came in on the same flight as Bryan." Hough aimed the beam of her flashlight at a dark-blue house across Cake Eater Road, then played it three homes to the right. "He lives right over there."

"I have a standing order that I get notified for any death investigation," the chief said. "In this case, I had the unfortunate experience of being the first officer on the scene after Lilian's neighbor shot the bear. His dog started barking around three a.m. He knew there was a bear lurking, so he came out with his rifle and ended up dumping it. I got contacted by the PD. There wasn't much point in calling an ambulance. I figure she probably came out sometime before dark. Maybe to watch the sunset, I don't know. Anyway, the bear apparently had several hours alone with its meal before George put him down."

Cutter tore his gaze away from the mutilated body. There were clues there, probably, but the sight of so much gore brought back memories of another time in another country. Stoic or not, he could only bear to look at it for so long.

"Have you been out to the suicide?" he asked the chief.

"Just came from there," Strawbridge said. "I knew Denny in passing. Didn't seem like the suicidal type . . ." The chief shook his head, hypnotized again by the sight of Lilian Egak's remains. "But then . . . who wouldn't be screwed up after seeing their girlfriend torn to pieces?"

"Chief," Hough said, "I'd like to do a postmortem on the bear."

"We'll need to, for sure," Strawbridge said. "To cross all the T's on Egak's death."

"That too," Hough said. "But also because I think this is connected to Dennis Foye's death."

"Of course, it was connected," Strawbridge said. "He saw what the bear had done to Lilian, then broke down and took his own life. What is an autopsy on the bear going to prove about that?"

"No idea," Hough said. "But I'd still like to be a part of it."

Strawbridge heaved a deep sigh, no doubt doing what chiefs of small towns had to do in any situation. Thinking through the politics.

"George Norbert feels like that animal is his," he said. "It was a predatory bear, and he shot it."

"Chief . . ."

Strawbridge stood in the rain for a full minute, staring silently across the blackness of the tundra.

"What we really want is the bear's stomach," he said at length. "Am I right?"

Hough shot a glance at Cutter, who nodded.

"That's exactly what we want," she said.

"You want to be a part of it," Strawbridge said. "Then knock yourself out. Get with George and tell him you want the guts."

"I'd like to check out Dennis Foye's scene first," Hough said. "Before he's moved."

"Of course, you would," Strawbridge said. "Jolivet's handling that scene. Call him and tell him I said to hang on until you've had a look around."

CHAPTER 23

DENNIS FOYE'S BODY WAS STILL BEHIND THE WHEEL OF HIS BATtered Subaru Forester, right where the borough employee had found him. His eyes and mouth were open. His head lolled back against the seat. A quick glance suggested he might be singing a song or talking with someone on his cell. Cutter suspected the body had been slumped forward over the wheel, but someone, probably multiple someones, had leaned him back to check for signs of life. Rigor had set in, locking his fingers like talons around the wheel. They'd left the windows up because of the rain. The whiff of exhaust fumes rolled out when Hough opened the door.

A length of garden hose ran from a slim crack in the window to the tailpipe, where it was held in place with silver duct tape. Heat from the exhaust had melted it in place.

Cutter looked at the ground. Useless. So many feet had tramped around the Subaru that any clues as to what occurred in the moments before Foye died had been obliterated.

"Does this make sense to you?" Cutter asked Hough, eyes narrow. It was obvious he wasn't convinced.

"You mean Denny Foye finds his butchered sweetheart and kills himself in a fit of despair? That I can believe. But he finds his sweetheart, trundles out to the storage shed—probably stepping over her body—gets a garden hose that is probably stored for the winter, cuts it to the right length to fit between the window and the exhaust pipe, goes back in the house and walks right past a couple of guns to get a roll of duct tape so he can keep the hose in place, then drives a couple of miles away to do the deed . . ." She scoffed. "Yeah, that's a load of horseshit."

"Agreed," Cutter said. "And where's the roll of duct tape?"

Hough pointed an index finger at Cutter. "You marshal guys . . . You're always thinkin' . . ." She shouted to the baby-faced detective working the scene. "Hey! Jolly! Anyone pick up a roll of duct tape from the car or maybe on the ground?"

"And any pieces of hose," Cutter said. "You're exactly right. It's difficult to believe someone out of his head with despair would take the trouble to measure at another location, then set it up when he got here."

Detective Shawn Jolivet, who went by the nickname Jolly, polled nearby borough employees and the other uniformed officers at the scene.

If Cutter had a resting-mean mug, Jolly Jolivet was a hundred and eighty degrees the opposite. The sparkle in his eyes was ever present, no matter the weather or the moods of those around him. He was one of those people who looked as though they were smiling even when they had bad news. Cutter found the look more than a little creepy.

"Nobody's picked up anything like that," Jolivet said. "You make a damned good point, though. I didn't see any obvious wounds or signs of struggle. Maybe we'll find something on the autopsy and tox screen."

"Outstanding," Hough said. "Mind if I see the note?"

Jolivet leaned into the driver's side of his SUV and came out with a clear plastic bag. "It's on his phone," he said. "Short and sweet. 'I'm sorry. Can't go on without Lilian.'"

Hough held the bag by the corner to keep from smearing any fingerprints and passed it to Cutter.

Cutter played his light across the device. "You'll be able to tell more when you dust it," he said. "It looks to me like there are smudges on the face, but the back's been wiped clean. I'm betting the only prints you find are from a single thumb—"

Jolivet's smile lit up. "Meaning someone used Foye's thumb to type the suicide note and then wiped away all their own prints."

"That's what I'm thinking," Cutter said. "But the prints . . . or lack of prints when you lift latents will tell us more."

"Lack of any prints is evidence that this wasn't a suicide," Jolivet said. "I'll give you that. But it doesn't tell us who killed him."

"One step at a time, Jolly," Hough said.

Jolivet raised a wary brow. "You have some kind of theory, Jan," he said. "I can see it in your eyes." Cutter decided the man was older than he looked and, with Hough only recently promoted to detective, senior to her. "Why are you here? It's zero dark thirty. You didn't have to respond."

"Come on," Hough said. "Something like this is an all-hands-on-deck callout. Or would have been eventually. Anyway, we were planning to talk to Foye later today. There are a couple of loose ends to tie up on the Willadean Benson case."

"I thought that was an accidental death."

"That's what it looks like," Hough said. "But she used to intern for Dennis Foye."

"And now he winds up dead," Jolivet mused. "That's a hell of a coincidence." He shot a wary look at Cutter. "And remind me why the US Marshals are interested in this again?"

"Come on, Jolly," Hough said.

"I'm pretty sure I get it," Jolivet said. "But run it all by me, anyway."

"You know why I invited him out to take a look at the Benson scene," Hough said.

Jolivet folded his arms across his chest, flashlight under his armpit. He looked Cutter up and down. "Ethan was your brother?"

"Yes, he was," Cutter said.

"Boats told me you two seemed really interested in those fossils the Benson girl had in her pocket. And you came all the way up from Anchorage to look at a few rocks from South Dakota. Jan spent the better part of a year trying to convince everyone on the Slope that Ethan was murdered. Is that what this is about?"

"That is exactly what it is about," Cutter said.

"Foye was from South Dakota," Jolivet went on. "You think he was involved with your brother's death?"

"We wanted to talk to him," Hough said. "That's all. And now he's dead. And just like you said, the circumstances are whacked." She heaved a deep sigh. "Keep this between us for now, would you? We still have a lot of dots to connect."

"Mum's the word," Jolivet said. "You made a good case after that rig exploded. To be honest, I've been on Team Jan from the get-go. I agree with you. Ethan's death was no accident."

Cutter shook the man's hand. "Thank you, Jolly," he said.

"What wouldn't I do for my brother?" Jolivet said and then turned and went back to work.

"Dennis Foye didn't kill himself," Hough said when she was back behind the wheel of her Tahoe.

"Agreed," Cutter said. "I don't believe in coincidences, but there are holes in the holes of this case."

"Do you think it's possible that the person who murdered Foye is the same one who killed Ethan?"

"That is exactly what I think," Cutter said.

Hough gripped the wheel with both hands, rocking forward and back in her seat before turning to look at Cutter, her face illuminated by the glow of the dashboard.

"You ready?"

"For?"

"To go cut the guts out of a polar bear."

Cutter gave a quiet sigh and muttered under his breath.

"The action service . . ."

CHAPTER 24

Anchorage

MOST OF THE LOCALS WHO LIVED AND WORKED IN THE NEIGH-borhoods along Spenard Road had worked hard in recent years to distance themselves from its reputation as one of Anchorage's red-light districts. Gone were the days when prostitutes stood at bus stops hawking their wares in short-shorts and tube tops—or, in the winter, froze their assets off in short-shorts and tight wool thermals. Hooking in the North was not for the faint of heart. Massage parlors still popped up now and then, tucked in among other business, and a handful of pay-by-the-hour hotels remained. Some businesses, like Gwinnie's, a famous former brothel turned restaurant, embraced the nostalgia. One cupcake and pastry shop sold T-shirts that read LEGALIZE FROSTITUION ON SPENARD!

It was still a likely spot to find Eddie Dupree.

Lola was a dog with a bone, spending all night running down five different hotels where Russel Whittaker said Dupree and his ilk might be filming movies. She'd called Blodgett and Alvarez—who were both excited to come in and act on the new information . . . at first. By four in the morning, they'd pounded on countless motel room doors and talked to three stoned-out-of-their-mind desk clerks. Joe Bill checked in when he could, but Anchorage after midnight kept him hopping.

The second to the last hotel looked like it might finally bear fruit.

"Check out the top floor," Lola said over the radio. "At first glance, it looks like all the lights are off, but focus on the second room to the right of the stairs."

"Screams at you when you look at it with night vision," Blodgett said. "They must use foil or something to black out the windows, but little slivers of light escape at a couple of the corners. Easy to see with the NVGs."

"Yep," Lola said. "Video lighting . . . and that's the only room with the lights on."

Like all the previous locations that night, Lola planned to conduct a knock-and-talk. No judge was going to give her a warrant to go on a fishing expedition at random hotel rooms on the word of a junkie. She did, however, have an arrest warrant for Dupree, which would allow the task force to boot the door if they needed to once they caught a glimpse of him inside.

They parked around the corner, donned ballistic vests, and eased their doors shut so as not to start a chain reaction of barking dogs and paranoid meth-heads. Alvarez requested a patrol unit so they could have a uniform on scene for a knock-and-talk in room fifteen. Spenard was in APD Area 22. Joe Bill, working 21, the adjacent area to the north, heard Alvarez on the radio and attached himself to the call. Two additional units arrived to cover the rear windows.

The team stacked up in the dark at the bottom of the metal stairs, guns out and ready. Not a run-of-the-mill knock-and-talk, but Eddie Dupree wasn't a run-of-the-mill fugitive. Blodgett, the caboose, gave Alvarez a pat on the thigh to signify that he was ready to go. She gave a similar pat to Lola, who repeated the process with Brackett, who was in the lead. He started moving at Lola's signal, padding silently up the stairs. The team split outside the room, with Lola and Brackett to the left of the door by the knob and lock. Blodgett and Alvarez posted on the right.

Joe Bill raised his hand to knock, but stopped, cocking his head to one side.

Lola heard it too. A high voice . . . like a whimper.

She cupped a hand to her ear, signaling to Alvarez to listen.

The sound came again. The whimper turned into stifled sobbing.

Joe Bill looked over his shoulder at Lola and frowned.

"Go!" she whispered.

He hammered on the door with his fist, shaking the entire floor. "Anchorage Police! Open the door!"

The sobbing grew louder, then went quiet.

Lola nodded emphatically at Joe Bill. He gave the door a more vicious beating.

"United States Marshals!" Lola bellowed. "We're not going away! Open the door!" The "or we'll kick it in" was implied.

The room went black. A series of shuffling thumps came from inside.

"Heads up in the back," Alvarez said over the radio. "They may be trying to come out."

"And watch the neighboring rooms," Lola snapped. "Some of these places connect like Habitrails."

The door opened a crack, revealing an eye—a very young eye, heavily caked with mascara.

Lola wedged her boot against the door before it could close. "Open up!"

A male voice growled unintelligible orders from somewhere in the background.

Lola caught a flash of bare skin as a frail looking Native girl ducked behind the door, pulling it open as she went. Only her face and one shoulder remained visible.

"Hands!" Lola barked. "Let me see hands!"

Joe Bill and the rest of the stack poured quickly into the room, getting out of the fatal funnel made by the doorway. A heavyset man wearing jeans and a black T-shirt made a break for the bathroom. He looked to be in his late fifties and, judging from the wheezing, was winded from the minuscule sprint. At first Lola thought he held a gun, but realized before she shot him that it was a handheld video camera. Sean and Joe Bill ran after the pudge. Alvarez took care of the kid behind the door.

A second girl cowered in the corner. This one was gaunt,

blond, and also in her early teens. She clutched a thin cotton sheet to her bare chest, the blinding glare of two umbrella video lights causing her to squint. Another man, this one taller, younger, and in much better shape than the camera man, hopped on one foot, naked but for a pair of gym shorts he'd managed to pull over one leg.

"What are you waiting for?" he screamed. "Get the bitch!"

The blond waif dropped the sheet, stutter-stepping toward Lola as if unsure of what to do.

The naked guy gave up trying to get dressed and let the shorts fall around one ankle. Unencumbered, he took a swing.

Her attention divided between Naked Guy and the blond, Lola found herself caught on her back foot. The swing glanced off the point of her shoulder. The blow infuriated more than it wobbled her. Naked Guy was obviously unarmed, so she couldn't shoot him, not just yet, anyway.

Lola sprang forward, closing the distance and taking the sting out of another wild punch. A snap kick to the man's unprotected groin doubled him over and sent him listing sideways. The young blond took another tentative step forward.

"Stay back!" Lola snapped, at the same moment delivering a wicked cross-elbow to Naked Guy's temple when he tried to get up again.

Nancy's voice came from close behind her. "Tase, Tase, Tase!"

Lola stepped out of the way as the twin darts flew past, trailing hair-thin wires. Nancy was so close the probes hit him less than a foot apart, one burying itself an inch above his navel, the other impaling him at the apex of his thigh and his groin. A larger spread between the darts would have locked up more muscle groups, but the sudden influx of molten pain brought on by fifty thousand volts flowing through this particular area did the trick nicely. Naked Guy fell like a sweaty tree.

Lola rolled him onto his stomach and cuffed him behind his back. Joe Bill and Sean frog-marched the cameraman in from the bathroom, also handcuffed behind his back.

"Idiot tried to toss his camera out the window," Blodgett said.

There was no need to pat the naked guy down for weapons, so

Lola left him where he was while she tossed a sheet to the blond girl. Nancy stowed her Taser and rolled him up on his side, looking down at the location of the darts.

"Yeah, we're gonna let the medical folks pull those out."

Lola moved both girls away from the couch. Far too many law enforcement officers had been injured or killed by someone they were in the process of saving.

Nancy gloved up and then checked the pile of the girls' clothes by the door before having them get dressed.

Naked Guy, whose name turned out to be Leonard Tice, sat cross-legged against the wall, hands still behind his back. Lola threw the filthy bedspread over his lap, much to everyone's relief. Sean put the cameraman, a beer-bellied man named Harris, on the floor along the same wall. Lola couldn't tell if it was because he was fully clothed or if he naturally had more of an attitude than Tice, but he threatened to sue with every other breath and warned everyone to keep their mouths shut.

Nancy ushered the girls out the door to the APD patrol officers who'd been watching the rear of the building. Lola would talk to them eventually, but she wanted to give them some distance between the two pukes and this awful room at the first possible moment.

The room secure, Lola allowed herself to take careful stock of the scene. The white blouse and short blue skirt of a Japanese schoolgirl uniform hung on the curtain rod. Video lights, candles, ball gags, and assorted unspeakable, degrading props littered the floor. If this was any indication, Dupree definitely showed a propensity toward torture and violence.

Lola had to restrain herself from snatching a leather riding crop from the tattered chair and whipping the two men bloody.

"Y'all are in deep shit!" Harris said snidely, as if he really believed it. "You assholes barged into a rented room without a warrant. It doesn't matter what you think you found. You ever hear of fruits of the poisonous tree!" He went on and on with more pseudointellectual bullshit he'd learned from his YouTube law degree. All Lola heard was "*Wa-wa-wahh-wa-wahh.*"

There was so much damning evidence on these two that the US Attorney was bound to deal them into talking if given enough time, but that was time Lola didn't have.

Tice hung his head in silence.

"Hey!" Harris said when Lola looked away. "Are you listening to me, sweetheart?"

She turned, head cocked and face passive, though her stomach roiled.

"Lawyer!" he said, enunciating the word so it was three syllables. "*La Wuh Yer*"!

Lola looked at Joe Bill and gave a toss of her head toward the door. She'd always wanted to separate the two but had wanted to make sure the girls were out of the way first.

Joe Bill tapped Harris on the shoulder. "On your feet! Let's go."

Harris grunted and heaved himself into a standing position. He glared over his shoulder at Tice.

"You keep your mouth shut—"

Joe Bill bodychecked him out the door.

Lola stood over Tice. He glanced up, opening his mouth to speak.

"Leonard!" she snapped. "Don't you say a word."

She read him his Miranda warning off a laminated card she kept in her vest pocket, then said, "You know your buddy's so fat 'cause he's full of shit, right?"

"That's kinda harsh."

Lola hunkered down beside him so they were at eye level.

"But true . . ."

Tice gave a dejected nod.

"I hear what sounds like a girl crying through the door," Lola said. "I am compelled to perform what we call a welfare check. And what do I find when I get in here but you shooting home movies with a couple of . . . how old are they? Twelve? Thirteen?"

"They said they were older than that," he scoffed.

"That's good," Lola said. She took a deep breath, tamping down her emotions. As enjoyable as it might be, ripping this guy a new asshole wouldn't help her find Dupree. Not yet, anyway. Instead, she played along with the lie he was telling himself.

"Maybe they're here of their own free will. The point is, Leonard, we heard what sounded like victims, and we came in and found you with underage girls. A federal judge is going to call that a lot of things, but I reckon an illegal search and seizure ain't one of 'em."

He gave another dejected nod.

"As bad as all this is," she said, "and I'm not gonna lie to you, Leonard, it's baaad, but I reckon you have the tiniest sliver of a chance to help yourself."

He stared at the floor. "You can get this to go away?"

"Oh no." Lola gave a slow shake of her head. "Not a chance in hell of this going away completely."

"Then you can—"

She cut him off. "But I can tell the US Attorney you cooperated, that you helped us get a dangerous man off the street."

"I'm not ratting out Harris," he said. "If that's what you're after."

"Your cameraman?" Lola scoffed. "I don't give two shits about him." In reality, she would have searched just as hard for these two as she was for Dupree had they been fugitives. But they were bought and paid for—caught in the act, on tape, even. The most liberal judge in Alaska—and that was saying something—would have a hard time letting them out on bond.

"Who are you talking about then?"

"Eddie Dupree."

His head snapped up.

"I know Eddie," he said, sensing a lifeline.

"I'm listening."

"I don't know how to contact him," Tice said. "He contacts us."

"How do you get him the videos?" she asked. "After you film them?"

"We upload it to the web," he said. "Then get paid in bitcoin." His shoulders began to shake with uncontrolled sobs. "I got nothing but shit luck . . ."

Either Tice was lying or Eddie Dupree had walled himself off so well his accomplices really didn't have any idea where he was. Either way, Lola didn't have time to deal with this now.

"Let's get you booked," she said. "Or else you're going to miss breakfast."

"I'm not hungry." Tice groaned.

"Again," Lola said. "I don't give two shits. You are under arrest for sexual assault of a minor—"

"They're getting paid the actors' going rate—"

She ignored him. "—sexual assault of a minor, human trafficking, and manufacturing child pornography."

He began to blubber.

"All that just seems like the same thing over and over again."

Lola rolled her eyes. "You're a hard man to feel sorry for."

He looked up suddenly, as if something had just occurred to him. "Hey," he said, sniffing back tears "Will . . . will the other inmates inside . . . you now, find out what I got arrested for?"

"They might," Lola said. "But I'd keep that to myself as long as I could if I were you."

CHAPTER 25

*L*OLA TRANSPORTED THE TWO GIRLS DOWNTOWN TO ANCHORAGE Police Department headquarters in her Tahoe. Putting the girls in the back of a caged police cruiser seemed beyond cruel after the fresh hell that they'd just been through. Nancy Alvarez rode shotgun.

Unlike the older two-story HQ building tucked in the trees off Elmore, the new digs were six stories tall and located smack downtown on Fourth Avenue. Almost entirely glass, the building always made Lola feel a little like she was walking into a fish tank. She used Nancy's proximity badge to park in the underground garage.

Blodgett stopped by the McDonald's on Northern Lights and grabbed a half dozen breakfasts. The girls ate two apiece, plus Lola's hash browns.

Lola couldn't blame the poor things. Both were gaunt and pale, with thinning hair and bad skin, likely from a steady diet of booze and drugs to keep them stoned into compliance.

The blond turned out to be a Ukrainian refugee who, after being assaulted by her sister's boyfriend in Portland, had run away to find an aunt who had settled in Anchorage. Harris had told her it didn't matter how old she was. She was just as guilty as he was because she'd been paid to perform in movies for the Internet. Tice assured her the US authorities would deport her back to Ukraine if she ever spoke up.

Her name was Valentyna Brutka, and she was fourteen years old.

Courtney Ashes from Russian Mission had a round baby face. The Yupik girl looked considerably younger than Valentyna but had just turned fifteen the month before. She, too, had run away from home—trading one abuser for a new one.

Lola had thought to separate them, but they appeared much more relaxed and cooperative when they were together. Now safe and full of sausage biscuits, both appeared willing to talk. Neither knew how to contact Eddie Dupree—not a surprise—but both picked him out of a photo array. According to them, he liked to personally inspect the girls who worked for him.

Both girls had been met initially by women who offered them modeling jobs for fast money. Courtney by an older blond woman, Valentyna by a redhead with very large breasts. According to the girls, both women wore large glasses and probably wigs. Though they were recruited separately, there were enough similarities in their descriptions to suggest they were recruited by the same person—a woman who appeared to be in charge of all the girls, known in the business as a "bottom girl" or "bottom bitch." Dupree was a boss, they said, but this woman might even be higher than he was in the food chain.

Lola looked at Nancy and then Joe Bill in turn. This was news. They'd been operating under the assumption that Eddie Dupree was the mastermind behind the trafficking.

"Where did she find you?"

"In front of the Native Hospital," the Native girl said.

"The bus station," the Ukrainian girl said.

"She's the one who told us where to meet Harris," Courtney heaved a weary sigh. "The asshole with the camera."

A female detective from the sexual assault unit arrived a short time later along with a representative from Child Protective Services to transport the victims to the hospital for sexual assault kits and treatment for possible STDs.

Lola met with Nancy, Sean, and Joe Bill to compare notes in the APD briefing room.

"This recruiter seems to be working all over Anchor-town,"

Nancy said. "The description is too vague to know exactly what she looks like."

"We could show these girls some photos of hookers with priors for prostitution," Sean offered. "Maybe one of them graduated to bottom bitch."

Nancy agreed. "It's a long shot, but sitting surveillance at multiple locations just hoping to spot someone recruiting is a waste of time." She caught Lola's eye. "We need bait."

Lola gave a slow nod, thinking it through.

"You know," Lola said. "I reckon that might really work."

Joe Bill cleared his throat.

"I mean this in the best possible way," he said, "but nobody in their right mind is going to confuse either of you two for underage girls."

"We're not trying to get anyone to recruit us," Lola said, her voice matter-of-fact. "We need this woman to think we're poaching on her territory."

"Get her to show herself," Nancy said. "Try and run us off her turf. Then we get her to lead us to Dupree."

"I can see it," Blodgett said. "You're going to be—"

Lola raised a hand to cut him off. "That's right," she said. "Meet Anchorage's newest bottom bitches."

CHAPTER 26

Utqiagvik

IT WAS ALMOST TEN A.M. BY THE TIME CUTTER AND HOUGH FINISHED retrieving what they needed from the bear—a massive boar that the locals estimated weighed well over a thousand pounds. George Norbert, a broad-shouldered block of an Iñupiaq man, did the technical work to ensure the bear's meat and hide stayed usable. The liver, toxic to humans, would go to his dogs. Both Cutter and Hough were flecked with bits of leaf and twig off the tundra and bathed in blood up to their elbows by the time they'd tied off the massive paunch and rolled it into a heavy-duty body bag. Garbage bags were far too flimsy. It took all three of them to maneuver the thing into the back of Hough's SUV.

"That, my good friend," Jan Hough said once they'd reached the Police Department and wrangled the ungainly bag full of bear innards into an empty evidence freezer, "is a once-in-a-life-time law enforcement endeavor."

"That is my sincere hope," Cutter said, catching his breath.

They'd worn gloves during the process and scrubbed their arms until they were pink afterward, but Cutter checked his hands for errant traces of polar bear blood, anyway. "I thought you North Slope coppers did this kind of shit pretty much twenty-four seven."

"Ha . . . ha . . . ha," she said, clearly not amused. "Anyway . . . I talked it over with Jolly. He's all good with us paying Beck and Associates a visit this morning. I'm hoping we can find something of use in Dennis Foye's office."

"They may ask us to get a warrant," Cutter said.

Hough reached in the pocket of her fleece vest and produced a folded piece of paper. "Voilà," she said. "Jolly was all over it, working things out with the judge while we were up to our chins in bear gall."

Cutter noticed the missing harpoon the moment he walked in the door. Surprisingly, Maureen was there, sitting at her desk in the reception area.

Hough greeted her with a smile. "I thought you were going out for caribou with your dad."

"He only takes me to use as a pack mule." Maureen gave a nervous laugh. "No, really it's because that part of the tundra smells like polar bear and death this morning. All the *tuttu* have moved out for the time being."

"They'll settle down," Hough said. "Listen, we'd like to take a look at Dennis Foye's office."

"Of course," Maureen said, as if she'd been expecting it.

"We have a warrant," Hough said. "If you need it."

"That won't be necessary," a low voice said from somewhere down the hall. Moments later, a tall man with a silver goatee and a stern eye walked out behind Maureen. He nodded to Hough and Cutter, shaking their hands in turn. Hough, he took by the fingers, bending them slightly as if he meant to kiss the back of her hand. He smiled benignly before turning to grasp Cutter in a firm, two-handed shake, like he was genuinely pleased this meeting was taking place.

"Leo Beck," he said. "I own the place." His lips smiled. His eyes flicked back and forth between Cutter and Hough as if deciding who was the greater threat. They settled on Cutter.

Not one to talk himself out of a win, Cutter didn't ask again for permission. "Which one is Foye's office?"

Beck gestured over his shoulder. "It's right next to mine," he said. "But I'm afraid you won't find anything."

"How's that?" Hough asked.

"Denny was here last night," Beck said. He looked at Hough long enough to let her know he was answering her question, then turned to face Cutter. "He was finishing up some quarterly tax filings I needed for one of our clients. I went to retrieve them this morning when I got in and found the entire office had been cleaned out."

"Cleaned out?" Hough asked.

"That's right," Beck said. Then, directly to Cutter again. "Files, photos, even a mother-in-law's tongue houseplant Lilian gave him." He scratched his goatee. "Awful business, what happened to her."

"You already know what happened to her?" Cutter asked.

"The whole town knows," Beck said. "And what happened to Denny as well. News travels fast across the tundra, Marshal."

"We'll take a look, anyway," Cutter said. "Dot the I's and cross the T's, so to speak."

"By all means." Beck waved down the hall with a flourish.

Just as Beck said, the office was completely empty, as if waiting for the next employee to fill it.

Hough opened and closed every drawer and cabinet, snapping photos from all angles.

Cutter stood at the door. Beck watched in silence, his hands low and quiet. What movements he did make were sure and direct. Nothing wasted.

"You mentioned Foye was working on some tax files for you," Hough said.

"That's right."

"What files?"

"Some quarterlies for an oil company," Beck said. "But they are gone. As I told you, that's what I was looking for this morning when I discovered the office had been emptied."

"Which oil company?"

"I'm afraid that would be privileged," Beck said, shrugging as if there was nothing he could do about it. "Client information. You'd need a different warrant for that. Get one that protects me

from getting sued by our clients, and I'll happily give you whatever you need."

"We'll do just that," Hough said.

Beck met Cutter's eyes, locking on. "Maureen tells me Ethan
Cutter was your brother. Is that right?"

"He was," Cutter said.

Beck gave a sad shake of his head, but the challenge in his eyes
remained. "Tragic what happened on the rig that day. I didn't
know him well, but to be so big, the Slope can seem a very small
place. We crossed paths more than you might think." He shot a
glance at Hough, then back to Cutter, watching for a reaction.
"His death must have been particularly hard on Jan."

Hough flushed red, coming up on her toes as if to speak . . . or
kick Beck in the face.

Cutter refused to engage with whatever game this guy was playing. He changed the subject instead.

"So, your office is this one next door?"

"It is," Beck said.

"I couldn't help but notice the harpoon on your desk," Cutter
said. "That's the one that was hanging on the front wall when we
dropped by yesterday?"

"Very observant," Beck said.

"I have to pick up on the small things in my line of work."

"I'll just bet you do," Beck said, ice cold. "The harpoons are
more than art. I like to keep them . . . you know, in good working
order, from the point to the bomb."

"I see," Cutter said. "In case you need to harpoon somebody
coming through your front door."

Beck smirked at that. "As one does," he said. He clapped his
hands together at his waist, shooing them away from his office up
the hall toward the reception area. "I'm sorry your search came
up empty-handed."

"So am I," Hough said.

Cutter paused in the cramped lobby beside the Mark Maggiori
painting and smiled at the young Iñupiaq woman. She sat tight-
lipped, looking as if she'd rather be on the tundra with a polar
bear than here with her boss lurking behind her.

"Miss Akpik," Cutter said. "When we were here yesterday, you mentioned Mr. Foye was visiting a brother in South Dakota. I wonder if you'd have that address in your files."

Maureen smiled back. She started typing on her keyboard but stopped suddenly and gave Beck a quivering sideways glance.

"I don't think we're supposed to give out personnel next-of-kin information without a warrant—"

"It's all right, Maureen," Beck said. He gave a magnanimous wave of his hand. He was a hell of a hand waver, Cutter thought.

"Denny was a good man. We want to be as cooperative as legally possible. I'm sure David won't mind. He'd want them to find out why his elder brother would do such a horrible thing."

Maureen scribbled something on a yellow legal pad, then tore the page off and passed it to Hough. "Here you go. David Foye. All I have is a phone number, but I did hear Denny say once that his brother lived on some ranch near a place called Bad River."

Jan Hough grabbed the steering wheel with both hands and gave it a frustrated yank.

"Leonard Beck really pissed me off."

"I could tell," Cutter said. "And so could he. He seems the kind to thrive on other people's discomfort."

"I don't know about you," Hough said, "but most of the people I arrest are generally good folks who did bad things . . ."

"I don't know about most people," Cutter said. "But I get your point."

"That guy is pure malevolence." Hough stared straight ahead, speaking through clenched teeth. "He's involved with Ethan's death. I know it in my bones. So much time has passed since the event, proving it is going to be a problem."

"There's proof that holds up in a court of law," Cutter said, "and then there's proof that is enough for us to be sure of what happened."

"I just don't know how I missed looking into Leo Beck right off the bat."

"No reason to until we had the connection with JBM Engineering."

Hough hit the ignition and nestled down in her seat, both hands still on the wheel.

"We're on a roll," she said. "What do we do from here?"

"You've got your hands full with this homicide," Cutter said.

"Possible homicide," she corrected.

"No," Cutter said. "It's a homicide. You know it—in your bones like I do. Keep me posted when you hear from the lab about the bear's paunch and the toxicology on Foye."

"I suppose you're going to Bad River?"

"Absolutely."

"You want some company?"

"Oh, I'm sure I'll have some."

Hough nodded. "Mim . . ."

"I doubt I could keep her from going if I handcuffed her to the radiator. She needs this."

"We all need this." Hough turned to Cutter. "I . . . I have a confession to make."

Cutter braced, resisting the urge to jump out of the SUV. "If this is about you and Ethan, there's no need for you to—"

"Arliss," Hough said, staring forward again as if in a trance. "I've kept something from you . . . from Mim."

He leaned against the headrest and waited. There was nothing to do but let her speak.

Tears welled in her eyes. "I should have given it to you the first time I saw you in Deadhorse. Really, I should have just sent it to Mim . . . Given it to her when she was here. But I . . ." She turned suddenly, locking eyes with Cutter. "I know it was selfish, but I had to have something to remember him by."

She pulled a hand from her jacket pocket and shoved it toward Cutter, uncurling her fingers.

Cutter, who was surprised by little in the world, found himself caught completely off guard.

"Ethan's watch," he whispered. He held the timepiece up in awe as if he'd just discovered a long-lost treasure. In fact, he had.

According to family lore Nana Cutter had given the Vulcain Cricket to Grumpy when he graduated his first police academy in Texas. Smallish by modern standards, the simple field-watch aesthetic and cricket-like manual alarm had been points of awe to the boys when they were young. Grumpy had told them every president since Truman had worn a watch like it. This, of course, meant nothing special to the boys when they were young, but they did like the stories about how LBJ would often set the alarm to get out of meetings. The way the alarm and movement could be packed into such a small, "water-protected" case was a fascinating mystery, especially to Ethan. Grumpy had eventually passed the coveted Cricket down to him when he graduated with his engineering degree.

Cutter held the watch up, at a loss for words.

Jan choked back a sob. "I am so sorry."

"How did you—"

"It was at the scene." She sniffed, gaining some semblance of control—at least outwardly. "Just lying out on the tundra. It must have . . . come off during the explosion. Arliss, I knew it was his, but I just shoved it in my pocket and kept my mouth shut. It was so wrong. Stupid . . . But . . ." She wiped her nose with the forearm of her sweater. "There's no excuse. I am sorry, though."

Cutter gave a somber nod, turning the watch over and over in his fingers, remembering all the times Grumpy had let him fall asleep with it when he was small, how he held it under the covers to marvel in the dark at the tiny glowing marks on the face. Neither boy gave a thought to inheriting Grumpy's things. Immortal men like their grandfather could not be touched by death. But Grumpy knew what suited each of them. Ethan got the Vulcain Cricket, and Arliss got the Colt Python, both items that the old man had worn virtually every day of his adult life, certainly as long as the boys had known him.

Hough touched Cutter's hand.

"I wish you would say something."

"There's nothing to say."

"I kept something from a crime scene that was not mine to keep," Hough said. "You could have my job."

"Don't worry about that." He swallowed hard. "Thank you . . . for taking care of this. If not for you, it might still be out there, rusting away on the tundra."

"Arliss," she said. "I need to know you believe me. About me and Ethan, I mean."

"I'll tell you what I believe, Jan," Cutter said. The watch felt warm in his hand, like it had when it had just come off Grumpy's arm. "I believe my brother was your good friend."

Hough began to cry again. "He was," she said. "He really was."

CHAPTER 27

THREE HUNDRED AND NINETY-SIX DOLLARS AND A COUPLE OF TAT-
tered books didn't make much of a stake, but Leo Beck had built
his empire on it. That and the backs of weaker souls who didn't
understand the natural laws of the North.

Now this nosey bitch and her marshal friend were about to
move in and rip it away from him.

Poets and those who had never spent a night on the ice or lost
toes to frostbite were quick to point out that the North was a cruel
mistress. They were dead wrong. The North was neither cruel nor
benevolent. The North simply didn't give two shits about you one
way or another.

In the North—and anywhere else for that matter—you had to
be a predator to survive. Jack London had known it—the law of
club and fang.

Leo Beck knew it too. Lived it, every single day of his life.

Beck slammed a fist into his bouncing knee, willing it into sub-
mission. It was not like him to be jittery, and he hated himself for
it. He leaned forward in his comfortable button-leather office
chair behind an expensive walnut desk—both out of place in this
Arctic edge of the world—and fanned the smudged and tattered
pages of his ancient copy of *Call of the Wild*, shoving it across the
desk beside *The Best of Robert Service*. An eight-by-ten photograph
of his wife, Inez, smiled back at him. His marriage to her had

been a means to an end, but she was not unpleasant to look at. She had surely snapped to the particulars of what really went on in his business ventures. She was also smart enough not to say them out loud, even to Beck.

Beck banged at his keyboard, mistyping his password twice while attempting to log on to the virtual private network. He cursed, unaccustomed to being so ham-fisted. The man he was calling had probably drunk himself to sleep by now. Too bad, he'd have to deal with it.

For all his business savvy and ruthless tactics, Beck had to admit that he'd made some very poor decisions in choosing his business partners. These men just could not bring themselves to admit that they were predators. No, his feckless associates had to hide behind the fairy tale that big oil and the businesses that worked with big oil—like Johnson, Benham, and Murphy Engineering— were the true criminals. They needed to reassure their fragile psyches that a decade skimming millions of dollars from client accounts was a victimless crime.

Then Ethan Cutter had started to tug on some loose threads he discovered in JBM's books. It was only by sheer luck and coincidence that Beck had learned of Ethan's snooping trips back and forth to South Dakota. The hapless engineer was days, maybe even hours, from unraveling the entire operation when they finally put an end to him.

Dennis Foye had spent three days vomiting.

His brother, David, had run home like a whiny little bitch.

The others stood fast, for a time, doing what needed to be done, but eventually, they, too, got nervous and planned more and more business trips to hide.

Fortunately, the authorities on the North Slope chalked everyone's distraught behavior up to mourning the loss of a friend. All of them except Jan Hough. She'd been a problem. He'd wanted to leave her out on the ice then, but the others wouldn't have it. They couldn't kill a cop. They envisioned themselves good men merely caught up in a bad situation. Dennis Foye admitted as much.

Good men . . . That was a joke. There were no good men, only strong and weak. Strong men knew the law of club and fang. Strong men did what needed to be done. Weak men sniveled and told themselves they were good.

Those *good* men didn't leave Jan Hough out on the ice when they should have—and now she was a problem again.

Leo Beck made no bones about what he was—a prospector mucking his due bit of gold out of the North. He'd do whatever he had to in order to hang on to what was rightfully his, even if that meant murdering a nosey engineer and one of his partners—or both of his partners if it came to that.

The whaling harpoon now leaned against the corner of his office. He wasn't ready to return it to the lobby, wanting it nearby so he could look at it, enjoy the craftsmanship, the elegance—and brutal efficiency.

If any boy ever heard the call of the wild, it was Leo Beck. The Liberty County High School library in Hinesville had a slim selection of books about the North. Leo had read them all by the end of the first quarter of his freshman year, so he read them again. Jack London had kept him company during the sticky Georgia nights under the box fan while his mother and aunts played forty-two on the folding card table in the front room where the window unit was.

He'd read other stuff too—a book about a boy who sailed around the world when he was sixteen years old, countless stories of Everest expeditions, and an epic poem about a gaucho in Argentina that he liked but didn't quite understand. But his internal compass had always pointed him north. He couldn't remember when he'd decided to leave, but he knew early on that the two-bedroom fourplex apartment held nothing for him but mildew and boredom.

His sophomore year, he'd swiped a map of Alaska from a *National Geographic* in the school library and pinned it to his bedroom wall. A month later, he'd carefully torn a copy of "The Spell of the Yukon" out of a book from his English teacher's personal collection. She'd caught him in the act, but instead of punishing him for the destruction, she'd made him tape the page back in place and then given him the book—*The Best of Robert Service.*

He'd left home the day he graduated high school, without wasting even a minute to interrupt his mother's dominos game to say good-bye. Now, thirty-two years later, he wondered if she ever realized he was gone.

His journey north was worthy of a Jack London tale, fraught with conmen and whores all looking to skin this green chee-chako out of everything he had—one hundred and seventy-four dollars. He'd realized just how far away Alaska really was when the Greyhound bus took him three days to get from Hinesville to Bellingham and the ferry trip from Washington to Seward took over five. He arrived in Anchorage with a grand total of three hundred and ninety-six dollars folded in his money belt, having done a little skinning of his own—and learning valuable life lessons.

Strong-arm robbers didn't win many brain teasers. Conmen were, on the whole, smart enough, but they rarely had enough stomach for the messy stuff. An intelligent person who didn't mind making someone bleed, well, the world was their oyster.

Beck even considered writing a book—*The Eight Day Educa-tion*—but that would only get him indicted or, at the very least, draw unwanted attention.

The garbled tone of his voice-over-IP call shook away the mem-ory and brought him back to the task at hand. Beck didn't care much for computers, but he was smart enough to use them to make money—and cover his tracks by speaking through an end-to-end encrypted "tunnel" via his virtual private network. The VPN made it difficult to trace the call's origin or contents.

"We have to talk," he said when the line connected.

The voice on the other end of the line was crystal clear.

"Tell me you're not behind this," the other man said.

"I am not," Beck said.

"Really?" the man said, unconvinced. "So, I don't need to worry I'm going to end up slumped dead in my car or lunch for some bear?"

"I don't know," Beck said. "You might need to worry a lot. That marshal is in town, running around with our little North Slope cop."

"Janice Hough?"

"That's the one."

"She was a problem after that all went down," the man said, stating what they both knew all too well. "We should have taken care of her then."

"I seem to remember saying just that," Beck said.

It was time for a little nudge, a fairy tale to make what had to happen next easier for the others to swallow. "It looks like Hough's decided to take care of us now."

"Knock it off," the other man said. "You don't expect me to believe Hough and the marshal had something to do with Denny?"

"The marshal's name *is* Cutter," Beck said. "Is it really that hard to imagine he could want some vengeance?"

"I'm not buying it," the other man stammered. "Denny Foye and . . . and his girlfriend . . . That's got your signature all over it."

"You can think whatever you want," Beck snapped. He would have been upset but for the fact that the other man was so scared of him he sounded like he might lose control of his bowels at any moment. "But Hough and the marshal are problems."

"Then we need to do something."

"That's why I'm calling," Beck said.

"Okay." Ice tinkled against a glass. Beck could picture the man looking over his shoulder for Beck's associates. A wise move, but it hadn't come to that. Yet.

"The marshal is heading to Bad River," Beck said.

"To take care of David . . ."

"I'm afraid the time has come for us to take care of David."

Silence but for a gurgling pour and more tinkling ice.

Then a tentative, "Right. Okay. What about the widow. Eventually, I'm going to have to talk to her."

"David Foye, the marshal, Hough . . . and the widow. The list gets longer."

"As long as I'm not on it."

"Not at all," Beck lied. "Now, let's put our heads together. I have an idea about how to deal with Officer Hough . . ."

CHAPTER 28

Anchorage

*C*HIEF PHILLIPS APPROVED CUTTER'S ANNUAL LEAVE BEFORE THE plane from Utqiagvik touched down in Anchorage. Mim had two tickets booked on the red-eye to Rapid City, South Dakota, by the time he got home.

The Marshals Service had prepared Cutter for travel on short notice both in and out of Alaska. Mim made frequent trips to gain practicum hours for her nurse practitioner license. It didn't take either of them long to pack. The face-to-face confrontation Cutter had planned with Coop Daniels was going to have to wait, but there was time to have a sit-down dinner with the family before he and Mim had to be at the airport.

The family . . .

Cutter was hesitant to focus on it too long for fear it would all evaporate. For the moment though, he sat back and enjoyed the fleeting comfort.

A chilly rain had followed him home from the Arctic, and now pelted the living room window, buffeting the glass with periodic gusts of wind, but inside . . . inside was heaven.

Snippets of Mim's heated conversation with her sixteen-year-old daughter, Constance, carried in from the kitchen on the rich, peppery odor of seasoned chicken broth. Cutter had learned it was wise to give those two a wide berth when they were in the middle of a debate, no matter what the topic was. He hid out in the living room with Mim's nine-year-old twins, Matthew and Michael, while they practiced their Grumpy "Man-Skills," whittling feather sticks for the fireplace.

The boys sat at opposite ends of the hearth, out of each other's blood circle, both working with rapt focus. Pocketknives out, they carved thin layers of wood off pieces of birch kindling. They left the curled shavings attached, resulting in a feathered piece of wood that would ignite easily and stay lit long enough to get a fire going. Cutter and his brother had grown up with Grumpy's two-matches-per-fire rule, which meant tinder, kindling, and larger fuel had to be prepped and organized before any spark was set. Grumpy taught Ethan, and Ethan taught his boys. All Arliss had to do was make sure they didn't cut their own thumbs off.

"Air, fuel, and a heat source," Michael said, half to himself, half to demonstrate to his uncle that he knew what he was doing. His dark hair and easy way with people reminded everyone of his father.

"Yep." Matthew was the spitting image of Arliss at that age, at least in the face. The shaggy blond locks and the resting-mean mug were the same. But Matthew was already well-muscled, where Arliss had been on the runty side. Both boys stuck their tongues out while they carved. Each with several fingers and at least one thumb already bandaged with first-aid tape. Once white, the tape was now gray from days of building forts and playing in the woods behind the house.

Old wounds. Scars they could tell their grandkids about someday.

It wasn't long before the boys had a fire of birch and spruce popping like gunshots in the fireplace.

"Uncle Arliss," Matthew said. "Is it true that that lady up north kept Dad's watch?"

"She found it," Cutter said.

"And then kept it?" Matthew said. "Isn't that like stealing?"

"It's complicated," Cutter said.

"Sounds like stealing," Michael said.

"You're right. It would be like stealing. But she felt bad and gave it back."

"I remember that watch," Matthew said. "Dad used to let us play with the alarm."

Michael gazed into the flames and sighed.

"We should invite Lola over for dinner again."

"And Joe Bill," Cutter said.

"Nah," Michael said. "Just Lola."

It was clear to Cutter that both boys had a massive crush on his pretty Polynesian partner. Michael was the only one comfortable enough in his own skin to admit it.

"She's busy catching bad guys," Cutter said.

Matthew nodded sideways toward the kitchen and then groaned, exasperated. "They're still at it . . ."

Michael said, "Monte! Play 'Ten Cent Pistol'! Louder!"

Moments later, the song from the Black Keys throbbed out of the electronic assistant in the kitchen.

"Monte! Stop!" Constance groused as Cutter made his way into the room. The music obeyed immediately.

Mim raised a wary brow. "'Ten Cent Pistol'? Seriously?"

"It's a good song," Matthew said.

Cutter shrugged. "It is a pretty good song."

He raised a brow of his own at the electronic assistant. This wasn't his house, but he made no bones about the fact that he considered so-called smart speakers too smart for their own good.

Mim tapped a long wooden spoon on the edge of her stewpot and wagged her head. "Yes," she said, ponytail bobbing. "Could that thing be spying on us? Yes." She gave a resigned shrug. "But is it also super-helpful for a harried nurse practitioner student and mother of three extremely energetic kiddos? Also, yes."

Cutter raised his hands. "Hey, you're the boss."

"I don't relish the idea of the boys having cell phones," Mim said. "This gives me the option of dropping in virtually when I'm still at the hospital." She brightened. "You should get the app, and I'll put you on the account. I'm telling you, it's incredibly convenient."

"You can send fart noises," Matthew said, stifling a giggle.

Cutter shot a glance at his nephew. "Put it that way, I guess I'm in."

"Great," Mim said. "We'll have a few minutes after supper before we have to leave for the airport. I'll show you on your phone." She switched gears. "The broth is done and ready for the veggies when you boys get them chopped. I'll shred the chicken while they work on that. Constance has dumpling duty."

Cutter inhaled the rich odor. "This is my Nana Cutter's chicken and dumplings recipe. She got it from her mother who grew up in Louisiana—"

Michael glanced up from the carrot he was chopping. "Dad told us that Nana Cutter's mom sometimes used squirrel instead of chicken."

"True," Cutter said. "Your dad and I used to make it all the time when Grumpy had to work late."

"With squirrel?"

"Once or twice." Cutter shot a glance at Mim. "Usually chicken."

Constance brushed flour off her hands and used a shoulder to push bangs out of her eyes. She was a natural blond like Matthew and Arliss, but she'd opted to color her hair to match most of her clothes, sullen and black.

She stared at the counter, gently mushing together the dumpling dough so as not to overwork it.

"I don't like the idea of you two running off together like this," she said, blowing the lock of hair out of her eyes.

"We're not running off together," Mim chided. "When you say it like that, it sounds like—"

"It sounds exactly like what it is?" Constance put her hands on the counter and looked directly at Mim. "Are you going to Rapid City?"

"Yes, but—"

"Is Uncle Arliss going with you to Rapid City? On the same plane?"

"Yes," Mim said. "But going together is different than going together."

"Sounds exactly the same to me." Michael held a piece of celery between his fingers like a cigarette and pretended to smoke it.

"Knock that off," Mim whispered.

He ate the celery. "Well, it does."

Constance shrugged, sure in her victory. She took the dumpling dough out of the bowl and put it on the floured counter. Softer now, almost sweet, she smiled at Cutter while she gently rolled out the dough. "Uncle Arliss, do you ever think about Aunt Barbara anymore?"

Cutter's fourth wife, Barbara, had passed away from breast cancer just months before Ethan was killed. There was no denying Cutter had a type. Like his three wives before her, she'd borne a striking resemblance to Mim. Barbara, though, had been the only one he'd really gotten along with.

Mim shot her daughter a look that let her know she'd gone too far. "We all loved your Aunt Barbara."

"I do think about her a lot," Cutter said. "She died way too young."

"Our dad died way too young," Michael said.

Matthew's lip began to quiver. "I think about Aunt Barbara a lot too. And Dad . . ."

Constance closed her eyes. "I'm sorry, guys. I didn't mean to—"

"It's okay, kiddo," Cutter said. "We're all still trying to navigate this."

Matthew brightened. "How about we all go to South Dakota? Mount Rushmore, the Badlands, Devil's Tower—"

Michael pointed a judgmental stalk of celery. "Devil's Tower is in Wyoming, igmo."

Matthew wagged his head. "I know that," he said. "But it's close to the border. We could go to visit both places while we're there."

"That sounds like an excellent idea," Cutter said. "But not this time. Your mom and I are going to South Dakota for work. It's not a vacation."

Michael raised a brow. "Whose work?"

"Both," Mim said. "And just so you know, Constance, your uncle travels so much with the Marshals Service he's got enough Marriott points for us to get two rooms."

"Good," Constance said. Her eyes locked on Arliss, then, under her breath with a look that reminded him of his seventh grade English teacher, she said, "Two. Rooms."

CHAPTER 29

South Dakota

THEY SHARED A SURNAME, SO EVERYONE FROM THE UNITED AIRLINES gate agent in Anchorage to the rental car clerk in Rapid City naturally assumed Cutter and Mim were married. That suited Cutter right down the bone. Mim did a lot of nervous grinning, but she didn't correct anyone.

As Cutter had learned shortly after moving to Alaska, traveling anywhere from the Great Land was a lesson in planning and patience. Mim took the middle seat next to Cutter on the first flight, sleeping fitfully for most of the five-hour red-eye to their layover in Denver with her head lolling on his shoulder. Cutter could have flown armed but opted to check his handguns in his luggage so he could at least try to sleep during the flights. There was a time he would have been able to work all day, then fly all night and hit the ground running the moment he landed. That time was long gone. They'd need their wits about them to negotiate all the unknowns they were facing with Dennis Foye's brother.

They arrived in Denver at six forty-five a.m., grateful for the four hours to stretch their legs and grab a leisurely breakfast at a place called Snooze, which was just what both of them wanted to do.

Mim spent the rest of the layover curled up in her puffy down sweater taking catnaps. Cutter was used to spending a great deal of dead time in airports, often with a handcuffed prisoner in the seat between him and another deputy marshal. Now he spent the time strategizing in his little black notebook—in between stealing glances at Mim.

The flight out of Denver put them in Rapid City at a quarter to one in the afternoon. Cutter rolled his checked luggage into the bathroom stall and retrieved his Colt Python along with the Glock 27 to keep him in compliance with Marshals Service policy.

They were on the road in a rented Toyota Corolla by two, heading east toward their rendezvous on Interstate 90 under a cloudless South Dakota sky. The information Maureen Akpik had provided put David Foye at a ranch somewhere near Bad River, which, according to the map, was southwest of Fort Pierre. Cutter had called ahead, identifying himself as a friend of Ethan Cutter. He'd not mentioned his name or said anything about being a deputy US marshal. Foye hadn't asked for specifics. If anything, he'd seemed resigned to the meeting, as if it was inevitable. Rather than provide the location of his ranch, Foye had insisted they meet in between, fifty miles from Rapid City at a crowded tourist mecca called Wall Drug.

"This must be a heck of a place," Mim said through a long shuddering yawn from the passenger seat. "There's a Wall Drug sign every quarter mile. Everything from nickel coffee to buffalo burgers."

"I did some checking with a deputy I know in Pierre," Cutter said. "Wall Drug's supposed to be one of *the* must-visit spots in South Dakota—right up there with Mount Rushmore and the Black Hills . . ."

"And 1880 Town," Mim said, nodding to another billboard, this one larger, advertising a historic Western town. "We should have met Foye there. You have the look of a frontier marshal. People would probably stop you and ask for autographs."

"Nope," Cutter said. "We have an hour. You want to grab a little more sleep?"

"Nope," she said, obviously mimicking him. Then, out of the blue, "What's the deal with Jan Hough keeping Ethan's watch for so long?"

Cutter drove in silence for a time, sure the question was rhetorical.

It wasn't.

"Do you think there's any way Ethan might have . . ." She turned to look directly at him. "What if. . . . ?"

"Did you ever meet Jan's husband?"

Mim shook her head. "No."

"He's kind of an asshole," Cutter said. "He called her Jessica Rabbit in a cop uniform while we were sitting at the dinner table."

"That is kind of an asshole-ish thing to say," Mim said.

Cutter sighed. "You know how Ethan always accused me of having a Tarzan complex?"

"Your compelling need to swing in and save the day?"

"Yep," he said. "Exactly that. Where do you think I learned the behavior? I'm thinking Ethan was just being his normally good-hearted self and Jan developed a crush. She's fallen on a lot of swords since we met her. I feel like she would have told you if . . . You know."

"You're probably right," Mim said. "But it still makes me want to kick her ass."

"Welcome to my world."

"I guess I just feel sorry for her."

"Me too," Cutter said. They passed another sign for Wall Drug. "We're close. Let's go over what we know about David Foye one last time."

"Right," Mim said. "He was a roustabout on the Slope, working on the same rig when Ethan was killed. He was injured but somehow escaped being one of the five fatalities, including Ethan. He quit his job for the drilling company right after the explosion and hightailed it to South Dakota the day he was released from the hospital." She turned to stare out the side window. "Do you think he was involved in Ethan's murder?"

"I think that's a possibility we have to consider," Cutter said. "I've seen more than one bomb maker with missing fingers. We know he was close enough to get injured, but somehow had enough foreknowledge or luck to be far enough away that he survived. That said, Ethan's phone records show three calls to Foye's cell. There's a chance he's who Ethan was coming to visit during his trips to South Dakota."

"For what though?" Mim said, half to herself, still staring out the window. "Ethan's South Dakota trips are a mystery to me."

"Foye knows something. He might not even know he knows it. People don't just pull up stakes and leave overnight without a reason. One way or another, maybe just tangentially, he's involved."

Mim gave a slow shake of her head. "I can't believe you still let me come on this trip with you. You're usually so overprotective."

"Would you have stayed home if I'd asked you to?"

"Oh, hell no."

"There you go, then," Cutter said. "We're meeting in a public place. That makes me slightly more comfortable with the whole deal. And it appears to be what David Foye wants as well."

Mim sat lost in her thoughts for a full ten minutes. Then, out of nowhere, "Don't you wonder what Constance said to me before we left?"

"Not especially," Cutter said.

"Liar." Mim laughed out loud.

He shrugged. "I've long since given up trying to decipher the secret ways of women."

"Anywaaay, I guess one of her girlfriends from church asked her, in all seriousness, mind you, if you and I were practicing a levirate marriage."

Cutter tapped the steering wheel with his thumbs and glanced sideways. "I don't even know what that means."

"I had to look it up," Mim said. "I guess levirate marriage is the Hebrew custom where the living brother marries his deceased brother's widow in order to . . . carry on his seed." She grimaced. "Constance used that word. It's no wonder she's a little freaked out thinking about stuff like that."

"What? Levirate marriage?"

"No," Mim said. "Seed. Anyway, after I looked it up, I pointed out that in our particular situation, since I already have children, I do not need your seed to carry on their dad's name."

"You do not need my seed . . ." Cutter mused, almost, but not quite, under his breath. He felt his face flush. "I'm sure she was thrilled with that conversation."

Mim chuckled. "It shut her up."

"Ethan and I knew Grumpy used to skip some verses when he'd read the Bible to us in the evenings."

"My mama would do the same thing," Mim said. "Pretty sure she skipped most of Deuteronomy and Leviticus. We read the Bible every night before bed when I was growing up, and I didn't even know "The Song of Solomon" was in there until after I met Ethan." She started to say something else but must have thought better of it and changed the subject. "Look! A prairie dog town."

"Yep." Cutter nodded to another road sign for Wall Drug. It was a relief to talk about something other than what the Good Book had to say about his responsibilities toward his brother's wife.

CHAPTER 30

Utqiagvik

JAN HOUGH NOTICED THE HITCH IN BUSH PILOT TONY'S VOICE AS
they flew through intermittent fog ten minutes out of Utqiagvik.
It could be difficult to tell with Tony, but his already jerky movements had grown much greater in scope than usual and the periodic self-validating grunts that came over the intercom throughout
most flights had devolved into something closer to strangled sobs.

They were in trouble. That much was as clear as the sweat
drenching the nape of Bush Pilot Tony's neck.

The single-engine Cessna 208 Caravan was on its way to Kaktovik, an Iñupiaq village three hundred miles to the east with
Tony in the driver's seat and Hough as the sole passenger. She'd
jumped on an already-scheduled cargo flight. Bush pilots would
often put the only passenger up front in the copilot seat. Hough
had no desire to see how the flying-sausage was made and declined the invitation, choosing instead to park her butt with the
cases of soft drinks and blue boxes of Sailor Boy Pilot Bread that
filled the cargo area.

Detectives had to be experts in triage and prioritization. New
cases came in every day. Time-sensitive investigations were often
sidetracked or even derailed because something new burned
brighter, requiring immediate attention. Hough had a million
other things to do, not the least of which was take a deep dive into

Leo Beck's background. The man was vile. This she knew. There was some connection to Ethan's murder. She just needed to connect the dots and find the evidence to prove it. But someone had called in a bomb threat to the Kaktovik school. The officer on the scene felt sure it was bogus. He even thought he knew who made the call, but Chief Strawbridge wanted a detective on the ground. Isaac Dundee, the officer on rotation in the village, was plenty capable. This was about appearances. Detectives were the "pros from Dover," people who knew more than the locals simply because they were . . . not from there. They were specialists who flew in when something big went down—or the chief wanted to show that the PD took some matter seriously.

Detective Jolivet was still buried in the paperwork on Dennis Foye and Lilian Egak. It was maddening, but Hough had hit pause on what she had going and hopped on Bush Pilot Tony's flight.

Now she was paying for it.

She leaned forward, straining against her seat belt to get some notion of why Tony was freaking out. He tapped a gauge on the console. The engine temperature was rising fast.

"We've got a problem," Tony grunted, probably to himself.

Hough unbuckled her belt and stumbled forward as Tony banked the aircraft one hundred and eighty degrees and began a steady climb.

"We're heading back to *Utqiagvik*?" Hough said. "What's happening?"

"Shut up and sit down, Jan," Tony shouted.

Gobsmacked by the kid's sudden shot of clarity, Hough complied.

Gaining altitude, Tony radioed Barrow Air Traffic Control and declared an emergency. Oddly, the worse things got, the more his actions calmed. Barrow ATC held all incoming aircraft. The runway ran almost due east and west, allowing Tony to line up straight in for his approach.

Two miles out, the oil line blew. Black gunk spewed from vents in the cowling. Prop wash threw it backward, covering the windscreen and completely obscuring any forward view. Seconds later, smoke began to pour from the engine. The controller gave him wind speed and direction—less than five knots on the nose—and cleared them to land. Hough pressed her cheek hard against the side window, struggling to catch some glimpse of where they were. With the runway ghosting in and out of view in the fog, Tony killed the engine, trying to avert a fire. He called ATC in the steady voice that sounded more like a seasoned disk jockey than a rattled Bush Pilot Tony and let them know he was on final— literally. He'd have only one chance at this, but he'd gained enough altitude from the moment he knew they were in danger that with a little bit of luck and skill, he just might be able to glide the Caravan straight in.

Hough checked her lap belt and settled back for a hard landing. Somehow, knowing that Tony Caprese had grown a pair brought a tremendous sense of comfort, no matter how this turned out.

CHAPTER 31

South Dakota

A QUICK DETOUR TO THE NORTH OF A LONELY STRETCH OF INTER-state 90, the tiny town of Wall turned out to be a virtual tourist mecca.

David Foye had agreed to meet them in one of the main thoroughfares between the interconnected warren of buildings and shops of the Wall Drug complex. He was supposed to be wearing a John Deere hat and holding a copy of *Farm Journal* magazine. Cutter had let him know he'd be wearing an Alaska Railroad ball-cap and a dark-blue shirt with a leaping marlin embroidered in white thread over his left breast pocket. Foye knew the meeting was with a "friend of Ethan Cutter," but Cutter still hadn't given his name or mentioned he was a deputy US marshal.

It was all like something out of a spy movie . . . in South Dakota.

The meeting wasn't scheduled for another hour, exactly as Cutter wanted. His grandfather's rule to "never go anywhere for the first time" meant doing a great deal of reconnaissance. Google Earth and hundreds of online photos gave Cutter the opportunity to study ingress and egress, choke points, dead ends, and so on before actually setting foot on the property. Getting the lay of the land was crucial, but only part of any battle plan. Getting there early allowed Cutter and Mim to have a look at the local clientele and check the general mood of the place. More important, it gave them a chance to sniff the air. Cutter had learned a long time ago that the "smell" or gut feeling he got when he first arrived at a protective advance or fugitive warrant service was usually on the money.

He made the block twice, windows down, watching, listening. RVs and pickup campers ruled the day. The streets were crawling with Q-Tips, a term Alaskans sometimes used for tourists—white haired on one end, gleaming white tennis shoes on the other. Evidently, everyone in South Dakota over the age of fifty had decided it was a good day to pay Wall Drug a visit. Often as not, the men wore black socks.

Cutter had to park the Corolla two blocks away from the hodgepodge of buildings that made up the store itself. His phone buzzed as he walked around to open Mim's door for her.

"Sorry," he said. "It's Jan Hough. I need to take this."

Mim waved away the apology.

"Arliss!" Hough said as soon as he picked up. "You need to watch your ass. I'm reasonably certain someone just tried to kill me."

She gave him a quick rundown of what had happened.

"The bomb threat was perfectly timed to make me jump on Tony's eastbound cargo run to Kaktovik on a sabotaged airplane. The mechanic says there's no doubt someone monkeyed with the oil line before we took off. And get this," Hough added. "According to Chief Strawbridge, Leo Beck's wife, Inez, is the one who nudged him into sending a detective."

"You're okay, though?" Cutter asked.

"Just rattled," Hough said. "Honestly, I think the scare helped Caprese."

"Caprese?" Cutter was eyes-up as she spoke, scanning for danger. So far, he saw only Q-tips.

"Bush Pilot Tony," Hough said. "Nothing like coming out the other side of a near-death experience to give you the confidence for a check ride."

"Ah," Cutter said, only half listening. He couldn't decide if something was off or if he was being overly cautious because Mim was there.

"Arliss," Hough said. "We need to get this son of a bitch. Find us something we can use to put him away."

Cutter assured her he would and ended the call.

Eager to get to their meeting with David Foye, Cutter gave Mim a quick rundown about the attempt on Hough's life as they walked.

"You want to check on the kids?" he asked.

"Yes, I do," she said. "But is there time?"

"We'll make time."

"There's nothing to connect me to where they're staying unless someone knows who my church friends are," she said, obviously trying to calm herself. "I'd imagine they're okay, but I'll call while we're walking."

"I'll ask Lola to reach out to her APD contacts and request extra patrols . . ."

They passed a tall camper on a long-bed pickup, bringing two men in leather vests and cowboy hats into view less than fifteen feet away. The men loafed along the curb outside the main entrance to Wall Drug as if guarding a vacant parking spot. A black GMC dually pickup and a white-over-candy-apple-red 1958 Ford Ranchero flanked the empty spot, each parked a couple of feet over the yellow line. The men had been looking up the street like they were expecting someone as Cutter and Mim came around the camper. Both looked away. Cutter's hackles went up. Conspicuous ignoring was as bad as staring at giving away one's intentions.

The larger of the duo was every bit of six four, towering even taller in a black felt hat. He had at least fifty pounds on Cutter, much of that in his arms. A gold rodeo belt buckle caught the sunlight. He appeared to stare at his own boots while he chewed on a toothpick. His partner, leaning against the Ranchero's rear fender, was no small fry, either, maybe six feet tall—an inch or two shorter than Cutter. This one had divided his graying beard into two long braids, held in place by small metal sleeves that glinted in the bright sunlight.

Cutter slowed and touched Mim's arm to get her attention.

"I see 'em," she whispered. "Are you looking at the Viking cowboy or that sweet Ford Ranchero?"

Cutter forced a smile. "Both," he said. As much as he craved her company, bringing Mim had been a horrible idea, an added layer of something to worry about during a fight.

He shot a quick glance over his shoulder. An ambush worked better if it cut off avenues of escape. Sure enough, a third man lurked at the corner behind them. This one was just a kid, early twenties, if that. Tight, impress-the-buckle-bunny Wranglers and a feedstore ballcap rounded out his pearl snap shirt. The Kid didn't look away, instead zeroing in on Cutter like he was about to rush him.

"I count three," Mim said from the corner of her mouth.

"That we can see," Cutter said. "The kid behind us is likely to have a friend hanging around out of sight. A pack of three very well could mean a pack of five . . . Stay beside me. We'll use the crowds to our advantage."

Mim walked on his left, keeping his gun-hand free.

Fork Beard rocked forward, using his hips to push away from the Ford Ranchero and then hitched up his belt to turn and face Cutter.

The ignoring part of this dance was over.

Cutter was far more comfortable when he led.

"What can I do for you?"

Fork Beard stopped in his tracks, hitching his belt up again to bleed off nervous energy. Black Hat stepped off the curb, fanning way from his partner. Closest, he puffed up his chest and peered out from beneath the hat, surely hoping to intimidate with his sheer bulk.

This was odd. If they'd been professionals, they would have killed him without all the fuss. But then, maybe they weren't professionals.

Cutter nodded sideways toward Mim. "You're scaring my friend," he said.

The men remained locked on to him.

Cutter felt her move. "That kid is coming up behind us," she said. "Thirty feet and closing."

Buoyed by their advancing friend, the two cowboys in front closed on Cutter, slowly, without saying a word. Their intimidation tactics were obvious enough that a handful of tourists began to gather along the sidewalk to see what was going on.

From a distance, it looked as if they were about to have an old-West gunfight.

Fork Beard moved first, waltzing in with what he surely thought was going to be a posturing shove. Done with dancing, Cutter snapped two lightning jabs into the man's unprotected nose. Rattled, the big guy collapsed flat on his rump, legs splayed out in front of him.

One down, Cutter shot a glance at Mim.

"Run!"

Black Hat roared in, swinging. His blows were clumsy and un-aimed, but deadly from sheer momentum. His imposing stature likely kept him out of many actual fights. Cutter took a sloppy haymaker on the shoulder but was able to mete out a snappy left-right combination. He just followed with a wicked left hook to Black Hat's liver when Mim screamed and something heavy slammed into him from behind.

The kid.

Cutter sidestepped, throwing his right elbow backward in an attempt to catch the kid in the face. It connected but was a glancing blow that staggered the kid but didn't knock him down. In the meantime, Black Hat, on one knee from the rattled liver, was in the process of pushing himself up. Fork Beard had recovered and now moved in.

Mim did the exact opposite of what Cutter had wanted her to do. She joined the fight, screaming with rage as she leaped onto Fork Beard's back, clawing at his ears and knocking his hat to the ground. The man yowled in pain and surprise, throwing himself against the door of the Ranchero again and again to try and scrape off this wild woman.

The Kid and Black Hat finally got their acts together and swarmed Cutter at the same moment Mim gave a muffled cry, mashed against the Ford.

The effect of her voice on Cutter was instantaneous.

Black Hat threw another sloppy punch. Cutter let it slip by, snap-kicking the man in the groin as his momentum carried him through the punch. At the same time, the Kid batted at the back of Cutter's head. If he'd known how to fight, it would have been devastating. With Black Hat stutter-stepping headfirst into the side of the dually pickup, Cutter spun quickly and slapped the Kid across the ear with an open hand. He followed with three quick cross-elbow slams, smearing the kid's nose across his face.

Mim cried out again from somewhere behind him.

Pushing away so he had all three men in sight, Cutter swept the tail of his jacket and drew his Colt. He pointed it directly at Fork Beard's head.

"US Marshals!" He roared, all but rattling the windows. Blood poured from his nose. "Get on the ground! Now!"

Fork Beard leaned away from the Ranchero and raised his hands in surrender. He shot a glance at Mim, who had slid to the pavement beside the Ford, wheezing, struggling to catch her breath from two hundred pounds of cowboy crushing her against the steel door.

"Do not move!" Cutter snapped. "I will end you right here!"

"Hey, hey, now," Fork Beard said. "I didn't know you was a marshal."

Mim rubbed a smudge of grime off her chin. "I'd say that's obvious."

Both the Kid and Black Hat stood rooted in place, their eyes glazed in confusion. "He's telling the truth," Black Hat said. "We thought Beck sent you."

"Wait," Mim said. "You don't work for Leo Beck?"

"That guy?" Fork Beard said. "Hell no." He eyed Cutter. "You mind showing me your badge?"

Cutter lifted the tail of his jacket to display the silver circle star badge clipped in front of his holster.

Black Hat took a deep breath. "What's your name?"

"Cutter."

A smile spread over Fork Beard's face, even though he had a Colt Python pointed at his head.

"You're Ethan's brother."

"I am."

"Well, sir, I wish you would have said that from the get-go." Fork Beard kept one hand raised but rubbed his jaw with the other. "You'd have saved us all a hell of a lot of heartache. I think my eardrum is busted, and I'm fairly certain you broke Junior's nose. Listen, we never intended to hurt the missus."

"That's good," Cutter said. "Because if you had, you wouldn't be standing right now."

"I believe you, Marshal Cutter," Fork Beard said. "Now, if you'll let us put our hands down and show us some actual ID, we'll get you in touch with the man you came to meet in the first place."

Cutter tentatively holstered his revolver.

On the sidewalk, the crowd of onlookers began to clap, thinking they'd just seen an extremely realistic street performance.

Black Hat rubbed the side of his neck, wincing at a spot beneath his ear.

"Hot damn, Marshal, you fight like you're stomping out a grass fire and the whole country is depending on you to end it."

CHAPTER 32

FORK BEARD'S NAME TURNED OUT TO BE BLAINE PETERSON. According to him, he'd grown up cowboying with the Foye brothers. He'd never cared much for Denny, but David was his closest friend. Most of what was going on was a mystery to him. He just knew that a couple of people were on their way to bother his friend, and they needed a little discouragement. After a short discussion with David on the phone, Peterson drew Cutter a map and apologized for the misunderstanding.

Cutter gave a grunting nod. He wanted to touch his own ear but didn't want to let these guys know how bad they'd thumped him.

"His ranch is near Bad River," Mim said after she'd buckled into the passenger seat and compared the hand-drawn map with the one on her phone. "Looks like it's north of I-90 on a hundred miles of two-lane and grassland."

Cutter bristled when he noticed a trickle of blood from a scrape on the apple of her cheek. He reached halfway across the middle console as if to wipe it away with his thumb but stopped short, gesturing instead.

"One of those assholes must have scratched you—"

She shrugged it off. "I'm fine," she said. "And they're not assholes. You can't tell me you've never gotten physical trying to protect a friend."

"Mim, I—"

"I know you think it was stupid of me to come." She set her jaw, eyes ablaze. "Arliss, you have got to let me share the weight." She sat there looking at him for a long moment, breathing hard but saying nothing.

She was here, and there was no changing that now.

He spent the two-hour drive to David Foye's ranch in silence, with little to break the monotony but cattle, grass fields, and the occasional swooping hawk. Mim looked out the window, lost in her own thoughts.

A bent man in a battered gray felt cowboy hat met them at the gate. His skin was weathered and brown but for the pink burn scars on his hands and one side of his neck. David Foye. He'd been on the drilling rig when it exploded and killed Ethan. He wore faded jeans and a light pearl snap shirt with long sleeves, the tail of which was half untucked, partially covering the butt of a Glock pistol. A red bandana hung from his left front pocket. He opened the gate and waved them onto the dirt lane inside a five-strand barbed-wire fence, where a red Honda ATV idled under a bright-orange wind sock.

Foye closed and locked the gate and jumped on the ATV, leading the way toward a white farmhouse that sat between two rows of cottonwood trees on a low rise to the north. Apparently, they would wait for introductions until they got to the house—well away from the road.

Cutter counted ten lone thousand-pound round bales of bromegrass hay, evenly spaced between the gate and the house. Fifty yards between each bale, five hundred and fifty yards.

"Weird," Mim said. "How he's got this hay out here but no cattle."

"I'd imagine he's got cattle somewhere," Cutter said. "He's using these round bails as distance markers. The sock at the gate gives him the crosswind if he needs to pick off uninvited visitors with a long-distance shot."

Mim looked out her window and shuddered. "I guess he has a right to be paranoid," she said. "Considering what just happened to his brother."

A small rectangular metal sign on the chain-link fence behind the farmhouse read BAD RIVER LAND AND CATTLE. Cutter assumed it had once hung beside the main gate, but Foye had moved it when he went into hiding.

The old cowboy saw Cutter looking at the sign and, as if reading his mind, said, "No sense in advertising where I'm at." He extended his hand. "David Foye, sorry about the misunderstanding."

Though stooped and spent, Foye's iron grip was exactly what Cutter would have expected from a man who'd made his living as a cowboy and oil-patch roughneck. He wasn't trying to be macho. He just didn't appear to know any other way to shake hands.

He took his hat off when he greeted Mim, and his face twitched a little when she told him who she was.

"I . . . you're . . ." He took a deep breath and waved them through the back door, giving Mim a polite nod. "Ma'am."

After a lifetime of looking for defendable positions, Cutter couldn't help but notice the field behind the house had round bales of hay spaced similarly to the front for marking distance.

Foye led them through a mud room that smelled like wet earth and home-cured bacon, then through a second doorway into a rustic kitchen. Mim caught Cutter's eye and then nodded to a simple wooden table covered with various rocks and fossils, sorted carefully into types. Oreodont teeth were the most prevalent, many of them imbedded in fossilized bone, two of which were almost complete oreodont skulls.

Foye hung his sweat-stained hat on a set of long horns beside the back door and then turned to catch them studying the fossils. "I've been finding those 'mountain-tooth' specimens on the ranch since I was a kid," he said. "I guess they're mostly out in the badlands, but we got some hoodoo formations on the ranch where you can dig up all kinds of old bones. I figure this place must have been crawling with the little beggars up until five or six million years ago." He patted the sheath knife on his belt. "I found a big piece of fossilized mammoth tooth kicking around between jobs on the Slope several years ago. Made a deal with Ethan to get us a couple of knives made with the mammoth and oreodont handles at that shop in Anchorage."

"Northern Knives," Cutter said.

"That's right," Foye said. "One for me and one for him. I don't know for sure, but I think his might have gotten lost when the rig blew."

"No," Mim said from behind a wan smile. "We still have it." She nodded to Cutter. "Ethan's brother carries it now."

"Good to hear," Foye whispered. He pulled the latch handle on a rounded avocado-colored fridge that was at least fifty years old. "Can I get you something to drink? I have water, iced tea . . . and water. If you want something hot, I have Caf-Lib that I get from Canada. Kind of a chicory root concoction. Coffee gives me the jumps . . . And this mess has me unsteady enough at the moment . . ."

Light from the open refrigerator illuminated the burns on the side of his face as he looked up at his guests and waited.

"Iced tea is fine," Mim said.

Cutter raised an open hand. "Nothing for me."

Foye poured Mim a Mason jar of iced tea and handed it to her. "I feel like I should offer Ethan's widow and brother some cake or something," he said. "But to be honest, most times I forget to eat at all, let alone think about sweets. This house hasn't seen a cake in years."

Judging from the coat of dust on the sparse furniture and the general state of disrepair, the house hadn't seen visitors in years, either.

"We're fine," Mim said. "I am exhausted though. Would you mind if we sat down?"

Foye moved a pile of magazines and a basket of dirty laundry off the couch and waved at them to sit. He moved aside to stand with his back to a blackened hearth. A sepia-tone photo of a long-dead relative hung in an oval wooden frame over the mantel. A scoped Winchester bolt-action rifle leaned against the corner wall, next to one of two living room windows. Cutter guessed the rifle to be a .300 Win Mag, judging from the magnum length of the action. He had one just like it. It was perfectly capable of reaching the five hundred and fifty yards to the gate and much farther if the need arose.

"I'm so sorry for your loss," Foye said. "Both of you." His chin quivered, surely near tears. Scarified hands flitted from pocket to belt buckle and back again like birds trying to find a safe place to roost.

"Thank you," Mim said.

"You've lost a brother as well," Cutter said.

"Yup," Foye said. "Sad day . . . but one I knew would eventually come. I expect he did too in the moments when he was honest with himself." He realized Mim was looking at his trembling hands, and he shoved them in the pockets of his Wranglers.

"Listen . . ." He shook his head slowly as he stared out the living room window next to the Winchester. "Would you mind terribly if we went for a short ride?"

Cutter looked at Mim and shrugged. "We can take our rental," he said.

There was no way he was getting in a vehicle with someone he'd just met who appeared to be teetering on the edge of a breakdown.

"I don't mean a country drive," Foye said. "I'm talking about a ride. Horseback. Some folks have emotional support dogs. I have quarter horses. I took the liberty of saddling a couple after Blaine called and told me who you really were."

Foye saw Cutter eyeing the holstered pistol on his waist and raised his hands. "I'll leave the Glock on my kitchen table, so you don't have to worry I'm going to shoot you in the back or something."

"No disrespect intended," Cutter said. "But judging from your setup, you don't seem like a man who wants to be too far from his sidearm."

Foye gave a sad chuckle. "I've got a .45-70 Henry in my saddle scabbard. Not as quick to get to—which should ease your mind some—but it'll do if we get in a pinch and I need a rifle." He nodded at Mim. "How about she hangs on to my pistol?"

Foye waited for a nod from Cutter before he unbuckled his belt and slid the holstered weapon off. "To be honest with you," he said to Mim, "after I get done telling you what I'm about to tell you, I wouldn't blame you if you just shot me in the brainpan with this."

CHAPTER 33

*I*T HAD BEEN YEARS SINCE CUTTER SET FOOT IN A HORSE BARN, MUCH less been on the back of a horse. He paused in the open alley and took a moment to breathe in the smells of hay and horse dander and manure. He and Ethan had both ridden quite a bit when they were younger, always on neighbors' horses that Grumpy had arranged. It was all part of the old man's master plan to make sure the boys were Renaissance men. Later, when Cutter had gotten older, he had often talked about getting a horse of his own, but the time and travel demands of man hunting always seemed to bump that notion aside. Still, he firmly believed in the axiom that "the best thing for the inside of a man was the outside of a horse."

David Foye's sun-bleached barn had seen exponentially more care than his house. The tack was clean and oiled, and the three horses hitched to a rail under a second-floor hayloft were well-groomed and in excellent flesh.

"How'd you know we'd be up for a ride?" Mim asked.

"I wasn't sure," Foye said. "But Ethan loved to ride, so I figured what the hell . . . Anyhow, that sorrel there is the one he used to ride. I adjusted the stirrups, of course."

Mim gave a slight nod, momentarily unable to speak.

"Mine's the big meathead on the end." He walked to a thick blood bay tied farthest from the door. He grabbed the saddle horn and speared the oxbow stirrup with the toe of his boot to swing the opposite leg over the animal's back. Every horse was tacked with a mild snaffle bit and a decent saddle, but there was no doubt that Foye's buckaroo rig with dally-wrapped horn, slick forks, and high cantle was the property of a working cowboy. Foye took the leather reins in his left hand. "The gelding on the end is for you, Marshal. Matt Dillon rode a buckskin, so it seemed fitting."

Cutter stepped forward to see if Mim needed any help to mount. As he suspected, she climbed up on her own.

Five minutes later they were settled into their saddles and riding north at a ground-eating walk across a wide-open pasture. They crested a small rise, and at least two hundred Black Angus cattle came into view. Cutter couldn't help but think how easy it would be to hide in a place like this. The terrain looked flat, but numerous cuts and draws looked like perfect ambush sites.

Foye rode in the lead, bent and crooked in the saddle. His left shoulder drooped considerably lower than his right. The nape of his neck and back of his head shone pink and hairless beneath the brim of his hat.

Mim took naturally to the saddle, shoulders back but loose, moving with the horse, hands low and quiet. The singular sight of her figure backlit against the open prairie forced Cutter to periodically look away if he wanted to keep his wits about him.

Mim clucked at her sorrel, urging it up beside Foye.

Foye rode on, sitting his horse like he'd been born a part of it. He looked to be aiming for a large hackberry tree on a low rise a quarter mile away. "You know that's all horseshit about Ethan and that lady cop, don't you?" He curled his lip like he'd just eaten something bitter. "A damned lie. Every last word of it. You listen to me, now. Ethan wasn't like that. Not at all. You likely knew this already, but there was this young Iñupiaq hunter from Wainwright who took him caribou hunting one winter way back when he was in college—before I ever knew him. The poor Native guy got into a bad patch of ice and went into the river. Froze to death, but Ethan promised before this Native guy died to look in on his family whenever he was in town." Foye nudged his hat back with a knuckle and turned to look at Mim. "And he kept his word too. Took 'em groceries, fixed shit that broke around their little house. Hell, he kicked the ball around with the boy so much

I'm pretty sure the kid thought Ethan was his daddy. People said ugly things about that too. I would never have known if his mom hadn't told me. As far as I know, Ethan never talked about why he was doing any of it. He just did it—and was still checking in on 'em until he died."

Cutter sniffed back a tear. That's exactly the way he remembered his brother.

Foye reined to a stop under the thick boughs of the lone hackberry tree, then turned his horse to face the sorrel and the buckskin. He put the low sun to Mim's left so no one had to look directly into it, then kicked a boot out of the stirrup and stretched his crooked leg before leaning across the saddle horn. "My granddad told me his father hung two horse thieves from this tree."

People often started conversations about serious matters with some innocuous factoid. Instead of speaking, Cutter looked at the ground. Horse tracks crisscrossed the thatched dirt.

He glanced up at Foye, then went back to studying tracks. "You come out here a lot?"

"It's a good thinking spot," Foye said. "High ground. I can see for over a mile in every direction. Plus, a hangin' tree seems like a good place to make a last stand."

"Let's hope it doesn't come to that," Mim said.

"No offense, ma'am," Foye said. "But I don't waste time on hope, not anymore . . ." Both hands on the saddle horn, he gestured at the ground with his chin. "I hot-shoe my horses," he said. "Build them from scratch out of bar stock. Most of these tracks are from horses that are cold shod, outfitted with generic preformed shoes."

"So these aren't yours?" Cutter said.

"Nope," Foye said. "Somebody . . . or, if I had to make a guess looking at the tracks, three somebodies have been up here watching me. I reckon it's not paranoid if someone really is out to kill you."

"Why though?" Mim asked, squirming in the saddle, clearly growing exasperated. The sun was sinking fast. "Why does someone want to kill you?"

"Oh, Ms. Cutter," Foye said, giving her a wan smile. "You'll want to kill me too after I tell you what I did."

Foye fell quiet for so long his horse gave a little start when he finally broke the silence.

"I'm sure you noticed that I got me some hellacious burns the
day the rig kicked."

"I did," Cutter said.

"They're all on my back," Foye said. "Looks like I was running
away, doesn't it?"

"You saw something?" Mim said.

Foye leaned down and scratched his horse on the side of its
neck. He gave a quiet nod, too choked up to speak. He swallowed
hard, then closed his eyes composing himself.

"My brother flat out warned me to call in sick that day," he said
at length. "I didn't put it all together until after, but Denny was up
to his ass in this mess." Foye looked forlornly at Mim. "Excuse my
French. Course, I blew it off and went in to work, anyway. There's
not a damned thing to do on the Slope if you're not on shift. Surprised me to see Ethan on the rig, but even then I still didn't snap
to what was going on."

Foye stopped to watch the setting sun for long enough that
Mim prodded. "Put what together?"

"Engineers don't normally spend their downtime hanging out
with roughnecks and roustabouts," Foye said. "But Ethan was just
sorta one of the guys. He'd play cards with us. Helped us out with
our taxes, that kind of thing. I heard he was making trips to South
Dakota, so I invited him out to the ranch to go pheasant hunting.
It wasn't until later that I learned he was poking around into shell
corporations he thought were being used to hide money embez-
zled from his company. South Dakota's banking laws aren't exactly the strictest in the world."

Cutter's horse shook its head to get rid of a bothersome fly, jingling the snaffle bit. "I didn't realize engineers spent much time
out on the rigs during the drilling process."

"They don't," Foye said. "Not usually, anyway. Somebody above
my pay grade reported an issue with the possum belly. That's the
metal box that takes in and slows down the drilling mud when it's
coming back up the flow line. This particular line and belly were
part of Ethan's design, so he came out to take a look and trouble-

shoot." Foye glanced up, looking at Mim and Cutter in turn. "You know what I mean when I say the well 'kicked'?"

Mim gave a tentative nod. "I think so. Fluid mud gets pumped down the drill hole with the pipe. If the downward pressure of the mud is less than the pressure of the gas or oil in the well, you can get a blowout. Is that the same thing as a kick?"

"That's right," Foye said. "I saw someone else at the rig that day too. A piece of shit named Karl Ditmar."

Mim sat up straighter at the mention of the name. Her eyes shifted to Cutter. "He's one of the guys who hassled me in Utqiagvik last June."

"That doesn't surprise me," Foye said. "I think that son of a bitch was a killer from the day he was born. I've lost count of the men he's put in the hospital. Peeled another roughneck's nose right off his face with a spanner wrench a couple of years ago. That one cost him his job, but he's like a cockroach. Just keeps showing up, mostly as a leg-breaker for hire now. He does work for a guy named Leonard Beck. I thought you might be friends of Beck's when you first called. Fact is, it could be him sitting on one of the horses that made the tracks we're standing over."

Cutter felt his face flush red. "Why would Karl Ditmar have been on the rig?"

"There's a couple of situations that can cause a blowout," Foye said. "One is when we pull the pipe too fast. Another is if the mud flow slows, and"—he gave Mim an approving nod—"like you said, the pressure of the mud becomes less than the gas and oil. Every one of us on that rig knew there was a shitload of pressure in this well. Hell, there's a big set of gauges right there that show the pressure coming off the strata we're drilling into and the mud that's supposed to be keeping it down. In order for that kick to occur, somebody had to disable the pressure differential alarm and then cut the flow on the mud. Nobody would be stupid enough to do that on purpose and then wait around for an accident to happen on the rig platform."

Cutter was getting the picture now. "You're saying Ditmar was on the rig but then left before it kicked?"

"That's why I'm burned on my back," Foye said. "I saw him

hauling ass and wanted to know what was going on. The guy's got a reputation. That's when I saw it . . ."

"What?" Mim asked. "The blowout?"

He shook his head.

"The oxygen bottle."

Cutter looked up. "There was an O_2 bottle on the platform?"

Mim's mouth fell open. "We get all kinds of warnings in nursing school about the dangers of Vaseline lip balm and patients using oxygen."

"That's right," Foye said. "Ditmar knew that well had oil and gas under a tremendous amount of pressure. I'm sure he's the one who caused the blowout and hid the O_2 bottle in the pipe stack next to the well . . . Probably turned the valve so it was spewing pure oxygen into the air." Foye choked back a sob. "I heard Ethan telling some story while he worked. It was loud on the rig, so he was practically screaming. Guys were laughing, working hard. I saw the oxygen bottle moments after I snapped to the fact that Ditmar was there. It all happened so fast I didn't have time to register how dangerous this was. Maybe I'm a subconscious coward, I don't know. Ethan was my friend. I should have warned him. Instead, I stepped off to confront Ditmar. I don't know if he had some kind of sparker or if the oil caught spontaneously when it hit the oxygen. Either way, the explosion blew me into the tundra, broke my back, my left leg, my jaw in two places, ripped my shoulder out of the socket, and shattered my ribs. I woke up in the hospital in Anchorage a week and a half later with my brother standing over the bed."

Cutter looked directly at Foye.

"The same brother who knew enough about the plot to warn you not to go in to work?"

"The very same," Foye said. "The one who still let the sabotage happen when I went in, anyway." He glanced up from under the brim of his hat. "You know what the first thing my beloved brother said to me when I came to? Not how you doin'? Can I get you a glass of water, Davey? Nope. The first words out of his mouth were 'Leo Beck will kill us both if you breathe a word about what you saw.'" Foye gave a resigned sigh. "So . . . I ran away and hid like a little bitch . . ."

"I don't understand," Mim said. "They blew up an entire oil rig just to kill Ethan?"

"That's exactly what they did," Foye said. "And my weak-willed brother had a hand in it."

"Who else?" Cutter said, his gut seething at finally putting names to the men behind his brother's death. "Who else was involved?"

"I have my suspicions," Foye said. "They're not enough to hold up in court."

Mim urged her horse forward, nose to nose with Foye's bay. "Who?"

"Ethan suspected someone with his company," Foye said. "He never gave a name. Fact is, he never mentioned Leo Beck. The only one I knew for sure was involved was Ditmar until my brother brought up Beck when I was in the hospital." He looked up, suddenly animated. "I'll tell you one thing. Denny didn't take his own life. Leo Beck either did it himself or had someone like Ditmar do it. I'm guessing there was an autopsy on his girlfriend?"

"Happening today," Cutter said.

"I can almost guarantee you'll find something with her body. Beck is behind this. I promise you. But he walls himself off so he never faces the consequences. He's smart enough not to leave any witnesses. And he's got a hell of a lot of influence on the Slope."

Cutter moved his jaw back and forth, vainly trying to get rid of the ache brought on by the recent fight—and years of clenching his teeth while he slept. "Leo Beck is just a man."

"Yeah," Foye said. "You obviously don't know him like I do. He's a force of nature. Quiet, never makes a fuss in the open. According to Denny, he has no qualms about throwing someone onto an ice flow. I've got no proof, but you can see it in his eyes. Pig eyes . . . Like one of them plastic dolls." Foye gave a cursory nod to the west. The last rays of the sun were turning the prairie grass orange. "We'd best get moving. I have trip wires and such, but I don't like being this far away from the house after it gets dark."

Foye turned his horse toward the barn. Cutter and Mim rode up on either side so they rode three abreast.

"I need you to think hard," Cutter said. "Who with JBM is involved in this?"

"No idea." Foye lifted his reins, bringing his horse to a halt. He turned and looked directly at Cutter, his exhausted face grim, eyes rheumy with fatigue. "But I'll tell you this. Whoever it is, they're either already dead or scared shitless that Beck is coming for them. Only reason I've lived as long as I have is because of my brother. I don't know what Denny did to piss Beck off, but now he's not even around to protect me."

Cutter didn't say it, but he knew exactly what had happened. He and Jan Hough had visited the office and stirred up a hornets' nest.

Leo Beck was cleaning house.

CHAPTER 34

*T*HE SUN HAD LONG SET BY THE TIME CUTTER GAVE DAVID FOYE back his Glock, then drove past his yardage markers and out the front gate.

Cutter glanced sideways at Mim in the reflection of the dashboard lights in a vain attempt to gauge her mood while he drove. The sky was a deep purple-blue. With only the brightest stars yet visible. His favorite time of night.

"So," he said, "given this new information from Foye, what's our thinking about Coop Daniels now?"

Mim raised a wary brow like she might get angry. It was dangerous to bring up a man who'd shown interest in her after Ethan's death—and Cutter knew it. She held her breath for what seemed like an eternity, then released it all at once.

"When you hear hoofbeats," she whispered, "think horses, not zebras."

Cutter shot her a quizzical look but said nothing.

"It's a nurse thing," she continued. "Like Occam's razor. The most likely answer is usually the correct answer. Coop Daniels did contract work for JBM Engineering. We know he made trips to South Dakota. The most likely answer at this point is that he is up to his eyeballs in this. I'm just not sure how."

"And he lied to you," Cutter said. "Or, even in the kindest terms, he withheld information—which I would call a lie."

"So would Ethan," Mim said.

"Well," Cutter said, "whatever you call it, he's got questions to answer. We're going to have a talk."

"Not without me, you're not. I need to be there when you talk. Arliss, you have to promise me."

Cutter nodded. "Of course. I'm sure you have questions of your own."

"There's that," Mim said, "and I don't want you to beat him to death with a ball bat."

"Now see," Cutter said. "I don't get it. Why does everybody always go straight to that?"

Arliss," Mim scoffed, "I have heard you literally say the words, 'I'm going to beat that guy to death with a ball bat.'"

"As one does," Cutter mumbled. He didn't do sheepish for most people, but Mim wasn't most people. "Seriously though, I say a lot of shit."

Mim scoffed. "Oh yeah, millions of words just spill right out of you."

"Okay," he conceded. "Maybe I'm not a brilliant conversationalist, but I think I keep my cool better than I get credit for."

"When it comes to yourself, you are fine," Mim said. "I think someone could spit in your face, and you'd stay cool as a cucumber. You wouldn't stand for it, but it wouldn't spin you up." She gave an exaggerated shiver. "But Lord have mercy, some bully so much as looks cross-eyed at me or any other person under your very broad umbrella of protection and woe be unto his mortal soul. You are lightning quick to take offense on behalf of someone else."

"Nope," Cutter said. "It's not about *taking* offense. It's about *seeing* offense and then doing something about it."

Mim appeared to chew on that for a time, then said, "I've been around you too long because that sort of makes sense."

"Yep," Cutter said.

Two more minutes of silence, then Mim asked, "Do you think we're in danger?" Cutter started to answer, but she cut him off. "It occurs to me that you are the absolute wrong person to ask. You always think we're in danger."

Cutter rubbed his jaw. "The bruises on my face believe we are."

"I guess I do too." Mim scrolled through her phone. "I mean, Foye's brother and his girlfriend dead in Utqiagvik . . . and you said someone sabotaged Jan's plane . . . The kids are staying at friends but . . . I can get us on a five-a.m. flight to Seattle out of Sioux Falls. We can be back in Anchorage by eleven thirty."

Cutter looked at his watch. He'd lost track of what day it was. "They'll be in school until . . ."

"Two forty-five."

"Okay," Cutter said. "Sioux Falls it is. We'll head east when we reach I-90 instead of west. It's—"

She finished his sentence. "Four hours away . . ." She held up the phone. "We're booked."

"Okay then, I have to run to the office as soon as we get in and take care of time sheets so my guys can get paid. We'll pick up the kids from school, get y'all someplace safe—"

"Get *them* someplace safe," Mim said. "I'm not hiding anymore."

Cutter stifled a groan. "Get *them* someplace safe," he said. "Then, I'm taking annual leave until we finish this thing."

Mim gave a groaning stretch. "We have all kinds of time before the flight," she said. "How about we get a late dinner someplace in Sioux Falls and you can tell me your plan."

"*My* plan?"

"You know what I mean. How do we intend to get Leo Beck?"

"Working on it," Cutter said.

Mim shrugged. "That's even better. We can hash out a plan together while we eat." She yawned, then leaned forward to look up through the windshield at the stars.

"You know, Alaska has a lot going for it, but it's nice to be somewhere that the nights are warm at the same time they're dark . . . To hear Ethan tell it, he wanted to move north from the time he was a kid."

"Yep," Cutter said. "He read me a Farley Mowat book about two boys surviving in the Canadian Barrens. I was eight, so he would have been around ten. He found a piece of cottonwood tree and carved a pair of Inuit snow goggles even though neither of us had ever seen so much as a flake of snow up to that point."

"I remember Florida getting snow a couple of times."

"And it was a big deal, especially for Ethan. We got maybe an inch in eighty-nine, I think, not too long after he carved the Inuit goggles. Grumpy was already out on patrol, and we wanted to try and build a snowman before the sun melted everything. My feet had gotten too big for my rubber boots, so Ethan gave me his and put plastic Wonder Bread bags over his tennis shoes. That way we both got to play in the snow."

"You just had a bunch of Wonder Bread bags on hand?"

"Oh yeah," Cutter said, remembering. "Grumpy wouldn't stand for throwing out something after just one or two uses. I remember a lot of good talks while we were darning socks on the couch, watching episodes of *Quantum Leap.*"

"Darning socks . . . Grumpy did make you Renaissance men." Mim gave a soft smile, nodding slowly as if keeping beat to a song in her head. "I'm going to be quiet for a few minutes," she said. "I need some time to process."

"You don't need to explain yourself to me."

"I just didn't want you to get the wrong idea," she said. "You know, to think it was a judgy silence."

Cutter grinned and did his best Lola Teariki impression—which wasn't very good. "No worries."

A half-moon turned the two lane into a silver-gray thread running between dark fields toward I-90 to the south. Periodically, farmhouse lights twinkled from behind pickets of tall cottonwood trees planted to break the prairie winds.

Mim's breathing grew deep and rhythmic, and for a time, Cutter thought she'd drifted off to sleep.

She had not.

He gripped the wheel tighter when she suddenly broke the silence.

"Pull over," she said.

"You need to . . . ?"

"No," she said. "I went while you were helping Foye put away the saddles. I just want you to pull over for a minute."

It was late, and the country roads were deserted, so Cutter found a likely spot on the grassy shoulder and rolled to a stop.

"Go ahead and kill the engine," she said.

Cutter complied, boggled as to where this was going.

Mim got out and shut the door behind her, quietly, like she was in church.

Unsure of what to do, Cutter stayed put, thinking maybe she needed a moment alone.

When he didn't get out, she pounded on the passenger window with the flat of her hand. She said something, but he couldn't hear it through the glass.

He opened his door and joined her at the back of the car, where she was leaning against the trunk.

"What can I do for you?"

"Look above us," she said. "We have plenty of time, and I don't want to miss this."

Cutter took a deep breath, noting the heat of the day rising on the dusty smell of prairie grass. Beside him, Mim shivered despite the warmth. Her eyes shown incredibly bright in the moonlight.

She stole a quick glance his way. "You don't mind stopping, do you?"

"Do I mind if you want to stop and look at the stars with me?" Cutter said, deadpan. "That is hilarious, Mim."

"The boys were just getting old enough for Ethan to teach them about the constellations," she said.

"He was always better at that than I am," Cutter said.

"Nice of you to say so," Mim said. "But I doubt that. Ethan was a wonderful husband and father, but he would be the first to admit that you're the better woodsman and sailor."

Uncomfortable with compliments, Cutter changed the subject, gesturing toward the horizon with his chin. "I've worked on astronomy some with them, but their attention spans for this sort of thing is inversely proportional to how cold it is outside."

"True," Mim said, distant, as if her thoughts were light-years away. Then, back to earth, she leaned in, almost, but not quite, nestled in the pocket of his shoulder. She pointed skyward. "What's that one?"

"The one that looks like a W?" Cutter let his head fall sideways, closer to Mim. "Cassiopeia."

"Right." She continued to gaze up at the blanket of infinite stars. "Arliss Cutter, I need to know your intentions."

He concentrated on his breathing, forcing himself to relax. "My intentions?"

She turned ever so slightly, facing him. Her hair fell across her chin. He was already looking at her. From his vantage point she was far preferable to any old star in the night sky.

"What I mean is," she said, "do you intend to pursue something . . . more serious?"

He gave a tight chuckle. "I'm not sure if I should answer that."

"Really?" she said. "Because I was under the impression that under your rules, withholding crucial information would be a lie."

"I . . ."

"Let me put it in simpler terms," Mim said. "As my grannie would say, are you going to court me?"

"Yep," Cutter said, popping the P. "That is, if you approve of being courted."

Eyes locked on the stars, she was silent for a time, then said, "I do approve. But we'll need to take it slow."

"Yep," Cutter said again. "I am a patient man."

"Maybe," she said. "In some ways you appear to have the patience of Job. Other times . . . you're just so . . . so full of rage."

"I guess I can't argue with that," he said.

She heaved a deep sigh, shuddering a little in the darkness. "We're what? About three hours from Sioux Falls?"

"About that," Cutter said. "We should be back on I-90 in a half hour or so."

"That works," she said. "So, here's the way I see it, Arliss. There are two ghosts standing between you and me. Ethan's . . . and whatever it is that filled you with so much anger. I'm working on the first one, the other—"

"Afghanistan," he said. "You already know most of it."

Her head snapped up to face him. "Arliss, I'm sorry—"

She'd done some digging, meaning well. His old Army Ranger buddy, Dr. Dave Carnahan, also meaning well, had spilled the beans."

"It's okay," he said. "Carnahan and I have walked barefoot over broken glass together. We're kind of like each other's AA sponsors. Sometimes we go a year without talking, then we'll call one another two or three times a month. Your call spurred him to check in on me."

"I'm so sorry I didn't tell you."

"I didn't ask," Cutter said.

"Still," she whispered, "I know how you are about that strict Grumpy Man-Rule. Keeping a secret is tantamount to a lie in your book."

Cutter gave a little shrug. "Some lies are okay."

"We'll dig a little deeper into that philosophy some other time," she said. "But I am sorry I went behind your back."

"I'm not," Cutter said. "I mean, I might have been a little grouchy when Carnahan first told me, but it just proves you care."

"Do you ever think you'd be able to tell me what happened? From your point of view."

"I could," Cutter said. "But as you know, it's pretty ugly."

"Arliss, I'm a nurse," Mim said. "I can do ugly."

"Suit yourself," Cutter said.

"We've got a three-hour drive ahead of us." She held out an open hand. "Keys, please. I'll drive."

Cutter adjusted his seat and buckled himself in, one hand on each knee, bracing himself for the story.

Behind the wheel, Mim did her "preflight"—seat, steering wheel, mirrors, then located the high beams. Thirty seconds later, they were back on the road.

Cutter took a deep breath, but before he could speak, Mim reached across the console and took his hand in hers. He thought she might give him a reassuring pat. Instead, she let her hand linger. Her peaches-and-cream cheeks glowed in the faint red glow of the dash. She turned to him, smiled, and gave his hand a squeeze, playing her thumb gently back and forth across his knuckles. All his angst crumbled away at the touch of her skin. Slowly, he built up the courage to speak, and words began to spill out of him into the dark car.

CHAPTER 35

MIM WONDERED IF SHE'D BEEN TOO FORWARD. MAYBE SO, SHE thought, but she was over forty—too old to dance around something this important. Arliss stared out the window for a time. Probably . . . hopefully . . . gathering his thoughts.

He was a man of few words in the first place, and now she'd put him on the spot and asked him to tell her about what must have been the most traumatic experience of his life.

She jumped in surprise when he did finally speak.

"I could give you a whole list of excuses and color commentary, but you got most of that from Dave Carnahan, my good buddy who can't keep a secret. Anyway, none of that really matters. The long and short of it is this—My men and I were sent to do a job and we . . . I . . . put that job over the life of a child. I will never, ever, do that again."

Mim said nothing for a time, then, softly, barely above a whisper, said, "Arliss, tell me the whole story. Please. I think it would be good for you."

He took a deep breath and let it out slowly.

"Do you know much about Afghanistan?"

"A little," she said. "I have to admit I read up on it because I knew you were there."

He gave her a rare smile, but it vanished as quickly as it came. He took a deep breath and then looked out the window again.

"There's a province called Nangarhar in the eastern part of the country on the border with Pakistan. It's a spectacular place—rivers, terraced fields, beautiful crops. Not what most people picture when they think about Afghanistan. It was also one of the deadliest provinces in the country. Most of us called it 'the heart of darkness.' We lost way too many good people there."

He shook his head as if to push away a thought and then leaned back in his seat to stare up at the roof.

"Anyway, my guys and I were tasked north of Jalalabad up the Kunar River valley to snatch this mullah who had information on an HVT . . . sorry, a high-value target responsible for killing a lot of American soldiers. We'd been hunting him for months. Our job was to lie in wait by this little bridge and snatch the mullah when he crossed the river with his entourage. We slipped in quietly since every other person in the valley likely wanted to kill us, or at the very least, turn us over to someone who did. We got there early, the middle of the night really . . ."

He choked back a sob, moved his jaw back and forth. The idea of Arliss Cutter crying broke Mim's heart.

"And then there was this little Afghan girl," he whispered. "Nine or ten years old—about the twins' age. She's up with the sun, skipping down the road from the east about forty yards below where we were hiding, singing her little heart out on the way to get water. One of the guys, I think it was Carnahan, started calling her Sunny over the radio, because of how cheery she acted smack in the middle of a country that was being ripped apart by war.

"Then three Chechens drove up in advance of the mullah's convoy, scouting the route. They reached this stone well about the same time as the little girl. So, we're all hidden, watching this go down . . . forty meters away. Close enough their leader's bad teeth fill my optic. The sneers on the Chechens' windburned faces, the dust in their beards—and the abject terror in that little girl's innocent eyes . . . green, like moss agate. She knew she was in trouble the moment these monsters drove up. They started hassling her right away, tossing her back and forth like a ball, and then . . . I'm zoomed in on Red Beard's ear. Finger on the trigger.

If I intervene, the Chechens fall out of communication with their convoy and our target gets spooked. My choice was simple. I save the mission, or I save that little girl."

Mim couldn't help but notice how the story had been about the team up until that point. *Their job, their tactics*—but now it was *his* choice and his alone.

"I considered taking them out," Arliss said. "It would have been easy to pop them all. But I didn't know if they had to give a final all-clear before the mullah approached . . ." He gave a slow shake of his head. Tears ran freely down his cheeks. "Mim, I ordered my men to stand by while that poor child was brutalized and murdered . . . all for the sake of a mission."

He rubbed a hand across his face, sniffed back his tears, then fell silent.

"Arliss," she said. "According to Carnahan, that mullah had information that would save hundreds of American lives."

"That's the intel command gave us," Cutter said. "But we got the guy, and he had nothing. Not. One. Damn. Thing.

"Carnahan told me how you gave the order for the men not to move so they would be spared the burden of making that decision themselves."

"I wish I hadn't," Arliss said. "Then one of them, hell, all of them might have done the right thing and blown those pieces of shit to hell where they belonged. Instead, we let them do what they did and then slip into the village to make sure it was safe for the mullah."

Mim shook her head but said nothing. It wasn't her place to argue with him.

"The point is," Arliss said, "a child suffered and died because I did not act. I won't ever be able to make that right, but I decided that day, that very minute, I will not let something like that happen in front of me again. If some shithead needs stomping, I'm going to stomp him. Right then. Get it over with. I don't care if he's the guy that signs my paychecks."

"That's got to be hard," she said. "Things are rarely so black and white."

"But they are," Cutter said. "It's surprisingly clear. I draw a bright line—and bright lines are easiest to see. I don't even have to think about it."

"I meant facing the consequences," she said. "That must be difficult."

"There are no consequences worse than what happened to that child in the Kunar valley. None. People think I'm always angry. I'm not. I'm just determined."

Mim waited for him to say more, but he didn't, seemingly content to keep holding her hand and stare out the window. Carnahan had told her about the aftermath. How Arliss and his team had taken Sunny's body to her father. That part of the story took on new gravity when she realized how dangerous it had been for seven US Army Rangers to go into a Pashtun village alone—a village that had been ready to receive the mullah these men had just abducted. But, like Arliss said, the decision had already been made. He and his men hadn't cared how dangerous it was, they were going to take the little girl's body back to her family—and find, fix, and finish the Chechens who'd brutalized her.

"Thank you, Arliss," she said at length.

He nodded, still looking out the window, his shoulders racked with periodic sobs.

She gave his hand a squeeze, sniffing back tears of her own.

CHAPTER 36

Anchorage

CHIEF PHILLIPS PULLED SOME STRINGS WITH THE PATROL CAPTAIN
at Anchorage PD and, with the promise of a halibut fishing trip
on her husband's twenty-seven-foot Hewescraft, got Joe Bill Brackett temporarily assigned to the Alaska Fugitive Task Force. Joe Bill
had been involved in the hunt for Eddie Dupree from the beginning, so it was an easy argument that it would be in the taxpayers'
interest if he kept that momentum going.

Lola and Nancy had worked several likely spots but got no
bites. Tonight, they were back at it again, trying their luck in front
of the downtown bus transit station on Sixth Avenue. Anchorage
was the biggest city in Alaska, with just under three hundred thousand people, but it could feel like a small town. Both women had
worked the streets long enough that the risk of them running
into someone they'd arrested was high, and even higher at the
bus station, which seemed to draw a particular clientele.

Alvarez covered dark shoulder-length hair with a curly blond
wig that, along with her other traits, made her look like Dolly Par-
ton. Temporary dental veneers aged her by a decade and gave
her the street-hardened look she was going for. Lola's Polynesian
features made changing her appearance a little more problematic. In the end, she left her hair down around her shoulders

rather than in her customary bun and wore a blanket-lined leather jacket that showed off the tightest pair of jeans she could
pour herself into. "*Trust me*," Joe Bill had assured her earlier with
a purring growl, "*with those jeans, nobody will be looking at your face.*"

A tall Hispanic woman in a white bunny-fur jacket stood inside
the building and watched them as they arrived.

Lola took a deep breath, steadying herself. "Jackpot," she said,
then described the woman over the radio.

"I see her," Nancy said from the other end of the walkway. "Didn't
one of the girls describe the woman who contacted them as being
a redhead?"

"They would have described you as a blond," Lola said into her
earbud.

"True," Nancy said. "She's definitely giving me the *mal oho*."

"Pink backpack," Lola said, so Sean and Joe Bill, who were providing overwatch, were up to speed. "She could have a gun under
her jacket, but I'd bet on the pack if she's carrying at all."

"Watch yourselves," Sean said. "You're taking money out of this
lady's pocket. That's serious business."

"Head on a swivel," Lola said. It was one of Cutter's favorite
phrases, during the rare moments that he talked.

She wondered what he'd think of her plan. The chief had
signed off on it, and Cutter had enough on his plate already. She
missed having him there, though, watching her back—and her
watching his. Her jeans were too tight and her jacket too short to
keep her duty sidearm concealed. For this undercover op she'd
gone with a Ruger SP101 revolver, giving her five rounds of .357
Magnum she could shoot from the pocket of her jacket if she
had to.

Both women paced the sidewalk in front of the station, stomping their feet against the cold. They conspicuously eyed any lone
females who arrived by bus, offering each of them a card with a
number that promised a hot meal and a modeling job, but would,
eventually, lead to a counselor at a youth drop-in facility for at-risk
teens. Bunny Fur stayed inside but watched them intently
through the glass.

At least a dozen homeless, both male and female, huddled in small knots, sharing drinks from brown paper bags and eyeing the two new women who'd taken over the block, obviously recruiting new talent. Bunny Fur had to notice.

Nancy made the rounds right up next to the building.

"Bunny Fur's on the phone," she said.

"Calling her muscle to shoo us away, no doubt," Lola said.

"I've probably arrested half the people on this block." Nancy stomped her feet again.

"At least you have a disguise," Lola said. "I'm trying to hide behind poofed hair and the hope that people just stare at my ass."

"Some of 'em probably wouldn't piss on me if I was on fire," Nancy mumbled. "But I still don't fancy getting them killed in a drive-by shooting."

Sean's voice came over the radio.

"We've got a lone female dragging a little cart your direction down Sixth," he said. "Short, curly hair, black beret, frumpy skirt. She's still in the shadows, but I think it's that lady from the airport doin' her bit to get to heaven."

"I see her," Joe Bill said. "Yep. That's her. She was at the airport last night handing out religious tracts and threatening people with hellfire."

"Hellfire is right," Nancy groused. "She tried to shame us with Bible verses. Sister Donna something . . ."

"Donna Do Good," Sean mumbled.

Lola chuckled. "Go easy on her. We got heaps of evangelicals in my family."

"We're all doing the Lord's work in our own way," Joe Bill said. "Donna with her preaching . . . and you with those heavenly jeans."

A bus squeaked to a stop in front of the station, disgorging its passengers into the cold night. Most had someone there to meet them. Some walked away alone as if they knew exactly where they were going. But one girl, probably Native, stood on the sidewalk, looking lost and very much alone.

Bunny Fur came outside and stood by a concrete pillar alongside the door. She lit a Swisher Sweets cigar and looked on but said nothing.

Nancy approached the young woman who'd gotten off the bus with a smile and offered a card with a number where she could get a hot meal. A car pulled up moments later. Her brother, the girl said. She thanked Nancy for the card and left.

"I know exactly what you're doing," Sister Donna Do Good called out from beside her little metal stand of religious pamphlets.

Lola turned and gave her a wide smile. "God bless you, ma'am," she said. "We're just out here like you, tryin' to help a few poor lost souls."

She kept one eye on Bunny Fur, who was still just standing by, blowing smoke rings with her cigar.

The woman in the black beret took a half step forward. "I know a liar when I see one," she said. "And a whore."

Lola recoiled, genuinely taken aback. She'd not expected this woman to be so forward.

A blue Mercedes pulled up to the curb. Bunny Fur climbed in, and it drove away. She'd gone, but Sister Donna was just getting started.

"Liars suffer damnation—and harlots . . ." The woman gave a low chuckle, hoarse like she was hiding a two-pack-a-day smoking habit. "Oh, honey, Jesus taught in no uncertain terms that the harlot should be stoned—"

That caught Lola's ear.

Joe Bill broke squelch over the radio. "And that, ladies and gentlemen, is our bottom bitch!"

Lola sidled up alongside the rack of religious pamphlets, wondering who Donna Do Good had stolen them from.

"You're getting your testaments bassackwards, sister," she said. "The Old Testament is violent as hell, but by the time Jesus came around, he was challenging the ones without sin to cast the stones. Matter of fact, he was pretty damned civil to the harlot—

wasn't about stoning her at all." Lola's eyes narrowed, drilling holes in the woman. "Seems like something a person in your line of work should know by heart."

Nancy closed in from the opposite side. "How about *you* move on. This is our spot."

"You two got no idea what kind of fresh hell you're about to unleash on yourselves." She raised her Bible. "Haul ass or . . ."

"I gotta tell ya," Lola said. "That frumpy housewife getup makes it hard to take you seriously."

"How about this?" Bible in one hand, Donna opened her bag with the other to reveal a Glock pistol and at least a dozen condoms.

Lola raised her arms, palms open as if giving up. "Holy crap, sister, traveling prepared for a gunfight and the rapture are we . . ."

Lola wanted everyone to know she'd seen the Glock but not to panic. Simply possessing a gun in Anchorage wasn't probable cause for anything.

"Look, hon," Donna offered with a saccharine smile, "I don't know what you think you got goin' on here, and frankly, I don't give a shit as long as you do it somewhere else. This is my spot. You two need to take your precious selves down the road."

Lola smirked. "Listen, ma'am," we're not hookin'. We're recruiting. I'd offer you a job but you're . . . well, you know."

Sister Donna put her nose in the air, giving Lola and Nancy a slow up and down scan. "So, you're looking for young ones, are you?"

Lola shrugged. "My clients don't care how young they *are* as long as they *look* young."

Donna scoffed. "You're so full of shit. It's not the age these guys are after, honey. It's the innocence."

"*Here's an idea*," Lola said. It was the pre-arranged signal phrase for Joe Bill to pull around. "We like this spot. *You* find somewhere else to be, and we can all stay friendly."

"Don't let this skirt fool you, sweetheart," Donna hissed. "I won't even need the gun to kick your pollywog ass."

"Oh?" Lola chuckled. "I'm beginning to think you're not really a missionary . . ." She slapped the bag out of the woman's hand.

Donna let loose a horrific growl, slamming the Bible edgewise, straight into the bridge of Lola's nose.

Lola swung instinctively, blinded by the sudden explosion of lights behind her eyes. A cupped hand caught Sister Donna in a brutal slap across the ear.

It turned out that getting smacked in the nose with a Bible hurt like hell. By the time Lola's vision cleared, Nancy had spun an equally stunned Sister Donna and cuffed her behind her back.

Joe Bill pulled the Tahoe directly up in front of the station, bouncing a wheel over the curb. Lola did a quick pat down and put Donna in the back seat. She and Nancy jumped in on either side of their prisoner, and Joe Bill sped away, with Sean bringing up the rear. Fights broke out all the time in front of the bus station. Few people took note of this one. Some might have thought Eddie Dupree's bottom bitch had made an enemy powerful enough to kidnap her. If anyone did, they kept it to themselves.

The woman's name was Donna Boone. An Ohio driver's license said she was thirty-two. She wasn't much older than Lola—but her occupation had put an undue number of hard miles on the odometer, leaving the check-engine light on—probably for good. Her criminal history showed convictions for nine felonies, ranging from vehicle theft to assault with a deadly weapon, all starting two days after her eighteenth birthday. Hard miles on the odometer, indeed.

The girls from the Spenard Road hotel were both easily able to pick Boone out of a photo lineup as the person who recruited them, introduced them to Eddie Dupree, and set them up with Harris and Tice to shoot the video.

Two hours after she'd been bashed in the nose with the Good Book, Lola stood with her back against the wall of one of the "Let's Make a Deal" rooms at APD. Donna Boone slumped over the table, head resting on her hands. She'd been to this party before and was surprised by none of it. Nancy Alvarez sat across the table from her, notepad and pen in hand.

"Felon in possession of a firearm," Lola said. "That's five years on top of . . ." She glanced down at Nancy. "What else we got Detective Alvarez?"

Nancy began to thumb through the pages of her notebook. "Let's see," she said. "Pandering, child trafficking, sexual exploitation of a minor, manufacturing child pornography, and assault of a federal officer."

"That's a hell of a lot of time when you stack it," Lola said. "And I gotta tell you, when it comes to crimes against kids, judges like to see sentences run consecutively."

Boone leaned back, rattling the chain of her cuffs as she dragged it across the table.

"So, you got my tit in a wringer," she said. "Now you're supposed to offer me a way to unwring it. If all you wanted to do was throw me in prison for the rest of my natural life, you woulda done it already." She sucked air through her front teeth, like she was trying to get at a piece of stuck food, then, mimicking Lola, said, "When are you gonna say those magic words—'*help me, help you*.' Tell me what you want me to say. I'll obviously say it to stay out of prison."

"Oh," Lola said, "you're not staying out of prison. But we can let the US Attorney know you helped us out. It could—"

"I don't want to know what a deal *could* do," Boone said. "I want to know what it *will* do. Tell me what you want from me."

"Eddie Dupree," Lola said.

Boone laughed out loud. "You want Eddie? That makes sense, I guess. You'll just turn him to get the next guy up the food chain."

Lola and Nancy exchanged glances but said nothing.

Boone nodded, sucking her teeth again. "Y'all thought Dupree was at the top of the food chain? Oh, hell no. There's real money above him. Dupree ain't a nobody, but he's not somebody, either."

"Enlighten us then," Lola said. "First Eddie Dupree, then the real money."

"First," Boone corrected, "get me my own lawyer and that US

Attorney in here to put this on paper. You saw my rap sheet. I've learned not to trust any deal unless it's in writing. Get it all signed, and I'll point you toward Dupree. You want anyone above him . . . you're on your own." She raised her eyebrows and gave a slow shake of her head. "Those guys are . . . Let's just say there ain't no deal sweet enough to make me turn on them."

CHAPTER 37

*C*UTTER SHOULD HAVE BEEN EXHAUSTED BY THE TIME HE REACHED his office at the James M. Fitzgerald US Courthouse and Federal Building in Anchorage, but he found himself sparking like a live wire. Spilling his soul to Mim had left him raw and exposed. He thought the feeling would pass, but he wasn't sure. Some things were meant to stay buried, too awful to see the light of day. Any rest he'd gotten on the flights from South Dakota had been fitful and far between. Mim had slept, but she felt the buzz too. The kids were safe at school for the time being, so she headed straight to the gym to swim and shower. Cutter rushed through time sheets and a couple of other mundane supervisory tasks at the Federal Building.

The corner of his cramped office, where some people might have a ficus or rubber tree, was stacked with two hard Pelican cases and three heavy-duty gear bags in "tacti-cool" colors like black, desert tan, and flat dark earth. This left just enough room for Cutter's desk and two side chairs, one of which was piled high with powder-blue warrant folders, each one representing a fugitive who needed to be located and captured. It wasn't a particularly good filing system, but it kept more than one person at a time from camping out in his office. Each time the operational supervisor or judicial security inspector—or anybody, really—dropped by for a visit, Cutter thought about stacking something on the other chair as well.

He checked his watch. Twenty past one. He'd finish here, then swing by and pick up Mim before getting the kids from school and stashing them someplace secure. After that, they'd sit down with Coop Daniels and finally get some answers—

The electronic cypher lock outside whirred and clicked as someone entered the task force suite. A moment later, Chief Jill Phillips poked her head in Cutter's office. She carried a nylon duffel over her shoulder, on her way to the USMS gym and mat room just across the hall.

"Hey, Big Iron." She gave him an accusing side-eye. "I thought you were only going to work a couple of hours today."

Cutter continued to click away at the keyboard, slogging through the mundane task of approving time sheets, leave requests, and overtime—the administrative bullshit that took him off the street.

"Finishing up time sheets and then I'm outta here," he said without looking up.

Cutter tensed when she stepped into the office, hoping against hope that she wouldn't sit down. Jill Phillips was the best chief he'd ever even heard of, but he didn't have time to chitchat, not with anyone.

Hands behind her back, she leaned against the door. "The task force is putting in some long hours. Lola giving you any updates on Dupree?"

"She called me and brought me up to speed when we were in Seattle," he said. "This bottom . . . girl . . . they popped at the bus station shows promise," he said. "They're just waiting on the lawyers."

"Lawyers," the chief said. "So close and yet so far away."

"Lola has matters well in hand," Cutter said. "Not to mention Nancy and Sean."

"And Officer Brackett."

"I gathered that," Cutter said. "Anyway, they'll get Dupree."

"Good," the chief said. "That guy's a real piece of shit."

"Yep," Cutter said, still typing, checking boxes.

"Sounds like you have a lot to think about after this South Dakota trip."

Cutter nodded.

"You know, Arliss Cutter . . ." Phillips said. She often used his

full name, like a mom wanting to stress a point. "It is my job to remind you that the US Marshals Service does not do homicide investigations."

"I get that."

"But we do hunt evil men." She stood up straight, tapping the
door frame to drive home her point. "Your grandpa passed on a
ton of rules to live by. But here's one from your chief. I want you
to memorize it. *Policies are not law. They are guidance.* Breaking one
might get you sued, possibly fired, but you won't go to jail. I can
provide you a certain amount of top cover on policy . . ."

Cutter finished her thought. "But breaking the law is a different story."

She gave him a finger-gun salute. "Yep," she said. "Be careful out—"

Cutter's desk phone rang. He looked at the caller ID before he
picked up. "Officer Hough with North Slope PD," he said.

Phillips didn't move from the door.

Cutter put the phone on speaker and grabbed a yellow government-issue wooden pencil from a mug beside his keyboard.

"Hey, Jan," he said. "I have Chief Phillips on the line with me."

"Hello, Chief." Hough brushed past any pleasantries. "Listen,
Arliss, we got back the preliminary postmortems. Both Dennis
Foye and Lilian Egak had fentanyl in their systems. The medical
examiner says it wasn't enough to kill them, but they were both
definitely stoned. They found bruising on Foye's wrists and the
small of his back—"

"Like someone restrained him," Phillips said.

"Exactly, Chief," Hough said. "Too much of Egak's body had
been consumed by the bear to be sure about her, but get this,
both of them had what appeared to be small puncture wounds on
the side of their necks."

Cutter drummed the pencil against his desk blotter. "The fentanyl," Cutter mused.

"That's what I thought," Hough said. "But the ME found traces
of something called succinylcholine in both victims' systems.
Sounds like it's metabolized pretty quickly, but there were also
traces found on Foye's neck around the injection site, so the ME

took the time to look for it in the tox screens. Some must have leaked out of the needle during the struggle."

"Sux," Cutter mused. "I've heard of that stuff. The Israelis apparently used succinylcholine to take down a Hamas operative in Dubai ten or twelve years ago. It's a paralytic. The victim can't move but is completely aware of what's going on."

"That's exactly what the pathologist told me," Hough said. "Their eyes are even open."

"Holy shit . . ." Phillips turned up her nose. "That means Lilian Egak was likely awake when the bear started to eat her . . ."

"It gets so much worse," Hough said. "If you can believe it. The ME found remnants of blackfish and Arctic char on Egak's body.

"And the bear?" Cutter asked, already knowing Hough's answer.

"You guessed it," she said. "Lots of blackfish and Arctic char in its gut . . . along with the portions of Lilian."

Cutter snapped the pencil in half with this thumb.

"Holy shit," Phillips whispered again. "She just laid there paralyzed and covered with dead fish . . ."

"Oh yeah," Hough said. "I'm telling you, Leo Beck's a malevolent son of a bitch. A cancer . . ."

"No doubt," Phillips said. "But do you have anything to actually tie him to these murders?"

"Working on it," Hough said. "I'll call you later, Arliss, after . . . We can compare notes."

Hough ended the call.

Phillips gave Cutter another side-eye. "What's she talking about? After what?"

"After I talk to Coop Daniels," Cutter said.

The chief gave a contemplative nod, eyeing him up and down. "Arliss, I want you to check in with me this evening after your talk with him."

"Roger that, chief." Cutter pitched what was left of the pencil into the trash can and turned back to his keyboard, tabbing through the last couple of time sheets. "Everyone can get paid now . . . So, if you'll excuse me, I'm outta here in five."

"Just talk to him, Big Iron," Phillips said. "Nothing else." It was an order, not a question.

"Due respect, Chief," Cutter said, "Coop Daniels and I are going to have a conversation. Just how that conversation goes is entirely up to him."

Cutter turned on his wipers against the heavy rain as soon as he pulled out of the underground garage. His phone buzzed while the door rumbled shut behind him. David Foye was on the other end of the line, out of breath like he'd been running. Cutter couldn't be sure, but he thought he could hear the creak of saddle leather and the jingle and crunch of a snaffle bit.

He turned onto Eighth Avenue.

"Cutter."

"Thank God you're okay," Foye said.

"Having some problems?" Cutter headed east on Eighth, toward the Chugach Mountains, barely visible through brooding gunmetal rain clouds.

"That's putting it mildly," Foye said. "Amateurs, though, at least as far as the way they handle horses. I imagine they'd be top hands at shooting me in the back if I gave 'em the chance. I ran 'em down and—"

"Best you remain silent on any details," Cutter said.

"Yeah, of course," Foye said. "I'm gonna hunt a hole and lay low for a while. You and the Mrs. should do the same. He'll be sending people for you too. I guarantee—"

The line beeped. Cutter held the phone away from his ear long enough to see it was Constance. His hackles went up immediately. She was way too cool to call her uncle.

"I need to go," Cutter said.

"Keep your powder dry," Foye said. "I'll let you know when I come up for air."

Cutter leaned forward slightly, keeping an eye on other traffic in the downpour. He tapped the phone's button once as he turned onto the Seward Highway, heading south toward home.

"Hey, Constance," he said. He waited, as was his habit. She'd called him, probably with something important to say, and he didn't want to tie up the line.

Nothing but dead air.

He checked the phone to make sure he hadn't inadvertently disconnected.

He started to speak again, but a breathy, almost inaudible whisper cut him off. It was Matthew.

"Uncle Arliss . . ." Breathing. A quiet sob. "Uncle Arliss, can you hear me?"

CHAPTER 38

"*I*'M RIGHT HERE," CUTTER SAID. "WHERE ARE YOU, BUDDY?"

"I'm in Mom's room," Matthew whispered. "Uncle Arliss . . . some bad guys have Constance . . ."

"Have her where?"

Cutter resisted the urge to snap. The boy would just shut down if he yelled. He checked his side mirror, then took the left lane, picking up speed as he whipped in and out of traffic, using the shoulder when necessary. APD might see him, but they would just become a tail he planned to drag all the way to Mim's house.

"I threw up on my desk at school," Matthew said. "Constance came to get me."

"Where is she now?"

"The living room, I think," Matthew said.

"How many bad guys?" Cutter willed an ancient Subaru Outback out of his way, shooting past it the moment he had enough room.

"Three." Matthew's voice grew quieter. "They have guns, Uncle Arliss."

"You're doing good, buddy," Cutter said. "Where's Michael?"

"He stayed at school."

Cutter worked to control his breathing. "I'm on my way. Do they know you're hiding?"

"I . . . I . . . don't think they do," Matthew stammered. "I was in the bathroom when they broke in. Only Constance was downstairs. One of them screamed. I think Constance scared them."

"Are all three in the living room with her?"

"I can go look—"

"No!" Cutter bit his lip to keep from cursing. "Just tell me what you saw already."

"I saw three of them . . . Sorry. I already said that. One is Native, the other two are white. Uncle Arliss, the blond one keeps pointing a knife at Constance. I heard him say he's going to finish her before Mom comes home. Does that mean—"

"I'm close," Cutter said, heart in his throat. He fought tunnel vision—pumped the brakes to keep from slamming into the back of a dawdling cement truck. The rain came down in buckets now, causing the little government-issue Ford to hydroplane. He counter-steered through it but kept up his speed. Killing himself en route wasn't going to help anyone, but neither would getting there too late. A truck driver laid on his horn. Cutter hissed a silent curse. "Do you think you can climb out the bedroom window and run down the hill to the cul-de-sac?"

"I don't think I should leave Constance," Matthew said.

"I'll take care of Constance," Cutter said. "But I need you to get to safety."

"The window squeaks so loud," Matthew said, his voice shrill with worry. "I think they will hear if I try."

"That's okay then," Cutter said. "Stay hidden for me."

"But . . . what if . . . I mean . . . Constance is in trouble. Mom's got a shotgun in her closet. Shouldn't I—"

"No, buddy," Cutter said. "I'm almost there. I need you to stay put. Got it?"

"Okay . . . but what if they—"

"Matthew, the best thing for Constance is for you to sit tight."

It occurred to Cutter that of all Mim's three children, Matthew's personality was the most like his—prone to wading into danger without thinking it through. The boy wasn't going to sit still when his sister was in trouble unless he had a job.

"Listen to me, Matt," Cutter snapped. He took a breath, willing himself to stay calm—or at least sound calm so as not to scare the boy any more than he already was. "You can really help me and the police if you stay right where you are, but quietly describe the men as best you can. Are they wearing masks?"

"No," Matthew said. "Not when I saw them. The blond one is the boss . . . I think maybe he could be . . . Russian? I don't know. He's got a weird way of talking. I don't like it. Hang on . . . I can hear Constance crying. I need to go—"

"Wait!" Cutter snapped. He all but ignored the red light and two lanes of oncoming traffic, drifting through a left turn onto Huffman toward Hillside. An angry chorus of horns rose up behind him.

He was minutes away—when every second mattered.

"I need you to tell me about their guns," he prodded. "This is important."

"Okay, yeah," Matthew said, as if convincing himself. "I can do that. The Native one has a shotgun. Super short, like yours. The other two have—"

Cutter waited a beat. At first, he thought Matthew had just fallen silent, but a series of beeps told him the call had failed. Either the boy had given in to the protective instinct to rush down and help his sister or the men had found him. Neither scenario had a good outcome. Cutter didn't call back for fear the ringtone or even the vibration would give away Matthew's location if he had managed to stay hidden.

Four blocks away.

Cutter tried Mim. The call went straight to voicemail. Her battery had been low when she got off the plane.

Shit!

Cutter pounded the steering wheel.

Three blocks out.

He called the first number on his speed dial.

"Hey, boss!" An insanely chipper voice came over the line.

"Lola," Cutter said. "Listen carefully . . ."

He gave her the down and dirty brief, including the descriptions of the men Matthew had provided, keeping everything professional and by the book. He knew she'd be questioned later. The last thing he wanted was for her to lie for him.

"Call 911 and get APD rolling this way," he said. "And remind them there's a plainclothes deputy US marshal on the scene. I'll be wearing my plate carrier."

"Arliss," she said. "You need to wait. I'm on my way. I will help you."

Cutter heard her call to Anchorage PD Dispatch over the radio—an officer-needs-assistance call. She gave Mim's address.

"I'm about to be offline," he said.

"Seriously, boss," Lola pleaded. "You gotta hang on."

"These men didn't come to negotiate," he said. "They came to find anyone asking questions about my brother—and kill them. They're not wearing masks. You know what that means."

"I'm begging you, Cutter." Her nerves brought out the full Kiwi, obliterating the R. "Dispatch has six APD units en route as we speak. ETA four minutes."

Cutter rolled to a stop in the cul-de-sac below Mim's backyard and killed the engine. Heavy rain pelted the windshield.

"Lola," he said. "One way or another, this is going to be over in three."

CHAPTER 39

Mim's split-level cedar house sat on a low hill surrounded by pockets of birch and a half dozen thick-hipped Colorado blue spruce. The living room was in the front, on the uphill side, with a large picture window that faced the street. Approaching from that direction would be tantamount to suicide. The back was the only option.

Cutter parked his Ford behind a stand of birch. Rain and wind stripped the thatch of yellow leaves off the trees before his eyes, but there were still enough to hide him in case one of the three happened to be looking out a window. A thicket of highbush cranberry bushes ran along the back of the property. It wouldn't stop bullets, but it completely hid the little G-car. Concealment, not cover.

He'd held out hope that he might arrive to find Matthew running down the hill in the rain.

No such luck.

Cutter rolled out of the little Ford and eased his door shut. He popped the rear gate to grab his green ballistic vest and throw it on over his shirt. The badge in front and the POLICE US MARSHALS placard on the back were there to keep responding officers from shooting him. The men inside knew exactly who he was and planned to shoot him, anyway.

He weighed taking the Heckler & Koch UMP stashed in the locking vault in the rear of his G-car. A .45 ACP burst-fire machine gun, the stubby H&K might come in handy—or it might get in the way. Where he was going, he'd need to crawl.

Constance bit down hard on the bandana the blond asshole had used to gag her. A nasty thing that he'd pulled so tight it cut into her cheeks, it tasted like motor oil and something else Constance came to realize was her own blood. They'd tied her hands behind her back with the phone charging cord. She thought she'd be able to wriggle out of it, but every time she even twitched her elbow, the blond backhanded her across the face. Between slaps, he brandished his hunting knife. One of his wild swipes had cut away three inches of her bangs and put a gash on the tip of her nose. Her left eye was swollen shut. Blood and angry tears covered her face and flecked the front of her T-shirt and gray sweatpants. This guy was insane, or he didn't care if he carved up her face—or both.

Constance had no idea what his name was, but his German accent made her call him Hans Gruber, like the bad guy in *Die Hard*.

An Alaska Native man they called Sherman stood beside the living room drapes, keeping watch out the front window. He held a shotgun down by his thigh.

The fat bastard they called Lovelace had been watching the back, but he'd heard Matthew. He must have found the hiding place because he dragged the poor kid down the stairs by his hair, kicking and crying. Animal. Matthew was barely nine, not nearly old enough to understand this kind of evil. Constance wasn't either. No one was.

Lovelace threw Matthew on the couch and stepped back without bothering to tie his hands. He pointed his pistol at Matthew's face, and for one terrible moment, Constance thought the man might shoot her little brother right then and there. And he might have, had Gruber not stopped him.

"I'm sick of all this boo-hooin'," Lovelace said, still aimed in on a cowering Matthew. Constance could see the poor kid's shoulders shaking from across the room. "Let's finish this and get ready. The marshal and his old lady come home to a couple of

dead kids, and it'll be easy enough to take care of 'em both without a fuss."

Hans Gruber cocked his head this way and that, eyes playing
back and forth between Constance and Matthew. "Not just yet,"
he said.

Gruber leaned in close enough that she could smell the mint
on his breath. He touched the tip of his blade to the wound on
her nose, bringing a searing pain. She jerked away, eyes blazing,
screaming against the gag.

The German glanced over his shoulder at the Native man they
called Sherman. "I have read that your people used to cut the
noses of a woman who disrespected you in some way."

"I don't think that was us." Sherman shrugged. "But it's not a
bad idea." He hawked up a mouthful of phlegm and spat it
against the wall.

Lovelace gave a low groan. "You idiot. You ever hear of a little
thing called DNA?"

"I thought we were burning the place down," Sherman said.

"Sure," Lovelace said. "In this rain?"

Hans Gruber rolled his eyes. "The rain won't matter."

"Well, then." Lovelace stuffed the pistol in his waistband and
leered at Constance, looking her up and down. "If we don't have
to worry about DNA, how about we see what this one has hidden
under those sweats . . ."

Matthew sprang from the couch, screaming with rage, clawing
at Lovelace's face. Caught off guard, the big man jumped backward, nearly tripping over his own feet before peeling Matthew
off and slamming him to the floor.

Undaunted, Matthew glared up at him, blood pouring from his
nose. "My uncle is going to kill you so hard!" he snapped, with the
certainty of a nine-year-old who hadn't lived long enough to learn
that things didn't always turn out.

Lovelace reached up and touched his eye, growling, then
yanked the pistol from his belt again.

"You coulda blinded me, you little puke!"

Constance screamed against the gag.

.

Hans Gruber raised his free hand. "Wait." He pulled the knot on the back of the gag. "I need to know when your mother will be home."

Constance wiggled her jaw back and forth when the cloth fell away. "I don't give a pinch of shit what you need to know!"

"Very well," the German said. "We'll see if the sight of your little brother's brains is convincing enough."

Constance laughed so loud it surprised even her. "You're going to kill us, anyway," she said. "It's supposed to scare me more what order you do it?"

The German gave an exhausted sigh.

Constance spat a clot of blood onto the floor, sobbing now, certain she and Matthew were as good as dead.

"He's right, you know." She sniffed. "My Uncle Arliss is going to mess up your shit."

A savage smile crept over the German's angled face. "Very well, then," he said, raising the knife. "If you do not care about the order we do things, the boy can watch us take care of you."

A sudden noise from the dining room caused the German to freeze. Lovelace glanced over his shoulder. Sherman half turned, lifting the shotgun.

A muffled voice drifted in from around the wall.

For the first time in hours, Constance felt hope. It was Uncle Arliss!

Then came a series of loud fart noises.

Constance slumped, deflated. Arliss was only "dropping in" on Monte, the smart speaker.

"Just checking in. Be home soon. Give me a call."

Then more fart noises.

The German gave a mock shiver, then turned back with the knife. He nodded at Lovelace, who scooped up Matthew, holding his little face so he would be forced to watch.

"Little boy!" the German barked. "I think you might learn something—"

Constance caught a flash of realization in the man's eyes a split second before his head turned into a red mist.

* * *

Cutter shot Karl Ditmar once under the nose, clipping the man's brain stem with 158 grains of jacketed hollow point from the Colt Python. Severing this "celery stalk," as they call it, stopped motor function and sent the knife clattering to the floor. The German's face was burned into Cutter's mind. According to David Foye, this was the bastard who sabotaged the rig.

He was the man who killed Ethan.

The smart speaker had been a useful distraction, allowing Cutter to squish across the kitchen floor in soaking wet clothes while everyone's attention was on the dining room. More important, it gave him a chance to do a quick peek and get a lay of the land—prioritizing the threats.

Ditmar down, Cutter turned immediately to the big guy hiding behind Matthew. Only the man's knee was visible, so Cutter took that, chopping him down. The fat man stumbled, presenting six inches of shoulder from behind a terrified Matthew. Cutter sent him another round, cheating left to keep from hitting the boy. The man dropped the pistol but held fast to Matthew.

Cutter caught a flash of movement to his left as Sherman Billy, one of the men who'd approached Mim in Utqiagvik the year before, raised the shotgun and fired. A rushed shot, the rifled slug struck Cutter's vest right of center, rolling off the edge of the rifle plate and slamming into the Kevlar that protected his side. The blunt force snapped at least one rib and probably two. Cutter staggered sideways, more from the sudden shock of getting hit than the actual force of impact, then fired twice, once center mass, then again straight through the center V of Sherman Billy's collarbone.

Cutter exhaled sharply, unable to draw a full lungful of air. He had one round left in the Python, and he intended to send it into the fat bastard's eye. Pivoting, he turned just in time to see the man bearing down on top of him, swatting the Colt from his grasp.

Cutter flew backward under the weight of the oncoming attack. The revolver hit the floor a split second before he did. Cutter fell hard, his head narrowly missing the oak corner of the couch. What little air he had left was driven from his lungs by the impact. He was able to get a leg up and shove the big man sideways, splintering the coffee table, but before he could regroup, the man was on him again, up on his toes, pressing down with his full body weight. Searing pain coursed through Cutter's broken ribs.

Cutter could feel the baby Glock 27 in the holster over his right kidney—trapped between his body and the floor. He'd managed to get a knee up, keeping himself from being completely crushed, but the fat guy's mass just folded around it, smothering Cutter with deadweight. Cutter tried to work on the man's shattered knee, but he couldn't reach it.

He gulped for air. Silver pinpricks of light danced in his vision. This guy was going to bleed out, but it would take time, time Cutter did not have. If he couldn't breathe, he couldn't fight.

Cutter trapped the man's good arm and posted a foot, bucking his hips in a vain attempt to roll the man off. It did no good, but in the process, Cutter's fingers slid across his buckle and brushed the handle of the Clinch Pick Lola had gifted him. He snatched the little knife with an overhand grip, slamming again and again like a sewing machine into the big man's ribs. The man laughed, thinking the blows were nothing more than Cutter's feeble punches. He flinched, as if bothered by a mosquito, exposing his kidney. Cutter stabbed and raked, over and over, shredding flesh, carving his way to something lethal. Pain finally overcame adrenaline and crept into the fat man's lizard brain, bringing a yowl of surprise. He arched his back, looking up enough for Cutter to bury the little blade in the side of his neck.

Cutter kicked out with his heels, crawfishing out from under the fat man's bulk, then rolled onto his side to draw the Glock.

There was no need.

CHAPTER 40

*B*EATEN AND BLOODY, CUTTER GAVE LOLA THE ALL CLEAR BY PHONE as soon as he made sure Constance and Matthew had no life-threatening wounds. She'd started an ambulance rolling as a precaution when Cutter had first called her.

The living room was in shambles, furniture splintered or flipped on its side. Blood pooled on the carpet and mopped the wood floors. The first .357 magnum round from Grumpy's Colt Python had scattered the wall with bits and pieces of Karl Ditmar.

The handle of the Clinch Pick quivered in the side of the fat man's neck with each beat of his heart. Cutter left it there for the paramedics to remove. It defied reason that this guy was still alive. Cutter handcuffed him behind his back anyway. There was no reason to handcuff Ditmar or Sherman Billy.

Cutter scooped up Matthew and took Constance by the shoulder, checking the wound on her nose.

She choked back a sob. "I'm fine. Check on Mattie."

Lola shouted from the front door. She knew where Mim kept her hidden key. "US Marshals! Coming in!"

"In here!" Cutter said. "We're all good. Three bad guys down."

"Holy sh—" Lola stopped, looked at the kids, then checked herself. "Holy moly, Cutter. You . . . Are you okay?"

"I'm fine," he said, more than a little loopy from the massive adrenaline dump after three days of running on fumes. He nodded toward the fat man, wincing even at that small movement. "That one needs a tourniquet."

Lola stooped to check his pulse, then shook her head. "Not anymore."

Cutter noted the scab on her nose and her swollen upper lip. "What happened to you?"

"Had a run-in with a Bible," she said. "Anyway, don't worry about me. I'm right-as."

She scanned the shredded clothing and torn flesh, settling on the Clinch Pick still lodged in the man's thick neck.

Cutter saw where she was looking. "Turns out you were right." He kept his breathing shallow. "I am always dropping my grandfather's revolver . . ."

CHAPTER 41

Utqiagvik

JAN HOUGH HADN'T SMOKED SINCE SHE'D LIVED IN LAS VEGAS. BACK then, she'd made an art of it, leaving piles of lipstick-stained stubs anywhere she spent more than a few minutes. Always non-filter Camels because that's what her dad had smoked. Her husband hated it and had asked her to quit a dozen times a day every day for two months until she finally did just to shut him up.

That in and of itself was reason enough to stop by the AC store and buy two new packs, the price of which had quadrupled since she'd bought her last carton at the market inside Bally's Casino on the Strip.

Now, it gave her something to do while she leaned against the fender of her SUV across the street behind Leo Beck's office, staring in his back window.

She was half a pack in when he finally looked out the window and noticed her. Eyes narrow and clearly perturbed, he watched her for a time, then shook his head and drew his mini blinds. She knew she had him then. He was still watching. Periodic movement in the blinds confirmed her suspicions. He would have been better off had he left them open and stared back. Hiding made him look weak. She knew it and so did he.

She continued to stand there, in the rain, staring, letting the cigarette burn down in her hand more than actually smoking it.

The first one had been a rush. The second, so-so. The third gave her a headache—or rather, added to the headache she already had. The only comfort came from knowing that Beck knew she was watching him. Not approaching, hassling, saying a word. Just a blonde Jessica Rabbit standing in the rain, smoking a cigarette—and planning to carve the black heart out of his chest.

Thirty minutes in, he came out the back door, raincoat pulled up around his neck, and shuffled off toward his truck, which Hough knew was parked down the street. She thought of following him, but he'd probably just call the chief. She stubbed out her cigarette on the bottom of her boot and held the butt in her hand, digging a baggie she'd brought along for that purpose out of her pocket. Gone were the days when she flicked butts willy-nilly to the ground.

"I got your message!" she yelled across the muddy street as he walked by. It was a stupid and impulsive thing to do—like starting to smoke again—but she didn't care. "Anything you want to add?"

If he would just stop and talk to her, she thought she might be able to antagonize him enough that he would turn on her, allowing her to shoot him or, at the very least, kick him in the nuts.

She tried again.

"I'm not going anywhere, Mr. Beck."

He stopped, turning slowly to face her, then trotted across the street.

He nodded. "I hear it's bad for your health."

Hough held up the cigarette butt and shrugged. "I'm too old to die tragically young."

"I'm not talking so much about the smoking, Ms. Hough."

She came up off the vehicle, standing up straight, shoving the cigarette butt in her pocket to free up her gun hand.

"Exactly what are you talking about?"

"The same thing you are, I'm sure," he said. He loomed over her, shoulders back, head up. It would have been more intimidating but for the telltale flutter in his right eye. She was getting to him.

"Anyway," he said. "I have a meeting with the mayor—"

"Go on then," she said.

Beck's lip curled, quivering for a long moment as if a word was working its way out, then he blew out quickly through his nose and turned to walk away.

"I'm easy to find," Hough said. "In case you think of anything else you want to tell me."

CHAPTER 42

Anchorage

THE VIOLENT ATTACK AGAINST A DEPUTY UNITED STATES MARSHAL'S family turned the streets surrounding Mim's home into a fortified wall of blue-and-white Anchorage Police cruisers and unmarked SUVs from virtually every agency in Alaska. Most were there for support and protection. A few were there to investigate. There was a better than average chance a small percentage had other motives in mind.

When a law enforcement officer used lethal force, the real bloodletting often happened well after all the shots had been fired.

The FBI would open a case of assault and attempted murder of a federal officer against the dead assailants. Bureau agents would assist APD detectives in their investigation into the OIS—officer-involved shootings (including Cutter's dramatic use of the Clench Pick)—while the USMS Office of Professional Responsibility (the Marshals Service's version of Internal Affairs) piggybacked with their own investigation to ascertain whether or not Cutter had violated any USMS firearms or deadly force policies.

Conventional wisdom would say the kids' trauma and the carnage at the scene spoke for itself, but Cutter knew better. He had plenty of friends in USMS OPR and the Bureau, but there was always some headhunter looking for a trophy. People like that would do backbends to twist the obvious evidence and surmise that Cutter had been too quick on the trigger, or worse, that he'd somehow orchestrated the circumstances that brought three violent assholes into his sister-in-law's home so he could murder them.

Cutter had been involved in enough shootings to know he should have had the Federal Law Enforcement Officers Association attorney on speed dial.

Chief Phillips pulled up shortly after Lola, armed with the official forms to document Cutter's injuries on duty. He reminded her he was on annual leave.

"Nice try, Big Iron," Phillips said. "You were wearing a ginormous ballistic vest with US MARSHAL stenciled all over it."

It wasn't long before the interior of Mim's house was standing room only, with squawking radios and a mountain of wet raincoats on the kitchen counter to keep from dripping water all over the crime scene in the living room.

Responding EMTs strongly recommended a trip to the ER. Cutter declined, but under the chief's withering stare promised to go in as soon as they'd come up with a game plan. Mim arrived a few minutes later with Michael and three of her church friends, just in time to ride in the ambulance with Constance and Matthew to the hospital. Chief Phillips had two deputies follow as a precaution until this mess was sorted.

Cutter sat at the kitchen table, away from the bloody scene, and sketched out what had happened for the chief. Lola stood by him, waiting for orders.

"You need to take a beat before you give a statement?" Phillips asked.

"I'm fine," he said, grimacing every time he took a breath.

Phillips watched him draw. "You know these guys?"

"I know of two of them," he said. "Ditmar and Sherman Billy confronted Mim last time she was in Utqiagvik. Tried to scare her off. It's a fair bet that Karl Ditmar is the one who killed Ethan on orders from Leo Beck. The fat one is new to me."

"Kenneth Wayne Lovelace," Lola offered. "Wasilla address. Pipe fitter's union card in his wallet."

Phillips pulled up a chair and, elbows on the table, leaned on her fists. "So, what's our thinking here? These three took the kids hostage to demand what . . . ?"

"The kids weren't even supposed to be here," Cutter said. "They stayed with friends while we were in South Dakota. We'd planned to pick them up from school. Matthew got sick, and Constance picked him up and brought him home."

Lola patted the table with the flat of her hand, thinking out loud. "So, Sherman Billy and friends come to Mim's in the middle of a school day. They are surprised to find the kids but decide to wait for you and Mim to get home to . . ."

"To call that a sloppy plan would be generous," Phillips said.

Cutter shrugged. "It didn't need to be intricate. Just kill us and slip away. No one else is looking into Ethan's murder or the oil rig explosion. If we're out of the picture, Beck skates."

"What do we have to tie Beck to these guys?" Phillips asked. "Or any of this?"

"David Foye's testimony," Cutter said. "But I'll get more. Nobody does something like this without leaving tracks. I just have to find them."

An APD detective named Nakamura poked his head in the kitchen. "Deputy Cutter," he said. "The morgue vans have gone. We're ready for you to do a walk-through if you're up for it."

"You're not required to do this," Phillips said.

Cutter waived off the suggestion. "I'm good. Happy to show them what happened."

Though he'd been sitting less than fifteen feet away for the past hour and a half, Cutter stopped cold at the living room door and stared at the scene.

Phillips put a hand on his shoulder and then pushed her sleeves up over her elbows. "Y'all are going to need a place to stay until we get a cleaning crew in here."

Contrary to what most people believed, it was the victims of a robbery or a home invasion who were responsible for cleaning up the mess—provided they survived the encounter. Cutter picked up a pair of nitrile gloves an evidence tech had inadvertently left behind.

Shards of a ceramic vase that Cutter had no recollection of breaking were strewn across the living room beside the splintered remnants of wood that had once been the coffee table. A framed cross-stitch of the Blue Boy lay broken on the floor. Blood soaked the carpet in at least four large spots. Fortunately, not too much of it belonged to Cutter or the kids.

APD detectives videoed the walk-through, noting time stamps along the way of sections they'd want to address later. Cutter explained how he'd slipped in through the back door, then used the smart-speaker app to send an "announcement" in order to draw the attackers' attention away from his actual approach.

He demonstrated.

An FBI agent who looked like he'd just gotten out of middle school gave a disgusted frown. His name was Reinhold.

"Really, Cutter? Fart noises? I'm having a hard time seeing the humor when your niece and nephew were being held at gunpoint."

Cutter chalked the attitude up to the can of whipass they'd probably poured all over the kid when he graduated from Quantico. Reinhold had not been on the job long enough for any of the officiousness to be knocked off yet.

Lola bowed up, ready to rip the young agent's head off. Cutter waved her down and gave an exhausted sigh.

"I wasn't trying to be funny, Special Agent Reinhold," he said. "My nephews only taught me how to use this smart-speaker app a couple of days ago. They downloaded the fart noises. It was the only drop-in tone I had."

The agent snorted and turned up his nose, unconvinced. He started to say something else, but Phillips stepped in and addressed Detective Nakamura, who was leading the OIS investigation.

"Let's all get one thing clear from here on out," she said. "My deputy is doing this walk-through as a courtesy. I'm sure his attorney has advised him he can have some time to get his thoughts together post-shooting. I was under the impression this is the time for him to provide his recollection of what happened. As a more seasoned investigator, Detective Nakamura, you will allow him to finish without the color commentary."

"No doubt," Nakamura said, deadpan.

Cutter gave the youngster a benign nod. This was probably his first office. He'd be in Alaska awhile, and there was no doubt they would cross paths again, hopefully when the kid had a little more sense. Cutter had plenty of enemies. No use in making another one if he didn't have to. Not while he was this tired.

The last of the law enforcement vehicles finally cleared the scene just before six p.m.

"You have somewhere to spend the night?" Phillips asked.

"I'll head to the hospital in a few minutes and talk to Mim," Cutter said.

Mim's voice carried in from the arctic entry. "You can talk to me now."

"I'm surprised to see you here," Phillips said.

"Really?" Hair plastered to her forehead, a smear of what was surely one of her children's blood on her cheek, Mim was all business.

Cutter stood when she walked in, clutching his side, stifling a groan.

"The kids?"

"They're okay," she said. "At least physically. Safe with friends from church. He's a big-game-hunting guide. Jill has two deputies guarding the place—so woe unto anyone who tries anything there. I know I should be with them . . ." Her eyes fell on Cutter. "Whatever happens next, I have to be a part of it." She walked toward the living room, but Phillips stopped her.

"I'm not sure you want to go in there," the chief said. "It's pretty bad."

"No," Mim said, matter-of-fact. "I've already told Arliss *we* are going to finish this. Not y'all. *We*. Am I clear? And if I'm involved, I need to see it all."

"Good to know," Phillips said.

Mim stood at the doorway and surveyed the mess. She hugged herself around the chest, speaking through her teeth.

"Karl Ditmar . . ." she mused. "He's the one who hurt Connie?"

"He was," Cutter said.

"So that's some of him . . . on the wall behind the couch? Where you shot him."

"Yes."

"Good . . ." Her eyes became distant—the thousand-yard stare. "He's the one who killed Ethan . . ." It wasn't a question.

Phillips stepped closer to Lola. "APD is clear of this scene?"

"They are," Lola said.

"We should help these guys gather what they need. They can't spend the night here."

"Right-o," Lola said. "Nancy's out on surveillance. I need to—"

"Go head," Cutter said. "We've got this under control."

"I'm not leaving you, boss," Lola said.

"And I appreciate that," Cutter said. "Go help Nancy get what she needs to locate Dupree and then come back."

Mim wheeled in the doorway. "Coop Daniels is supposed to be here at seven." She waved her hand at the gore. "Arliss, do you really think it's possible he had something to do with this?"

"I don't know," Cutter said. "My gut tells me Mr. Daniels seems the type to hire thugs. He's too much of a worm to do this himself."

Mim checked her watch.

"You think he'll show?"

"He'd better show," Cutter said. "If he doesn't, he and I are going to have a conversation . . ."

CHAPTER 43

JAN HOUGH TURNED OFF THE WATER OF A MUCH-APPRECIATED HOT shower to the sound of her husband's ringtone—"Fat Bottomed Girls" by Queen. She stepped out, grabbed a towel to keep from dripping everywhere, and nudged the Glock 23 on the counter out of the way with the back of her hand before picking up her phone.

She dabbed her face with the towel as she answered.

"I ran into someone you're gonna want to talk to," he said.

"Okay," she said. "Who?"

Mumbles in the background, like Bryan had covered the receiver. Then, "Not over the phone."

Jan gave a low groan. The shower was great, but it had made her a little lightheaded.

"It's late, Bryan. Tell whoever it is to come by the office. When are you planning to get home?"

"Listen," he came back abruptly. "I need you to come here to me."

"Where's here?"

"Down from the airport," he said. "Knowing you, this is something you'll want to hear."

"Stop playing games," she chided. "Just tell me what this mystery person wants."

More muffled conversation.

"Jan—"

"Put him on the line," she said. "And stop covering up the receiver!"

"He says he's got information on Cutter," he said, his voice tight.

She'd expected some question about a citation or warrant. "Arliss?"

"Ethan," Bryan snapped. "Your old pal . . ."

She dropped the towel.

"Bryan, quit jerking—" A thought suddenly occurred to her. "Is someone making you call me?"

"What? Knock it off, Jan. Just come talk to this guy."

She pressed. "Tell me the truth. No one's got a gun to your head?"

"Okaaay . . ." Grudgingly, "All . . . systems . . . go." It was their code phrase that all was well. "Seriously, Jan. The sooner you get your ass down here and talk to this guy, the sooner I can come home and have dinner."

He gave her directions to a warehouse not far from the Alaska Airlines terminal building.

"You think he's for real?" she asked. "It's not exactly a secret that I think Ethan Cutter was murdered. How did he approach you?"

"I know him, Jan. All right? He came up to me outside the airport when I got in from Kaktovik and said he needs to talk to you in person."

"Why didn't he come to me?"

Bryan's voice dropped to a whisper, toying with her.

"He didn't say." Then louder. "I do not give a shit."

She heaved a deep sigh, lightheaded from all the steam.

"Okay," she said. "I'll be there in half an hour."

"Hurry," Bryan said, then whispered. "I'm getting hungry."

Jan ended the call and stood there dripping on the bathmat, phone in one hand, pistol in the other. Was this mystery someone telling her things she already knew, or did he have some magic-bean evidence? And why the secret meeting? Unless . . . If Beck was tying up loose ends, maybe one of his guys was spooked bad enough he'd want to rat.

Bryan had to be pissed just to hear Ethan's name again. And he had conveniently forgotten to mention Dennis Foye had flown in on the same plane . . . Was this a trap? Was Bryan involved with Leo Beck? No. No way. Surely, her husband wouldn't lure her out to be killed. At least not on purpose.

Probably.

She wrapped a towel into a turban around her wet hair and then thumb-typed a number into her phone as she made her way to the bedroom to dress.

Most, if not all the other officers at the North Slope Borough PD were sick to death of hearing Hough's theories about how Ethan Cutter died. Detective Shawn Jolivet was probably just as tired of it, but at least he kept an open mind.

"Hey, Jolly," she said when the other end of the call picked up. "You busy?"

"Taking the wife out to Niggivikput for a cheeseburger and onion rings," he said. "Why? What do you have going?"

"Hi, Jan," Missy Jolivet said in the background. She was one of the few police wives that didn't stare daggers at Hough every time they crossed paths.

"I don't want to wreck your date night," Hough said.

"We're not there yet," Missy said.

"What do you have?" Jolivet asked again.

"Nothing, really," Hough said. "You guys live out by Leonard Beck, right?"

"We do," Missy said.

"I have to be somewhere, and I was just going to ask if you'd mind swinging by his house to see if he's home."

"We can do that," the Jolivets sung out in unison.

"I'm about to drive past his office," Jolly said. "I'll check there for you too."

"I can do it," Hough said. "I'm closer than you if you're already in town—"

"Stop," Jolivet chuckled. "We're already in the car and rolling. You do whatever it is you need to do."

"You know Shawn lives for this stuff," Missy said. "We'll let you know what we find out."

Hough thanked them and ended the call. She pitched her phone on the bed and used the turban towel to dry her hair.

Was her own husband luring her into a trap?

Probably not . . .

CHAPTER 44

*L*EO BECK WAS ABOUT TO OPEN THE DOOR OF HIS WIFE'S TOYOTA 4Runner when a pair of headlights turned and came up the side street next to his office. As was his habit, he'd parked down the block. Normally, a vehicle cruising by wouldn't have given him a second thought. It wasn't even eight p.m. There were plenty of cars still crawling and splashing through the streets. But Karl Ditmar had not called. Ditmar was a maniac, but he was Beck's maniac. He always called. No matter if things went well or turned to shit, he let Beck know as soon as was practical.

There were a couple of posts online about an Anchorage police presence at the Cutters' address, a home invasion, three dead—but no press release, no details. No names of the dead. Beck had paid for two bodies, the marshal and Ethan Cutter's old lady. Three meant there'd been a problem. He'd sent three men and still hadn't heard back from any of them. It was impossible to imagine anything happening to Karl Ditmar. The man was a cockroach. Beck had no doubt he could survive a nuclear winter. No way the marshal could have killed him. But what if he'd been arrested? Cockroaches knew when to phone home and when to spill their guts to the cops to protect themselves.

Beck recognized Detective Jolivet's dark-blue Explorer, caked with Utqiagvik mud. He slouched in his seat as it made the corner, slowing slightly in front of the office entrance and then continuing past, toward the lagoon. There was someone else in the Explorer with Jolivet, riding shotgun, but Beck couldn't make out who. Absent the probable failure in Anchorage, even two cops driving past his office would not normally have been an issue. Utqiagvik was the hub for the North Slope PD. They all trained here, turning the place into Cop City on any given day. You couldn't swing a dead cat without hitting a badge.

This was a problem. That bitch Jan Hough was up to something. She was baiting him. Trying to trip him up. Her little stunt earlier, smoking outside his window, was meant to intimidate. It had very nearly worked. He'd seriously considered walking out the back door and shooting her in the face.

Still slouched down in his seat, Beck checked his rearview and caught a second SUV idling a block up from his office. Another cop? Had Ditmar talked? Foye? Someone else? Was it possible this bitch actually had something concrete?

Beck threw the Toyota in gear and eased onto the street without turning on his headlights, following the muddy Explorer.

Three blocks ahead, Jolivet headed south like he was going to the hospital, but then turned left on Ahgeak Street . . .

Beck grabbed the wheel with both hands and cursed. The bastard was going toward his house!

Cutter must have gotten Ditmar. Beck could picture the sullen German sitting in an interrogation room, selling his soul for a deal. Maybe it was Sherman Billy or that fat slob they took with them. Someone was talking.

A new set of headlights played across the street to Beck's left, illuminating the soggy tundra. He cursed again, a rat caught in a trap. It was her. Jan Hough turned her SUV directly toward him. Beck briefly considered running her off the road right then and there, but she was surely on the radio with Jolivet—and whatever other shithead cops were lurking around his house and office. He thought of calling his wife but pushed that idea out of his mind. They'd be up on his phones, listening to everything. Hough had the feds helping her now—Ethan Cutter's brother no less, if he'd managed to stay alive.

Hough passed without a sideways glance, busy trying to drive and dial a number on her phone at the same time. Coordinating raids, no doubt.

Beck had known the day might come when he'd have to run. You didn't take three and a half million from the good old boys at big oil and expect to live a cushy life out in the open. He had go-bags stashed—one at his office, another at his house. They might as well have been on the moon for all the good they'd do him now. Hough had someone watching his office, and Jolivet was heading to his house.

Beck made the block and fell in behind her SUV. He'd have to find another way out.

CHAPTER 45

MIM'S DOORBELL RANG AT FOUR MINUTES PAST SEVEN.

She forced a smile and pulled open the door.

Coop Daniels stood with an umbrella in one hand and a bottle of wine in the other.

"Fashionably late," Mim said. She had to concentrate to keep from gritting her teeth as she pulled open the door. She'd never been a good fake smiler. "Come on in."

Seemingly oblivious, Daniels closed the umbrella, shaking off the water before he stepped inside. He handed her the wine.

"Should I take off my shoes?"

"I'd leave them on if I were you," Mim said, earning a shrug and an arched brow.

Daniels followed her through the entry alcove. He grimaced at the muddy trail of boot prints through the dining room. "Did you have plumbers in or . . ." His voice trailed off when they reached the threshold to the living room, then he gasped, recoiling like he'd hit a brick wall.

"Holy shit, Mim! What . . . what the hell happened here? Is that blood? Because it looks like blood."

"That's exactly what it is," Mim said. "Among other things."

"Are you okay?"

"Coop, I'm not even close to okay," she said. "Someone just tried to murder my family."

"But . . . why?"

Mim leaned back against a clean spot on the dining room wall and folded her arms across her chest. The fake smile bled from her lips. "You tell me."

"I . . ." His head snapped up. "What makes you . . . Wait. What? You think I had something to do with this?"

Arliss's voice boomed from the kitchen.

"You're telling me you didn't?"

Daniels flinched, visibly shaken. His eyes darted back and forth like a terrified rabbit. For a moment Mim thought he might try to hide behind her.

Holy shit, had she misjudged this guy . . .

"Ar . . . Arliss . . ." Daniels licked his lips in a desperate attempt to find enough saliva to form words. "What . . . what are you . . . ?" His face clenched as if stricken with a sudden pain. He clutched the top of his head and began to sway in place. "I . . . Is this about the money?"

Mim cocked her head, staring him down.

"Is it?"

Arliss strode quickly across the room, closing the distance, surely meaning to protect Mim from Daniels. She gave a slight shake of her head. The man looked like he might throw up.

Mouth hanging open, hand still on top of his head, Daniels looked from Mim to Arliss and then to the blood-stained floors. His words came out hollow and breathy, stunned.

"W . . . what?"

Just then, Jill Phillips stepped out of the powder room off the back hall. She channeled her pissed-off chief deputy voice.

"It doesn't do you any good to keep saying that. I need you to get a grip and talk to us."

"Are . . . are you guys going to kill me?"

Mim shot a glance at Arliss, ready to back his play. He gave a little shrug, like the idea had certainly crossed his mind.

It was her turn to be dumbfounded.

"You can't really be that dense," she said. "Of course, we're not going to kill you, Coop. You're the one who's been lying to me . . ." Her voice rose with each successive word. "For. Two. Years! I want to know why."

"Lying? No, I—"

Arliss moved a step closer.

"Sit down."

The chief took up a spot against the far wall, arms folded, badge and sidearm prominently displayed on her belt.

Daniels held his breath, crouching, seeming to shrink before their eyes. Mim got the impression he would have jumped out a window if they hadn't surrounded him. Instead, he raised his hands and collapsed into one of the dining room chairs.

"I'm sure Ethan must have talked to you about the missing money?"

"Missing money?"

"Nope," Arliss said. "This is where you tell, not ask."

Daniels blew out hard through his mouth.

"Then you don't know," he said. "Okay . . . JBM was bleeding funds. We're talking millions of dollars from some very big contracts. Double billing, fake subsidiaries. They brought me in as a contract consultant to find out what was happening."

Mim no longer attempted to hide her dripping disgust for the man. "And Ethan knew about it?"

"Oh," Daniels said. "He knew about it all right. The firm started noticing discrepancies about thirteen months before he died. The board hired a firm to do a forensic audit . . . and two of the worst-hit accounts were on Ethan's projects. They had a pretty good idea he was involved in the theft but hired me to get the proof."

"To get the proof that he was guilty?" Mim scoffed. "Not get to the bottom of what was happening or find out who was stealing their money? What a dick move."

The chief nodded in agreement but said nothing.

"How do you sleep at night?" Mim said.

"You think I do? I felt . . . I feel like shit. Especially after what I found out."

The tendons along Arliss's neck tensed. Mim could tell his ribs were killing him, and she pushed an armchair across the floor so he could sit down before he fell down. He ended up facing Daniels, their knees less than four inches apart.

"Let's hear it," Arliss said. "What is it you think you found out?"

"You're not going to like—"

Mim stood above him. "I wish you'd knock it off and tell me the truth for once in your miserable life."

"I *am* telling you the truth . . ." Daniels's hand came up again like he was scared she might hit him. "I took a trip to South Dakota." He looked up at her, chin quivering, near tears. "Ethan was there, Mim. I didn't want it to be true, but it was. He never saw me, but I saw him. He was leaving a law firm that represented two of the shell companies."

"Okay," Mim said. "What was he doing there?"

Daniels looked from Mim to Arliss, incredulous. "Meeting with his contacts? Laundering money? What else could he have been doing?"

Arliss let out a slow breath, a rumbling growl.

"I'm guessing you made zero effort to confirm anything?" Arliss said.

"With the law firms?" Daniels scoffed. "They weren't going to tell me anything."

Mim glowered down at him. "Did it ever occur to you to ask Ethan why he was there?"

"I wasn't allowed to," Daniels said. "I wrote up my findings, then presented them to the JBM C-suite guys. That was one week to the day before the rig accident."

"Hang on now," Chief Phillips said. "How much money are we talking?"

"Two million and change," Daniels said. "And we're only talking about losses incurred by JBM. I'm certain other companies doing business on the Slope were losing at least that much."

Phillips looked like she wanted to spit.

"And throughout all this, no one thought to get law enforcement involved in this investigation?"

The lawyer gave a timid shrug. "The oil patch is like a fraternity. There's too much risk of losing large accounts if people stop trusting the process."

"What if Ethan had seen you first?" Mim asked.

"How do you mean?"

"Say Ethan saw you hanging out around one of those South

Dakota law firms," Mim said. "You think he would have run straight back to the board and told them you were ripping them off?"

"It wasn't like that," Daniels said. "I was trying to get to the truth."

"Maybe Ethan was trying to get to the truth," Mim said. "Sounds to me like you were just trying to finish your report and grab some billable hours."

"That's not fair . . ."

Arliss scooted sideways in the chair, taking shallow half breaths, guarding his injured ribs. It was obvious to everyone in the room that he was hurting, at the end of his rope. The pained look on his face made him more frightening, not less so.

"That is the shoddiest excuse for an investigation I've ever heard of," he said.

"Tell me," Mim said, "did you ever connect Ethan directly to money in South Dakota?"

"I did not," Daniels said. "But that's the whole point of why he used a shell company. Anyway, it didn't matter. Johnson, Benham, and Murphy is a large enough firm that they're self-insured. There's no outside insurance company for their employees. Absent a ruling from the court, the shadow of guilt was as good an excuse as any to keep them from paying the death benefit."

"The shadow of guilt put there by you," Mim said.

"I'm the one who finally convinced them to pay you—"

"You mean pay me off," she said.

"No," Daniels said. "Just pay you."

Mim closed her eyes. She'd thought she was beyond crying, but she'd been wrong.

"Let me get this straight," Arliss said. "Is my brother still your sole suspect?"

"Of course not," Daniels said. "But the details of the case are proprietary—"

"Oh, buddy," Arliss bellowed. "I do not give a pinch of shit about what you think is proprietary."

"Look," Daniels said. "I feel awful about Ethan. He was my friend—"

"No!" Mim said. "You don't get to say that anymore! You can't call a man your friend while you lie your ass off to his wife after he's murdered, and then spend the next two years trying to charm your way into her pants by pretending to help. You make me sick."

Daniels sat dumbfounded, blinking as if he were looking into an oncoming tornado.

"Mim," he stammered. "I never meant to—"

Arliss took a deep breath, seething in his seat. For a fleeting moment, Mim thought he might spring out of his chair and snap the other man's neck. She sure wanted to. Instead, he rested his elbows on the arms of his chair and folded his hands, as if to restrain himself. The folded pocketknife disappeared inside his fist.

"What *did* you mean to do?"

Daniels slumped in his chair.

"People are dying," Arliss said. "And we need to stop it." He dropped his hands and leaned forward in his chair. His withering glare left no doubt that he'd just as soon twist the man's head off as look at him.

Daniels shot a hopeful look at Chief Phillips.

"He's on annual leave," Phillips said. "Not my responsibility."

Mim closed her eyes. "Coop, just stop yanking us around and tell me who did this to my house!"

"I am telling you I do not know. I suspect another JBM engineer is involved, possibly even the ringleader. I haven't even told the board about him. His name's Hopkin."

"Phil Hopkin." Mim nodded. That made sense. On her last trip to Utqiagvik, he'd asked her to meet him in a place known for attracting polar bears and then neglected to share that little tidbit of info.

Chief Phillips prodded. "Anyone else?"

"Dennis Foye," Daniels said.

"Who conveniently happens to be dead," Arliss said.

"I heard about that," Daniels said.

Arliss's chair chattered across the floor as he scooted forward, crowding Daniels so their knees were touching.

"Who do *you* think killed Foye?"

Daniels jerked sideways as if he'd been burned. "Hopkin, if I had to guess. But I don't have any proof."

Mim bit her lip to keep from asking about Leo Beck. Daniels was a piss-poor investigator if that name had never come up—or he was holding something back.

Arliss rolled the pocketknife back and forth in his hand. "Does Hopkin know you were investigating him?" he asked, clearly going somewhere with the question.

"I'd imagine so," Daniels said.

"Amazing that you're still upright and aboveground," Arliss said.

"Hold on." Daniels's head began to bob. "You think I'm in danger?"

"Of course, you're in danger you feckless asshole." Mim motioned at the carnage spattering the walls, the blood-soaked floors. "Someone held a knife to my daughter's throat! He would have killed her if Arliss hadn't shown up. Hopkin and whoever he's working with have already tried to murder us and a North Slope Borough police officer. And don't forget, they blew your dear old friend, Ethan, to hell."

Arliss put his hand flat on the dining room table. "Anyone who's snooped around regarding this missing money is a target." He drew the closed pocketknife across his own throat to make his point. "You need to watch your back."

Daniels squirmed like he might lose control of his bladder. "What do you want to do?"

Mim threw her head back and stared at the ceiling, stifling a scream. "I want to make sure my children are safe. I want the person who had my husband murdered to pay for what he did."

Arliss started to say something, then paused and took a long, slow breath, obviously thinking better of it.

"Coop," he said at length, his voice low and measured. He tapped the pocketknife against the table to punctuate each and every phrase. "I want company records, investigative notes, recorded voice memos, doodles you made on napkins, dreams you've had at night. I want every scrap you have if it has to do with JBM's missing money."

"And we will give all of this to the Troopers and the FBI," Chief Phillips said. Her eyes settled on Arliss. "Eventually."

"No problem," Daniels said. "I'll need to bring in JBM's attorneys. My files are their work product."

"That's fine," Phillips said. "I'm sure JBM would prefer cooperation to misprision of a felony."

Arliss bounced his fist on the table again, softer this time, like he was thinking through a plan. Every move of his arm brought a tight grimace to his face and a flinch from Coop Daniels.

"This isn't over until we root out everyone involved." A drop of blood dripped from Arliss's nose and landed with a plop on his thigh. Another followed, painting his upper lip. Eyes red with a fury Mim had never seen, he continued to speak, unaware. "You, the kids, David Foye, none of us are safe . . ."

"Arliss," she whispered. "You're bleeding."

He looked down at his side, where the pain was, saw the blood in his lap, then grabbed the handkerchief he always carried from his hip pocket.

Mim had a fleeting memory of him getting nosebleeds as a teen. They'd been his Achilles' heel. His kryptonite.

His head tilted back, Arliss rose from the chair. He gave Daniels a wicked side-eye. "You stay put until I get back."

He made it halfway down the hall before his phone rang. One hand holding the handkerchief to his nose, he answered with the other.

"Hello, Jan," Mim heard him say before he shut the bathroom door. "Yeah. We're all just fine . . ."

CHAPTER 46

*J*AN HOUGH PARKED HER SUV ON THE MUDDY BANK ACROSS AHKOVAK Street from the Wiley Post–Will Rogers Memorial signpost.

Jolivet had gone the extra mile and driven by Beck's office before checking his residence. The office had been empty, but Beck's truck was in his driveway and the lights were on in the kitchen.

Maybe this mystery man with Bryan really was scared enough to rat on his boss.

Instead of backup, she'd called Arliss Cutter, whose voice now resonated through the AirPod in her ear, warm and comforting . . . like fresh-baked bread out of the oven. She wondered if he realized how much he sounded like his brother.

He'd given her a blow-by-blow rundown of the home invasion and told her in no uncertain terms that she was crazy for going to this meeting alone.

"Hey, Ethan . . ." She paused, flushing, certain her face was beet red. "Did I just call you Ethan?" She blew out a heavy breath. "Sorry about that. A lot on my mind. Anyway, did I tell you Tony Caprese did a hell of a job when Beck sabotaged our airplane? The kid was amazing."

"Focus," Arliss said. "Cooper Daniels seems to believe Phil Hopkin is behind all this."

"That's horseshit," Jan said.

"I'm passing on the intel as it was given to me," Cutter said. "But you're right. It is horseshit."

"Oh, Hopkin is involved," Jan said. "But I like Beck as the head honcho."

"Yep," Cutter said. "Listen to me, Jan. You know you're walking into a trap, right?"

"Maybe," Hough said, chuckling a little at her own bravado. "Probably. Bryan's an asshat, but I have to think he loves me in his own way."

"Speaking of your husband," Arliss said, "have you got eyes on him?"

She shook her head out of habit, though no one was there to see it. "Not yet," she said. "His Toyota's here, though. Parked across the street where he usually leaves it."

"How about your backup?" Cutter asked. He sounded stuffed up.

"Are you coming down with a cold?"

"A bad case of fist to my nose," he said. Then he prodded her. "Your backup?"

"They're all busy," she said. "I'm being careful, taking it slow."

Hough killed the engine and then rolled down her window to listen.

All was quiet but for the drip of rain and a periodic whine of a power tool from the guys at the rental car shop down the street, who were putting in a new floor.

"No one around," she said, voice low as she climbed out of the vehicle.

It was late evening, dark. The last Alaska Airlines flight of the day had already come and gone, leaving this little stretch of the only paved street in Utqiagvik like something out of a ghost town.

The side door to the large metal hangar where she was supposed to meet Bryan stood ajar.

"I'm going to go in," she said.

She heard Arliss give an exasperated groan. *Damn but he sounded like Ethan.* "Hang on a minute," he said, mother-henning her. She didn't mind. No one else seemed to give a rat's ass what happened to her. "Are you seeing anything out of the norm?"

"Hell, Arliss, I'm just looking for the normal stuff," she joked. "You know, marauding polar bears and guys who want to kill me in my car."

"Jan . . ." Cutter chided. "Be serious."

"I am," she said.

She padded swiftly across the wet street, shiny under the street-lights, closing the distance to the open door.

"Stay on the line with me," she whispered, peeking inside.

"You bet," Cutter said.

Hough tapped the Glock .40 in the holster on her belt, com-forted by the weight of it.

The smell of aviation fuel and rubber tires hit her in the face as soon as she stepped out of the rain. Early in her career those odors had made her think of adventure. Now, they were a reminder of how much she traveled and made her miss her own bed.

Rather than allowing direct access to the hangar, the entry boasted a rough plywood wall that blocked the wind from blow-ing straight in off the tundra. Hough took a step left to move around the wall, giving herself a chance at another quick peek be-fore committing completely.

Gymnasium-style lighting illuminated the front half of the cavernous interior, leaving her a no-man's land of freshly waxed concrete floor that she had to cross before she reached a blue-and-white Cessna 185 taildragger that would give her some sem-blance of cover. Like many such hangars in the North, this one did extra duty as a place to store bulky winter items. From the looks of the cot and mini-fridge in the corner to Jan's right, it was also a decent man cave.

Overhead blowers poured heat into the large open space. Hough would have been happy in a T-shirt and shorts. "It's hotter than hell in here," she said to herself.

Arliss gave an exasperated groan. "Tell me what you see."

She pushed the sleeves of her jacket up to her elbows, then stopped, straining to hear above the drone of the blowers.

"I hear voices," she whispered. "But I don't see anybody."

Arliss said, "Wait for backup."

"I think we're good," she said. "Anyway, we need this. Ethan de-serves it . . ." She crept forward a few feet, scanning the fifty-by-fifty-foot hangar. An ancient Taylorcraft squatted forlornly on blocks a dozen feet from the cot. The little tandem-seat aircraft was missing a prop, wings, a tail wheel, and much of its torn yellow fabric skin. The little engine was torn down, with many of the components setting on the floor by the hole where a door would be. A fifty-five-gallon oil drum served as a tool table. Cluttered and tidy at the same time.

"I have eyes on Bryan," she whispered. "Holy shit, it's Phil Hopkin." Her heart began to beat faster.

Bryan Hough sulked in the shadows at the far corner, partially hidden by the large balloon-like tundra tires of the 185 and tail section of a Piper Seneca.

"I've seen that Cessna before." She read the tail number to Arliss. "Not sure who it belongs to . . . Could be Phil's. Pretty sure he's a pilot."

Bryan, who'd been surfing on his phone, glanced up at the sound of her voice.

"Finally!" he said, a throaty grunt. Impatient. Hangry. His usual mood this time of day.

Phil Hopkin leaned against a metal worktable, hands stuffed in his pockets and hunched up like he was cold. Bryan looked relaxed enough, but Hopkin, a JBM engineer who spent much of his time bouncing back and forth between Alaska and JBM's North Sea offices, was drawn and tight like he wasn't used to the chill. He was dressed for a trip—bright-orange Grundéns rain jacket, flannel shirt—both crisp and unfaded—and khaki hiking pants. His boots were blocked by the tundra tires, but she imagined they were new enough to give him blisters walking out to catch a taxi. The proverbial city mouse, Hopkin never had quite taken to life in bush Alaska.

"Phil Hopkin is our informant," Jan whispered. "I love it."

"Or it's a trap . . ."

"Have faith in people's ability to rat out bigger rats," Jan said. She stood up a little straighter, relaxing a notch. It made sense that the one scared of Leo Beck would be an accountant or engineer.

"I think we're good to go," she whispered to Arliss as she made her way past the Cessna. She had to duck slightly to keep from bumping her head as she walked under the wing. "I'll let you know what I . . ." She paused when she reached the aircraft's cowling. "Weird," she said to Arliss, low, under her breath. Bryan and Hopkin stood less than fifteen feet away. They might have thought she was talking to herself. "This 185's engine is still warm. Hopkin must have flown in."

Past the Cessna, she got a better look at Hopkin's face.

"Holy shit, you've aged," she said under her breath. Then, louder, in her firm Officer Friendly voice. "Hey there, Phil. I need you to take your hands out of your pockets for me."

"Yeah, sure, okay."

Hopkin straightened up and showed her his hands. Empty. Good.

"Okay then," Bryan said, as if he were running the show. "Let's get this over with so we can all—"

"You've got your car," Jan said. "Haul ass. I'll be . . ."

Bryan's eyes flew wide. He shook his head as if to clear his vision. It took Jan a moment to realize Phil Hopkin's face had suddenly fallen slack, as if he'd been kicked in the liver.

Before she could say a word, the crazy-eyed engineer grabbed a handgun from under a shop rag on the metal table and spun toward her, firing twice.

Bryan flinched at the sudden gunfire, inexplicably throwing his hands out in front of him.

"No!"

Both of Hopkin's shots missed Jan completely, flying past her shoulder to thwack against something metal behind her.

A half a breath after his second shot, Jan's pistol was in her hand, her finger convulsing on the trigger.

Hopkin shot again. Missed again.

She did not.

CHAPTER 47

JAN HOUGH'S FIRST AND SECOND ROUNDS CAUGHT HOPKIN CENTER mass. Her third . . .

This couldn't be. Her third shot should have hit Phil Hopkin inches from the first two, but somehow, Bryan had a neat red hole in the center of his forehead.

Hopkin's pistol clattered to the concrete floor. Only then did Jan find the breath to call out to her husband.

Bryan pitched forward, landing face first, arms dead at his sides. The impact of his head on the concrete seemed as loud and sickening as the shots.

"Bryan," Jan sobbed. "I didn't . . . This can't be happening . . ."

Hopkin just stood there, blinking, a look of utter dismay spreading across his face. He took a tentative step backward and then grasped the edge of the steel worktable to stay on his feet.

"Look . . ." A breathy murmur. "Watch out . . ."

Jan was vaguely aware of Arliss's voice in her ears. Stunned from the gunfire, she had no idea what he was saying.

"Look out . . ." Hopkin said again.

A sharp pain seared the side of her neck, as if she'd been prodded with an electric wire.

For a split second, she thought she'd backed into the Cessna.

"I think he was trying to warn you, dear," a voice behind her said.

Beck!

She attempted to turn, but the muscles in her torso refused to comply. The Glock slipped from her hand. Her head fell to the side, no longer supported by her useless neck.

Beck caught her under the arms as her legs collapsed. Coarse stubble on his face burned her cheek. "This is all on you, you know," he said, lips buzzing against her ear. "Good old Phil was trying to shoot me until you took care of him."

She could no longer turn her head, but she thought of Bryan dead or dying six feet away.

"You malevolent bastard," she said. It came out of her mouth as "*louvegymlvetturg.*"

Beck dragged her backward on her heels, growling directly into her ear. "Foye talked, didn't he? I should have . . . Everything was just fine until you sent your dogs to watch my house!"

Hough struggled to focus her thoughts through the sudden shock and soul-crushing panic. *What was Beck talking about?* Guilty at heart, he must have been out when Jolivet drove by and suspected he was there to make an arrest. The guilty had a million reasons to be paranoid. Hough tried to speak again but got nothing more than a grunt before everything shut down—her jaw, her vocal chords, nothing worked.

"Ohhh," Beck's voice trembled with emotion. "I hear anyone outside, I pop you first. PD or pizza guy, it makes no difference to me. You're dead. You get that?"

It took her a moment to realize that he'd seen the AirPod in her ear. The message wasn't just for her.

He gave a tight chuckle. "You thought you killed your own husband, didn't you? Oh, it is your fault he's dead. I pulled the trigger, but you're the one who made me pick up a gun."

She managed to clench her jaw. A tear ran down her cheek.

"You idiots forced my hand. You know that don't you." Beck lowered her to the floor. "You have my house and office covered, what the hell else do you expect me to do?"

Silent screams echoed inside her head. *What the hell was this guy talking about?* She had to talk to Arliss, to tell him what was happening. Was he still listening? Could he hear all the insane banter?"

"Don't fight the sux," Beck said. "It's just no use. Once I make sure you're not gonna die, I'll give you a little something else to help you sleep."

Jan Hough's entire world became about drawing her next breath. An unbearably heavy weight pressed against her chest. Unable to even twitch, she could do nothing but lie on the concrete floor. In her mind, she flinched at the sound of duct tape being torn off a roll. In reality, she merely closed her eyes. She'd worn low Salmon Sister boots, allowing him to wrap directly against the skin of her ankles. He moved higher, kneeling beside her elbow to loom over her body. She would have cringed or tried to kick in his teeth—had she been able to move more than her eyelids. He made eight wraps around her wrists, tight, turning her hands purple almost immediately. Finished, he sat back on his heels and used his teeth to tear a short piece of tape off the roll.

He glared down at her, face twitching, eyes burning with hatred and fear. As terrified as Hough was, it was some consolation that she'd managed to rattle a man who was normally so calm and calculating.

He stood, arching his back from the effort of taping her up. "The sux goes through you too fast." He licked his lips, searching for moisture. "I was careless with Lilian and didn't give her enough." He shook his head, remembering. "That polar bear sure enjoyed her thrashing, though."

A string of spittle ran from the corner of Hough's lips. She may as well have been staked to the ground.

Beck began to mutter to himself. She could hear him shuffling around, banging, scraping, a man on a mission each time he walked past her peripheral vision. He came back moments later, dragging a dusty canvas wing cover. Essentially an insulated sleeve that slid over an aircraft wing to protect it from the elements when tied down, when used in conjunction with the duct tape, the cover made a passable straitjacket.

"You idiots brought this on yourselves," he said as he rolled her into the cover and pulled the Velcro tabs tight. "Giving me no other way out."

Only her head was left exposed. One more flap and even that would be covered. She wondered if she'd be able to breathe.

Beck stood and admired his work. "There's a chance that someone heard the gunfire. Unfortunately, one of Hopkin's shots hit the fuel tank on his 185." He gave a tight laugh, clearly tense. "What would we do in the bush without duct tape . . ."

He squatted beside her and rubbed his goatee in thought, sighing heavily as if he'd come to some conclusion. He pulled back the Velcro straps on the wing cover and dug the phone out of her pocket before taking the AirPod out of her ear and putting it in his own.

CHAPTER 48

*C*UTTER PRESSED THE HANDKERCHIEF TO HIS NOSE, STANDING IN front of Mim's bathroom mirror and listening to the whole horrible episode. He heard the shots. The screams. The pitiful cry when Jan had been injected, no doubt with succinylcholine, made his teeth hurt. The sound of duct tape nearly sent him into a frenzy, ready to break Leo Beck in half. He put the phone on speaker, low so Mim and the others couldn't hear it, and started for the living room to bring Jill Phillips in on this. She'd be able to call North Slope PD while he kept this asshole on the line. He stopped cold when Beck threatened to kill Jan at the first sign of backup.

His hand was still on the doorknob when Leo Beck came on the line and addressed him directly.

"Are you alone, Marshal?"

Cutter dropped the blood-soaked handkerchief and stepped back from the door. "I am."

"Good," Beck said. "I'm glad for Jan's sake it's you she's talking to. I suspect anyone else would blindly call in the cavalry—Troopers or FBI SWAT, but not you. You don't strike me as a rule follower . . ." His words came on the back of an odd hissing sound that Cutter couldn't quite make out. Then Beck gave a little grunt. "You want to handle this personally, don't you?" The metallic squeak of a door opening. Then another grunt.

He was moving Jan, loading her in something.

Beck caught his breath, panting. "No, he continued, "you want to get your own hands dirty. Am I reading you correctly?"

Cutter's thumb moved quickly over the keypad, typing a hasty text to Lola. "Tell me what you want from me."

"You people have backed me into a real corner here," Beck said. "It's important for you to know something. I don't behave well when I'm cornered. If I hear so much as tires on gravel, the first thing I do is put a bullet under Miss Jan's ear. She dies. End of story . . . Well, her story, anyway. I seriously doubt I'll come out the other side of this alive, but I do hold onto a sliver of hope. That said, my reputation means a great deal. There are things to me that would be much worse than death . . ."

Cutter paused before sending the text. North Slope PD officers were good, but it would take them time to get organized—and if he took this bastard at his word, Hough would be dead the moment they rolled up.

Beck went silent for a beat. "Are you still there?" he asked.

Cutter closed the text box without hitting send.

"You sounded like you wanted to make a speech," he said. "I was letting you make it."

There was a rumble, long and low like distant thunder.

Beck gave a tight laugh. "I want to get away, marshal, but I'm not afraid to die."

"Yeah," Cutter said, sounding completely unconvinced. "A lot of people say that. They might even believe it until the moment comes, then—"

"Then they call for their mother?" Beck cut him off as the rumbling stopped. "Is that what you were going to say? Because if it is, I'll tell you I'd just as soon leave my mother on the ice to rot as—"

"Whoa there, scooter," Cutter said. "Is this what we're doing? Hashing over unresolved issues with your mama?"

"You are one cold son of a bitch," Beck said. "You obviously don't care what happens to our poor Jan."

"Not true," Cutter said. "I just don't give a rat's ass about you and your mother. Now tell me what you want me to do so I can do it!"

"Let me leave," Beck said.

"Is that all? You expect me to believe you'll just let her go."

"It's just that simple," Beck said.

"I don't make deals."

"Don't think of it that way then," Beck said. "Think of it as waiting me out. I see you or anyone else and I kill poor Jan." His voice was tight again, straining. He was lifting something heavy. "Let me leave and I'll drop her off when I don't need her anymore. Come after me and she dies. Stay away and you can save her life."

A door slammed in the background. Not heavy like a door to a building, but softer like a car door . . . or an airplane.

"You forgot another possibility," Cutter said.

"Is that so?"

The whir of electronics. Airplane magnetos coming up.

"I show up alone in the dark and you never see me coming."

An engine coughed to life. A propeller thumped and began to thrash the air.

"You'll have to find me first."

"It's what I do."

Cutter thumb-typed a new number.

The whine of the propeller grew louder, more impatient. Cutter imagined Beck holding the brakes, getting ready to roll.

Beck chuckled. "I already told you. I'm not afraid to die."

"Oh, Leo," Cutter said. "The next time you and I meet, dying is going to be the least of your worries."

"I'll sleep with one eye open." Beck laughed, nervous, bleeding off energy.

The engine roar grew garbled and exponentially more intense. There was a sudden crack, and the engine noise gradually faded into a whine.

Beck had thrown the phone out the window onto the tarmac.

CHAPTER 49

A SUDDEN RATTLE PULLED MIM'S ATTENTION TOWARD THE FRONT door. Jill Phillips braced, her right hand dropping to the Glock on her belt. Coop Daniels cowered low in his chair, attempting to make himself look as small as possible.

The door from the arctic entry opened a crack, and Lola Teariki announced herself before walking in. A wise move considering recent circumstances.

She eyed Daniels with a look that was a mixture of disdain and threat, like she might bite him, but he wasn't worth the trouble.

"Any news on Dupree?" Phillips asked.

"None, Chief." Lola's expression softened when her eyes fell on Mim. "Nothing positive, anyway. You all good?"

"I'm fine," Mim said.

"Hmmm," Lola said, clearly puzzled. "Where'd Cutter go?"

Phillips hooked a thumb, gesturing down the hall behind her. "That fight was harder on him than we thought," she said. "He's in the bathroom taking care of a bloody nose."

"How long's he been in there?"

Mim looked at her watch. The chief had been busy questioning Daniels, and she'd lost track. "It's been a while," she said. "Fifteen minutes, maybe."

Daniels raised a hand.

"What do *you* want?" Lola snapped.

"I was just going to point out, it's been closer to thirty," he said.

"This is odd, boss," Lola said to Phillips. "Cutter texted ten minutes ago and asked me to come make sure we keep protection up on Mim and the kids."

Mim pushed away from the wall, a nervous pit growing in her stomach. She padded quickly down the hall and knocked on the bathroom door.

"Arliss!"

No answer.

"Arliss!" she called again. The door was locked. She leaned in, cheek against the door. "Arliss, hon, are you all right?"

"He's not in there." Lola used the tip of her pocketknife to pop open the door and confirm her suspicions. "Just a rubbish bin full of bloody tissue."

Lola stepped into the hall. "Which one is Cutter's room?"

Mim nodded to the door on the right.

Lola looked in, scanned the room, then glanced over her shoulder. "I'm guessing that's where he keeps his second set of boots."

Mim blushed. "I never . . . I mean I don't come in here."

Lola gestured toward a vacant spot in a line of footwear under the window arranged by size, from running shoes to the tall Tony Lama cowboy boots he hardly ever put on since coming to Alaska.

"His other boots were soaked from the rain," Lola said.

"And probably covered in blood," Phillips said.

"Right," Lola said. "I'm thinking he grabbed his second pair of Zamberlans."

"The window's open," Mim said. "You think he—"

Lola leaned out, studying the grass and leaves below.

"Cutter, you wily son of a bitch," she said under her breath. Then, to Mim, "Yep. He's gone out the window and done a runner. I can't tell for sure from here, but it looks like his G-car is gone from down in the cul-de-sac."

Chief Phillips shook her head, phone pressed to her ear. "He's not picking up."

Lola tried from her phone with the same result.

"You call him, Mim," the chief said.

Mim nodded emphatically. "Maybe he'll answer me."

"I reckon it's worth a try," Lola said. "But he's not going to answer. He knows you're safe. That's why he contacted me."

Mim lowered her phone and gave a sad shake of her head. "Lola's right. It went to voicemail."

"Okay," Phillips said. "Lola, get Nancy on the line and have her ask APD to ping Cutter's cell. I want to know his location, and I want to know it now!"

"He'll have it in a Faraday bag, chief," Lola said. "He knows our methods—"

Cooper Daniels piped up from the dining room. "Can I go?"

Lola glanced at Phillips and whispered, "Want me to take him to jail?"

"For what?" Phillips asked. "If being a dumbass was a crime, he'd get consecutive life terms." She thought for a moment, then shook her head. "No. I think we've already put the fear of God into him. If he knew anything more, he'd tell us."

Lola Teariki wanted to do something, even if it was wrong. Cutter didn't have to teach her to err on the side of action. Sitting around on her thumbs while her partner was out there, probably needing her help, made her want to scream. She would have, had the chief not been sitting three feet away at Mim's dining room table.

"Let's think about this," Phillips said after Daniels had slinked out the door. "Arliss got a call on his cell before he went in the restroom."

"From Jan Hough," Mim offered. "She must have given him some new information. I have her number in my phone."

Mim called it. As with Arliss, it went to voicemail.

Mim closed her eyes. "Oh, Jill," she said. "What has he done?"

The chief gave a contemplative nod, then looked at Lola. "Do you have the number for North Slope Borough PD?"

Lola scrolled through her phone. "I do." She put her cell on speaker and held it between them. "Chief of police is Morgan Strawbridge," she said while she waited for the other end to pick up.

A young woman answered.

"This is Jill Phillips, chief deputy with the United States Marshals Service, Anchorage office. It's important that I speak with Chief Strawbridge."

"He's out on a call, Chief," the dispatcher said. "I can give him your number."

"I'll get straight to the point," Phillips said. "One of my deputies has gone missing, and I believe a Detective Janice Hough may know where he is. Can you have her call me as soon as possible?"

A tentative pause fell over the line. Then, "I . . . I shouldn't be telling you this," the dispatcher said. "But Chief Strawbridge just arrived on a homicide call near the airport."

"Homicide?" Chief Phillips said.

"Yes, ma'am," the dispatcher said. "Is your missing deputy named . . . Cutter by chance?"

"That's right," Phillips said. "Arliss Cutter."

"He's the one who called in the homicide."

Teariki was about to bounce out of her boots by the time the chief's phone rang ten minutes later.

Phillips put it on speaker.

"This is Strawbridge. I understand you want to speak with me."

"I do," the chief said in her endearing Kentucky drawl. "Jill Phillips here, chief deputy with the Marshals Service in Anchorage."

"And you're looking for Detective Hough . . ." Strawbridge paused as if deciding how much information he should give out. Lola started to say something, but Phillips held up a finger to stop her. Strawbridge continued. "I appreciate your man's call, but I'm afraid this doesn't look good."

"How's that?"

"Deputy Cutter said we'd likely find a dead or wounded Phil

Hopkin along with Jan's husband, Bryan. We found Bryan all
right, with a bullet wound between his eyes. No sign of Hopkin.
Head wounds bleed like hell, as you probably know, so it's hard to
tell yet if some of what we're finding here belongs to Hopkin or if
it's all Bryan Hough's."

"Wait," Phillips said. "Cutter said you'd find Hopkin, but he's
not there?"

"That's correct," Strawbridge said. "And his plane is missing.
A blue-over-white Cessna 185 with tundra tires. The tower said
he flew out just before your Deputy Cutter called us with the information. Fog's thick as cotton candy at the moment. I'm surprised they made it out." Strawbridge paused. "I hate to
mention it in the middle of all this, Chief, but the marshals are
usually good about letting me know if you're operating here on
the Slope. I was under the impression Cutter had returned
home to Anchorage."

"He did," Phillips said. "I was with him as of half an hour ago.
He was speaking to Detective Hough on the phone in the other
room and then left out the back without explanation."

"Curious," Strawbridge said. "And you think your missing
deputy is somehow related to the homicide in this hangar."

"Without a doubt," Phillips said, rolling her eyes.

"Something's sure as hell going on," Strawbridge said. He was
apparently one of those people who had to talk through ideas as
they crossed his mind. "Here's an odd coincidence for you. A few
minutes before we got the request for a welfare check from
Deputy Cutter, Phil Hopkin's wife called in demanding to talk to
Jan Hough. Someone, she didn't say who, let it slip that Jan and
her husband were in the middle of some torrid affair."

Phillips shot a glance at Mim, who shrugged.

"Were they?"

Strawbridge groaned. "Chief, there is something about Jan
Hough that makes half the women on the Slope imagine their
husbands are sleeping with her. And I've got to tell you, a good
many of the men wish that the rumors were true. Normally, I'd

take up for Jan, but it looks like this rumor might actually have some basis in truth."

"How's that?"

"Well, at first blush, the evidence in front of me suggests she and Hopkin murdered her poor husband and then flew off together in his airplane."

"Are you saying Jan Hough murdered her husband while she was on the phone with Deputy Cutter?"

"It's not likely," Strawbridge said. "I'm saying the evidence suggests that could be the case. There's a small puddle of avgas on the floor. A stray bullet might have hit the fuel tank. Not a big leak, but whoever flew out of here left in a rush."

"What exactly did Cutter say when he called this in?" Phillips asked.

"I can get you copies of the logs," Strawbridge said. "But from what I've been told, he gave this location, said he'd heard shots, and asked us to do a welfare check. It wasn't much. Dispatch said he sounded like he was in a hurry."

Mim, who up until now had been silent as a mouse, spoke up. "Does the name Leo Beck mean anything to you?"

"It does," Strawbridge said. "As a matter of fact, one of my other investigators, Detective Jolivet, said Jan called him a little over an hour ago and asked him to swing by and see if Beck was home."

"Was he?" Phillips asked. "Home?"

"His truck was in front of his house," Strawbridge said. "According to Jolivet that was all Hough wanted to know. He assumed she just wanted to talk to Beck and left it at that."

"Is Beck home now?"

"I haven't checked," Strawbridge said. "It's on my list of things to do . . . which, I might add, is getting longer as we speak."

Lola grimaced, giving a thanks-for-nothing glare at the phone.

Phillips waved her off. "Got it," she said. "I'll let you get to your rat killin'."

"I apologize for being so abrupt," Strawbridge said. "We get more than our share of homicides on the Slope, but they don't customarily involve one of my best officers. I really do hope you find your deputy."

"We will," Phillips said.

No, we won't, Lola thought. *Not until he wants to be found. By then, it might be too late to help him.*

CHAPTER 50

J AN HOUGH WAS VAGUELY AWARE SHE WAS IN THE BACK OF A PLANE, hands and feet duct taped so tight she'd lost all feeling, wrapped up like a burrito in the moldy wing cover, and shot full of some kind of drug that made her feel like she might throw up. They were in the air. She could tell that from the turbulence and the chatter of the radio . . . The radio? For some reason, Beck had taken the time to clamp a headset over her ears. He just had to have an audience.

Her eyes fluttered shut, and she drifted off to the hum of the engine and sway of the little Cessna as it wallowed on the wind. Thirty seconds or an hour later when she came to—she had no way of knowing—the radio was quiet. She'd lost control of her bladder at some point while she'd been out. It couldn't be helped so she put it out of her mind. She had a lot more to worry about than being embarrassed. Bryan was dead. The thought of it brought a crushing pain deep in her chest, like she'd already spent days crying over the loss. He could be a real idiot, but he was her idiot. The sux had worn off, allowing her to move her neck inside the cramped wing cover and take some of the pressure off her aching muscles. The small movement brought waves of nausea, first making her dry heave, then slowly subsiding into a woozy sleepiness, almost euphoric, like she didn't really care who was dead or that she was trussed up in the back of a crazy man's airplane. Her head lolled to the side in the filthy canvas—putting her face-to-face with a very dead Phil Hopkin.

She yelped reflexively, angry at herself the moment the sound left her lips.

Beck's baritone voice clicked over the intercom.

"Ah," he said, soft, pleasant, like they were old friends. The hollow sincerity made it all the more terrifying. "You're awake. I thought you might sleep longer. We're only about half an hour south of the village of Atqasuk. Not much there, I know, but I was worried we might lose fuel from that bullet hole. Don't you worry. We're good to go."

Hough arched her back, trying in vain to caterpillar away from Hopkin's body. There was no room. She gave up and collapsed, panting, still only inches from the pallid corpse of the man she'd shot to death when she believed he was shooting at her. She wanted to thrash, to crash the plane, but even the smallest movement made her stomach churn and her head feel as if she'd been stabbed in the back of her neck with an ice pick.

She used her lips to maneuver the tiny boom mic on the headset into place so she could speak.

"Whwheego . . . ?" She wanted to ask where they were going, but it came out breathy and jumbled. She wondered if she might be having a stroke.

Beck gave a sad chuckle, almost as if he felt sorry for her.

"So . . . the succinylcholine wore off a long time ago. Shortly after we took off, I'd imagine. I gave you a little ketamine at first, to keep you from trying to take my head off—and tearing your arms and legs out of their sockets in the process."

"You . . . you're . . ." She swallowed, gathering her thoughts. "That's . . . big of you." If she focused very hard, she could make entire sentences. "Whatda you care? You . . . kill me anyway . . ."

The intercom clicked with Beck's sigh. "You're probably right," he said. "But maybe not. Either way, I may need you to walk on your own. A hostage I have to drag around by the hair makes for a poor human shield."

"You can . . . kiss my ass," Hough managed to say.

He chuckled again, this one more vile, malignant. "I suppose the ketamine's worn off too. Tell me, did you see spiders? I hear people on ketamine dream about spiders. Keeps me from touching the stuff."

"You're . . . a twisted . . . man . . ."

"You feeling queasy?"

"Kiss my ass," she said again.

"I imagine you are," he said. "Can't have you going berserk in the air while I'm trying to fly the plane."

Her words were thick, like she was talking with a mouth full of marbles.

"What did you give me?"

"Just a little skin pop of black tar."

The pain in her head grew exponentially at the news. A liquid flame pulsed in her brain with each beat of her heart.

She choked back a sob.

"You shot me up with heroin?"

"I did," he said. "A bubble under the skin of your forearm. We're looking at two and a half hours of flight time. I wouldn't rub it if I were you. There might be enough in there to kill you if it hit you all at once. But you needed a slow burn to keep you docile."

She began to sob.

"You . . . you . . . asshole!"

She screamed until her voice was raw, then caught her breath while she waited for the agony in her head to subside. Perhaps it was the sudden shot of adrenaline or maybe the effect of the drugs wearing off, but little by little it became easier to speak.

"Are you done?" he asked. "You can see now why I did what I did. I could tell the first time I met you that you were a fighter. Go down fighting. That would be your motto. No compliant prisoner just hoping to bargain for a few more breaths." He snorted. "I respect that. I can't have it, but I respect it."

This guy loved to hear himself talk. She could use that.

Her chest still heaved, but she willed herself to calm. If she hoped to get out of this, she would have to use her head.

"Where are we going?"

His laugh came over the intercom again, drawn and tired, but just as malevolent.

"Have you ever wondered why the bad guy in the movie, when he's got the hero in his clutches, always takes the time to spell out the minute details of their criminal enterprise, all so the hero can somehow get free and muck everything up? I always think—how stupid can you be."

"So, you're not going to spell out the minute details of your criminal enterprise?" The heroin still slurred her speech enough that he probably couldn't tell she was mocking him. A shame, because in her head she was spot-on with his officious drone.

"I am not," he said. "Because all my criminal enterprises are behind me. I just want to get away . . . and you are making it next to impossible."

"How?" she asked.

"You know how," he said. "By watching my house and my office and harassing me by smoking outside my window like a smug little bitch."

She craned her neck outside the edge of the wing cover so she could just make out the back of his head, the green headset mussing his silver hair. The tension in his voice made her imagine bloodshot eyes and a throbbing vein along his temple.

"I meant how are you getting away," she said.

More than a minute went by before he answered—ages in the middle of this kind of conversation. Hough kept quiet, knowing that he could not.

Finally, static crackled over the intercom again.

"I guess there's not much to it," he said. "I need a few things from the cabin."

Hough licked her lips. She was so thirsty.

"What could you possibly need from your cabin?" she asked. "You gotta have all your money in secret accounts somewhere."

Beck gave a genuine laugh. "You're right," he said. "Gold. Where I am going, is . . . somewhat off the grid. I can't risk running out of money because my phone won't get a signal."

"Off the grid," Hough said. "What could be more off the grid than your cabin?"

"The cabin is only a stopover," he said. "I'll top off with fuel and then fly to Russia."

Hough let that sink in through her brain fog. Was this guy really that crazy.

"Just . . . fly away to Russia?"

"Shishkabob is a little over three hundred miles from the cabin," he said, joking about the village of Shishmaref. "I can fuel up there if I run into problems. Then, it's only an hour across the Bering Sea to Cape Dezhnev."

They hit a pocket of turbulence, tossing the little plane. Something heavy slid across the floor and pressed hard against Hough's ribs. She shivered when she realized it was Phil Hopkin's knee, locked stiff with rigor.

"You make it sound simple," Hough said.

"It will be simple," he said. "Very simple. But not easy. That stretch of the Bering can be a nasty little bitch, and, of course, I'll have to fly low to avoid Russian radar, but . . ." He twisted his neck around to look over his shoulder. A cruel sneer crossed his lips behind the tiny microphone. His voice crackled in her ears. "Don't worry your pretty head about anything beyond the cabin. One way or another, your trip ends there."

Earlier, she'd been worried she might accidentally knock the headset off. Now, she raked it hard against the wing cover until she freed herself from Leonard Beck's taunting voice. She fell back against the musty cloth, exhausted from even that small effort. He could talk all he wanted to. She didn't have to hear it. On her side now, she looked at Phil Hopkin's corpse and listened to the drone of the Cessna's engine as it flew deeper into the night.

" *'Your trip ends there . . . ,* ' " she muttered, mocking Beck's tone and cadence.

Two minutes earlier, she'd discovered a thin metal stay running through the fabric of the wing cover. Slowly, ignoring waves of nausea and the excruciating pain in her dying fingers, she began to gouge at the duct tape around her wrists.

"Your trip ends at the cabin too, asshole," she whispered.

CHAPTER 51

Fifty Minutes Earlier

CUTTER FIGURED HE HAD ABOUT TWENTY MINUTES, MAYBE HALF AN
hour before the chief started pinging his phone to try and locate
him. He took a chance and called the Peanut Farm sports bar,
paging Tony Caprese as soon as he ended the call with Leo Beck.
It was Thursday, the day of Tony's celebration party—if he'd
passed the check ride for his float plane rating. He had. Fortunately, he'd just arrived at his party.

"Hi, Marshal!" the young pilot said, giddy that Cutter had
called to congratulate him.

"Proud of you," Cutter said. "But here's the thing. I need your
help on something that's extremely sensitive."

The background noise suddenly grew quieter. Cutter pictured
the kid standing at the reception desk, turning away from his
friends to talk treason over the phone. If anything, he sounded
more excited to help with a sensitive assignment than he was
about passing his flight test.

"Yeah, sure," he said. "Anything. What do you need?"

"You might want to listen to what I'm asking you to do first before you agree. I need a pilot. This is your party. How much have
you had to drink?"

"I only just got here," Tony said. "Half an Alaskan Amber, if
that."

"Would you feel comfortable flying?"

"Yeah . . ." More tentative now. "Weather's shit out there now, but it's supposed to lift some by morning."

"Right," Cutter said. "I need a pilot tonight. The sooner the better."

"I flew down commercial," Tony said. "I don't really have an airplane—"

Cutter looked at his watch. "Jan Hough is in trouble."

"What kind of trouble?"

"The kind that she won't come out of alive without our help," Cutter said.

"Where do you need to fly?"

"Shungnak," Cutter said. "But I don't necessarily want to tip my hand by flying straight in—"

"How about Ambler," Tony said. "I've flown there a bunch of times. I used to date one of the teachers."

"What about Kobuk?" Cutter asked. "Upriver might be better." Cutter wanted to be able to drift down quietly, but he didn't say it.

"I don't know anybody in Kobuk," Tony said.

"Ambler it is, then," Cutter said.

"When would you want to leave?"

"As soon as you can get a plane."

"Can I talk about this to my float plane instructor?"

"If you trust him to keep quiet. Small circle on this one."

"Understood," Tony said. "He's back and forth to the Slope all the time. Pretty sure he's got a crush on Jan."

"Doesn't everyone?"

Tony gave a shrill whistle, no doubt waving over his float plane instructor. He came back on the line less than a minute later.

"We're good to go," he said, breathless with excitement. "How fast can you get to Lake Hood?"

"Hang on," Cutter said. "That's a seaplane base."

"Trust me," Tony said.

And Cutter did.

Cutter took five minutes to search online for maps of the meandering Kobuk River, specifically the tributaries to the south near the Iñupiaq village of Shungnak. It took some searching, but he was finally able to find one map, dated 1911, that identified the Black River as the place where the Becks were supposed to have their cabin—*Imigiksaaq*—"fresh water."

Cutter knew there was a chance he was dead wrong. Maybe Beck wasn't going to the cabin at all. But a quick call to Utqiagvik tower had confirmed that a Cessna 185 had departed shortly after Cutter's telephone conversation with Beck. The plane had continued due south for as long as they'd had it on radar—making a beeline for the Kobuk. Adding the fact that Beck had no idea Cutter knew of the cabin's existence, and that he seemed extremely addled on the phone, probably making plans on the fly. For whatever reason, the man believed law enforcement was preparing to raid his home and his office. He needed something, probably travel documents, maybe money, though Beck seemed the kind of man who'd have the bulk of his fortune squirreled away in Swiss or South Dakota accounts. This purely circumstantial evidence—and more importantly, his gut—told Cutter that Beck would head for his cabin. Beyond that, Cutter flat out did not know where else to look.

Now he had to get there before anything happened to Jan. To do that, Tony Caprese would fly him to Ambler. At night. In the snow.

Twenty-five miles downriver from the Shungnak, Ambler did look like the better choice of places to land, especially if Tony knew someone there. Almost twice the population of Kobuk with some two hundred and fifty souls, it wasn't really a booming metropolis, but chances were Tony's friend would either have a boat or know someone who could get him one.

Semi-satisfied with the rough idea where he was going, Cutter dropped his phone in the Faraday bag from his glovebox and headed toward Ted Stevens International Airport.

Traffic in South Anchorage was light, and fifteen minutes later, he found himself a parking spot on Lakeshore Drive facing the aircraft tiedowns north of the lake between the water and the gravel runway. Piper Super Cubs, de Havilland Beavers, Cessnas from diminutive 152 trainers to station-wagon-like 207s, all stood out in colorful contrast to the yellow birch and blue spruce. It was postcard Alaska—as was the sign on Lakeshore Drive that reminded motorists that on these roads, aircraft had the right of way.

Lake Hood—actually, two connected lakes, Hood and Spenard— was the busiest seaplane base in the world. With the weather turning colder, a few of the planes were already out of the water and on wheels or skis, but Alaska bush pilots had to be a die-hard breed. Most would leave their birds on floats for at least another week.

Tony Caprese drove up ten minutes later and got out carrying a backpack and a small duffel. A bush pilot, he knew better than to leave home without things he would need to spend the night away, possibly in the woods. Cutter was surprised to see Neil Olufsen—the taciturn, Elmer-Fudd-hat-wearing pilot who'd flown him from Utqiagvik to Wainwright just days earlier. A bush pilot for the past thirty years, he flew primarily out of Anchorage but regularly filled in for friends on the North Slope. Uneven shoulders and a noticeable gleam in his eyes told Cutter he'd been at the party much longer than Tony and was, by now, well into his cups.

He turned out to be Caprese's float plane instructor.

"I understand you are in need of an airplane to go save Jan," he said. "I think we can fix you up."

"Neil's going to rent us his Husky," Tony said.

Olufsen homed in on Cutter, his eyes narrowed to fine slits. "Is the government paying for this, or are you?"

"All me," Cutter said. "But I'll leave you my open credit card."

Olufsen waved his hand. "Never mind that. Just fill it up with gas when you bring it back." He looked at Tony. "If you crash, I'll tell my insurance company you stole the damned thing."

"Well," Tony said. "I know the marshal's in a rush, so—"

Cutter paused. "Hang on, how are you getting home, Neil?"

"Not to worry," Olufsen said. "If I was in any shape to drive, I'd be flying you myself. My wife's on her way to pick me up."

Cutter grabbed his duffel from the Ford and followed the men out to the plane—such as it was.

A box kite with wings would have been a better description. Like the venerable Piper Super Cub, Neil Olufsen's Aviat Husky was a high-wing fabric-covered taildragger with tandem seating—that is, the pilot sat directly in front of the single passenger. Cutter had known he should bring minimal gear, but with both men's bags, the compartment behind the rear seat would be packed to the gunnels.

"Remember," Olufsen said to his young protégé, "She'll do an easy one hundred and forty miles per hour at seventy-five percent power, but you'll gain well over a hundred miles of range if you keep the throttle at fifty-five percent and cruise at one-thirty."

"Roger that," Tony said.

"I don't really like this rain," Olufsen said. He held onto the prop to keep from toppling over as he leaned back to look sky-ward. "But the ceiling is plenty high to get out of here. Weather's squirrely in the Alaska Range during the daylight hours. Fly the Parks Highway to be on the safe side, then make your turn toward the Kobuk once you get through the pass. If you get into trouble, set her down somewhere and wait out the weather."

"Roger that," Tony said again.

He folded the door down and showed Cutter where to put his feet to maneuver himself into the little airplane. The rear seat had a stick and rudder pedals too, identical to the pilot's, who sat up front, or from Cutter's point of view, sitting in his lap. The cracked ribs made climbing in a lesson in pain tolerance. A big man to begin with, crammed into the small plane, Cutter couldn't shake the feeling that he'd somehow squeezed himself into a shirt that was too tight—and the buttons might start popping off at any moment.

Tony buckled his harness and put the headset over his ballcap. He tapped his right earpiece, a signal that Cutter should put on the headset that was hanging on the wall with a small bungee cord.

"All settled in, Marshal?" he asked when they were both on the intercom.

"Good to go," Cutter said.

"Thanks for trusting me to do this," Tony said.

Outside, Neil made sure the doors were all buttoned up on his bird, then patted her on the fuselage, pulling the wheel chocks and stepping well back before Tony turned over the prop.

Bush Pilot Tony had grown some honest to God swagger since Cutter had seen him last. What had once been jittery, indecisive movements now flowed easily from task to task. He sounded like a different man when he contacted Ground for instructions on the radio. Four white-knuckle minutes later, the capable little Husky leapt off the gravel runway and roared into the night sky. Spattering rain trailed along the trapezoidal windows as Tony banked to the northwest. Cutter shrank into his seat the best he could, trying to keep his hands and feet off the controls so he didn't interfere with Tony's work.

"Think we'll have to stop for fuel?" he asked when Tony was flying straight and level. They passed over Eagle River under the right wing.

"This airplane should give us six hours of seat time if we need it," Tony said. "But we'll make it to Ambler in three and a half, give or take. I'm not too worried about fuel."

"You say that like you might be worried about something else. Weather ahead?"

"There is weather," Tony said. "But it's not too bad. We can skirt it if we need to."

"What is it then?"

"Flying at night is no different than flying during the day—as long as you avoid flying into a mountain."

Cutter pressed a cheek against the chilly window and peered out at the intermittent streaks of rain in the flashing wing lights.

"Okay . . ."

"Landing at night is a little trickier," Tony said. "Neil said I should stop overthinking it. He says the hardest thing about landing at night is finding the damned runway. He's right too. Ambler's got a good runway. As long as I can find it, I'll have no trouble landing at night.

"Won't you see the lights?"

"I'm not sure," Tony said. "I should be able to see the river, and the GPS will put me right over the village, but my friend said they're having a little trouble with the lights."

"Trouble?"

"You're supposed to be able to turn them on by clicking your radio mic a couple of times," Tony said. "Evidently, that system's got some problems at the moment."

"Can't they just do it from the ground?"

"You'd think," Tony chuckled. "But she'd have to find the airport maintenance guy. She's just a teacher."

"So how will we land?"

"My friend said she's working on it."

Cutter nestled himself in, slowly coming to grips with the fact that he wasn't going to fall through the fabric sides.

"I hate to ask," he said. "But I've got a lot to do when we arrive. Would you mind if I shut my eyes for a few minutes?"

He folded his arms, feeling the thrum of the engine against his earpiece as he tried to keep the pressure off his injured ribs while not putting too much weight against the painted fabric that separated him from the cold outside world by a measly half a millimeter.

"I'm glad you can relax," Tony said. "Forgive me for saying this, but after our last flight, I was under the impression you didn't much care for small airplanes."

"I don't." Cutter shut his eyes. "There's nothing I can do about it, so when I get on a plane, I just give up hope."

CHAPTER 52

LOLA TRIED CUTTER'S CELL AGAIN, WILLING HIM TO PICK UP, CURS-
ing under her breath when he didn't.

"Strawbridge said Arliss sounded like he was in a hurry," Mim
whispered. She looked hard at Phillips. "Do you think he's done
something stupid?"

The chief took a deep breath but didn't answer.

No," Lola said. "I don't. Think about it, Mim. You know him.
Arliss Cutter might blast off like a missile, but he's a guided missile. Everything he does has a purpose. We may not see it in the
moment, but he does. I trust him."

"So do I," Mim said. "And that's the problem. He's all about law
and order, but when it comes to me and the kids . . . he'd do
whatever it took to keep us safe. Laws or no laws. He won't care
what happens to him."

"We'll find him," Phillips said. "It's what we do."

Lola brightened. "Yes, we will, Chief!" She held up her phone.
"Cutter has me make our flight reservations all the time. I know
his Alaska Air number and password."

"And?"

"It looks like he made a reservation on the next smokin' jet to
Fairbanks."

"What's the flight number," Phillips asked. "I'll call Airport Police and get them to stop him."

Still scrolling through her cell, Lola shook her head. "Looks
like that flight left five minutes ago."

"At least we have something to work with," the chief said. "It's a one-hour flight, give or take. I'll get the Fairbanks DUSMs to meet him when he gets off the plane and shove a phone in his ear. He'll have to talk to me."

Her gaze lingered on Lola, tight-lipped. It was easy to imagine her as a parent. Jill Phillips was, in fact, "Mom" to the fifteen deputy US marshals assigned to the district of Alaska.

She gave a disappointed shake of her head.

"Teariki, tell me you wouldn't cover for him."

Lola scoffed. "Of course, I would, Chief! I reckon I'd cover for him any day of the week. Twice on Sunday if he asked me to. But you know Cutter better than that. He'd never ask." Her lip began to quiver. "Arliss is my partner, Jill. I want to find him as bad as you do."

Phillips's phone rang fifty-eight minutes later. It was Deputy Ryan Madsen. Paul Gutierrez had been the lone deputy in the Fairbanks suboffice until Madsen, a thirty-eight-year-old lateral transfer who'd been a special agent with the United States Department of Health and Human Services, had graduated the Marshals Academy a month prior. Both Madsen and Gutierrez were solid deputies who worked hard and played hard. Only one week before, both men had donned colorful luchador masks—red and blue—and worn them down the hall to the US Clerk's office. Luckily for them, the deputy clerk of court had a strong heart and a wicked sense of humor. Phillips, and virtually anyone else in the district, prefaced every interaction with either of the two Fairbanks deputies with some version of, "Don't bullshit, now. This is serious."

"No joy, chief," Madsen said.

"What do you mean, no joy?" Phillips rarely snapped at her troops. The fact that she was doing it now only illustrated how worried she was.

"I mean Cutter was not on the plane," Madsen said.

Lola could tell the chief was gritting her teeth. Phillips had been a plain old deputy once. She knew the rules about covering for a partner. "Don't feed me that," she said. "Are you absolutely sure Arliss Cutter wasn't on that airplane? I'm not going to be mad if you tell me straight right now. But, remember, you're still on probation. I like you, Ryan, I really do. But consider yourself fired if I find out you're lying to me."

Madsen chuckled. "A hundred percent he wasn't. The gate agent even let us do a walk-through and check the restrooms."

"Could he have gotten off on the tarmac?" Phillips knew she was grasping at straws. "I wouldn't put it past Cutter to James Bond it out the landing gear or some such thing."

"Afraid not, Chief. The flight attendant showed me the manifest. Cutter wasn't on this plane."

"Thank you, Ryan," Phillips said. "I apologize for threatening to fire you . . . I meant it, though. In case you're wondering . . ."

"I have no doubt, Chief," Madsen said. "We're here if you need us."

Phillips ended the call and pitched the phone to the center of Mim's table. "Cutter played us." Chin on her chest, she peered up at Lola. "He was never going to get on that plane. But he knew you would look at his account."

Two and a half hours after they'd last seen Arliss Cutter, Lola, Mim, and Jill Phillips sat at the dining room table, still with no idea where he'd gone. Mim had given them everything from their visit to South Dakota. They'd yet to hear even a peep of news from Chief Strawbridge.

Lola called Joe Bill, who was an hour into a busy shift.

Mim called to check on her children, talking in hushed whispers to Constance and each of her boys in turn. She was a good mother, fierce. Lola respected that. She figured she'd be a straight-up Polynesian version of Arliss Cutter whenever she had kids. Hell, just about every Māori mother she knew was basically a female Arliss Cutter. Maybe that's why she got along with him so well. He reminded her of her aunties in the Cook Islands. She'd have to remember to tell him that when she saw him next.

Chief Phillips called her husband, Muncy, to tell him she was going to be even later than expected and to check on their toddler, whom she referred to as "the runt," especially when she was tired or stressed. Now she was both.

Their obligatory calls made, the three women put their phones in the middle of the table.

Phillips clapped her hands. "All right, ladies," she said. "Let's go over what we know one more time."

Lola leaned her elbows on the table and rested her chin on her fist, glum as she'd ever been in her life.

Mim sank into her chair, arms folded across her chest. "My money's still on Leo Beck."

"Agreed," Lola said, her words muddled from talking against her fist. "Nancy and Sean are staying late. I'm heading to the office in a minute to help them and do a full workup on that shit-bird. Credit history, traffic tickets, overdue library books. I mean to crawl so far up this guy's caboose I can check his tonsils from below."

"How can I help?" Mim asked.

"Honestly," Phillips said, "I'm not even sure what *I* can do. We should hear from North Slope PD again before too long. That might give us some—"

Faceup in the middle of the table, Lola's phone began to dance, the caller ID clear for all of them to read.

CUTTER.

CHAPTER 53

JAN HOUGH FELT THE FAMILIAR POP AND WHINE WHEN HER EARS cleared. They were descending. She'd been so focused on sawing through the tape binding her hands that she'd lost track of time. Unable to look at her progress, she estimated she was only half as far through the tape as she needed to be in order to rip it with her cramped muscles—not to mention being strung out on heroin.

Beck's voice buzzed in the headset that lay beside her ear. "Buckle up," he joked. "We're ten minutes out . . ."

He fell silent again, focusing, no doubt, on finding his airstrip in the dark.

Wind buffeted the little plane as they came down. Even from her vantage point on the floor, Hough could see snow zipping by out the right-side windows in the green glow of the nav lights.

Beck cursed under his breath, barely audible over the headset that lay beside her. No false bravado for her benefit this time. He was really worried about something. She heard a faint click, click, click over the radio as he repeatedly keyed the mic. He cursed again. Her body grew heavy as he added power and climbed, banking back the way they'd come. He'd missed his landing and had to go around.

He leveled off, flying straight again. The plane's bright landing lights reflected off low clouds and blowing snow outside the windows.

Click. Click. Click.

Beck attempted to turn on the runway lights again.

"It's about time," he muttered.

Hough's stomach rose against her chest as the Cessna dropped out of the sky.

"For the love of—" Beck added power and pulled up, climbing and banking. "Get off the runway, you dumb shits!"

He continued to curse a herd of caribou as he came around for yet another approach.

The runway lights must have turned off. Beck clicked the mic again. Evidently to no avail this time, judging from his frantic curses. The plane continued to settle lower and lower.

Hough stopped picking at the tape with her metal stay and braced herself as best she could against the back of the copilot seat and Phil Hopkin's rigored knee.

Beck was going to chance the landing—at night in the snow on a dark runway crawling with caribou. Hough couldn't help but wonder if she'd even get the chance to kill the bastard.

Three hundred miles to the southeast, at the stick of the Aviat Husky, Tony Caprese heaved a sigh of relief. "Okay, he said. "We made it through Broad Pass."

"You say that like you were worried we wouldn't," Cutter said.

"It's not that," Tony said. "Just happy to be out in the open again, that's all. Not many mountains to run into up on the tundra. Anyway, Healy will be coming up off the right wing. You should be able to get a cell signal any minute now."

Cutter leaned the side of his head against the window and watched the twinkling lights of the tiny mining town of Healy come into view along the black ribbon that was the Parks Highway. Condensation from his breath froze when it hit the plexiglass. Temperatures dropped dramatically north of the Alaska Range. Autumn in Anchorage was already winter in the Interior.

Just as Tony predicted, he was able to get a signal.

Lola answered on the first ring.

"Boss! I've got Mim and the chief on speaker."

Cutter smiled at that. Good partner, warning him from the get-go not to go off the rails with anything he said.

"Sorry to be so abrupt, Chief," he said. "But I'm not sure how long I'll have a signal."

"Go head," Phillips said, her displeasure clear enough with just those two words.

Cutter gave them a quick rundown of what he'd heard go down between Beck and Jan Hough in the hangar. He explained his reasoning, however flawed, and his plans to rescue Jan Hough without getting law enforcement involved—everything but where he was actually going.

Tony flew a slow loop around the cell tower so they could keep a signal.

Jill Phillips could no longer contain herself. "Arliss, this is insane," she said. "I am telling you—"

"I'm going to stop you there, Chief," he said. "You're the best boss I ever had. Normally I'd jump off a moving train for you, but I am not turning around. If you give me a direct order, you know I'll disobey it, then you'll have to do your job and show me the door."

"If you survive long enough."

"There is that," Cutter said. "Anyway, if you feel like that's the way you need to go, I understand."

She was quiet long enough that Cutter thought the connection might have dropped.

Then Mim said, "Arliss, don't kill him unless you have to."

"I won't," Cutter said, more quickly than his heart actually believed.

"Be careful, boss," Lola said.

"I'm about to lose this signal," Cutter said. "Y'all are good enough investigators to figure out where Beck has property. I'm just asking you to take your time. Give me a chance. With any luck, I'll be there waiting for you when you come to pick me up . . . or throw me in jail."

Mim sniffed. "What if you're not?"

"Don't worry about that," Cutter said. "This, this thing I'm doing right now. It is exactly what I'm good at."

Cutter motioned north, urging Tony to fly on.

The line grew spotty almost at once.

"I've got your back, boss," Lola said. "We'll be there to pick you up."

The call dropped before he could answer.

"All good, Marshal?" Tony asked over the intercom.

"About time you call me Cutter, I think."

"Sure . . . Marshal Cutter," Tony said. "Listen, we're looking great on fuel, and we have a smokin' forty-knot tailwind coming off the backside of the Alaska Range. I've kicked up the power a skosh to seventy-five percent of max. That gives us a ground speed right at a hundred and eighty miles an hour. Flight computer says we'll arrive in Ambler at ten minutes past midnight . . . if this tailwind holds."

"That would be outstanding." Cutter thought for a moment. "What do you hear from your friend on the ground? Did she ever find the maintenance guy to fix the runway lights?"

"I guess he's down in Anchorage getting a heart valve replaced," Tony said, as if the guy's heart problems were his fault. "My friend says she's coming up with a work-around, though."

Cutter watched his breath freeze on the plexiglass again as he spoke. "What sort of work-around?"

"She didn't say," Tony said. "Honestly, I'm not sure she even knows yet."

Leo Beck wasted almost forty-five minutes flying circles in the sky, doing low passes of the runway and trying to get the lights to work. A thousand thoughts flooded his mind as he lined up on the black void below him to touch down. His first order of business was to get this damned airplane on the ground in good enough shape he'd be able to take off again. The caribou had scattered on his last pass, disappearing into the trees along the runway, but those damned things could be suicidal. Chances were high that one of them would lumber out in front of him and stop, turning to stare like an imbecile and killing them both. Now the lights had gone tits up again. Beck told himself he needed to get that fixed if he made it through this, then, laughing perversely, realized that if he survived, this would be the last time he ever put wheels on this airfield.

He worried about the snow. It was just a skiff now, barely enough to cover the ground, but taking off again might be problematic if it got too deep. And then there was the problem of what to do with Hough. He had to kill her. That was a given. It was all because of her that he'd been forced to run—leaving his business, his wife, a stellar reputation. But how would he do it? He'd been forced to take care of a fair number of adversaries early in his career, almost as soon as his feet hit the ground in Alaska, but eventually, he'd hired others to do the dirty stuff. Dennis Foye and his pitiful little girlfriend had been his first hands-on work in years. Another shot of drugs would kill her . . . The heroin and ketamine were gone, but he still had a little sux left. Or he could just leave her out in the cold to freeze. However he did it, he hoped Marshal Cutter would eventually figure out where he'd taken her, so he could see what the wolves had done to her body.

A bump of turbulence shook Beck out of his stupor, bringing him back to the here and now of landing the plane—or crashing it.

He adjusted himself in his seat, using his rudder pedals against a persistent northern crosswind. The grass strip ran generally on headings of sixty and two hundred and forty degrees—northwest to southeast. Not because of prevailing winds but because that was the only flat and relatively level ground close enough to his cabin to build a runway.

He added flaps and pulled back on the throttle, slowing, sinking, working the rudder pedals like crazy against the crosswind. The stall warning blared. He leaned forward, stretching his neck to watch for caribou on the runway ahead. Any minute—

The tundra wheels slammed into the runway, hard enough to slam Beck's teeth together.

Hopkin's body flew forward, hitting the back of his seat with a sullen thud. Hough gave a muffled scream.

They bounced, suddenly airborne again. Beck reduced power even more, willing the airplane to stop flying. Then it hit the ground again, just as hard as the first time. Beck clutched the yoke and let her roll, staying off the brakes to keep from ground-looping and eating the dirt with the prop. Slowly, the tail wheel settled to the ground.

Just when he thought he was in the clear, his right wheel veered off the manicured portion of the runway, catching on mud and bouncing over rocks. The wing dipped precariously, lifting the opposite wheel off the ground. Beck instinctively threw his weight left, adding power. The wingtip thwacked against some bushes but careened upward, leveling the airplane long enough that he was able to steer back onto firmer ground. Cursing through clenched teeth and very nearly yanking the yoke off the column, he was able to wallow the battered Cessna to a shaky stop less than a hundred feet from the end of the runway.

A bull caribou, frozen in the beam of the landing lights to his right, stared at him from the tree line before turning tail and disappearing toward the river in a flash of white rump.

Beck used the engine and brakes to spin the little plane around at the northeast end of the runway. He wanted to take advantage of the winds that would likely be coming out of the mountains to the south by the time he took off again. He killed the engine and sat completely still for a long time, thrumming with adrenaline and listening to the sounds of metal as it cooled.

He'd need to give the gear a good inspection before he took off again.

Behind him, Jan Hough sobbed softly in her cocoon, still loopy from the effects of the heroin skin pop, surely more terrified than he was at the hard landing. She wasn't going to be a problem.

He looked at his watch. It was eleven fifteen.

CHAPTER 54

*L*EO BECK DRAGGED HOPKIN'S BODY OUT BY THE FEET, FEELING more than a little queasy when the man's head thudded against the wheel strut on the way to the ground. That was the thing about killing someone. It was impossible for Beck not to imagine that it could have been him bouncing his brain pan off the wheel instead of good old Phil.

The ground was too hard here to bury him. Beck didn't have the time, anyway. Bears and wolves would take care of all that. Rigor made it relatively easy to drag the body a good hundred feet off the runway before dumping him unceremoniously in the bushes—a buck brush burial, Sherman Billy had called it. Beck looked at the body, then back at the silhouette of the airplane on the runway, judging it far enough away that if a bear claimed the corpse before he was ready to fly out, he would have time to get a shot off. You had to think like that in the North. Especially here. Bears were a real problem.

"Now," he said to himself when he trudged back to the plane. "What to do about Jan?"

He found her writhing on the floor and gave her a smack with the flat of his hand on the top of her head.

"Knock it off!" he snapped. "Quit moving around."

She moaned and then went limp immediately.

"That's better." He nodded, still pondering on what to do with her and when he should do it. He considered dumping her in the buck brush with Hopkin. The bears would have a good old time tearing into that burrito, and maybe he would leave her like that when he was ready to go. Until then, he'd bring her along in case there was a problem or the marshal somehow caught up with him. No reason to get rid of that insurance policy yet. Besides that, he didn't mind having someone to talk to.

She lay on her side now, wrapped in the ridiculous wing cover with her face exposed from the chin up.

"You know," he said. "I thought of staging it so it looked like you and Hopkin were lovers, you know, a murder suicide. I could have made something like that work if I'd had enough time."

"Wouldn't work," she said, eyes still at half-mast. The bubble of heroin under her skin was doing its job. "Hopkin's blood is all over the scene. They'll run tests—"

"I know that," Beck snapped. "That's why I didn't waste my time with it."

He dragged her to the edge of the aircraft so she was seated, her legs dangling over the edge.

"You should lose the look," he said.

"What look?" she sneered, swaying like a worm in her wing cover. She swallowed hard, and for a moment, he thought she might throw up.

"The look that says you want to gouge out my eyeballs."

"You're going to kill me," she said. "What do you care what look I have?"

"You don't know that," he lied. "Your friend might make it here before I leave."

"Oh, he'll figure it out." She choked back a sob. "But not for a while. I'm not stupid, Leonard. Anyway, you murdered my husband, you bastard. I wish you'd go ahead and put a bullet in me."

"In time," he said, and threw her over his shoulder, wing cover and all. She proved to be much lighter than Hopkin, but still deadweight. With his arm across the backs of her knees, her head and shoulders bounced against his back in time with her whimpering moans. It was awkward, but it worked. He didn't notice until they reached the house that she'd lost control of her bladder.

"You're not such a tough cop after all," he muttered. "Just remember, my dear. This is all your fault."

Muffled sobs came from inside the wing cover.

"Quit your crying," he said. "I've got a couple of steaks in the propane freezer. You can talk to me while I eat them."

"You awake?" Tony asked. Then, before Cutter could answer, he said, "The booming metropolis of Ambler coming up on the left side of the airplane. Snowing like hell now. I'm gonna be glad to get on the ground."

Cutter could see a few lights from town through the blowing snow. Below them was a dark, winding ribbon.

"That's the Kobuk River below us, meandering back and forth in those big oxbows . . . and . . ." He pointed forward with an open hand. "I'm ninety percent sure that's the runway. Hard to get a read in the snow."

"What about the other ten percent?" Cutter asked.

"Could be a tributary off the river," Tony said. "Or a mud bog between the trees. Either way, it won't be good if it turns out not to be the runway."

"I guess not," Cutter said.

Tony kept flying toward his best guess, making frequent minor adjustments to the flaps and throttle like he fully intended to land.

Then the ground ahead of them lit up like Main Street.

The work-around at the Ambler airport turned out to be two pickup trucks parked at either end of the strip with their headlights pointing down the length of the runway and four ATVs, two on either side, shining their lights across the patchy snow.

"I told you she would come through," Tony said as he brought the little Husky down in a textbook landing. Before, he'd wrestled with the plane. Now, he played this one like an instrument he'd been familiar with all his life.

"You've come a hell of a long way since I first flew with you a week ago," Cutter observed, once they were on the ground and turning to taxi toward the small crowd of people waiting on the gravel apron.

"I guess it was almost dying with Jan," he said. "Once you have one of those, everyday flying is a piece of cake. You just rely on procedures and stop worrying about the wings falling off."

"What if a wing does fall off?"

"Like you said when you got on the plane. You just give up hope."

Tony brought the plane to a halt alongside four people waiting on the gravel. Cutter presumed them all to be bush teachers.

Cutter gingerly unfolded himself out of the little plane, trying in vain to hide his injuries from the audience.

"Cracked rib," a middle-aged man with Albert Einstein hair observed, giving Cutter a shoulder to brace on as he climbed down.

"I'm thinking bruised," Cutter lied.

Cutter gave Tony his credit card. "To fuel up the airplane. I'll get it back from you later. Thanks for the ride on such short notice."

"Thanks for asking me. Are you sure you don't need any help from here on out?"

"The boat?"

"Oh yeah." Tony turned to a short Native woman wearing a black wool beanie and insulated Carhartt coveralls. "This is Shawna, my friend—"

"His girlfriend," the young woman said. "You'd think he would have figured that out since I'm out here in the snow on a school night helping you guys out when I gotta be up in five hours."

"My girlfriend," Tony said. "She has you fixed up with a boat."

Einstein came up to listen, and two other teachers Cutter judged to be husband and wife crowded in beside him. All were dressed in Carhartts or wool. Einstein, Shawna, and the other young woman all had rifles. The male half of the young couple carried a large-frame revolver in a Diamond D holster on his chest. A man after Cutter's heart. They would have made a formidable platoon if he hadn't been worried about getting them killed.

"You want to go upriver, right?" Shawna said. "After someone dangerous."

"That's correct," Cutter said. "He's holding a friend of mine hostage. A female police officer named Jan Hough from Utqiagvik. He's killed at least four people in the last week—two in the past five hours. One of them was Jan's husband."

"Holy shit," Einstein said.

"I have reason to believe he's stopped off for a few hours at a cabin off the Black River."

"Black River . . ." Einstein scratched his fuzzy head. "That's east?"

"I'm not sure they even call it that anymore." Cutter opened his phone and showed the group his 1911 map. "Looks like it's a little over halfway between here and Shungnak. I'll need to move quiet and fast."

Shawna looked to Einstein. "What about your canoe?"

"Sure," he said. "It has an electric trolling motor. Quiet enough, but the battery won't last to get you that far upriver though."

"I'll use my boat to get us upriver," Shawna said. "Then you can switch to Evan's canoe while we're still out of earshot. We'll have to be careful, though. The Kobuk meanders so much you can be less than a couple hundred feet away from someone in the next oxbow over and not even know."

"You're all by yourself," the young man with the revolver said. His named turned out to be Justin. "We could help you."

"I have no doubt that you could," Cutter said. "But more people means more noise. You've been a huge help already."

"So you're going alone?" Tony asked.

"From the point where you and Shawna drop me off with Evan's canoe." Cutter gave a nod to Tony. "That credit card I gave you doesn't have a balance. There's enough on there to fill up the plane and, just in case something happens, to buy Evan a new canoe and trolling motor."

Tony's baby face darkened. "You'll make it back."

Justin nodded at the badge in front of Cutter's Colt Python. "I get that a US marshal is going after a killer, but where's your backup? Where are all the other cops."

"About that." Cutter handed Justin a business card, on the back of which he'd written Lola Teariki and Jill Phillips's cell numbers. "If you'd do me a favor and call the top number and tell them where I'm going."

"Of course," Justin said.

Cutter unclipped the star from his belt and slipped it into his pocket. "Until then, I'm it. Just a man trying to save his friend."

CHAPTER 55

SHAWNA'S BOAT TURNED OUT TO BE AN EIGHTEEN-FOOT OPEN SKIFF that her father had given her. The snow fell in earnest now, huge flakes that were really dozens of flakes clinging to each other. Cutter dug a set of Merino wool long johns and a quilted Zero Foxtrot hoodie in black camo out of his duffel. He rarely went the tactical route anymore, preferring the wool a hunter might wear over gear with a military bend, but the black hoodie was light and warm. Sometimes it was too warm, but not tonight. Layered in a Merino wool hat and underwear, the wool plaid shirt he'd been wearing, the hoodie, and a parka shell, he'd be good to around fifteen above for a while—unless he fell in the water. Then it wouldn't matter what he had on. Rafts of ice the size of his hand rattled periodically down the side of the skiff on the current.

Shawna stood by the boat wearing insulated XtraTufs as Cutter climbed over the gunnel. "Started to freeze upriver," she said. "Another day or two and we wouldn't be making this trip."

Evan secured the bowline of a fourteen-foot forest-green Old Town canoe to a cleat at the rear of the skiff before sloshing back to the bank beside Justin and his wife.

"Good luck!" the three of them said, almost in unison.

Hand on the tiller of the seventy horse Tohatsu outboard, Shawna looked to Cutter and Tony. Both gave her a thumbs-up.

The dark water burbled as she threw the motor into reverse and backed them into the current. She let the bow drift around to deeper water before she opened the throttle and took them in a wide arc to point upstream against the sluggish current. Snow slapped Cutter in the face with wet kisses. Sitting amidships, across from Tony, he turned toward the stern and bowed his head against the frigid air. The boat jumped up on step at once, cutting a silver V in the water. Behind them, the little green canoe trailed obediently, dancing on the wake.

Shawna whistled to get his attention from her perch on an old ice chest at the tiller. She pitched him a baggie of something.

"Salmon strips," she yelled above the engine noise and water chattering against the boat. "They'll give you energy."

Cutter took one and passed the bag to Tony.

"Keep them," Shawna said. "It's getting colder. I got a feeling you're gonna need all the energy you can get."

The river swept back and forth in great, meandering oxbows, some of them, as Shawna had said, divided only by a thin strip of land.

Twenty minutes after they left Ambler, Shawna let off the throttle, slowing the little boat enough that it came off-step but still putted upstream, barely staying ahead of the current. She motored slowly toward a cutbank covered in willows and then motioned for Tony to tie off the bow. He did, and she killed the engine.

"Can I see your phone again?"

Cutter gave it to her with the map open.

"We're here right now," she said. "I'm thinking the place you're looking for is three oxbows up, at the confluence of what they used to call Black River. It flows in at the bottom of a deep oxbow to the south. There's a cabin back up in there off a little clear stream. A woman from Shungnak owns the land. I can't remember her name."

"That would be the place," Cutter said.

Shawna drew a line with her finger between the bottom of the oxbow and the Black River. "They got an airstrip here, between the cabin and the clear water creek. If I was gonna say, sneak up on a moose, I'd climb up the bank of the Kobuk here, downstream a bit from where the Black River dumps in. That'll put you right behind the airstrip."

Cutter thanked them for the ride and climbed into the little canoe while Tony steadied it alongside the skiff. He made sure the electric trolling motor worked and then cast off, buzzing silently upriver. Tony untied the skiff from the willows, and Shawna started the outboard again and turned the boat toward home, burbling along just above idle. She let the current take them first, as if she didn't want to disturb the silence of the river.

Cutter chewed on another salmon strip and checked his watch.

A quarter to one.

The trolling motor pushed him upriver at a steady four miles an hour. Fortunately, he didn't have far to go. Every bend was new territory, with unknown trails and new dangers. This was why Grumpy had rules about thoroughly scouting a place if possible before taking any action.

Cutter motored beyond the place he thought Shawna had advised him to climb the bank, making it past the mouth of the Black River. He couldn't see the lights of a cabin, but he could smell the smoke from a wood fire. Cutter wasn't positive, but he thought he got a whiff of something that might be cooking meat.

Beck was still there.

Cutter turned off the electric motor and let the river take the canoe, drifting back the way he'd come. He used a paddle to steer, keeping close to the south side of the river. Paddling at once brought pain and relief. Pain to his injured ribs, relief to be doing something physical and not sitting on a plane or boat while others hauled him where he needed to go. Apart from the spitting snow, frigid water, and the strong possibility he'd run into a brown bear, it reminded him of canoeing the bayou with Grumpy and Ethan when he was a boy.

He counted the oxbows on his way back downriver to make sure he was back at the spot Shawna told him about, and pointed the canoe to the bank, coming in alongside the willows and tying off. He caught the smell of cooking meat again. Maybe Beck had eaten his fill and then gone to sleep with Jan tied up in the corner.

Cutter dismissed the idea as quickly as it occurred to him. Nothing was ever that easy.

Beck was as paranoid as any tweaker Cutter had ever seen. He was likely to have booby traps all over the place. Game cameras were so cheap now everyone had them. With the proper equipment, Cutter would have been able to locate and disable them. But he had little beyond his guns and his brother's mammoth-tooth knife.

That had to be enough.

He'd watch out for trip wires. If he missed a game camera, there was nothing he could do about that.

CHAPTER 56

*T*HE BANK WASN'T AS STEEP AS IT LOOKED, AND CUTTER USED THE willows to pull himself up with no trouble. His ribs would be on fire in the morning, but for now, he was growing numb to the pain.

Cutter moved deliberately, looking where he would have placed booby traps if he were setting a perimeter around his place. Approaches from the water, choke points in the vegetation and terrain, natural lines of drift. He came across nothing but a very large pile of bear scat.

Snow fell harder by the time he reached the airstrip and the 185. It was cold and wet, but muffled his approach. Heartened to see lights burning in the cabin a hundred or so yards away, he found remnants of tracks leading to and from the aircraft, disappearing fast beneath new snow. He recognized Phil Hopkin's body from the driver's license photo he'd pulled after Mim's incident in Utqiagvik. The brush pile seemed a good place for him.

The Cessna's high wings had preserved some of the tracks around the door. From what Cutter could tell in the ambient light reflected off the snow, there were no tracks but Beck's and the single set of drag marks where he'd moved Phil Hopkin into the brush. Meaning Beck had either pushed Jan out of the plane somewhere en route or carried her to the cabin. And if he carried her to the cabin, maybe she was still alive.

A small copse of half a dozen spruce trees separated the runway from the cabin. Cutter put them between him and any windows and trotted closer, keeping his breath slow and quiet. Panting killed his ribs, and he wanted to be able to shoot. Though he relished the idea of ripping off Leonard Beck's arms and beating him to death with them, the last thing he needed in his present condition was a hand-to-hand fight.

The front of the thirty-by-sixteen-foot cabin faced the runway, with the fresh water creek running alongside. A low wooden porch ran the full length. Hazy orange light spilled out of dusty double windows that flanked the front door. It was difficult to tell from a distance in the dark, but the top half of the door looked to be decorated with some kind of wrought iron.

The west wall had a single window. Probably the bedroom. The lights were off. A decent place to approach. Cutter ran toward it, closing the distance as quickly as possible, swinging wide from the spruce trees to stay out of direct line of sight if Beck happened to be looking out the front.

Sparks rose from the chimney at the back of the cabin, orange streaks against a blue-black sky.

Cutter pulled up short a few feet away from the cabin, catching his breath, listening. He could hear Beck's voice, brash, threatening. Cutter chanced a peek through the dark window. The room was vacant, but the door leading to the main room with the fireplace was open. Furs and Native masks and other art adorned the log walls. What looked like a filthy quilt was rolled up and leaning against the far wall. Jan's face poked out of the top. She said something Cutter couldn't quite make out. Beck stopped in front of her, reared back like he might hit her, but turned and walked away. Jan screamed at him, then her head lolled as if exhausted from the effort—she was injured, but alive.

Beck paced back and forth, coming in and out of view, fireplace poker in hand. He raised it now and then, threatening her, then continued his walk. Sooner or later, he was going to follow through.

"That is enough," Cutter said under his breath.

He knew where Jan was. There was no point in attempting to kick the door. He'd shoot the lock and offer Beck one chance to

surrender. If the fire poker didn't hit the ground immediately—
well, Cutter could say he tried.

He drew the Colt and padded quickly through the soft snow
around the corner, taking a quick moment to test the wooden
porch with the weight of one foot. It was new and solid, like something a rich man would have on his remote cabin. No squeaks. He
stepped up with the other foot.

Now it squeaked.

If he went backward now, Jan was dead. He was committed,
squeak or no squeak.

Cutter bounded forward covering the fifteen feet to the front
door in a flash. Too late, he realized that the decorations were not
wrought iron, but an array of sixteen penny nails driven through
the door so the business end pointed outward. The spikes were
meant to keep grizzly bears from pushing their way inside the
cabin when it was left unattended.

Heavy footfalls sounded inside. Beck had heard his approach.

Cutter had just come up alongside the door when Beck threw it
open, catching him from the top of his shoulder and down his
arm and wrist with over a dozen three-and-a-half-inch nails. At
least two missed his arm and went straight into his side, scraping
bone on his already injured ribs. The force of the swinging door
should have knocked him off the porch, but the uneven points
snagged on his coat and carried him all the way through the arc,
pinning him against the wall. He stifled a groan, slumping for an
agonizing moment, his body suspended by the nails. He regained
his footing and attempted to tear himself away when the door
bounced. Beck put his shoulder into it, driving the nails in deeper
before Cutter could slide himself free.

He growled at the searing pain. The sudden shock of steel
spikes tearing muscle and grinding against bone caused his finger
to convulse on the trigger.

The round tore through the bottom of the door. It missed Beck
but caused him to jump out of the way. Cutter fired again, trying
to angle the barrel upward. The second shot missed as well but
chased Beck off a step. Cutter let loose another fearsome roar as

he jerked himself free of the nails. The overwhelming pain sent waves of nausea through his body. He dry-heaved, staggered sideways, stumbling clear of the nails before Beck tried to impale him again. His arm dangled by his side, useless, staining his coat with blood from countless gaping punctures. The Colt slipped from his fingers and hit the porch.

Inside the cabin, Jan was up, hopping forward, the top half of her body somehow free enough to throw herself into the fight. Beck caught her hard across the face with the poker. Screaming, he struck her again on the backswing, sending her to the floor in a tangled heap of blood and quilts.

Cutter tried to reach behind his back, clawing at the Glock over his right kidney, but his right arm refused to work. He twisted to reach it with his left but saw Beck going for his pistol at the same time. Cutter rushed forward, driving Beck backward with the point of his injured shoulder, ignoring the pain. Beck stumbled but caught himself. He swung the poker, intent on taking Cutter's head off. Cutter lunged, closing the distance. He took the blow across his shoulder, bringing another wave of nausea but robbing the swing of its power. Cutter pressed, driving Beck backward again before he had time to chamber for another attack. A brutal headbutt all but peeled Beck's nose from his face and sent him reeling. He swung the poker again, blindly, but with plenty of force. Cutter thought to swat it out of the way, but his arm just would not go where he wanted it to. The poker took him in the head, a glancing blow but enough to send him staggering. He grabbed for the wall with a bloody hand, struggling to keep his balance. Beck finally had the distance he needed to go for the pistol tucked in his belt. Instead, he stuck with the poker, emboldened, swinging again for Cutter's head. This time, it whistled past. Barely.

Then Cutter saw the whaling harpoon on the wall.

He turned. Beck laughed, thinking he was running away, until he saw the weapon too.

By then it was too late.

Beck dropped the poker and dug at his waist, hunting for his pistol. His shirttail had come out during the fight, making the search all the more difficult.

Cutter snatched the harpoon off the pegs with his left hand and ran forward, holding it under his arm like a jousting lance. The brass head was nearly four inches across, razor sharp and meant for a sixty-ton bowhead whale. It hit Beck at the point of his sternum and slid neatly beneath his ribs. Eyes wide, mouth open, Beck continued the vain search for his pistol. Blood painted his teeth. Cutter drove forward with his legs, growling at the molten pain in his arm as the point went through Beck and kept going into the fireplace.

A loud boom shook the walls. At first, Cutter thought the plunger on the harpoon had activated the brass "bomb."

It took him a moment to realize that it wasn't the bomb at all, but his own Colt Python revolver fired by Jan Hough. The .357 Magnum round tore a jagged hole above Beck's collar bone. She'd managed to free her hands, but they were dark blue, almost black from lack of circulation. The recoil from the single shot had knocked the Colt from her grip.

Cutter let go of the harpoon. He secured the Colt and Beck's pistol before staggering over to Jan who stood against the wall, shoulders heaving.

Her ankles were still partially bound with duct tape. Cutter cut them free with his working hand.

Wracked with sobs, she tried to tend to his shredded arm with her ruined fingers. She stopped, turning to dry heave from the effort, then spat a clot of blood—and a tooth—onto the floor.

"Look," Cutter said—a low moan. "Both of us are in shock, but help is on the way." He took a look at her eyes, her swollen face. "My entire right side is hamburger and I'm pretty certain you're rockin' a concussion."

"He shot Bryan," she whispered.

Cutter held her shoulders and they slid down the wall together, side by side, each one keeping the other from toppling over.

His flesh ripped and torn by countless jagged nails, his body spiraling into shock, Cutter suddenly felt lighter than he had in years. He stifled a single sob, then perked up when he thought he heard the thump of a helicopter in the distance. He wondered if he might be dying.

Jan leaned away and tried to look up but winced at the pain of simply moving her neck. In the end she fell panting against his good shoulder.

"We got him," she said. "We got the man that killed Ethan."

Cutter closed his eyes and let the sobbing overtake him.

"Yep."

CHAPTER 57

Anchorage

GONE WERE THE DAYS WHEN A CLEAN USE-OF-FORCE INVESTIGATION could be resolved with the Office of Professional Responsibility/Internal Affairs in less than a week. Even incidents captured on video in which the deputy's actions fell clearly within the bounds of both USMS policy and the law often bounced from investigator to recommending official to deciding official for interminable months. Some deputies found themselves on desk duty for well over a year while they waited for state or local authorities to decide whether or not to bring criminal charges. Cases where the deputy used a weapon other than a firearm—say a Clinch Pick—were problematic but not unheard of. Death caused by whaling harpoon was a first for the USMS and the Alaska State Troopers.

Hough gave a detailed statement from her hospital bed. Fortunately, the testimony of a law enforcement officer who was also the victim of a kidnapping packed a good deal of weight. Carrying a badge meant the color of law followed you, on duty or off duty, even when you were on administrative leave. The gruesome injuries from the sixteen-penny nails had gone a long way in showing self-defense. Jill Phillips had been able to ramrod Cutter's use of force investigation through the byzantine process in a lightning-fast two weeks.

The civil cases that were sure to follow would drag on for years. But, as Grumpy often said, if someone wasn't at least threatening to sue you, you weren't doing your job.

Seven of the nails had scraped bone, two had punched holes in tendons at Cutter's shoulder, but only one had actually broken anything, a small triangular bone in his wrist. He didn't even know he had the damned thing, but it turned out he needed that tiny triangle in one piece to make a good fist. Nineteen days after the confrontation with Leonard Beck, his right wrist was still in a cast and his arm looked like a pin cushion. Even so, Arliss Cutter found himself in the passenger seat of Lola Teariki's Chevy Tahoe peering through the rainy windshield at a sullen gray clapboard house.

He could shoot left-handed, but Phillips let him participate with the express orders that he was only an observer. No throat punching. He'd argued with her enough lately, so he kept his mouth shut and did as he was told. Mostly.

David Foye had called the day before to invite Cutter and Mim out pheasant hunting. He came across light and hopeful and ten years younger from the time of their visit.

The FBI was still trying to suss out how much Beck's wife knew about what was going on. She was, after all, the one who got Jan Hough on the sabotaged airplane and called Phil Hopkin's wife about the rumored affair. She claimed she'd done it at the behest of her husband and had "no earthly notion" that he'd planned to harm Officer Hough in any way. She didn't seem particularly saddened by the fact that her husband was dead.

Cutter and Hough had both been flown to Anchorage by air ambulance. He was given a tetanus shot and pumped full of antibiotics and then released with a cast on his wrist and a gob of follow-up appointments. She'd spent hours in surgery. Cutter and Mim had been to visit her the next day after the FBI finished raking him over the coals, again. He'd known she was badly injured but was surprised to find the left side of her face one solid purple bruise. She looked much worse than the last time he'd seen her. The swelling around her eye had gotten so bad, she told them, that there had been real danger of losing her sight for good. A third-year ophthalmology resident in the ER had made the on-the-spot decision to break the orbital bone below her eye with a pair of hemostats in order to relieve the pressure so she could keep her sight. Cutter could handle even the most brutal violence—except when it happened to his friends. Hough's description of the barbaric procedure made him queasy enough that he swayed on his feet. As an ER nurse, Mim was highly impressed and said that doctor was a badass.

Hough put her husband's funeral on hold until she could get out of the hospital and fly to Nevada, where his family was from. After that, she said she didn't know, probably just go back to what she did best, policing the Arctic.

Cutter was glad to hear it and told her so.

Cutter may have been injured and on administrative leave, but the hunt for Dupree had not stopped. Lola and the rest of the Alaska Fugitive Task Force were busy getting an affidavit for a T3, or Title 3 wiretap, on known telephones and Internet-capable devices for Eddie Dupree. The two young women Lola and the task force had rescued from the hotel on Spenard provided the probable cause. Donna Boone, the bottom girl they'd arrested at the bus station, agreed to give up the numbers in return for a four-year sentence and a government recommendation she serve her time in a camp. Four years at a place like the women's federal prison camp in Bryan, Texas, where the "fence" was nothing more than a yellow line painted on the ground, seemed like less than a slap on the wrist for her part in a child sex-trafficking conspiracy. But it got them closer to Dupree, so they swallowed their misgivings and made the deal.

Even with the T3, the trail had gone quiet for over a week. Both Boone and Tice, the porn actor they'd also arrested, attempted calls as part of their plea agreements, but Dupree must have gotten wind of their arrests and kept his head down.

Four days later, while Cutter was suffering through the final hours of his administrative-duty hell, a low-level heroin dealer and known associate of Dupree who went by the name Rooster, got an incoming call from Squish Merculief, who was looking to score some "slow." Rooster made a VOIP call to an IP address that was up to that point unknown. The location of the new computer was spoofed, bounced to five different countries around the world, but the person speaking was clearly Eddie Dupree. Dupree arranged a heroin delivery through an intermediary, saying it was "too hot" for him to come out himself.

Deputies gained little information from the contents of this call, other than that their target appeared to still be in Alaska. Now it was only a matter of time.

They had his number.

Task Force officers watched and waited, recording license plates and physical descriptions as they observed four separate deals go down without intervening.

Dupree made frequent calls to various cell numbers and IP addresses, allowing the Task Force to build a web of associates linked to both his narcotics and sex trafficking businesses. He also made numerous calls to a Kodiak number, always to the same woman. They spoke in a code that involved face cards and poker hands. Presumably, the suits and numbers representing people or product. Three times, two while Cutter was still on admin leave, the Task Force set up on possible locations where they hoped to find Dupree. Three times they were disappointed.

Then, four hours earlier, just before midnight, Eddie Dupree had received a call from a number that came back to a Kelli Gilpin at an address near Dimond High School. Her voice was heavy with fatigue, congested like she had a bad cold. A baby squalled in the background. Dupree urged her to use his face-card code, but she apparently wasn't up for any of his games.

Cutter read over the transcribed contents of the call while Lola kept an eye on Kelli Gilpin's residence across the street and four houses down.

Dupree: *I told you never to call me at this number.*
Gilpin: *Then you should answer the other one once in a while. When are you coming home, Eddie?*
Dupree: *Soon. I promise.*
Gilpin: *You said that last time. The baby's got colic again, and we're all out of formula.*

Dupree: *You're gonna have to go pick it up yourself.*
Gilpin: *I told you I can't go out. I'm really sick. Haven't slept at all in two nights. Look, Ed, you're the one who wanted a baby. Come home and do your part. And don't you dare forget to bring formula. The can's completely empty.*
Dupree: *I'll be home soon.*
Gilpin: *I need you now!*
Dupree: *Kelli, I—*
Gilpin: *Eddie, if you don't get your ass over here—*
Dupree: *Okay, okay. Has anyone stopped by . . . you know, to talk to you?*
Gilpin: *Like who?*
Dupree: *Like anyone.*
Gilpin: *Nobody . . . or I would have sent* them *to the store for me!*
Dupree: *Okay, I'll come over, but I've got some bad folks after me. It's dangerous. That's why I've stayed away, to protect you and the kid.*
Gilpin: *Hurry up, Eddie. Your baby wants to see you . . . and I just gotta get some sleep.*

Half a block up the street, the kitchen lights in the target house flicked on. Cutter noted the time. 4:05 a.m. A shadow, stooped under the burden of a crying baby and the weight of the world, shuffled back and forth, casting forlorn shadows on the dingy sheet that acted as a curtain.

Kelli Gilpin, Eddie Dupree's supposed baby-mama.

Lola sighed, eyes glued to Gilpin's shadow. "This explains the pacifier in shithead's pocket," she said. "I usually don't believe it when the wife or girlfriend tells me they had no idea that bad boyfriend was up to a life of crime. But this lady seems genuinely clueless."

"Sounds like she's just trying to get by," Cutter said. "Considering what Dupree's doing on the Dark Web, we'll have Child Protective Services check in with her, just to be on the safe side . . ."

An hour ticked by, steady rain tapping out the minutes on the roof of the G-car. Some of the raindrops turned to snow, splatting against the windshield. Snow mixed with rain. Snain.

"You think he'll show?" Lola asked. Then, in typical Teariki fashion, she answered her own question. "I think he'll show." She gave a smug nod. "He has to show. What is that you say? '*Gas, grass, or ass, there's no free rides.*'"

Cutter couldn't help but chuckle. "That does not sound like anything I would ever say."

"Tomato, tomahto." She shrugged. "You're always preaching how outlaws get tripped up by money, dope, or love. Gas, grass, or ass. Same, same."

The radio on the console between them broke squelch.

"Hello, Cutter."

It was Nancy Alvarez.

Lola reached down and keyed the mic, leaving the radio where it was, low and out of sight. "Go for Cutter."

"The T3 shows two calls outbound from the residence phone in the past five minutes," Alvarez said. "Going to Dupree. Our guy never says anything direct, but it sounds like he's coming over."

She keyed the mic again. "Did we get a ping on the phone when he answered?"

"He's showing up south of Tudor," Alvarez said. "Somewhere around Great Northern Guns. The phone went dark again right after the last call."

Cutter raised a brow, meeting Lola's eye. Tudor wasn't far at all.

"Thanks, Nance," Lola said. "Fingers crossed he's heading our way." Then to Cutter, her eye on Gilpin's house, "You ever want to be Batman when you were a kid?"

Cutter gave a little start at her abrupt change of tacks. He should have been used to it by now.

He looked at her, stone-faced, his normal expression. "Batman?"

"Yeah," she said. "You know, a crime-fighting caped crusader." She tapped her steel rifle plate in the center of her ballistic vest. "Utility belt and whatnot . . ."

"Nope," Cutter said.

Teariki snorted. "Who then? Every kid wants to be somebody."

"I wanted to be my grandpa," Cutter said.

"Grumpy?" She gave a contemplative nod toward the Colt Python on his belt.

"Hell of a lot better than Batman," he said.

"Well," she said, "I don't know if you *are* Grumpy, but you sure as shit can *be* grumpy."

Cutter gave a slow nod, staring straight ahead. "And I guess I went through a phase where I wanted to be a musketeer."

"Are you serious? Sweet as!"

"Grumpy got Ethan and me a couple of fencing foils when I was around six and he was eight. He would tie balloons to our masks and then let us duel until one of us popped the other's."

She turned and looked directly at him now, eyes sparkling in the dim glow of the streetlights. "You do have that swashbuckling way about you."

"I was in the first grade," Cutter said, stone-faced again. "I grew out of it."

"I'm not so sure about—"

Joe Bill Brackett, sitting in an unmarked Impala at the end of the block, came over the radio and cut her off.

"Movement on the south side of the street," he said. "Across from Gilpin's residence. Subject's wearing a dark raincoat, but I got a look at his face. It's our guy."

"That's confirmed," Sean Blodgett said, from the opposite end of the street as Joe Bill. "Subject approaching the target house is Dupree."

"*Popongi!*" Lola said.

CHAPTER 58

*L*OLA HIT THE IGNITION AND THREW THE TAHOE IN GEAR.

"No way this perv is getting into the house with the kid," she said.

Four vehicles roared up from either end of the dark residential street, throwing rooster tails of rain as they converged. Dupree, overwhelmed by the screeching tires and blinding headlights, stood momentarily rooted in the middle of the roadway, arms out to his side as if for balance. His head snapped this way and that. Alvarez hit her air horn to anchor him in place. The sudden noise had the opposite effect. Dupree bolted for Kelli Gilpin's front door.

Coming in hot in the Tahoe, Lola cut sharply to her left. Cutter hung on to the grab rail as she hit the gas, bouncing over the low curb.

"That's how it's done, Teariki!" he said, caught up in the moment, even with the aching ribs and broken wrist.

She stomped on the brakes, plowing deep furrows in the waterlogged yard as her rear tires came around, putting the body of the Tahoe between Gilpin's house and Eddie Dupree.

Eye to eye with her fugitive, Lola bailed out, knocking Dupree to the muck with the door as she flung it open.

Cutter ripped away his sling and jumped from the passenger side, running and sloshing his way around the rear bumper.

"US Marshals!" he barked. "Do not move!"

Dupree scrambled to his feet, stumbling a few steps before he half raised his hands. Bits of mud and leaf plastered his forehead. Caught in a pool of light from the task force vehicles, he hunkered slightly as he looked left and then right, getting ready to run even though he was surrounded. Running was in his blood. He couldn't help himself.

Lola never slowed once her feet hit the ground, rounding the rear fender of her SUV in a flash of green, head up, arms pumping, powerful legs driving her forward. She came in low for a textbook rugby side-on tackle, wrapping her arms low around his legs as she planted the point of her shoulder low on his rib cage, driving the wind from his lungs and surely snapping more than one rib.

He never saw her coming.

Lola rolled away immediately so she didn't get trapped in a ground fight. She needn't have worried.

Upended and flat on his back in the muddy yard, Dupree blinked up at Cutter, who now loomed over him, Colt Python in his left hand.

"Hands!" Cutter said. "Show me your hands!"

Joe Bill Brackett jumped out of his sedan and ran up beside Cutter. Both provided lethal cover for Lola while she rolled Dupree face down and then, on her knees in the muck, slapped on the handcuffs like a rodeo roper tying up a calf. She gave the small of his back a quick pat down for weapons before rolling him to a seated position.

"There's something about the sound of those cuffs ratcheting on a guy like this," she said.

"Outstanding work," Cutter said. "All of you."

Two white APD patrol cars screeched up half a breath later, red-and-blues strobing against bullets of driving rain.

The front door of the house creaked open, and Kelli Gilpin stepped into the downpour. Frantic squalls of a hungry baby poured out the door behind her. Wind and rain whipped at her loose knee-length T-shirt. She raised a hand to her brow to shield her eyes.

"Did you get it?" she yelled over the weather, as if her baby-daddy wasn't handcuffed and surrounded by law enforcement.

Dupree looked up at her, rain and saliva running down his chin. He squinted from the lights and probably the pain of several broken ribs, if Cutter judged Lola's tackle correctly.

"I told you people were after me." His mouth fell open as a sudden thought occurred to him. He glared at her. "Did you know about this?"

"Eddie!" Gilpin screamed through gritted teeth, her tears mixing with the rain. "You worthless son of a bitch! I never asked you for anything in my life except to bring me a can of baby formula. She's sick. I'm sick. I can't take her out in this!"

Lola stood Dupree up and took a half step back, still controlling his arms.

Cutter shook his head. "I thought you'd be bigger."

Lola and Joe Bill Bracket performed a more thorough weapons search now that Dupree was on his feet and then put him in the back of the Tahoe for transport. It was an unwritten custom in the Marshals Service that the junior deputy locked up their gun and rode in the back seat with the prisoner if there was no cage. But this was Lola's arrest. Cutter elected to secure his guns. Once they were in the lockbox, he grabbed a plastic sack from his gear bag in the rear of the Tahoe and brought it around to Lola, who stood next to the open rear door. Dupree was already buckled in, staring dejectedly into space. Cutter had seen the look countless times before—a wolf turned into a puppy, stupefied that he was finally captured.

Cutter nodded down to the deep trenches the G-car's tires had carved into the front yard.

"We may need a tow truck to get out of here."

"I've been in worse," Lola said. "She'll crawl out."

Joe Bill, who'd run back to his patrol car, came trotting up from the street, carrying a plastic sack similar to the one in Cutter's hand. He glanced at Gilpin, who held her crying baby just inside the front door out of the rain, watching the drama in her front yard.

Lola touched Joe Bill's arm. "What's all this?"

He gave a sheepish shrug.

"I heard over the Title 3 that she needs baby formula so I

stopped by Walmart and picked some up on the way. We all knew Dupree wasn't going to bring her any."

Lola grinned, then gave a slow nod, eyeing her boyfriend up and down.

Cutter passed his bag to Joe Bill. "Coincidentally, I happened to stop by the store as well . . . You can add this to yours."

Joe Bill took both bags of formula and trotted them up the walk to an extremely grateful Kelli Gilpin.

"Hang on to that guy," Cutter said.

Lola gave him a friendly jab to the shoulder.

"I reckon I'll keep the both of you . . ."

CHAPTER 59

*T*HE FIRST REAL SNOW OF THE SEASON CAME ON THE SECOND WEEK in October, early for southcentral Alaska. It started on Friday afternoon, sifting gently over Anchorage and kindly giving evening commuters plenty of time to make it home before the roads got bad. Sixteen inches fell by Saturday morning, covering streets and cars and memories of recent violence.

Temperatures hovered in the midtwenties. Downright comfortable in a place where elementary school students were expected to go outside for recess until the mercury dipped below minus ten Fahrenheit. Cutter had used the snowblower on the driveway first thing that morning amid the throaty drone of a half dozen others up and down the block doing the same thing with their snowblowers—the winter song of the urban North.

The boys had been up since dawn—eight thirty this time of year. With only a short lunch break to warm their toes and eat a quick PB&J, they were still outside building snow forts and sledding down the back hill with their neighborhood friends at two in the afternoon.

A spruce fire popped and snapped in the fireplace. Constance was in her room, leaving Cutter and Mim to their own devices, making pies in the close warmth of the kitchen.

Mim's house was a different place than it had been just a few short weeks ago. The living room had been stripped down to the studs. New walls, flooring, and throw rugs all came courtesy of Johnson, Benham, and Murphy Engineering—their way of saying

"Please don't sue us." Cutter worried that Matthew and Constance might have a problem coming back to where they'd seen so much trauma, but the smell of fresh paint appeared to calm them. Even so, they met regularly with counselors, as did Michael and Mim (and Cutter at Chief Jill Phillips's insistence).

With the fireplace popping and the rich voice of Andrea Bocelli on the smart speaker, Mim worked on her pie dough while Cutter took care of the frozen blueberries they'd picked on a family outing up toward Matanuska Glacier in August. It had barely even been six weeks, but so much had happened that it seemed like forever ago.

He'd dispensed with the sling but wore a hard plastic brace to protect his wrist while it continued to heal.

He dumped a pint of frozen raspberries from one of Mim's church friends in a mixing bowl and opened the plastic baggie full of blueberries, popping one in his mouth and giving a satisfied nod. If anything, a few weeks in the freezer had sweetened the little gems even more than when they were fresh.

Mim brushed a bit of flour off the tip of her nose with the back of her forearm and nodded at the blueberries.

"We must have been in a hurry with that batch," she said. "Looks like more leaves and twigs than berries."

"Nothing that a baptism in make-believe water can't fix." Cutter dumped the berries into a bowl of water, lukewarm to keep them from bursting, and then swished them gently with his fingers. There were enough crushed ones the water immediately turned wine red.

Mim pulsed her food processor a couple of times to blend the flour, salt, shortening, and butter into what would soon be the best pie crust Cutter had ever tasted.

"Make-believe water." She chuckled. "Ethan used to call it that too. Another Grumpy-ism. A bath to make us believe we'd washed away all the little critters."

Cutter pinched a small green worm, still frozen, that was floating in the berry bowl and dropped it down the garbage disposal. "We would have never even noticed this little beggar if we'd accidently baked him into a pie."

Mim gave an exaggerated grimace. "Let's make believe he's the last one," she said. "So, anyway, tonight it's raspberry, blueberry, and—"

"Blueberry-raspberry," Cutter corrected. "The blueberries are the star."

"Okaaay." Mim gave him a wink. "Blueberry-raspberry pie for dessert along with a beef potpie for dinner tonight. I'm making enough crusts so I can freeze some for Thanksgiving and Christmas."

"Good plan—and I am always up for your beef potpie."

She shrugged. "It's basically Grumpy's venison stew inside a piecrust."

Cutter smiled. "And what's not to love about that?"

He gave the blueberries and make-believe water another gentle swirl.

"I like this," she said. "Cooking together."

"Me too."

"Don't get me wrong," she said. "I love that you spend so much time focused on the boys, teaching them all the skills and rules Grumpy taught you and Ethan. But I have to admit, it's nice to do something that's just you and me . . . besides solving murders."

"Yep."

"It's kind of like courting . . ."

Cutter froze. His hand still in the berry water, he glanced up to try and get a read on Mim's face.

She was frozen too, looking straight at him.

"I suppose it is." He wondered where this was headed. "You said before there were two things standing between us."

"I did say that."

"Okay . . . So, you've become my sin-eater and listened to every awful detail of what happened in Afghanistan. But what about Ethan's ghost?"

Mim gave him another wink. "Must be outside visiting with the boys."

Cutter used the dish towel to dab a smudge of flour off Mim's face. It was useless.

She tiptoed up to kiss him, lingering there for a long moment.

He took a deep breath when she stepped away. "I'm not much of a courter," he said.

"I don't think I'll notice," Mim said. "It's been a long time since I've been courted."

He held her by the shoulders and kissed her again, taking his time, the kiss he'd been waiting to give her for twenty-five years.

"I don't know." She fanned her face with an open hand when he came up for air. "You seem pretty good at this to me . . ."

"Mim—"

The squeak of Constance's door down the hall gave them enough of a warning they had time to resume their pie making duties.

"Hey, kiddo," Mim said when she walked into the kitchen.

Constance chuckled. "You guys are adorbs."

Mim's face flushed red as she and Cutter exchanged glances.

"What?" Cutter asked.

"Uncle Arliss," Constance said. "You and Mom both have flour on your noses, and Mom's got a blueberry handprint on the shoulder of her blouse. What is it you call that? Prima facie evidence . . . ?"

Cutter wiped his face with the dish towel and tossed it to Mim.

"You're turning into a heck of a tracker," he said.

Constance pulled up a barstool beside him and slid the Vulcain Cricket watch across the counter.

"Did you tell him already?"

Mim shook her head.

"Mom and I talked it over," Constance said. "We think Dad would have wanted you to have this, for a while, anyway, until one of the boys gets old enough to wear it. I forget sometimes that he was your brother long before he was my dad."

Cutter pushed the watch back to her, gently bumping her hand. "You wear it," he said. "Grumpy had *Man*-Rules because he only had men to raise. I am one hundred percent certain that if he were alive, he'd want you to have this."

Constance held the Cricket up in front of her face and smiled. "It is nice to have something of his—Dad's and Grumpy's." She choked back a sob. "Uncle Arliss . . . Thank you for saving us."

He gathered her to his chest in a great bear hug. The truth was, she'd saved him. They all had.

Mim, shedding tears of her own, suddenly tensed. She leaned away from the counter a little so she could peer out the front window to where the boys had built their snow fort. The sound of their laughter had fallen off. They were talking to someone.

A visitor.

Still on edge, Cutter flipped the dish towel over his shoulder and started for the door with Mim on his tail.

"Probably the mailman," Constance called after them.

Cutter opened the door to find a tall woman wearing a heavy peacoat and fur mittens standing just off the porch at the edge of the driveway. Her back to the door, she chatted amiably with the boys. Her long blond hair spilled from beneath a green woolen hat.

Snow fell in huge popcorn flakes.

"Can I help you?" Cutter called.

The woman turned, her soft smile hitting him like an uppercut to the chin. His heart pounded in his ears. He had to grab the door frame to keep his feet.

"Arliss?" the woman said. Her voice was Southern and buttery smooth. She nodded softly to herself. "Well, just look at you . . ."

Cutter tried to speak, but the words wouldn't come. Finally, he said, "Ursula?"

"Who?" Mim said from behind him.

Cutter let out a slow breath and whispered.

"My mother . . ."

ACKNOWLEDGMENTS

One of the best things about writing books based in Alaska is exploring the state. Some of that exploration and research was done specifically for this book, but much of it came over time during my career with the United States Marshals Service and the twenty-six years my wife and I have lived in the Great Land with our family.

My old USMS partner, Ty Cunningham, has not only been a dear friend for the past thirty years, but a valuable resource for all things man-tracking and martial arts. We have talked through or walked through virtually every fight scene in all the books I've written. Another dear friend, Brain Kroschell, led my wife and I on a two-week trip from village to village down the Kobuk River where we talked to students in Shungnak, Ambler, Deering, and many other villages about how they could write their own stories. And they have plenty, believe me. The bush teachers, the students, the wonderful Iñupiaq culture, and the Kobuk region itself have all provided amazing inspiration that will continue, I'm sure, to influence many books. In the fall of 2023, Brian accompanied me on a research trip to Utqiagvik where he'd worked for the North Slope school district. Without his introductions, I'd never have met Jen Brower and the other educators at the Kiita Learning Center where high school students talked to me about traditional whaling practices, their family ice cellars, and favorite traditional foods. As we left the building, two of the boys called us back in to demonstrate their drumming and singing skills. Though the drumming didn't make it into the book per se, I hope the boys' spirit did. It was a terrific experience, and one I won't forget.

Friends and aviation experts Sonny Caudill and Steve Szymanski constantly let me bounce ideas—like how can I sabotage a perfectly good airplane? As well as keeping me honest about the capabilities of the type of aircraft we fly in Alaska.

Thanks to the South Dakota Humanities Council for inviting

me to speak in their festival of books in 2022 and to Professor James Reese for having me stick around a couple of days and speak at Mount Marty University after the festival. If you're ever in South Dakota, I highly recommend a visit to Wall Drug. As soon as we got out of the car, my wife looked at me and said, "you want to set a book here, don't you?"

I've been retired from the US Marshals since 2013. Things have changed. I owe a huge debt of gratitude to former and current deputies for keeping me honest about how Arliss and Lola would carry out their mission in the here and now. And a special thanks to my old buds in the USMS District of Alaska, a few of whom are still around from my time.

Anchorage PD is one of the finest police departments I've ever worked alongside—and written about. I am fortunate to call many of them friends.

Same goes for the Alaska State Troopers. They are the experts in rural policing—and from my personal experience, genuinely good souls doing an extremely demanding job.

I don't know what to say about the folks at Northern Knives. They are just terrific. I explained what Cutter's knife would look like and they made one, complete with mammoth and oreodont teeth. It's a one of a kind—and so are they.

Books don't get produced in a vacuum. I have the best agent in the universe with Robin Rue at Writers House. We've been working together over twenty years now. She and her assistant, Beth Miller, have become family friends with me and my wife. I've been working with my editor, Gary Goldstein, for over twenty years. A big thank you to him and the great folks at Kensington for believing in these books.

Above all, I need to thank my wife, Victoria, who not only stuck with me, but offered constant encouragement during the decades of rejection letters before we inked our first book deal.

Patience and then some.

RECIPES

Nana Cutter's Chicken and Dumplings

Chicken Soup
1 medium onion
3 carrots
3 stalks of celery
¼ cup butter
Salt and pepper to taste
1 Tbsp poultry seasoning
6 cups chicken stock
3+ cups of cubed/chopped cooked chicken

Note: You can make your own chicken stock by boiling chicken pieces—whole carcass or thighs with seasoning—or you can buy a rotisserie chicken and use the meat from it and add water and bouillon in place of stock.

Note: Add more or less vegetables and poultry seasoning according to your taste and the number of people you are serving.

Chop onion, carrots, and celery, and sauté in a large pot with butter. Add salt and pepper and poultry seasoning as they soften.

Next, add chicken stock and chopped chicken. Bring to boil as you prepare to add the dumpling dough. Taste and add more seasoning as needed.

Dumplings: Can be easily doubled
1 cup milk or buttermilk
2 Tbsp oil
2¼ cup flour

1 tsp salt
½ tsp baking powder

Mix milk and oil together in a measuring cup.

In a bowl combine flour, salt, and baking powder.

Add milk mixture to dry ingredients and stir to combine.

Add more flour as needed to handle the dough, as it will be sticky.

Method 1: Drop the sticky dough by spoonfuls into the boiling chicken soup.

Method 2: Add enough flour to be able to roll out the dough roughly. Cut into various dumpling sizes and then drop into boiling chicken soup.

Depending on which method you use, soup may be more clear or thicker.

Reduce soup to medium and cook for 15 minutes. Stir occasionally to submerge all the dumplings.

Bonus: Mim's Piecrust

Ingredients:

2½ cups all-purpose flour (You will use more flour when you roll out the dough.)

2 Tbsp sugar (Brown sugar works great too.)

1 tsp plain salt

12 Tbsp cold butter cut into chunks (Some suggest unsalted.)

8 Tbsp lard cut into chunks (Lard is preferred but other shortening is fine.)

¼ cup ice-cold vodka or vinegar

¼ cup ice-cold water

Directions:

In a food processor add the flour, sugar and salt. Pulse briefly to combine.

Add butter and shortening a little at a time. Pulse 2–3 times each. Should be the texture of peas or crumbs. Scrape down the sides between adding shortening.

Note: This can all be mixed together by hand, cutting in the lard and butter.

Transfer this mixture to a bowl and sprinkle with the vodka/vinegar and water. Slowly combine by folding gently. (Rough handling crushes the butter/shortening pockets and results in less flaky crust.) Should be slightly tacky. Use more flour if needed for easier handling. Divide dough in half and shape into two discs.

Can be used immediately, but if time permits wrap in plastic and chill for 45 minutes.

Can be stored (properly wrapped, of course) for 2 days in the fridge or frozen for the future.

Yield: Top and bottom crust for 1 pie

Book Club Discussion Questions

1. Ethan's murder is finally explained in this book. Were you satisfied with how it was solved? Do you think justice was served?

2. Some aspects of Iñupiaq culture, including whaling and food storage, were depicted in the early part of the book. What were your impression of these?

3. The relationship between Arliss and Lola has changed and grown through the series. How do you feel about where it is now and where it is headed?

4. The geography and climate of Alaska influence the plots of the Cutter books. How might this story change if it were set in a different part of the United States? Could this plot be realistically set anywhere else? Why or why not?

5. What is your assessment of Janice and Bryan Hough's marriage? Is it a happy or successful marriage? How does it compare with the blossoming relationship between Mim and Arliss?

   What are Mim and Arliss's chances at having a successful romantic relationship?

6. Mim persuades Arliss to divulge the traumatic experience he had in Afghanistan that is shaping his decisions and behavior. This story was revealed in an earlier book. Why was it necessary to retell it in this book? How did it influence you as a reader if this was the first time you had read about it?

7. The home invasion chapters were particularly brutal in their descriptions. What is your opinion about how Arliss

acted? Have you made mental plans about how you will react to violence against yourself and/or your family?

8. The final twist at the end of the book is the arrival of Cutter's mother at the door. What do you predict will be the reactions of the individual members of the family to her arrival? What do you think will be Arliss's reaction? How would you react?

9. What do you think of the family cooking scenes? Are you likely to try one of the recipes? Why or why not?